The Parlour Game

The Parlour Game is book one in:

The Corvidae Hauntings.

The corvids are no ordinary family of birds.

Magpie, Crow, Jackdaw, Raven, and Rook.

Each one with a purpose and a distinctive trait.

Collector, Thief, Mesmerist, Trickster, and Oracle.

Nobody is safe from their influence in Victorian London.

Coming soon...

Book Two: *The Crows - There is a thief in the night!*

To receive news and updates about future releases, including a welcome gift of an original Victorian ghost story.

Sign up: www.JenniferRenshaw.com

Follow Jennifer on

Instagram: @ jen_renshaw

Pinterest: jen_renshaw

The Parlour Game

Jennifer Renshaw

The Parlour Game explores Victorian themes of death, violence, suicide, addiction, abuse, and mental health.

ISBN: 9798356121159

Magpie Luck

One for sorrow,

Two for mirth,

Three for a wedding,

Four for birth,

Five for silver,

Six for gold;

Seven for a secret,

Not to be told;

Eight for heaven,

Nine for hell,

And ten for the Devil's own self!

M. A. Denham's Proverbs and Popular Saying of the Seasons (London, 1846)

Part One

Chapter 1 ~ Funeral

1873

Ivy ~ Godalming, 9th November.

My cousin Edith does not fear a funeral. In truth, I believe she prefers every opportunity to buy a new outfit from the tailor; her enjoyment of the process almost outweighs her belief that old mourning attire is bad luck. How another black dress differs from the last is a mystery. With an unhealthy obsession for the pageantry of dying, the woman exudes an unsettling confidence that irritates me.

Our carriage drives towards the town of Godalming. A village burial would not be enough today. Our family is too well-known. I should be focusing on our journey, composing myself in the carriage for the funeral ahead, but instead I am letting my mind wander into dark thoughts, lingering on relations that are still alive. This day would end much better with Edith buried in the ground instead of my mother. I would be content to leave her abandoned amongst the graves and not to think of her again. The metallic taste of blood seeps into my mouth as I bite my lip too hard; a bad habit I know only too well.

Upon previous demises in the family, Edith has watched like a hawk to ensure we are upholding the expected grieving protocol. Her scrutiny should have protected us from bringing more death to our door, but her endeavours appear to have been wasted. For loss affects her more than most; her husband and closest companions, the dead, drop around her like flies. Maybe Edith poisons them with deliberate intention to buy herself a pristine hat or another pair of kid gloves.

A wry smile plays on my lips. If Father could read my mind it would shock him. I should make a diligent effort to avoid Edith when we arrive, especially when lack of sleep loosens my tongue. Any thought could escape, exposing my secret disdain for her; an uncomfortable situation for all.

We pass a narrow cottage set alone on the side of the road; the walls bowed under the weight of the thatched roof. Two crows perch on a neighbouring withered oak tree. They follow our progress with their shrewd, beady eyes, passing judgement on our procession of grief. The branch juts out over the lane like a signpost pointing to the graveyard. A third crow flies down and joins the pair, all fixed on our moving parade. Three feathered bodies together - a premonition of death.

My body shudders involuntarily. I am not superstitious, but as the tree disappears from view, their presence concerns me. A fitting message for today of all days. Sent by what ... and by whom? Mother always acknowledged the birds and sang whenever she saw a corvid to ward off bad omens. I have a song that is on the cusp of recollection, hazy in my memory, but I cannot quite grasp the words. Already I am forgetting her.

The absence of her reassuring words is a cruel void on this lifeless morning. Grey washes over the countryside, draining all colour, leaving bare trees stripped of their summer livery. Each one stands sombre and stark, isolated, and bereft, as we move past them down the bleak rural track.

I imagine the tincture I could make, which would put an end to my misery. For what purpose do I have now? A small dose of foxglove or the berries of belladonna would suffice. The plants are growing in the garden already. Mother always insisted I wear gloves when touching them. My pursuit of botany has gifted me the knowledge I need, but it would be a slow, painful death, and although I have the conviction, I fear I lack the courage. I could research another method. I've heard arsenic eaten like sugar, sprinkled on fruit would be faster. My studies are the only saving grace I have. If I could put all my energy into becoming a botanist, surely that would be enough to live, to find meaning in this world in which I no longer feel tethered to.

I steal a glance at my father and my half-brother, David. Although our bodies are close in the confined space, they seem like strangers. I doubt my absence would be missed if I also died before Christmas. My thoughts are as macabre as the day. We inch towards the church, stretching out the future, prolonging the inevitable. At least we are not walking, a small mercy for us in the icy weather. The vehicle struggles over a pothole and comes to a hasty stop at a crossroads. My father thumps twice on the door, opens the window and leans out.

'What is the holdup?' My father shouts towards the coachman's seat, agitated by the delay to our journey.

'Someone is blocking us, sir,' a deep voice bellows back.

A woman sways in the middle of the road. She wears a simple white smock, unsuitable in the biting wind. She seems oblivious to the cold, frozen in place as she watches the spectacle in front of her. Suddenly, she rushes forward. The window is still open, and she reaches for us, leaning inside. We are near enough for her to touch. She is old, unwashed. I resist the urge to shrink away in disgust. She fixes her attention on me, her bony fingers encroaching upon my cheeks.

'They are not at peace... They will follow you everywhere.' Her eyes are watery, and her voice is hoarse, perhaps with fever. A flicker of panic and then hope passes over me. If I fell sick and died now, this feeling would be over; no grief, nothing, only relief from the burden of continuing alone. There is something familiar about this crone, but I can't place her, my mind blanketed by the thick fog of grief, every thought unfolding in slow motion.

'What on earth are you talking about, woman? Move away at once!' My father blusters, startled by this sudden intrusion.

'The spirits, young mistress, they're in you!'

'Do not listen to her, Ivy. She is clearly mad.' Father bangs his cane against the door to scare her away.

Her words spark a memory deep within me. Images flash before me like a magic lantern show I once delighted in from a travelling salesman. As a child, maybe eight or nine years of age, I woke to find a moving shadow in the corner of my room. It drifted to the foot of my bed, gradually forming the outline of a towering, misshapen figure, terrifying me. I hid under the blankets, but I knew the spectre was there until dawn, hanging over me in the darkness.

My nursemaid, on hearing my tale whilst helping me with my outfit the following morning, stated my imagination was fanciful, tutting, 'I have never had a dream like that in my whole life!' And as she tugged the skirt around my waist, her tone pensive, she whispered into my ear, 'Everyone has demons, Ivy. I guess you were unlucky enough to see yours.' Even as a young girl, I realised then that the Devil had found me.

I told this story to my mother, and she promptly responded by asking the maid to bring us something sweet – a treat for breakfast. I never saw the apparition in the shadows, nor the nursemaid again. From that night, Mother brought me into her room and slept next to me in the same bed until she became ill. I had forgotten the reason why until now.

My father bangs on the door once more. Two quick thuds shake the panel. 'Drive on now and be quick about it!'

We jolt in our seats, trying not to collide with each other as the horses start to move, pulling us away. The old woman staggers back. I try to give her a coin, as she must need help, but the woman lets it fall through her fingers and into the mud. Glancing behind, I see she does not flinch from the dirt kicked up from the wheels, the hem of her dress becoming caked in filth. She stays fixated on us as we drive off.

The interruption leaves us shaken. David, in a surprising moment of empathy, leans over to close the window and exchanges a furtive look with me, but the awkward atmosphere remains. I remove my black leather gloves and rotate the unfamiliar ring around my forefinger. According to Cousin Edith, no other jewellery should be worn for a year out of respect for the departed. But at least mourning decorum allows me this solitary grieving piece now.

It is fashioned in the shape of a signet ring with two swallows engraved onto a gold square surrounding a lock of my mother's hair, the silver and red strands woven together in an emblem of a forget-me-not flower. It is a queer sentiment to keep a memento taken from the dead, but it does give me a small degree of solace, being the closest thing I have to Mother's presence.

Apparently, they are all the fashion in London, but I note Edith does not boast a keepsake from her late husband.

When Father hurried the order through at the jeweller's shop in the adjoining town, the invoice was an immodest cost. He gave the gift to me as we ate breakfast. A painful, stilted exchange.

I had helped brush Mother's auburn hair every night, and a surreal sense now fills me as I trace the strands gently through the glass, once part of her soft, breathing body. A fragment of her life that I refuse to let leave this world; preserved, everlasting. My mother is with me, and yet she is not.

A deep coldness sinks into the pit of my stomach, forcing me back into the damp seat. The odour of decay, old wood, and pungent earth wraps around us. Sickness threatens to rise in my throat. Even the attempt at a modest breakfast had been beyond my ability. My breath mists before me. I am chilled despite the heavy black gown and a coat smelling of mothballs.

Winter descended prematurely this year, smothering autumn with an unforgiving frost. Its chilled temperature encloses us, encasing the wooden cab like a tomb. I concentrate on nothing but a spider in the window's crook, striving to save its web, the delicate fibres destroyed by the repeated rocking motion on the uneven track.

'Ivy, are you well? Your pallor is quite profound.' My father bends across to me, one hand bearing down on his ivory-topped cane. His voice is distant, his brow furrowed in the strain of regard. 'You are white as a sheet. The arrangements have taken their toll on you.'

'Please, do not concern yourself with my health, Father. I am well enough.'

Mirroring his language is all I can manage. He means well, but I accept he struggles with me, using my mother as a vessel to communicate more often than not. If I had been a boy, my life would have been an easier fate.

With this, he straightens his back and glances at my brother for support in this uncomfortable dialogue. A slight man in his late twenties, David is a younger representation of my father in nature, but without the full beard speckled with silver. Where my father has become more rotund with age, struggling to fit into his morning suit, he towers above us, tall and lean. He also hardly converses with me and much prefers the company of other men to women.

'David, please say something encouraging to your sister.'

The term 'sister' is a loose reference. David was born to Father's first wife, who died of consumption when he was an infant. I imagine my father hoped my mother's death would bond us, but only an uneasy truce exists between the three of us.

My half-brother removes his interest from the farms and woodland to study me. His lips taut, he twitches to find the right words to form a sentence. The sound released is an indifferent grunt. A shake of his head dismisses his grapple with communication, and he shrugs, curving his back away from us to the fields once again. With fumbling fingers, he checks the buttons on his overcoat and flips up his collar for warmth, or for a more probable purpose, to distance himself from me.

My relationship with him has never been anything other than superficial. Mother encouraged me to think of him as a brother, but without her, do I still feel obliged to pursue this laborious task? To push through his frigid personality, hoping to find a crumb of affection, seems like hard work. But I have no one else to confide in; acquaintances do not linger and grow into friends. I do not share my heart easily.

'We are here,' David mutters. His words are abrupt, his first since we left our village of Fernecome. He directs them, not at us but at the door, fingers firm on the handle, plotting his departure before the horses come to a standstill. His jaw clenches. He will be happier once he is outside, free from the enclosed proximity of his family.

We enter the churchyard as the bell chimes noon and the sounds echo across the many headstones, half-buried in the graveyard. The ringing is deafening enough to disturb the dead. The idea amuses me, although I am not sure why. Part of me revels in the rebellious opportunity to wake their eternal slumber.

I cannot believe Mother passes by me in a wooden box, carried by the unfamiliar hands of local pallbearers. The notion is painful to comprehend. She was too alive to be consumed by the earth without a trace. Her spirit aligned itself with nature, rooted in the natural rhythm of the seasons. She understood that when she left her body, the cycle of life would not end. She reassured me that she would return to me like the swallows after the winter had passed.

Standing separate from my father and brother, I watch as they welcome those who have come to pay their respects. A fair number are in attendance, his valued patronage in the town, reflecting how well my father is esteemed. He is the true reason they came, not my mother. Heads bow low in unison with murmured polite apologies for a life at forty, taken too soon. They remind me of a flock of birds scratching the ground for worms.

Father and son look at ease next to each other, but they converse awkwardly with Anne and Elizabeth Cowley, two sisters renowned for being spinsters, now residing in the same house as constant companions – one plump and the other lean. The Jack Sprat nursery rhyme comes to mind: "But, together both, they licked the platter clean." I can smell their potent lavender perfume from only two steps away.

Anne is so earnest in her worry for my father that she is on the verge of tears. 'Of course, you would honour us if you all came to dine with us one evening. Elizabeth's mutton stew is delicious and not to be overlooked. We insist you must not be friendless during this arduous trial.'

Their fretting is fascinating to watch. A newly widowed, prosperous man is a rare find in this part of the country. The sisters are not the only women interested in my father. Subdued young women of marrying age flitter about nearby next to their mothers, attempting to catch his eye, no doubt in their best mourning finery, ready to be pushed forward for condolences and fleeting introductions.

I must have overheard the suggestion of dinner invitations a dozen times at least. It seems my father will be well-fed in his grief.

'Ah, there you are, my dear.'

The shrill voice of Edith makes me jump. In observing my father, I have missed my cousin's approach. I berate myself for being such an obvious target. She gives me a light tap on my arm and my body stiffens. Her back is poker-straight, with an unnaturally small waist and a hand-span narrower than mine - the corset so tight that her shoulder blades almost touch. I half expect her to faint from the restriction to her breathing. Her pale blonde hair drawn back beneath her raven-black bonnet gives a severe expression to her features. There are no laughter lines. I find it challenging to imagine her as a mother. She is so unlike my own. If she smiled, there is a chance she could be considered attractive, but it is hard to tell. In my opinion, her temperament eclipses any hope of beauty.

Her mourning gown is trimmed in the traditional ebony crepe, but I can't help noticing the unfading intricate lacework on her matching gloves. They could have been sewn yesterday. The back of my neck aches with the stress of restrained politeness, the beginning of a headache working up the base of my skull. Soon the pressure will move to the back of my right eye, and I will need a dark room to lie down in to lessen the discomfort.

'The minister is eager to start the proceedings. There was a forecast for bad weather this afternoon, perhaps a storm, and he is watchful to avoid the downpour.' Edith waves over to the smocked man who paces beside the open porch.

Indeed, the vicar shifts from one foot to the next, grimacing at the overcast sky and casting anxious glances at the burial ground. A rain-soaked ceremony would never do, a most undignified experience for the ladies in their long dresses and polished shoes. I wonder if he prays for the clouds to abate, or does he conserve his talks with God only for an expectant congregation?

'Look at him, poor man. He is in such a state,' reflects Edith, her face frowning with apparent concern. 'I have taken the liberty to instruct the service to begin early. I trust you do not mind?'

This is not a proper question. The request is already underway as everyone files into the church obediently under Edith's instruction.

'Where is Timothy?' I ask.

Her son, at twenty-six years old, is two years my senior – also unmarried, but apparently that is no problem for a man. We should socialise, but I hardly ever find him at events; he always seems to be afflicted with an illness. His sallow skin is a striking contrast against his red hair, and a somewhat haunted expression is always in his hazel brown eyes. He has a tendency to sicken often, despite Edith's superstitious efforts; his grave might be dug next. After my cousin returned from the city, leaving her husband to fester from typhoid fever in a London grave, her young son was all she had left. Over the years, she has guarded him well, preferring to keep him at bay from commoners who could bring on a fatal disease.

She ushers me down the aisle to a bench situated at the front, disregarding the fact that she knows I would like to sit further behind. I do not want to be on show like an animal on market day. 'Apologies, but Timothy is obliged to take care of business this week, but he sends his sympathies.' I am sceptical that he was ever given a choice in the decision not to attend. Edith ensures she is sitting next to my father, right at the front of the church, the most prominent seat for all to behold.

The vicar's voice is dry and monotone. His sermon cites the book of Matthew: 'God's love for the meek and the mild.' Somehow, the bland lecture soothes me, calming my thoughts; the anticipated pain in my temples is kept at bay, for now.

When the vicar refers to my mother as an obedient, gentle character, I am dubious about his research. The assumption is false. When passionate about a topic, Mother often became animated or emotional. Then Father usually recommended one of her special Kendal Black Drop drinks to calm her nerves. His answer to most female problems was an opium tonic to make everything better.

I am uncertain if she ever imbibed one. Many nights, I caught her leaning out of the window, tipping the liquid into the garden onto the rotten grass below – a contrast to the thriving garden we had created and a conundrum to the gardener who tried to make a perennial bed against the wall, but inevitably nurtured a lost cause as the plants always perished.

A short duration of illness had swiftly aged Mother beyond her years, confining her to her room. With little appetite, she wasted away; every minute the clock ticked by stole more from her body. Her bright auburn hair, once so lustrous, became brittle and flecked with silver, her expression tired, a mere ghost of her former self.

I look around to scour the flock of mourners with a yearning to seek out my mother. Naturally, I cannot find her, but my heart skips when a woman walks through the doorway, her high-heeled shoes click-clacking on the stone floor. A late arrival, she sits alone on a pew under a stained-glass image of the Virgin Mary. For an instant, I believe it's Mother. She shares the same elegant posture and shapely physique, but unlike my mother, she seems much younger and despite an ethereal melancholy, has a vibrant glow about her.

This stranger exhibits the obligatory lack of colour suited to the day; her elegant ankle-length gown consisting of many layers of rich jet-black silk adorned with lace trim and ebony beads, the pleats sweeping around into a splendid bustle. My ordinary attire is drab by comparison. She appears hesitant to sit nearer, satisfied to witness the vicar's address from a few rows back. Taking a white handkerchief, she holds the cloth to her lips, perhaps to stifle a sob. Her profile is masked by a black veil, and I am intrigued by her identity. It is remarkable to find such a refined lady in this area without a chaperone.

As expected, no one is present from my mother's side of the family, no relations or friends – only mourners linked to my father. The lone woman gives the impression of searching for someone. Then, I discern her looking directly sidewards at me and continuing to do so until the end of the vicar's eulogy.

Reluctantly, around thirty minutes later, we leave the shelter of the chapel to brave the weather and watch the coffin being lowered into the ground. I am numb to the events, apart from the strangest sensation that I am somehow being held captive under this mysterious woman's unwavering gaze.

Chapter 2 ~ Mystery Lady

Outside, after the last hymn dies away, the congregation disperses. The sunlight has already started to fade, reflecting shades of burnt orange on the carved marble headstone. The evening is threatening to devour the afternoon. November days are becoming shorter.

Back at our house, the servants will be busy preparing a spread for the mourners. The family home, Elm House, was built on a secluded estate on the edge of Fernecome Village. The name is adequately derived from the tall line of elm trees overlooking the kitchen garden. Our wealth is made from new money; my father made a success from judicious investments in farmland and textile factories. The cotton industry has been good to us.

The expectation of a fine fruit cake will be high, considering my father's position in local society. Our cook will only use the best ingredients; extra measures of cinnamon and nutmeg were purchased with no expense spared. The funeral biscuits were collected from the baker as soon as the sun rose, their caraway scent filling the kitchen, each wrapped in white paper imprinted with the mourning poem Edith had chosen. The prospect of consolation with warm wine and fresh baking holds no temptation for me, so I choose to take solace in the churchyard and the comfort of my mother's grave. I have never derived enjoyment from idle chatter.

I watch Edith walking in the opposite direction as she struts in front of the guests, leading people back to their carriages and restless horses. She doesn't acknowledge me on my separate journey because she is so engrossed in the conversation. The occasion becomes her party. A transfer of ownership has silently taken place. Now that my mother lies consecrated in the earth. She has surrendered her role as mistress of our house.

After a few minutes, I am no longer standing alone. The dry leaves crunch with the gentle pad of footsteps approaching from behind. I know it to be the veiled woman without looking. She draws up beside me and, I assume, prays in silence. I appreciate her not intruding on my solitude. I am desperate, aching to hear the muffled tinkle of a bell I have placed in the coffin. This is foolish. I know she can only be in Heaven now, but I still cannot believe she is gone.

'Ivy, is that you?' The woman's voice cracks, quivering with emotion.

I turn, but I still have no recognition of her and am taken aback by the use of my name. Under closer inspection, her apparel is magnificent and more lovely than I'd imagined. She wears no coat – each button of her bodice is covered in onyx silk, and elaborate ruffles edge along her cuffs and sleeves, a pattern not familiar in these parts of Surrey. They could be a French design. I believe they wear exquisite garments in Paris decorated with velvet ribbons – but her accent is not foreign.

She opens a large midnight-blue velvet purse, taking out the purest white rose I have ever seen, completely undamaged and perfect in every petal. She lays it gently on the grave. 'It was never my intention to...' She breaks off, the words falling away.

'Yes?' I ask.

'Please forgive me for attending uninvited.' She looks at the gravestone, reading the inscription surrounded by carved acanthus leaves:

'For the Grace of God, our burdens on earth are vanquished,
"Thorns also and thistles shall it bring forth to thee, and thou shalt eat the
herb of the field." Genesis 3:18.'

'At least my mother is free of the pains of this earth.' I mumble, breaking the silence.

'It is a small comfort.' She replies. 'Acanthus also means immortality. The verse is perfect.'

'You know the meanings of flowers and plants?' My cheeks glow under her nod of approval. The engraving was the only part of the service I was able to choose.

'To understand this world is to learn that everything is connected and has meaning.' She closes her eyes briefly and places her hand over her heart.

I smile in agreement. 'That is also what Mother thought – we have always wanted to understand what grows and why.'

'Lillian had a love for the small details of nature. I am not surprised she passed the knowledge onto you. What else did she teach you?' Her tone is conspiring, behaving as if we have always known each other.

I pause. There is something about this woman that makes me want to tell her my secrets. 'I am studying to become a botanist... I was, with my mother's help before she died. Now I worry that will no longer be the case.'

Her eyes examine me through her veil. 'Yours is a worthy pursuit, Ivy. You should continue with your work, come what may. It is possible that I could assist with your studies; I have an orangery of my own. It would be yours for your plants. A safe place to work that you can call your own.' My heart skips a beat at the stranger's suggestion, but there is something unsettlingly familiar about her.

'My apologies, but have we met before?'

'I am Rosetta. Your mother and I were dear to each other ... in another place, a world away from this one.' She lifts her veil up over her hair and holds out her hand, and we shake our gloved hands like men.

Up close, her face is striking. Men must find her attractive, her eyes are the most extraordinary mix of colours: green and amber, complementing the gilded leaves of autumn, but they contain a deep sadness which must mirror my own.

'It is astonishing. You have the same bright emerald eyes as Lillian,' she exclaims, smiling, pleased at her observation.

I drop my gaze, becoming self-conscience under her scrutiny. Compliments are rare.

'The city was the wrong place for Lillian. I like to think country life suited her, that she found contentment in the end.

Could you tell me, did she...' She gulps, a breath taken too fast. 'Did she ever mention me?'

The chapel bell strikes one o'clock, and the hollow metal clang interrupts us. No one has ever referred to my mother in such a manner. Someone once told me she'd lived in the neighbouring parish her entire life. I rarely saw her socialise, and certainly no one resembling this woman ever visited the house. She is about to say more, but she falters, her attention caught on something else. My father approaches us. He is still some distance away, and I am unable to read his expression, but he marches down the path, his arms moving with force by his sides, determined to reach us quickly.

When she speaks again, her face is strained with tension. 'There is something else, a matter of the utmost urgency that I must share with you.' She takes my gloved hands again in hers. 'This is perhaps not the best time, but it is the only chance I have.' Her voice lowers. 'There are forces working against us, dark spirits, even now.' Her change in tone is unnerving, her fingers tighten, squeezing mine until her rings dig at my skin through her gloves.

'How do you know of this?' My voice rises in surprise.

'You and I are family, your mother—'

'Related?' I interrupt. 'But this is absurd; it is not possible! My mother would have told me, and you would have been invited today.' I pull my hands from her grip.

'There is a whole world that you are yet to learn about. You have been protected for a reason, but now the time has come when you must know who you really are.'

'I am afraid that you are not making any sense!' I declare, my blood boiling with defiance.

She looks into my eyes, searching like she is delving into my very soul, and then gives a tender smile. 'I can see your struggle, for it has also been mine in the past.'

'How can you be aware of my predicament?'

'I do not doubt you are different from those around you. You may feel unaccepted at times?'

I shrug at her pertinence, attempting indifference.

'We are alike, kindred spirits. You must come to London. I can teach and protect you. The cards have been clear, forces are at work, spirits which mean you harm. We will be stronger together.'

'What cards? What spirits? Surely, this is the story of madness?'

'Sweet Ivy.' She touches my cheek with such tenderness that I am certain my heart will break. 'I know you must have had your fair share of troubling dreams and heartache, but this is true, I assure you.'

I am shocked. How can this stranger know what I try to hide from others? 'The voices from my bad nightmares are nothing but childish notions.' My tone is stubborn, defensive. 'And we had no secrets.'

'Sometimes a lie is nothing but a delicate veil masking the ugliness of the truth – they do not last for long.'

'You must talk with my father; I am certain he can shed some light on these … revelations.'

She looks towards my father, who, quickening his stride with determination, is approaching ever faster. Even on this cold day, he wipes his forehead with a handkerchief. 'It is you who needs help.' She speaks with haste. 'Do not trust your father with this information, he will never understand or confirm it. You must choose your next path carefully. Death is not calling you yet, and you must not chase it.'

I am bewildered by her meaning.

She exhales. Her small sigh is one of defeat. 'There is still so much to say, but we have run out of time. I must keep an appointment in London and travel back without delay. Most of my work is to help those left behind. Both the living and the dead.'

Stepping closer, her hand quickly delves into her fabric purse again and withdraws a fine case made of silver and tortoiseshell, snapping open the clasp with a single click. She produces a cream card with black swirling letters printed in the centre. She takes my gloved hand again, pressing her palm firmly inside mine. 'You must come to me; you have a greater purpose, more than you can imagine.' She nods in the direction of the town houses. 'I cannot help you here. There is danger everywhere, but in London we can truly be together. My home can accommodate you for as long as you need.'

Her tone is on the brink of pleading as she gathers her skirts in preparation to move. I remain stunned. Knowledge of my mother, especially as a young woman, has always been out of my grasp. Now before me, is a real link to her past, but everything she says is confusing. The urgency to learn more blooms in my chest.

'Please wait a little longer,' I beg, but my father's voice is already upon us.

'Ivy, Ivy!' he shouts, most indiscreetly in such a religious place.

'I will see you in London, but you must not delay. Time is not on our side – there is much work to do. Do not stray from the path of safety.' I catch her last words as she turns in the opposite direction, striding away. I ensure the card is concealed well in my own purse and prepare to greet my father. He pants, out of breath and flustered, his face red and blotchy from the exertion.

'Who was that woman you were talking to?' The abruptness of his speech surprises me. His usual disposition is generally reserved. His eyes trail the woman as she vanishes behind a row of willow trees by the cemetery gates. Still wheezing, he clutches my hand, attempting to calm me, or perhaps himself. His behaviour is confusing. Even in Mother's death, he never turned such a crimson colour. Perhaps he is having a turn; bereavement is an unpredictable master.

I speak slowly to him, calming my own heartbeat, which is beating fiercely in my chest. 'Father, the lady is like all the other mourners. Surely it is heartening that an old friend of Mother's came to give their condolences – she said they were close?'

Undeterred by my efforts to appease him, he leans forward, his hands shaking. 'No!' he barks. 'Lillian did not familiarise herself with strangers. Her life was here with you, me, and your brother. This vulgar woman you talk of is an imposter, an opportunist trying to find fortune at this grievous time.' He inhales sharply. 'I would counsel you not to entertain her. I am pleased she had the good grace to exit the grounds at the precise moment I discovered her trespassing … proof of her guilt.'

Unease stiffens my posture, reawakening the uncomfortable bones of my corset. 'A discreet woman with wealthy clothes … yes, a little eccentric, but no thief or fraud.'

'You are mistaken, daughter.' Taking my arm in the curve of his elbow, he guides me to the carriage, away from Mother in the ground. Each step away is harder to take than the last, until at last we arrive at the carriage. It is empty. David must have gone with the others to start consuming the refreshments.

'Remember, Ivy, this is an affair for invited guests only. We do not give our goodwill to strangers with false stories. You must pay no heed to them, nor encourage them. It will only lead to trouble.' He closes his eyes and loudly exhales. 'Please, wait here. I will find the driver.'

Climbing up the steps to the carriage and sitting out of sight, I take out the card from my purse, studying the print:

Miss Rosetta Earnshaw
34 De Vere Gardens
Kensington
London

On the reverse side is a small drawing of a blackbird, perfectly stamped with ink. I know little of London, but her smart attire would suggest her address is located in an affluent part of the city. A burning desire builds to discover who she is and what her connection is with Mother. If her words are true, I am obligated to see her out of family duty. Especially if there's a chance she shares my unsettling dreams and understands my antisocial personality, for I've always preferred the company of plants to that of people. We could comfort each other in our grief for Mother, and perhaps I would not be such an oddity in the world.

But am I swapping one kind of madness for another? Her words concerning dark spirits against me are confusing, causing me to doubt her legitimacy and state of mind, and yet there is something about her that gives me hope on this miserable day.

I will keep my thoughts from Father. His adamant claim that she was a deceiver before they had even spoken is uncharacteristic. Does he know of her? Perhaps she might have a claim in the will if one existed? The possibility that he is hiding something creates a leaden weight on my chest. I do not like secrets. We had only put a discreet notice in the provincial paper. How she found the date and location of the ceremony is a puzzle.

After we arrive back at our estate, the stable boy comes out to help with the horses. He gives me a small smile, a genuine emotion at last. I am relieved to be home – the journey was barely fifteen minutes, but the awkward silence was straining on both of us.

Without a backward glance, my father heads into the house ahead of me. His attention to me has always wavered between indifference and polite tolerance. He does not understand my ways, but I do his, and I know at this moment he is hungry, keen to take his fill of the remaining spiced cake. But we are late and have arrived after the handing out of mourning biscuits, for there is no longer a servant to greet us at the entrance. He will have to seek out the housekeeper and catch up on the eating protocol. Uninterested in food, I sidestep away from the front door and around the side of the house, needing the cold wind to dull my sorrow.

The threat of rain still hangs in the air, and thunder rumbles overhead. I watch the dismal party through the garden window, my face hidden by draped curtains. The men and women gathered in the drawing-room are going through the motions of the wake: eating and drinking and making mindless chatter. The social crowd splits into smaller, more intimate groups. Once the ritual of a burial is over, these gatherings become a hive of activity for exchanging news and gossip.

One of the windows is open, and my ears prick at the sound of my name. I recline against the rough brick wall of my home and listen in to the voices carrying over my potted plants lined up along the sill. I think it is the vicar's wife who speaks over the others.

'What a shame. She has always been a timid creature. I worry for her without Lillian. She's so reclusive and will never amount to much.'

A new voice chimes in. 'She is lucky to have a cousin such as you to support her through this traumatic event.'

I wonder if this is one of the unmarried women presented to my father before the service. The girl knows nothing of my life. I can't imagine how she'd contend with being judged so openly.

Edith's voice is easily recognisable, commanding the conversation. 'I do my best, but I am pained to say that bearing children may be more than she can cope with. She lacks the strength of character, you see. She can barely look anyone in the eye or hold a conversation and is always so pale and tired-looking.'

'I heard you were considering marriage options on her behalf?' It is Elizabeth who cuts through the brief silence, the older sister of the two spinsters, who have set their sights on feeding Father up for Christmas.

'Of course, I will do what I can ... but becoming her guardian has been difficult. Sometimes I contemplate whether there are more appropriate places for her to live.'

'You can't mean to send her away?' Replies Elizabeth.

'Oh no, of course not. It would be a brief stay somewhere that would be better suited to her unique temperament. I have heard of several excellent establishments. Money would not be an issue if she had to stay longer. I would ensure Ivy has the best care.'

Edith's words make my heartbeat skitter. I know she wants me out of this house one way or another.

'Alternatively, as you mentioned, there is the marriage option, but I am afraid Ivy makes no effort to make the best of herself. She can't help being plain, but is it not our duty as women to make ourselves presentable to the male sex? I suppose being timid appeals to some.' She gives a dramatic pause before raising her voice an octave louder. 'But I do have a small amount of interest, which I hope will turn into an engagement. All I can do is pray on the matter and hope that my efforts will be enough.'

My face flushes hot with shame. I do not class myself as timid, although I am quiet around people I dislike. I smooth down my dress, sorely aware that my appearance has been found lacking.

'A predicament to be overcome indeed. You are too kind, Edith.'

I recall that high-pitched voice. It's Mary, the wife of the proprietor at the inn nearby. Her vain attempt to sound upper class to impress Edith is laughable. I hear the clink of crockery as cups of tea are served – she talks over the noise. 'Perhaps, after the grieving period is over, she will improve her prospects by taking your advice. I find her disquieting... the way she hovers in corners, always watching and never speaking.'

An additional well-wisher joins in the discussion about my attributes. 'She also gave me a fright on my last visit to the house, half hidden with the plants behind a curtain, quiet as a mouse. It was most troubling. I heard she follows the servants around the rooms.'

I can't say who this voice belongs to, but supposedly my strange reputation is well-known.

Elizabeth's sister, Anne, pipes up. 'Leave the girl be. She is just a little peculiar and shy. She will grow out of her oddities.'

I balk at her reply. She is brave to challenge Edith in public. They must not be properly acquainted.

'She is past her prime of marrying well, and at twenty-four, she is older than she looks. If she were my daughter, I would nip her odd tendencies in the bud if she is ever to achieve anything,' Edith says, relishing the final say on the matter.

My stomach bubbles with hatred for my cousin, and my fingers flex with the itch to slap her … to show her up for the hideous person she is. But bravery fails me. Edith wins again.

Outside, at the bottom of the garden, is the glass garden house where Mother and I used to sit and do much of our planting and sketching together. We pressed flowers through the seasons and planted herbs, keeping a note of where they grew best. Our work became a diary of sorts. And of course, the birds … the birds are my joy. I know each of their songs even with my eyes closed, imagining them conversing with one another.

The door is unlocked, a safe refuge to hide from my home full of unwanted guests. The temperature is cool, with the first sparkles of frost glistening on the glass panes, struggling to capture any warmth from the weakening sun. Empty plant pots line a long wooden table, waiting for my attention to fill them with seeds and cuttings in spring. I draw my cloak tighter and pull at a thick woollen blanket, which sits folded on a chair next to the day bed.

Lying on the day bed, my gaze travels over to the only bookcase in this glass sanctuary, a combination of my own and my mother's personal collection – all the spines packed together like old friends whispering secrets to each other in their closely confined space.

I am grateful Mother's well-thumbed books on garden plants, botanical herbs, and astronomy still remain in this special place, along with my favourite book: a thick volume of fairy tales. I recall the whimsical stories of witches and princesses, frogs, and princes – each with a lesson, a secret message. Happiness never arrives without a price.

But now I spot a new book, hidden in plain sight, a volume slightly different from all the rest. I get up and carefully remove it from the shelf. Midnight-blue leather casing with silver thread knotted delicately into the material gives the impression of stars in a midnight sky. My fingers brush over the uneven texture. The cover is beautiful, expertly bound. The letter 'L' for Lillian is gilded in gold, surrounded by an ornate pattern of lilies and vines.

Settling back onto the day bed, the thick pages crackle as I turn them, old and well thumbed. Handwritten notes with drawings fill the sheets, but the words are not in English, or indeed in any known foreign language. What marks them is an unfamiliar use of symbols: drawings of geometrical shapes and overlapping patterns; the moon and a sun, half in shadow, the other half with the wings of a bird cast upon it. The markings are almost like Egyptian hieroglyphs and are grouped into nonsensical formations, clustered together on the pages. Upon further scrutiny, they could be interpreted as words formed into sentences and paragraphs. Written on the inside front cover, it says: 'To my dearest Lillian, let words and the beating of wings forever bind us together.'

I assume the drawings are of me, but the more I carefully turn the pages, the more they come to reflect a remarkable likeness to the woman at the funeral. Some sketches are in light pencil, where others are heavy-handed with deep shadows. I flick towards the back, where there's a section of drawings separate from all the others, where the paper edges are crumpled and dirty. These pages are almost black, the residual of charcoal coating my fingers.

Pausing to study them more closely, I find there's something disturbingly familiar about them. I recoil in horror as the shadows remind me of my childhood nightmares, the ones that have recently returned. Why would my mother have drawn these? I shut the book; the grief is too much. If she were alive, no doubt she'd give me a plausible explanation for this strange discovery.

I'll never understand why I still carry my childhood fear of the dark, but perhaps I am more honest than most. Living in the countryside, there were many strange noises I heard in the blackness of night: foxes with their high-pitched howls and owls with their hooting calls. My room was next to my mother's, with an adjoining door, but we always shared her bed. She understood my fright and ensured we had a lamp next to us in case we should wake. Father had long moved to his own room and left us to create a world of our own in the far corner of the house, overlooking the forest.

I suddenly sit up, startled, my mouth dry. I must have dozed off, the beginning of another bad dream taunting me. The sunlight has faded rapidly, and now dusk has emerged, bringing nightfall closer by the minute. People will have started to wonder where I am.

The blue book splays open again on my lap – a new image laid bare before me. This picture is so vividly drawn that the paper is torn in places with the sharp pressure of black chalk strokes. The image is more lifelike than all the rest, with glowing eyes and a grinning mouth set in a disturbing doglike face. The evil, tortured soul owns the page with gross monstrosity.

For many years, memories of him have escaped me. Now, twice in one day, he has returned to intrude on my thoughts. The fear slowly ebbs through my blood. I don't remember describing my childish apparition in such explicit detail to my mother, nor the devilry of its features, but the eyes glare back at me with evil delight. My mother has captured the exact likeness of the creature, almost as if she had witnessed the beast herself.

Chapter 3 ~ Ghosts

Master Blackham ~ Blackham House, 10th November.

Hunched over his desk, sleep slipping away, a cruel awakening settles over Master Blackham with a familiar despair. His back aches from the unforgiving, straight chair as he groggily looks around at the many shelves of books in his library, soothing companions to his pounding head. The bright light from the lamp on his desk makes him squint, the dark wood of the furniture matching his mood. The room is stuffy with stale air. Coal embers in the grate lay in dusty piles, their heat having dissipated hours before. Where the blazes have the servants gone? He sighs with exasperation at the stopped clock above the mantel before pulling out his pocket watch from his lounging jacket breast pocket. The effort is almost too much. The expensive timepiece reveals it is four in the morning, an hour before the maid rises to begin her duties.

In the earlier hours, he had taken a small, framed portrait from the top drawer of his desk, but now he can't bear to look at it. That exquisite face with fair hair, gentle grey eyes, and plump lips, the corners raised in an enigmatic smile. He can conjure her up easily with little effort, seeing her standing in all her fragile beauty by the fireplace, pale porcelain skin with that haunting aura of sadness. His mind wanders against his will, to the locked room facing the garden. His struggle to repress the memory of her takes a gut-wrenching effort; his guilt stalking him night and day. Even after an empty bottle of whisky, there is no escape.

Since he'd brought his new bride into the house, the ghost of Miranda constantly visits his dreams. Angelica was a necessary replacement – another Mrs Blackham entering the doomed family. His mother had said to correct the vacant position in the household as soon as possible, and now the familiar spiral of negative thoughts has come creeping back. He'd made such a disastrous mistake by marrying again. A gentle knock at the door brings his attention back into the room.

'Yes?'

'It's Bancroft, sir.'

'Enter,' Master Blackham groans, relieved that there is, at last, some sign of life.

Immaculately dressed in a waistcoat and black suit, his butler opens the door and walks into the room carrying a silver tray with a coffee pot, a small jug of milk, and a white china cup and saucer. He emits a sense of organised calm. Only in his mid-twenties, the butler has the presence and grace of an older, more experienced manservant. 'There you are, Master Blackham. I took the liberty of assuming you've been working late, and you might enjoy a coffee before retiring to your room.'

Diplomatic as ever, the young butler whitewashes the truth – no work has taken place within those library walls over the last month. Instead, the room had become the master's refuge, a place to catch his breath from the world.

'Thank you, Bancroft. The prospect of a hot drink is most welcome. Perhaps it is an illness that approaches.' Master Blackham presses his palms over his eyes and mouth, feeling the scrape of stubble across his jaw. He'd had no intention of staying out so late, but since the day the doctor had sent Angelica to the countryside to recover, he'd sought comfort in old habits. The men at the club were spirited and forceful in their insistence for him to remain. How could he refuse? Besides, playing cards delayed the inevitable misery of returning to the house.

Mr Bancroft sets down the silver tray on a small table nestled beside the desk. Without further comment, he pours out the coffee, adding only a dash of milk, and places it in front of his master. Master Blackham's right hand quivers involuntarily as he lifts the cup of steaming brown liquid. No emotion passes over the servant's face when confronted with the dishevelled man before him, except for a fleeting glance of compassion. He moves with ease, a practised art. He has placed a hot face cloth on a dish next to the saucer – a morning ritual which has become normality.

Mr Bancroft picks up the damp white fabric and dabs the brushed cotton against his master's face. A sigh escapes Master Blackham's lips as he responds to the warm comfort.

'If there is nothing else you require, may I suggest retiring to your room, sir? It has been prepared, and the fire has been lit.'

Master Blackham glances up at his servant. He knows from catching himself in the hallway mirror that his bloodshot eyes with deep shadows beneath them, along with his grey pallor, give him a shockingly aged appearance. 'I should like that. What would I do without you?' He focuses again on his coffee, lifting the cup to take another sip.

'Then, sir, when you're ready, I will escort you to ensure you are settled and comfortable.'

Master Blackham puts down his cup and scrapes his chair back, the noise muffled by the woven rug, and hauls himself up against the table with visible strain. Although only in his thirties, his slumped physique could almost be the figure of an old man. The constant drinking has taken its toll.

The butler takes his master's elbow and helps him out of the study. A heady, sweet scent of opium, mixed with the metallic tang of alcohol and tobacco, clings to his clothes.

Escorting him upstairs, he delivers Master Blackham to his room before descending the narrow servants' staircase at the back of the house to instruct the maids with their daily tasks.

Chapter 4 ~ Dinner

Ivy ~ Elm House, 14th November.

The mahogany dining room table is set; the evening meal is roast chicken, carrots, and boiled potatoes. A small chandelier hangs above us, the glass-encased candles shimmering. The loss of my mother aches in my chest as I sit opposite David and beside my father at the head of the oval table. I am reminded by the little things: the absence of her chair, and the space next to mine where her plate should be.

During the last few days, a strange sense of unease has crept into the house, creating a heavy atmosphere and an awkward edge in conversations. Numerous times, I have walked past closed doors to hear hushed words between my father and men from the nearby town. Although he appears happy in himself, an underlying tension exists between us. I want to ask him about Miss Earnshaw and demand to know if he has been lying to me, but I already know it would be pointless. He would deny anything but the life we have led. His reputation is everything to him.

'Now then, Ivy.' My father does not meet my eye as he holds the porcelain gravy jug in his hand, tipping it slightly, smothering his chicken in the steaming, thick, brown liquid. 'There is excellent news for you. I am pleased to have accepted a proposal on your behalf, which I believe will be to your satisfaction.'

He places the gravy jug back on the table, briefly gauges my reaction, and then resumes attention to his meal. I hold my knife and fork in my hands but do nothing with them as I watch him eat, waiting for him to decide whether to eat another mouthful of food or put me out of my misery.

'You are of an age now for marriage, and without your mother in the house for company and guidance, it is opportune that I place you into a family where you will be taken care of and evolve into a lady suited for convivial society.'

He continues on, oblivious to my feelings. A slow dread seeps through my body. So, this is going to be my new purpose. I think of the foxglove again and berate myself for my lack of courage to join my mother in her grave. At no point have I expressed a need to marry. I have an idea of who he wants to pair me with, Mr Whitlock. But it would be a loveless match; the man repulses me. He reminds me of a weasel, with his small shifty eyes and protruding ears, and the way he scurries about with his long body and thin legs. But Mr Whitlock is a well-respected undertaker, and if he is interested in me as a wife, I doubt I will have much say in the matter.

'Father, I do not want to sound ungrateful, but...'

He dismisses my sentence, talking over me as though my words were nothing but dust motes in the air. My defiance sounds pitiful, even to my ears. My fingers tighten around the silver knife as my fork presses against the soft potato.

'As I mentioned, I have found a suitable husband for you, Ivy. In this difficult time, we mustn't neglect your future. A marriage will be just what's needed to bring you out of yourself. A fine man from good stock. He knows of your ... shall we say, sensitive nature, and assures me personally that it makes no difference to him. We entrusted the details of your mother's casket to him, and I thought he did a fine job.' He chews a mouthful of chicken almost thoughtfully before continuing. 'He went above and beyond with the cost, and I expect it was his way of showing not only his condolences, but his intentions of being a worthy match. A union between our families would be a credit to all. We have arranged to announce the engagement at Christmas and the wedding will take place on your next birthday.'

I blanch at the statement. July is only eight months away. A wave of nausea engulfs me. They have discussed me as little more than a sack of wheat to be bartered for at the best price, my flaws and virtues highlighted as part of the sale. This is not how I see my future.

I swivel round to face my father. 'I do not wish to be married and most definitely not to Mr Whitlock – he is not what he seems.' My dress clings under my arms with perspiration; the fire is stoked too high in the grate nearby, and I can barely breathe. 'What about Mother's will? I appreciate you may not approve at first, but Mother wrote to the director of the Royal College of Science about how much I know about plants, and they said they might help me become a botanist if my work showed promise.' My stomach churns, 'in that case, I need not marry. I could get a job at the British Museum – the need to record all the varied species of flora is becoming more important. I would be independent and wouldn't be a burden to you at all.'

'There is no such thing as an independent woman,' he blusters, his cheeks tinged with pink. 'Your mother's dream for you was nonsense. No one can argue that an amateur interest in botany is not a pious pastime. Being surrounded by God's nature is an excellent pastime for a girl – but you are a woman now. Leave the professional ambitions to the men.'

'But Father—' My blood simmers beneath my skin.

'I do not envisage the museum will be interested in your flower arranging and amateur painting skills. Your efforts in trying to study will come to nothing. You must put all notions of taking this hobby any further.' He waves his knife in front of him as if he were drawing a stem and petals in the air between us.

'The study of botany is not about arranging flowers, it's so much more. It is a proper vocation. Each plant has a purpose, and I believe they can communicate with their surroundings in some way. There is much research being conducted on the subject.' For once, David looks up from his food, showing interest in my words and giving me the confidence to continue with my defence. 'Also, medically, there are many uses for their properties. Take the nightshade, for example. It can be poisonous, but in a small enough dose it can be used as a healing remedy.'

David screws up his face in the manner that he has eaten something distasteful. 'Now you sound like a common witch making potions. You will be selling them at the market next.'

'I am not a witch, you know that?' I give a nervous laugh. 'And besides, Mother told me that those women were misunderstood because they did not fit into society. This is a different age.'

'No,' he mutters, 'there is no difference between a deluded woman touched by madness, then or now. You must take care not to drag the family name down in the real world because of your fantasies.'

'All I am asking for is a chance to prove myself. I have my own ambitions, which do not include being someone's wife.'

'Whatever are you thinking? If you continue like this, you will bring shame to the family. This is exactly what Edith warned me about.' My father snaps at me, finally exasperated. 'God knows I saved your mother from the madhouse once. Do not say history is repeating itself?'

I want to retaliate; the words rage in my head: How dare you mention Mother in the same breath as a madhouse. You lie to me as you lie about Mother having no family. But I remain mute. I do not want to antagonise him further, suddenly wary of what might become of my unruly tongue.

'Your mother, God rest her soul, was also my wife. She had her own struggles that you were not party to.' As if he predicts my rebellion, he lowers his voice. 'Do not question me, daughter. You would do well to remember your manners under my roof.'

He is talking nonsense, and I refuse to validate his ridiculous words. Mother was the sanest person I know. It is my father who is not of sound mind. I remind myself that he is grieving.

He tugs at the lapel of his maroon velvet smoking jacket, his cheeks matching in colour, ruddy with quiet rage. 'This is all because of that blasted woman at the funeral. She was a nobody, filling your head with nonsense! Your mother had no one else but us; believe anything else at your peril.'

Both my father and brother resume their dinner, unfazed by my barely restrained emotion. Am I nothing but a slave to be sold if this is not my choice? Even our servants are treated better than this.

The meal continues until my father speaks again, the food and wine calming his spirits. 'It is well past the time to grow up and leave any childish notions in the past. Your mother indulged you too much.' My father pauses. 'Besides, it is a misgiving that your mother had any fortune of her own.'

I gasp out loud. 'Yes, she did. She told me the money was from her father. She'd saved it for me.'

'I am sorry to disappoint you, Ivy, but there is no fortune. The fever must have affected her senses, and even if it did exist, it would be required elsewhere since your mother's money would also be mine. I am afraid she filled your head with impossible dreams.'

'I have money of my own.' I stammer. 'Nonsense, a few coins saved will not last long, and I will certainly not give you any to indulge these ridiculous fancies of yours. You are so like your mother...' His shoulders slump, and then, as though he's put on a mask, he befriends denial. 'I refuse to discuss this matter any further. I am sorely disappointed in your attitude. A man burying his wife and his daughter turning on him within the same month is unforgivable.'

I know in my gut he is wrong. There is money somewhere – Mother told me she had been sent some long before she became ill. She must have hidden it. But there appears to be no argument left to defend. I am at the mercy of my father's decisions and have no voice in the matter. If I were his son, I know this conversation would be very different.

The heat of embarrassment spreads through my stomach and up to my neck. Deeply conscious of my physical presence, I want to shrink into nothing and disappear, my body wanting to expel this sickening sensation. The dinner before me sits untouched. My upper lip moistens with the heat of shame. The shame of being me, the shame of being the wrong sex – merely a woman.

Father turns towards my brother. 'When the summer is done, David, you must come to the factory and learn the trade. It is about time, and it will build your character. The family name must continue.' He glances at me. 'Ivy, your efforts would be best directed towards your future husband and ensuring you become a good wife.' As an afterthought, he considers me again. 'Perhaps you would benefit from spending some time with Edith. You will find her counsel valuable, as I have. She can educate you on how a young woman should behave. I am afraid your mother, unfortunately, did not guide you well in that respect – too much time in the garden and not enough on proper education. Your kind cousin brought the problem of your future residence to my attention and was instrumental in the good fortune of this proposal too. You should be grateful for her attention; she will make a lady out of you.'

As Miss Earnshaw predicted, there are indeed forces working against me. The silver cutlery glints in the firelight. If Edith were here, I would take the knife to her throat and silence her interfering voice.

Chapter 5 ~ Edith

Ivy ~ Elm House, 16th November.

'I thought I might find you here.' Edith stands hesitantly in the doorway to my mother's bedroom, watching me sit on the bed reading a book. It is not her usual style to be so restrained. 'May I come in?'

Two days have passed since the conversation at dinner about my future. I have become absorbed in reading about the deadly nightshade family. My usually favoured volume on The Language of Flowers sits discarded on the shelf, gathering dust. Avoiding company has become my focus, taking all my meals in my room, becoming the recluse I am already accused of being. My botanical hand lens, a gift from my mother for my twenty-first birthday, is carried everywhere. My fingers are constantly sliding the three-fold-out magnification lenses open and shut. Perhaps I am hoping to find evidence, no matter how small, that my mother is still here. At times, I can almost feel her presence. My father has assumed I am either sulking or grieving and leaves me alone.

I cannot stop speculating about Miss Earnshaw. Her words echo in every silence, urging me to come to her at once. The single white rose she laid on my mother's grave symbolises a new beginning and everlasting love. Am I reading too much into her words and actions? Her offer of help, an orangery to work in, is a glimmer of hope to the alternative I am reading in the pages in my lap. Am I acting out of pain? But I cannot breathe. The heaviness of existing is too much. For in each suffocating moment that follows the last, there is no world I can see myself in without my mother and my plants.

Edith enters and takes a seat by the window, despite the fact that I barely acknowledge her. It is my mother's chair with the best view of the garden. She looks out over the lawn. 'Such a lovely room. Your mother had fine taste.'

I baulk at the use of the past tense. Sitting in her room, I can maintain the illusion that she is still present. I can smell her, touch her hairbrush and hairpins as she left them, as if it will only be a short moment until she returns to me, as she said she would.

Edith's presence disturbs me. She is out of place. I watch her smooth down her dress. She is biding her time. But for what?

'The fact has not gone unnoticed. You may feel somewhat alone now.'

'Loneliness is not a sin,' I say, blurting out my reply.

'Sweet girl. Of course, but...' She looks out of the window.

I try to imagine that she is my mother, but her frame and colouring are too different. This false image cannot fill the void.

'We must try to be strong in these circumstances. Goodness knows I have suffered my fair share of loss. I understand your grief.'

Does she? Her words betray her face, her expression is righteous.

'I spoke at length with your father. You must trust that we have your best interests at heart. Why don't you come and join me over here in the light, and we can talk properly woman-to-woman?' She motions to the empty chair beside her. Mother and I often sat together in the warmth of the window. It's also my favourite place in the house.

'Consider me your confidante now, your...' The words fade away. 'I always wanted a daughter.'

I move reluctantly, not wanting to listen, but I won't leave her in this room alone. It would be disrespectful somehow. This space needs to be protected and preserved.

'You do understand how much your father cares for you?'

Nodding, I only give a slight agreement. I cannot control the basic ticks of politeness. I realise he holds some degree of care for me, but underneath it, I sense I've been tolerated only for the sake of my mother. He would have preferred another son to join him in his work. Now I am redundant; a loose end to tie up and move on from.

'Oh, yes, he told me how deep his regard is for you. And perhaps you remind him too much of your mother? You know how men are when they are bereaved... We must account for his emotions in this too. It is up to us to guide our dear menfolk through everything. That is why they look to us during the changing phases of life. They would be lost without us.'

Edith glances around the room. I have removed the covering from the mirror and allowed the clock to persist with its ticking. The superstitious custom of stopping time at the hour of death has not been extended to this part of the house. I am aware this disrespect to the dead displeases her by the agitation of her fingers, which flutter in her lap, itching to rectify my errors.

'But I agree with him,' she continues, 'that perhaps it is best you focus on your future now. You are a woman with a certain value to others and are attractive ... to the right person.'

The compliment twists inside my gut with a barbed edge. Self-consciously, I touch my mousey brown hair, neither straight nor curly. I do not have the same vibrant flame tones as Mother once did. Appearances have never been my forte. I had hoped to embrace a feminine fascination with lace and bows, but the desire never came. I prefer practical over fussy decoration.

Edith sees my hand movement as a sign of agreement. 'If you want my help, you only have to come and ask. I could assist you with the current fashion. I assure you; it would be no trouble. Your mother was a natural beauty, and perhaps with a little assistance, you will blossom yet.' She appraises me like a doll in need of a new outfit. 'It would make the prospect of marriage much easier for you. A husband looks more favourably on a pretty wife.'

I focus on her thin lips as they move, opening and shutting like a fish caught on a hook.

'We could start with small things, like cleaning the soil from your nails and drawing your corset tighter to cinch your waist in. Your posture and health will be much improved.' She looks at my hair. 'I could pin your unruly locks and decorate them with some green ribbon to bring out your eyes.'

Her words buzz like bees around my head, an uncomfortable hum of noise. I pick at my nails with their ingrained dirt around the edges, considering her statements.

She sighs, cupping my chin gently as she tries to get me to sit straighter. 'But we must work together. Must you always angle your face so awkwardly when you're thinking? It is so unbecoming. That is one habit we will have to work on changing.'

I can't help but shake my head in irritation. The hurt from overhearing her conversation about me at the funeral is still raw, but she ignores my reaction and continues speaking.

'I trust you will be pleased with your father's choice. I personally suggested the pairing with Mr Whitlock. I think you two will be a good match – I heard you took a stroll together only last month. He has been admiring you from afar for some time now.'

I flinch at the use of his name. I remember Mr Whitlock's sweaty hands on my wrists, his sloppy lips on mine. Pushing my sleeve up a little, the purple bruises have gone, but the memory hasn't faded. The mottled blotches of fingerprints haunted me for days until they healed – my skin so pale, they looked like a ruined watercolour painting. He had accompanied me on my outing to collect more examples of ferns to press into my sketch book. I understood too late that he had directed our walk to a secluded part of the garden. All of my belongings had been cast from my hands as I struggled against the weight of him. My beautiful hand lens lay covered in dirt, and the vasculum was thrown open and abandoned; my careful cuttings trampled into the soil.

A call from my maid, Nellie, had thankfully startled him, and I was able to wrench free and run to her through the trees as she searched for me on a pathway nearby. Later, he returned my possessions to the house, clean, but the vasculum was empty, as though I had lost interest and merely forgotten my most treasured belongings. Anyone who knew me properly would have known this was a lie – I would never leave them behind willingly.

It was the same day that Mother's illness took a turn for the worse, and I tried to forget the whole horrid ordeal. My wrist still aches from his grip. I had managed to hide the red marks from Nellie when dressing, yet she was unusually gentle with the corset for days. I am sure she knew what had happened, and it was no coincidence she was out in the garden when I needed her.

Edith has stopped talking and is waiting for my response. This woman must always command the full focus of her listener. 'I am good friends with his mother. So naturally, I could visit you often. Wouldn't that be nice? I am sure they would consider your delicate nature, and his mother would guide you in all matters of your future.'

Her words are much softer than Father's, but they mean the same thing.

'What about my plants?'

Perhaps I could still work. I push the image of Mr Whitlock's unpleasant face away and think of the many cuttings safe in their plant pots, lining the sill of nearly every window downstairs. I had cared for each one, making sure they had enough light and water and noting their growth preferences. Some were years old.

'You could take one or two with you, I suppose. Besides, surely you are not hoping to stay here on your own, indefinitely, by choice. What would you possibly do all day, apart from pressing leaves?'

'I would continue with my work. If I am to become a botanist, I must be rigorous in my studies. There is also a lot of work to be done on the grounds. Mother and I had planned a new flower garden. And the hedgerows will be abundant with new life in the spring. I must document everything that grows.'

Edith rolls her eyes. 'I would be driven mad at that prospect. Gardening is not enough to occupy a young woman. What a waste of time, and besides, your father has made his wishes clear. You must leave the plants in the garden where they belong.'

'But they are my plants,' I state slowly, as if spelling out each word.

'No, they are God's plants. Why, with my encouragement, you could be the lady of Whitlock House!'

'If I cannot be with my plants, then I truly have nothing to live for.'

She sighs, not understanding the serious nature of my words. 'But don't you want more?' Edith leans forward, inspecting me with her disconcerting attention. 'You are a strange girl. It is fortunate you have my attention. You are lucky to find a husband who will take you as you are now. Besides, you can no longer stay in this house. You would be better off married or living in an estate which is more suited to your needs.'

I recall the conversation I overheard at the funeral about her wanting to send me away.

She smooths her caramel hair, although not a strand is out of place, swept back in a tight bun. 'Life is fragile, Ivy. I would be grateful to be young again, as you are, and with such an opportunity. You are not widowed like me. Being a single woman is a hard burden to bear. Therefore, I like to help others, like your father. And like you, my poor dear.'

I wrinkle my nose in distaste and find my stifled voice. 'This is my home; I will not leave, and I don't need your advice or your pity.'

'Now don't be ungrateful.' Her eyes widen, shocked at my outburst. She regains her usual composure, folding her hands in her lap. 'This attitude of yours is why a private estate could look after you better than your father. Goodness knows I would if I lived here, but I have my hands full with my own house and my charity commitments.'

'You would send me to an asylum? I am not mad.' I can hardly say the words.

'Of course not. It would be a private institution where you would find other wealthy young ladies like yourself.' She pauses. 'They are treated considerably better than if they had been left to their own devices. You must admit that you have certain... shall we call them mannerisms that deviate from the norm. Even I have heard you telling people to leave the room when you are quite alone.'

I open my mouth but am lost for words. She is correct, of course. I know I am on my own, but the voices that escape from my dreams are at times too much to bear. Edith seems satisfied with her answer, although I know these institutions are just another word for an asylum, only the type she refers to take people with money. I question Edith's motives for wanting me gone from this house. Perhaps she has ideas of being the lady of the manor now that my mother is buried.

'But if you do not wish to live in an institution, it would not be a wise decision to turn down such a generous proposal. In time, you will see sense, although we do not have long. Mr Whitlock has made it quite clear he does not want to wait. We would like to set a date for early January.'

I notice the slip of her tongue. The alternative to marriage is nothing more than a glorified asylum. Her eagerness to avoid the shame this would bring and the prospect of a wedding to organise is brimming under the surface, alongside her frustration with me. How I must disappoint her with my lack of enthusiasm. Even at my wedding, she would manage to be the centre of attention.

She leans forward with a thin smile stretched across her face. 'I could arrange a trip to London to fit you for a dress. Only the best for you. Would that cheer you up? I have friends in the city who could act as your chaperone. Naturally, I would prefer to come myself, but I cannot be away from my son. Timothy has been ill of late.' She briefly touches her brow as though the recollection causes her pain. 'You could take tea at a nice hotel. I hear the Midland Grand is lovely.'

She continues, oblivious to my pinched face, as I imagine an appalling day. If she took the time to examine me closely, she would see that I am empty. Grief has stolen me away; living in the footsteps of my mother provides my only solace. I push my mourning ring firmly onto my finger.

With the mention of London, I drift out of the conversation until something else galvanises me. Thinking again of Miss Earnshaw, a new, absurd possibility lies before me: a chance that a visit might happen, despite my father's restrictions; a faint light in this tunnel of desolation.

'If I do agree to go to London, I wish to pay a visit to a lady who came to Mother's funeral. She said we were related.' My reflection in the mirror above the dressing table wavers ever so slightly, I glimpse what I might look like in London, taking tea with Miss Earnshaw in an elegant dress, my wayward hair styled with a fine hat perched on my head.

Edith's eyes bulge in their sockets. 'I am afraid that is out of the question. That was all a lie. Your father mentioned the intruder; you know nothing of her reputation. She might rob you in your sleep, leaving you alone in the city with nothing. Even associating yourself with her could lead to all sorts of embarrassment for our family name and disgrace us all. Your father and I would not agree to such a foolish demand under any circumstances. A young woman as delicate as you must protect herself from evil influences.' She tuts under her breath. 'You must look to God, not ungodly strangers.'

I snap the book shut with a thud, making Edith jump, but her unwanted advice continues.

'We must concentrate on the wedding. It is a better arrangement for everyone. Some might argue the arrangement is against mourning protocols – marrying so soon. But I am sure people would understand.'

My gaze falls to my mother's sketchbook, and Edith's voice fades away. I have placed it on her dressing table. Amongst the swirling leaves engraved in gold on the front cover of the sketchbook sits a tiny bird, almost hidden. It's the light from the window that reveals the miniature creature. The same little bird was printed on Miss Earnshaw's calling card: a blackbird! It is identical in every aspect and clearly created by the same hand.

I turn my eyes back to my cousin and she takes my silence as acceptance. These walls, once my favourite sanctuary, are starting to close in on me. Edith is right on one account: I can no longer stay here. Finding Miss Earnshaw is the only path of safety I see. If I don't have the blessing of my family to go to London, I will go without it.

Chapter 6 ~ Journey to London

Ivy ~ Bramley, 17th November.

My maid, Nellie, has asked her brother to help me journey to London. We find him in the early hours, waiting in a nearby road with a pony and trap. He takes us the short distance to the coach station with only a small nod of acknowledgement. The air is humid, and heavy black clouds form overhead, appearing to suffocate us at any moment; a sure sign that a storm is brewing. But I try to fortify myself for the journey ahead. I pray to God that my family does not come looking for me because I will not be taken to an institution or handed over to Mr. Whitlock. For all my doubts, I am sure my sanity is the same as any other. My mother wanted better for me, and I will do anything it takes to avoid the fate I will face if left in their hands.

In the next village of Bramley, I give Nellie two silver shillings before she leaves me. She is hesitant at first, but I reassure her that I have left a letter to my father stating I have acted alone. I try to swallow the guilt of running away. The scandal will no doubt become an infectious conversation in the town. But it is a small price to pay for me. I am already talked about, dissected like a science experiment in a public show.

The journey from Godalming to London should take under five hours, with a break past Guildford to refresh the horses. As I settle myself inside the coach, Miss Earnshaw's veiled face appears in my memory again. The details of her features and dress are sharper than those of my mother's image, which to my dismay, is already losing focus. Despite her ominous warnings, I hope that she is the answer to my freedom. But I do not possess the strength of body or mind to be dragged into any unsavoury business if she is a fraudster. If that is her ambition, she will be disappointed to find that I have no money of my own. Father's negative reaction still haunts me, but I will prove him wrong on all accounts. I couldn't bear it if he was right.

The more I reflect, the more my suspicion increases that she is not a stranger to my family. If that is true, it will be such a reprieve to be in the company of someone who will not quieten me in my memories. My grief aches to be acknowledged, but I force it down, the depth of emotion all-consuming. At my mother's funeral, I felt numb, but now reality has taken hold – the finality of death, the separation from the only love in my life. The pain is too deep to bear. I sob until there is nothing left of me, grateful for the noise of the horse's hooves to drown out my cries.

I watch the fields pass by as the carriage rocks me, pulling me forward along the uneven track. With each mile travelled, my mood slowly improves, banishing some of my fears, although the grief never leaves.

My attention finally falls on my mother's sketchbook, nestled in my magenta and gold embroidered carpet bag. Along with my small navy reticule, I am comforted by my most precious luggage close by my side; my leather case full of my clothes is strapped to the top of the carriage roof. Inside my carpet bag, I have even brought my vasculum, hand lens, and plant reference book in the hope of making studies within Miss Earnshaw's orangery. I am only sorry I did not have space for my screw-down plant press.

Touching the book gently, I know the language of symbols and drawings is important – a code of some kind. If I can unlock it, perhaps I can understand the hidden secrets my mother took to her grave. I recall again that the book and the card have the same little blackbird design. Are they part of a strange link to her past?

'We will be stopping soon!'

I can barely hear the driver with the noise of the wheels and the clatter of horses' hooves. I lower the window and lean out. 'Excuse me, already?'

'I said we'll have to stop. The sky has turned with the storm. I won't risk the horses.'

'Very well, if we must.' I shout back. 'How far away is an inn?'

'We'll arrive in about an hour, enough time to miss the worst of the weather!'

In the fields, the cows sit huddled in small groups, heeding the warning. The back of my neck tenses with foreboding as I anticipate the headache, which seems to arrive more frequently since Mother's death. I am truly alone for the first time in my life. Did I make a mistake in sending the maid away?

I last saw Mother alive on a day like today, when the sky was heavy with thunderous clouds and expectation. I sat next to her bedside, watching her fall in and out of consciousness, reading verses aloud from the Bible that drifted over her body like a blanket. As dusk fell, and I lit the candles on her bedside table, she called out, 'Ivy, Ivy?' When she saw it was me, she took my hand and drew it to her lips. 'My love, you must be strong. Remember that you are enough.'

My eyes watered. 'Please, don't leave me.'

'I will always be with you. Look to your plants, the ones we planted together. The earth will help you after I've gone.' Each word was a struggle as she gripped my hand, her knuckles whitening as pale as her face. 'And please remember, you will not be alone in the dark.'

I took much comfort in our last moments together, but I have not yet been able to return to the same ground we once tended together. The act is still too painful without her. But now that I think about it, did I misinterpret her final words? Were they a warning instead? For each night since she died, my childhood nightmares have worsened, spilling into the sounds of the night when I wake. Whispered voices: some mutter in anger, others cry in anguish. I can never understand the words, but they leave my blood cold.

The daylight disappears fast, even though it is not yet mid-day. Heavy rain clouds hover even lower, appearing within a hand's reach. The sky threatens to break as the coach pulls up alongside an old building at the crossroads. An orange glow emanates from the iron-crossed windows, and smoke billows from the chimney. Already, my joints hurt from the constant jostling of the carriage and the horses' stumbling steps on the ground, which is still hard from the frost and bumpy from potholes.

'We'll have to stay.' He mutters as I climb out of the carriage. 'The storm coming looks too bad. We cannot ride further.' He motions to the building beside us. 'This is the White Hart. They do a good bit of grub and a bed.'

I nod in agreement, although I am disappointed I will not make it to London for the evening.

'I'll bring your case in presently, miss.' He barely glances in my direction and dismisses me from his presence now that we have arrived. He's already focused entirely on the two horses, patting and examining their horseshoes with a practised, careful eye. Stooped in his bearing, his gaunt face appears to be around two score years and ten, his face aged from driving through many unpredictable seasons. Even though he is older and moves more slowly, he still has strength and agility.

I enter the inn alone with false confidence and my two pieces of hand luggage. I had expected to find a full room filled with pipe smoke and conversation. Instead, only a couple of tables are occupied by workers – countrymen with simple clothes and hands that turn the earth. They lean forward to watch me as I cross the room to the serving counter.

'There's a bad storm coming. Are you wanting board and a meal?' A woman with a florid complexion and coarse grey hair swept back from her face shouts across the room. She must be the wife of the innkeeper. She is busy. Not stopping for a minute, she continues to serve two full plates of steaming food to the men by the fireside. She directs her voice with ease over the seated patrons. 'We do a rabbit pie or a hearty beef stew, and a nice red wine or a local ale if the drink takes your fancy. Board is three shillings a night and includes a breakfast of muffins.'

I try to repress the rumble of my stomach. My hunger has risen fast in response to the meaty aroma. 'Yes, thank you,' I reply. The sight of a comfy seat and the smell of the food is a welcome respite from the potholes.

'I will take a night's stay. The coach driver will soon be inside with my luggage.' I nod towards the door expectantly, but it stays closed. Only the faint patter of rain on the cobbles outside and the drizzle sliding down the windowpanes show the quick change in weather. I hope he has not left my case out to get wet. A couple of the tables are empty. Would it be acceptable for a lady to eat with strangers in a place such as this?

The woman catches my eyes surveying the room, and sensing my question, returns with a key. 'Why don't you get yourself settled in your room and I'll bring you up some food... The beef stew, was it, Miss...?'

'Miss Granger,' I say, smiling and relieved. 'Yes, that would be most kind.' I am thankful for her sensitivity that I dine alone. I am weary, and an afternoon of solitude and rest beckons.

A cold blast of air rushes in from outside, whipping at my ankles. I watch as the coach driver finally pushes his way through the narrow doorway with my case and I am relieved to see it is not too damp from the rain. I found the luggage in the main house's attic. The brown leather seemed to be in good shape, even though it had been hidden in the eaves.

He exchanges a greeting with the innkeeper's wife and seems familiar with the place, already navigating the way to my room. I follow him up the stairs a little way behind and find him waiting at the end of a fair-sized corridor. Perhaps nine or ten doors span the hallway. I had not thought the inn was so large from the entrance.

He waits next to the furthest door, and I wonder why he doesn't enter until I notice I still hold the key. 'Here you are,' he says, as the door opens. 'I'll be seeing you in the morning. We leave at eight.' He mumbles, awkward from being alone in a private room.

I stride over to the dresser, which holds an unlit lamp. He places my belongings down inside the doorway and stands while I fumble with a candle to light the room. The afternoon sun has almost completely vanished. Maybe he is reluctant to leave me without company. Does he sense I am afraid? This is the first time I have left the family home.

The room is dismal and lonely compared to the bright fire and calm chatter of the people downstairs, so even though I want him to go, I'm grateful to him for staying longer. But as soon as the flame becomes strong, he leaves, his firm footsteps hitting each step of the wooden staircase.

I turn and appraise the space, simply furnished with a small bed, a table and chair, a dresser with a dish of water, and a wardrobe. The furniture is made of dark oak, which doesn't give the room a welcoming appeal. Instead, the gloomy colour enhances the loneliness of the room. With only a couple of hours of travel, homesickness is already trying to creep in.

I remove my cloak and gloves and place them on the bed. When the landlady enters with the meal, the aroma from the hot food is delicious, my mouth watering at the sight of the tray with a bowl of thick gravy and a large chunk of fresh bread on a small plate.

'I'll make you a nice fire and get this room warmed up.' She sets the dishes down on the table and then kneels, placing kindling and logs onto the grate from a neat stockpile in a wicker basket. I fumble to hang my cloak inside the wardrobe. The door is stuck, warped against the hinge. With a sharp pull on the handle, it reveals ample space for my cloak and luggage.

My hunger is demanding. Sitting at the scuffed wooden table to eat, I try to chew at a slower pace, but the meal is so delicious, the sauce dribbles down my chin. Such poor manners would never be accepted at home, but somehow, I have already shed some of the rigours of restraint, abandoning polite etiquette. I dab my lips with my handkerchief from my dress pocket as the landlady stokes the fire, none the wiser to my lack of décorum.

'A tasty dish,' I add, glancing up at her, placing my spoon back in the now empty bowl.

'It's a family recipe, some secret ingredients,' she replies, standing up and turning to face me.

With food this good, I would expect the downstairs to be filled with people eating. 'Do you get busy on this road? You have a large building. I imagine you can accommodate many?'

The woman hesitates. 'I suppose we could, but not all the rooms are for rent. It's best that way. But yes, people do come for our food now and then. We were full once.' She does not elaborate further. The conversation has taken a melancholy turn, and I do not wish to press her. 'We have dinner tonight and then we start breakfast at six,' she continues. 'If that's too early, we can prepare something for you to eat on the way. I understand the carriage is set to leave at eight?' She picks up the dirty crockery, smiling at the empty bowl in approval.

'If something was prepared, I would be grateful. Thank you. I rarely have an appetite before nine.'

'It is no trouble, Miss. I'm directly below your room should you need anything. Though I expect, after your journey and the stew, you'll want to rest now. Come down later if you're hungry again this evening.'

Before she closes the door, I consider the remaining rooms in the corridor. 'Is there anyone else staying on this floor tonight?' I ask loudly. She must have heard, but the door shuts without a reply.

Taking out a book I've brought with me about spring herb planting, I sit on the bed intending to pass the rest of the afternoon reading, but my attention is short-lived. The pull of sleep is too tempting, and the book slips from my grasp as I close my eyes. When I open them again, it feels like only a brief moment has passed, but it must have been hours, for it is now completely dark outside and the inn is quiet below. I have missed dinner, but I am still full from the stew, so it is no matter.

I make my evening ablutions using the chamber pot and the small dish of cold water left on the dresser and change into my white flannel nightgown and knitted grey shawl, grateful for the long sleeves and high neck – a small protection against the draughty room – and pull the bed-covers aside. I already miss Nellie, my maid; everything takes longer. The sheets look clean enough but are cold and slightly damp. I move into the middle, waiting for my body to warm up, my feet unwilling to stretch out.

A lone branch taps on the windowpane. I imagine a desperate ghostly skeleton, his bony fingers trying to pry open the glass, seeking shelter. Even the drawn curtains do not prevent the room from harbouring an eerie atmosphere.

As I lie there watching the shadows cast from the lamp dance across the wall, my thoughts wander. My limbs are still tired, but now my mind is restless. I leave the lamp on the table burning as it brings comfort, easing my loneliness in such an unfamiliar place.

After a time, I must have drifted off again, because suddenly I am wide awake, startled and cold. What disturbed me, I do not know. The light and fire have both dimmed considerably, the wood reduced to glowing embers. Tiny smoulders of orange and red dance about the room, but the desolate atmosphere encroaches towards me, threatening to engulf the bed. I tuck myself further into the sheets, attempting to sleep once more.

I have almost calmed my spirits when a door in the corridor slams shut with such a violent force, I nearly cry out. It comes from somewhere in the distance, near the staircase. A few minutes of silence pass until there is a faint muffled sound and another slam of a door. This time it's closer. The storm has picked up, and the wind is rushing loudly through the trees. This is an old building and draughty in bad weather, a far cry from the comfort of my room back in the family home.

Rhythmic heavy feet make their way down the hallway, opening and closing every door in turn. One sounds like it's being thrown shut. Irritated by the absence of empathy towards fellow guests, I decide to raise the issue in the morning. Yet now, the noises have become ever more erratic, as though this disreputable stranger is working themselves into a temper. What or who are they looking for?

Jumping from the mattress, I hurry towards the door and feel for the key in the lock to reassure myself of safety. Yes, I'd locked it. But anxiety overtakes me. Combined with the remnants of panic from my nightmare, my nerves are on edge, and I am clammy under my nightdress. I keep my palm on the door as though my touch can somehow prevent it being opened if the lock fails. The banging progresses closer to my room, then there's a hush – someone is standing on the other side of the hallway.

A dull light shines under the crack of the door. The handle gently starts to turn. Or is it my eyes playing tricks? I try to focus on the lock, but the image remains unfocused. I cannot make out if the key is moving or if it's my imagination. My mouth becomes completely dry. Should I scream for help? But the door doesn't move, and the light gradually fades away. Trembling with cold and trepidation, returning to bed only provides a meagre comfort in the terror of this strange place.

As I climb back between the sheets, I have a strange sensation of being watched. The movement in the hallway has left me greatly unsettled. Perhaps there is still someone waiting on the other side of my door after all, inconspicuous in their movements. I cannot tell what gives me this feeling. Trying to calm myself once more, I put it down to the storm. I am prone to headaches when the weather changes for the worst. A familiar dull pain creeps behind my temples, making my vision blur. But the anticipation of waiting for something to happen remains.

My eyes try to adjust to the dimness. There is no sense in the notion that someone could be in the room watching me. I will not succumb to these childish fears. Finding something to distract my imagination, I recite all the ferns I have collected, their Latin names calming me: Gymnocarpium robertianum, the scented oak fern, is my favourite.

A muffled voice comes from the shadows; the tone rises and falls, a desperate, melancholy sound. There must be a drunken patron somewhere in the building who is talking to themselves.

Mother always told me the things I heard escaping from my dreams were merely the result of an overactive mind. If only she were here with me now, for I fear the whispers of madness have returned. Perhaps I am destined for an institution, as Edith implied. I force the unwanted thought away, ignoring the faint words of desperation that echo in every crack of thunder and howl of the wind. My weak show of bravery is an embarrassment. Turning the gas lamp up full, it splutters for a moment with a burst of dim light, and the scratching takes on a more frenzied energy. It comes from the furthest corner by the window.

To my disbelief, the drawing of roses and vines on the front of the wardrobe door starts to move. I have always loved roses, but I suck in my breath as the vines around the blooms appear to grow. Holding out the lamp before me, the image begins to pulse. The greedy vines spread out, wrapping themselves around the wardrobe handles and doors, strangling the flowers until they are all crushed and suffocated. An ugly mass of thick green stems and thorns is all that remains. 'Ivy!' In between the bright bolts of lightning and the cracks of thunder, I hear my name called. I almost throw the lamp onto the table before I retreat back under the blankets, pulling them firmly over my head.

Only at dawn, when sunlight filters through the cracks in the curtains, does the storm quiet down and the roses bloom again, as if the night-time terrors never occurred.

Chapter 7 ~ The Parlour Game

Master Blackham, Blackham House, 11th November.

The servants have cleaned the house thoroughly. Each room is
polished and aired from the beatings of curtains and rugs,
especially the parlour, which is prominent in displaying their
wealth at the front of the house. The smell of beeswax drifts along
the corridors, mingling with the dried flowers adorning the side
tables, their preserved summer blooms boasting of a long-past hot
summer day.

Master Blackham retires to his library, avoiding the
commotion that the evening preparations have created. He is
determined to put his melancholy behind him and focus on his new
wife, Angelica, but first he needs a drink. He pours himself a large
measure and takes his usual seat beside the fireplace.

A flurry of activity follows each maid, who moves objects
aimlessly from room to room at Angelica's whim. She is in her
element, revived from her recent visit to the countryside – a rest to
recuperate, recommended by the family doctor. With plenty of
clean air and forest walks over several weeks, she has returned
with a vigour Blackham had enjoyed when they first married a
year earlier, the fragility and paleness of pallor banished. She is
now attired in a new gown in the vibrant hues of pink and green.

But this is not love, only attraction. Perhaps in time, the
emotion may evolve into more, and the suspicion that he has made
a mistake will lessen. Angelica, bright and enthusiastic, expresses a
simple interest in politics, and he takes pleasure in indulging her,
listening to her Italian accent and her modern views, spurred on by

her discovery of the suffrage movement. It will not come to anything, but the subject is an interesting pastime.

This marriage overshadows his previous attempts to block out thoughts of Miranda, the empty comfort he had sought in heartless love affairs and the secluded corners of his favoured opium dens. He shakes off the negative intrusion, the familiar clutches of dread threatening to drag his mood under. No, he will not think of her today; only the living will occupy his thoughts from now on.

Tonight's party has been meticulously planned. The idea arose from their doctor and was presented to his new wife as a pretext to occupy her time, a social gathering to bring some laughter back into the house.

Angelica has embraced the event, sending out invitations and engaging the entertainment for the evening. It is to be a night of parlour games, starting with the usual blind man's bluff and ending with the arrival of a special guest. She has organised it as a surprise for everyone, including her husband. He often finds these events tedious and turns to the decanter of whisky to help him through, blunting the tiresome game routines.

But something about tonight suggests a different evening. Energy buzzes in the house, and for the first time in a long while, a spark of excitement builds within him. He has watched his wife peruse the pages of Mrs Beeton, learning everything about English food, keen not to make a mistake. She has carefully selected a menu for dinner, choosing the popular dish of roasted duck, a current favourite amongst his peers.

The butler knocks and enters with his pressed suit, smelling faintly of the lavender pouches stored in the press box. No lingering scents from the gentlemen's club, not a single detail left to chance.

This will be their first occasion as a couple in public. They had planned to host a party when they returned from their wedding and subsequent six-month honeymoon in Europe, but soon after settling in London, Angelica fell ill. A fall down the staircase had ended an early pregnancy, causing a nervous condition diagnosed by the family physician. But after a trip to the countryside that was recommended for her health, he is relieved that she is now ready to make a suitable first impression on his two closest friends and their wives.

'The mistress is almost ready, Sir. They should be finished by the hour. We arranged everything to start at seven o'clock.'

'The candles are all lit? This was Angelica's particular requirement. We must display plenty of candles, especially in the parlour.' He drums his fingers across his glass of whisky as he waits for a reply. The alcohol should have calmed him down by now, but his underlying anxiety still prevails.

'Yes, all is well, sir. We should expect a fine evening.'

'Thank you, Bancroft,' he replies. 'I hope this means our luck is changing.' He tries to smile as he drains the last drops from his glass, but he cannot shake the notion that there is something amiss about tonight.

Several hours later, the guests arrive: two women, wealthy and of high social class. Their husbands show up thirty minutes later, their carriage drawing up loudly in the street with the clattering of hooves. Master Blackham appears from the library as Mr Bancroft greets two men at the front door: Mr George Ashdown and Captain Philip Lynch.

Captain Lynch, already inebriated, bellows out every word in the entrance hall. 'I expected you to be in the heart of the ladies, not waiting out here for us. It is a shame you did not join us at the club first.'

'On the contrary, you have caught me in mid-errand,' Master Blackham replies, holding up a book depicting sketches of Italy. 'Your wives are fascinated with the previous home of Angelica; they insist on seeing proof.'

'So, where are you hiding your lovely new wife? I cannot wait to meet her myself!' He opens his eyes wide in mock excitement. 'Has she recovered? That fall was bad luck. Still, I'm glad she has returned to you in one piece.' Captain Lynch pats the master's shoulder. We've missed you at the club the last few weeks, haven't we, Ashdown? Has this whirlwind marriage changed you from your usual habits of debauchery?'

They toss their winter coats and top hats to the butler as if he were nothing more than a hat stand. Both men wear black bespoke-tailored suits and bow ties.

'Not what we expected you to bring back from your travels. 'I must say, you have outdone your father in terms of spoils for the Blackham collection.'

Master Blackham only responds with a wry grin.

'Yes, it's not been the same without you sat brooding by the fire,' Ashdown says, with lips puckered down in exaggerated sadness. 'And besides, I've not played a decent game of poker in days.'

Both men laugh in unison. Captain Lynch wraps his arm around Master Blackham's shoulders in a tight embrace. 'I may be nearly forty, but we are still young, and you left an awful space to fill. Why don't you come back with us tonight after this little soirée?' He lowers his voice to a loud whisper. 'My wife arrived early, and no doubt she will leave early too.'

Ashdown interrupts, his eyes bright with eager anticipation. 'As I'm sure will mine. The ladies tire easily in this cold weather, but we can take a trip through Cleveland Street and get sozzled together. I heard there is a new place open.' The statement is laced with excitement and conspiracy. 'Although, after the news of last night, we might have to be more careful. They say a killer is on the loose.'

'Have you had a cup too many?' Master Blackham forces a laugh. 'You are talking nonsense, my good man.'

'Don't you know? The body of a woman has been found strangled and with her throat cut. Most disconcerting and extremely gory by all accounts.' Ashdown mimes a gruesome death, his bearded face animated as he plays dead. Their joviality is lost for a moment as the sad scene hangs heavy between them.

'Most terrible, I'm sure. But isn't that London for you? There is always some madman on the loose wreaking havoc.' Master Blackham does know London. Especially with these men who have accompanied him down the backstreets and into the hidden doorways to the opium dens on numerous occasions.

He glances towards the parlour, where the voice of his wife mingles with the others. Her gentle sing-song melody comforts him, and he prefers to know exactly where she is at all times.

With another burst of conjured joviality, he brushes their words aside: 'Gentlemen, when you meet her, you will completely understand the reason for my absence! I am quite unable to leave her company at the moment.'

Captain Lynch releases him and pats his back with a hefty slap. 'I am not surprised you have netted a treasure. Ladies have never been able to resist your charming conversation or those devilish blue eyes of yours. I hear Italian women are famous for their beauty.'

'I am sure she is the most delightful creature, old man, but do not abandon us for too long. We will wait until the honeymoon shine fades, as it inevitably will. She cannot charm you for much longer; otherwise, I will claim her as a witch with ungodly powers.' Mr Ashdown's voice is loud enough to carry throughout the house.

Master Blackham fidgets with his suit, uncomfortable in the spotlight of his friend's attention.

'Leave him be, Ashdown. Can't you understand that the man is in love? I'm glad to see you this happy, and I, for one, like your renewed positive spirit. Marriage suits you.' Captain Lynch pauses. 'Just like the first time, I recall. I trust you will treat this one better?'

The butler coughs, intercepting any awkwardness as a strained silence hovers between them.

Mr Ashdown shoots the captain a warning glance to shut him down. 'Come on, Lynch, don't bring up the past and spoil the evening. Blackham doesn't want to be reminded of all that. We are just sore we haven't found another player to thrash us at poker quite like you do.' He takes a step forward and grins. 'Now lead me to your new wife. Perhaps she might have the power to reform me, too.'

Master Blackham smiles, but his mood has truly soured.

Mr Bancroft leads the three men to the parlour opposite the library, where they each take a glass of champagne from the maid with a silver tray. The atmosphere is convivial, as expected. The wives, dressed in bright colours of lemon and mulberry, resemble tropical birds against the dark mahogany furniture. Angelica greets his friends with a sweet smile, her rich satin gown framing her like an exquisite oil painting in the firelight. Everyone is in high spirits, and glasses clink together in toasts and salutations.

The butler enters the room carrying a small calling card on a silver tray. 'A lady has arrived, Mistress Angelica. She is waiting in the hallway and told me you were expecting her?'

Angelica's face lights up as she picks up the card. 'Yes, that is correct. Thank you, Bancroft. I will accompany you and greet her myself.'

'What is all the chatter over there?' Mr Ashdown booms from across the room.

'I won't be a moment,' Angelica replies with a furtive smile. 'It appears that our final game of the night has arrived.'

'More games?' Mr Ashdown responds. 'I am worn out with all these charades. I couldn't possibly think up any more stories after imbibing so much port.' Taking out his pocket watch, his face stretches in mock horror. 'Nine o'clock already! I always lose track of the hours in this house.' He looks over at Master Blackham. 'Isn't it about time to get the clocks working again?'

The master's smile is thin. 'Have you forgotten my mother? She is still in mourning.'

'Ahh, yes … quite,' he replies, returning his watch inside his jacket, patting the pocket twice. 'We wouldn't want to upset the old lady now.'

'Well, this is a different type of game. Mr Ashdown, I hope it will not disappoint.' Angelica laughs; the sound blusters through the sudden tension in the room. The mystery awakens her guests' curiosity as she stands up and leaves, returning a few minutes later with a woman dressed impeccably in ruby-red velvet and black lace, her outfit in stark contrast to the garish gowns worn by the assembled ladies in the room.

'May I present, Miss Earnshaw. She will now kindly join us in talking to the spiritual realm!'

Angelica glances around the room at the intrigued faces of their seated guests. For this was no ordinary person, but a renowned spiritualist, written about in *The Times* newspaper, resulting in her popularity soaring to new heights. Angelica was determined to hire her for a séance, ensuring it would be an evening to remember.

The butler and a maid carry the round oak table into the centre of the room, and the space at once takes on a new atmosphere in contrast to the light-hearted games a moment before. The new arrival does not unveil herself of the black netting covering her face. Instead, she ambles over to stand in front of the fireplace, resting her hands on the marble mantel. She then turns slowly, appraising each individual in the room. The guests exchange curious glances, unsure of how to proceed. They wait with bated excitement, stifling drunken laughs. Master Blackham sits quietly in the corner, holding another glass of whisky and watching the evening unfold.

'Is this a good idea?' Mr Ashdown remarks loudly. 'You know, with the history of the house and everything? I remember stories as a child when it was an empty building and held a sinister reputation. We would always run, never walk past. And that was before the unfortunate events of your family. Who knows what things lurk in the shadows?'

'Superstitious nonsense,' declares Master Blackham loudly and with conviction.

'Yes, I am sure. Sorry old chap, it's the brandy talking. I am only joking, of course. The house is quite changed now.'

'Would you like us to sit around the table?' Angelica's voice breaks the strained silence, and all eyes travel towards Miss Earnshaw.

She turns and raises the black netting, revealing that she is perhaps in her late thirties. Attractive with a scarlet gloss on her lips, her green eyes lined in charcoal command their attention. Mahogany hair frames her face, styled in curls and pinned elaborately. Her body is bestowed with gold: several bejewelled necklaces hang around her neck, along with a gold bracelet on each wrist nestled against her lavender-coloured lace gloves. She is a wealthy woman, but she looks more like a lady going to the theatre than a woman at a séance.

Still, the spiritualist does not speak but considers the guests as if she were entering the minds of every person, holding them captive. Expectancy weighs heavily in the air. 'That would be acceptable. Yes, I see there are seven of us. A fortuitous number for our needs,' she says, her voice soft and low as she motions with her gloved hands to the chairs situated around the table. Each guest, obediently, finds a place, bringing their drinks and creating a circle in the centre of the room.

Taking the seat opposite the fireplace, the spiritualist rests her hands on the table. 'My name is Miss Earnshaw,' she says firmly. 'I have been invited here tonight to connect with the spiritual realm. Please be aware that I am but a messenger and a mere gateway to this world.'

'Are we to do some spirit rapping?' asks Mrs Lynch.

'No, the spirits will talk to me directly and not through the tedious manipulation of the alphabet.' She sits up straighter in her chair, casting an imposing silhouette against the wall.

'Ha, what poppycock,' murmurs Mr Ashdown to Captain Lynch's pretty young wife. 'I have heard of this, and it is all a hoax.' He examines the room. 'No doubt this parlour hides many hidden mirrors and tricks. I recognise your name, probably a fake too... Were you not the subject of Mr Hereward Carrington who exposes so-called spiritualists?' His face is flushed with the effects of wine and the flaming hot fire. He puffs out his chest, enjoying the attention and the sound of his own voice.

'Yes! I saw a humorous cartoon in Punch on the subject.' Captain Lynch pipes up.

Master Blackham focuses on Miss Earnshaw, who remains unresponsive to the drunken taunts.

'I can assure you my name is real, as is its meaning, but that is private. I believe that when jokes are made at the expense of another, they are made out of fear. Do you have a reason to be frightened by talking with the dead tonight, sir?'

Her reply stuns him, and everyone else, as the entire room becomes silent. Only the spitting of burning kindling on the coal fire and the rumble of carriages in the street can be heard.

'You are correct.' She assesses him, measuring his reaction, and this time addresses all the guests: 'Mr Carrington and I have been associated in the past, and it is true, he met me with the express desire to expose me as a fraud. He was not the first. But I can assure you, ladies and gentlemen, that despite his best efforts, he found no validity to justify his investigation. A conversation with his late mother, however, gave him much to think about. Now, if we may continue without further interruption, I would be grateful.'

'I also don't believe in ghosts.' Master Blackham felt moved to challenge her; something about this woman unnerved him. His awareness shifted when she entered the room, an awakening of some forgotten memory.

'We shall discover what you believe at the end of the evening, sir.' She smiles politely and continues to gauge everyone with a small nod.

Watching her movements, she evokes a sense of familiarity, and yet Master Blackham knows for certain he has never seen her before. He appraises her as he sips his whisky. She wears a jewel-encrusted brooch on the front of her gown, which continually catches his attention. Made of jet-black precious stones, it forms the shape of a bird, perhaps a mockingbird, a joke at the whim of the audience.

The spiritualist unconsciously touches the brooch as she talks, explaining how the evening could unfold if the spirits are willing to engage. Perhaps the jewellery was a lucky amulet? It was not a trinket purchased in an alley from a pawnbroker, but the product of a fine jeweller. He thought the woman had a deep mystery about her. But how had she come by such wealth, unmarried as she was? He reflected on the scenarios, a distraction from the apprehension building inside of him.

A sensation of déjà vu washes over him. A sense that this is not the first time he has found himself sitting at a table with this stranger, studying that same brooch.

She catches his eye. A polite smile is given, but he offers nothing in return. He broods over his glass, perplexed at why this woman, who has entered his house with her strange ways, has unsettled him to such an extent. He shudders, unsure if he wants to remain, but curiosity and politeness root him to his chair.

'Now is the time to lower the lamps and let the candles light the way.' Her voice has a note of melancholy about it. She nods at the butler and the maid standing at attention by the door. Obediently, they move around the room, extinguishing the gas lamps until only a flickering candle flame illuminates each corner and the pale faces of the guests. The maid leaves, but the butler stands unseen in a dark corner, his eyes transfixed on the woman.

Bringing out a miniature brass candelabra and matchbox from her reticule, she lights the three small candles with a single strike of a match, the scrape of sandpaper, the only noise in the room.

'You all contain a desire to connect with someone. Maybe you are not aware of it yet; the name may be buried within you. Others may have the name of a loved one who recently crossed over on their lips. But I can assure you, they are already waiting on the other side to make contact.' She then takes out a pack of cards from her reticule and spreads six of them in an arch shape across the table. The audience leans forward as her black-laced fingers slowly turn over each card. She focuses on one card at the end of the horseshoe, hovering her finger over the illustration a little longer than the others. Sitting opposite, Master Blackham thinks he can make out the drawing of a knight on a white horse carrying a black flag, but the knight seems to have no face. He can see her brow crease upon looking at the card as she shakes her head ever so slightly.

'Do they mean anything?' He asks, deliberately pointing to the card under her hand.

'Yes,' she replies. 'They foretell the future of this night is death. We are certainly not alone tonight.'

A shocked gasp escapes from Mrs Ashdown. 'Perhaps Gerald will come?' Her voice is abrupt and strident. 'My dear brother, who passed away only in January?' Her face is earnest and without pretence. It is an honest request driven by grief.

Miss Earnshaw smiles kindly at the woman. 'I cannot say who will join us, only that we must prepare to welcome them. Everyone, please take the hand of the person sitting on either side of you and create a circle around this table. We must not break this chain, for it is the connection that will keep the gateway open.'

The guests take each other's hands. Master Blackham sits between his wife and Captain Lynch, who, on the surface, appears to be taking it all in good humour, nodding in acknowledgement to the spiritualist's instructions. Everyone but him appears to have settled into the new parlour game. Or is it a game? The question is as strong in his mind as the whiskey he reluctantly places on the table. He has drunk at least three measures of whisky already, and yet his mind is still sober. Despite the heat from the fire, Master Blackham's skin reacts with goosebumps. He had heard of these occult evenings before, but never deemed that he would ever be part of one. This woman has only succeeded in making him feel worse. He hankers after the relaxation he sought at the gentleman's club. Perhaps there will be time for a late-night visit after they finish this evening. His body aches with tension and the need to release it, to remedy himself as fast as possible.

Apprehension is familiar to him; it drifts at the back of his mind, especially since they'd returned from their honeymoon. The place, this house, where he most expected to seek solace, was often the one he sought to escape from. Despite what had happened to his beloved Miranda, even in childhood, he could not say what motivated him to find reasons to stay except loyalty to his mother, to avoid upsetting her at all costs, but the nagging push-and-pull relationship with his family home refused to leave him.

During their travels in Europe, he had finally found freedom by leaving England. The fables of discovering artefacts and his new marriage had filled a void in his life and he had returned, renewed with hope for a happier life. However, recently, a smothering blackness had crept back, an increasing disquiet within his soul – and now this permanent sense of dread invaded his thoughts.

'If we are ready, we can begin.' The spiritualist holds the hands of the guests at her sides, completing the circle. She takes a few deep breaths and starts a low hum vibrating at the back of her throat. 'If there is anyone in this room who wishes to communicate with us, please make yourself known by tapping on the table.'

The room becomes quiet in anticipation. There is nothing but the noise of street-sellers hawking their wares and the faint clatter of crockery in the kitchen basement.

'Take your time, we will be patient.' She emits a sharp breath. 'I can sense there is a spirit close to us.' Miss Earnshaw lifts her eyes to the ceiling. A dull thud is heard from the corner of the room, like the sound of a dead bird falling down a chimney. Eyes turn to the candlelit shadows, but no movement can be seen. Excitement and nerves ripple around the room.

'Please ensure the chain of hands remains intact. The communication begins.' She closes her eyes and resumes humming to herself. 'There is a woman, stepping forward into the light. She is gentle, with a kind face and golden hair. Her lips are trying to move... No, there are no words, it is a tune she sings.'

Master Blackham screws up his eyes. Surely not his first wife – it couldn't be Miranda?

Miss Earnshaw begins to hum the melody, simple and haunting. 'I am not acquainted with this music. Is there anyone here that might resonate with this?'

The young wife of the captain stammers, her eyes widening, her face turning white. 'Why, that sounds like a song my aunt would sing.' She turns to her husband, animated with excitement. 'She would sing me to sleep. It is a German lullaby she learnt abroad as a governess. She died last winter of pneumonia... I was ever so fond of her.' The emotion wavers in her voice as she touches upon her grief.

The tone of the evening has now changed. An undercurrent of nervous excitement still charges the air, but mixes with a foreboding, more sombre vibration that only comes when death is near, when fear of the unknown reveals itself even to the bravest of men.

'Could it be real? Is she here for me?'

The spiritualist nods. 'Take care not to break the circle. The realms beyond this world are not bound by the same restrictions as this one.'

'Are you related to this lady?' she says with authority, searching the room with her eyes. 'Come forward – knock once for yes, twice for no.' There is a pause, and then another dull thud from beside the window, causing everyone to jump in their seats.

'My God are you well, my dear?' The captain says to his wife, seeing her sway in her seat. 'Do you wish to return home? This might not be suitable for your nerves.'

He raises his eyebrows at Master Blackham, whose face, passive and noncommittal, gives no response. He is still struggling with the possibility that any truth exists in this madness of so-called entertainment.

'I am fine. Please don't fuss. I want to remain and hear what she wants to say. After all, I may not get another chance.' She sits up straight. 'Aunt, I am here for you. Will you speak to me? I miss you greatly.'

The spiritualist sings again. The notes, starting soft and serene, slowly become louder and haphazard, almost frenzied, until it is no longer a natural tune, but a noise emanating from beyond her throat, abstruse and unworldly. Until she stops.

Two loud thuds shake the table. As they tighten their grip, their hands tangle and their knuckles turn white. The candles flicker in the shadows, and the fire, blazing with wild abandonment, fails to cast out warmth. There is an all-pervading chill in the air that expands, resting its fingers on exposed skin, finding the uncovered napes and shoulders exposed and vulnerable.

'No, you must let her speak!' Miss Earnshaw shouts into the shadowed corner of the room. 'There is another here who has pushed forward. He demands to be heard. The lady, your aunt, stepped back. She is fading, I cannot keep her...' She keeps her eyes closed.

Every person at the table stays poised, their expressions frozen, too polite to move, to break the spell.

'The connection is broken. There is a force that works against me.' Miss Earnshaw breaks the circle. She picks up the card she discarded earlier and checks it again. 'As always, the cards do not lie.' She sucks in her breath, drawing her lips together in concentration.

'Now, if I may, I wish to take a walk around the house, for I am being drawn to a different room.' She stands at once, blowing out the candles on her candelabra and sweeping her cards in a fluid movement from the table. With no further words, she leaves the parlour and walks up the marble staircase to the first floor, as the rest of the group follows behind, until she comes to the closed door of the back room.

Her hand pauses on a door handle in the hallway of the first floor.

'Surely you have no interest in this room?' Master Blackham steps forward. 'We use this as a storage room now and it has not been prepared for viewing.'

The prospect of them all entering this small room with their bright clothes and drunken laughter alarms him. A sense of panic beats inside his chest and his starched collar becomes uncomfortably tight.

'My dear, I am positive all will be well; covered furniture or a little dirt will not offend your friends,' his wife murmurs, but still within earshot. She laughs awkwardly to diffuse his abrupt manner.

The guests pace restlessly, waiting in the wings, their conversation pulsing with disappointment. He runs his hand over his face. Who is this woman invading his house and opening any door she sees fit? 'I don't want to spoil your party, but I fear continuing with this farce will be a bore for us all crowded in there.' His words seem lost in the hallway.

Miss Earnshaw continues to stand still facing the room, her eyes on the door as if listening to something coming from within.

'Are you going to let us in or not, old man? As nice as it is standing here, I can't help but notice we have moved too far away from the port for my liking.' The captain flexes the fingers of his empty hand.

'And this hall is a bit draughty without the fire!' Mr Ashdown's voice presses forward for entry. 'I say, "open sesame" and let's be done with it. Yes, "open sesame!"'

The chorus of voices becomes a jolly chant until Master Blackham waves permission to continue. The spiritualist tries the handle, but the door is locked.

Mr Ashdown shuffles to the front of the small gathering. 'Is this a joke? Who keeps a room locked up unless there is something to hide? Unless,' he stammers, 'this has got something to do with Mira—'

'If I may be of assistance, sir,' the butler interrupts loudly, stepping from the back of the hall with a set of keys. He finds a

62

key within seconds, and the door opens with a soft catch of the lock turning.

The room lays open before them. Several furnishings have been pushed against the far wall and covered with white dust sheets, the shapes resembling a wardrobe, table, and chairs. A musty odour of rotting flowers escapes the room, although no vases can be seen.

Master Blackham hesitates, stepping only a foot inside the door and leaning against the faded damask-papered wall. He lets everyone crowd into the small room, leaving the door open. He dislikes this space. The undisguised view of the graveyard unsettles his nerves; a hundred eyes are watching him, moral judgement en masse.

He remembers his naïve idea from long ago: dreams of a nursery overlooking the once beautiful garden. That hope died along with his family; the plants rotted and the trees became infected. Until now, he had almost successfully buried the memories that lingered, taunting him. Now, back inside the room, his past crept back. Could history repeat itself? They should not be here. He had made a mistake before, the error costing him everything: his sanity, his wife.

'This is a tad on the creepy side. I didn't realise you were so close to the church. It must be a hoot on All Hallows' Eve.' Mr Ashdown pulls at one of the white coverings. It slides to the floor, revealing a tall, silver-gilded mirror.

The joke pulls at Blackham's civility, but he must not react. They have rarely seen him buckle. He scolds himself for not having the power to resist the trepidation that claws at his heart. His legs are already beginning to tremble. How long can he stay without someone noticing he is nothing better than a child wanting his mother in the night? She had never come to his aid in his youth. Why would he wish for her now when her bitterness has only increased during the years since his brother died? He prides himself on never indulging in superstition or indeed being inclined towards religion, but at this moment, his past decision to abandon this room is reinforced. He wants to forget.

The butler tuts and then turns to the maid standing by the doorway. 'We must make a point of airing this room regularly, especially if it is not in use. It is not healthy for the rest of the house if it remains so stagnant. 'What is that foul odour?'

'I have tried, but the window won't remain open,' the maid replies. 'There is something amiss with the fastening. I asked William to fix the clasp, but nothing has worked.'

'Why has the gardener been involved with this room?' Master Blackham's voice is laced with anger.

'Sometimes he has a way with the house, sir. Apologies, it will not happen again.' The butler bows his head low in submission.

The guests look through the large windowpane. It is easy to view the church and its grounds; no curtains or netting blocked the rows of headstones laid bare in the moonlight.

An air of hesitation hovers. They are waiting for something to manifest. Without instruction, the guests gather around Miss Earnshaw, who stands in the centre of the room. She appears to be listening again.

Master Blackham steps closer to his wife, noticing for the first time her anxiety is mirroring his. Their fingers entwine, a rare public display of affection. 'Do you think this is a good idea?' she whispers to him.

'No. This party has taken a turn for the worse,' he replies. 'I am taking no pleasure in this game.'

She keeps her eyes on him, and he can sense them boring into his face. 'But you are certainly enjoying her!'

Did he mistake his wife's words? It was true. He cannot take his eyes off the spiritualist. Something about her is cracking him open. 'What did you say?' He mutters as he shoots her a look of disdain, pulling his hand away from hers.

'I didn't know the evening would turn out like this. I'm sorry,' his wife says. 'I should have told you of my plans, but I hoped it might be a fun surprise.'

'This will upset Mother; I am sure of it.' He hisses the words between his gritted teeth.

Miss Earnshaw raises her arms and stretches them to the corners of the room, her pallor changing to an almost deathly shade of white, her make-up now contrasting sharply with her pale features. Someone stifles a nervous giggle as she forms peculiar words, foreign to them; not a language Master Blackham is familiar with. It starts with a low mumble, building in strength until strange noises emanate louder from her lips.

The temperature plunges even lower. Everybody waits, holding their breath to hear her next sound, to witness proof of another world beyond this one. Despite the frigid air, small beads of sweat form on Master Blackham's forehead. The very walls surrounding them appeared to move closer, unforgiving to the life they'd left outside, a distant cry from the warmth and comfort of the parlour.

He knows he will regret the decision to unlock this part of the house. This room conceals a truth that resonates in his bones. Death lives within these walls. He has no concept of how long they stand there, how much time they spend waiting. When will the spiritualist answer the question of why they are here? How has she found this place, the one hidden room which he tried to remove from his life?

Miss Earnshaw has dug under his skin and found the creeping dread lying dormant, for he is not afraid of many things. All the men in the room have had their share of unsavoury encounters and have faced the dangers of back alleyways and the shadowed doorways of London streets. But now, along with his guests, there is a new emotion: fear. Freezing them to the spot, the room emanates a mixture of excitement and consternation.

Surely, it was never his wife's intention to make him so uncomfortable, but doubts crack open the perfect image. Does she want to test him, force him to talk about the past? Was this all an elaborate plan to assert herself as the new Mrs Blackham, above his mother, above the memory of Miranda? Perhaps he does not know her as well as he thought. Her profile reveals her state of rapture towards the spiritualist. She has no idea how wretched he feels, his stomach churning with the heavy sense of something bad unravelling, something he cannot prevent.

The moonlight dims until they become nothing but shadows. The butler leaves momentarily, returning within minutes with a lamp. It projects a dull glow that is bright enough to highlight the spiritualist's face. She opens her eyes wide in shock. 'My God, it's you!'

The gas lamp flickers out, and they are plunged into darkness. A scream curdles in a woman's throat as the room vibrates, the house moaning in protest as the walls creak and the floor shudders. The mirror shatters. Large shards of glass fall to the ground with a crash... and the door slams shut.

Part Two

Chapter 8 ~ London

Ivy ~ White Hart Inn, 18th November.

I learn a little before eight o'clock that the strong winds have brought down an old tree during the night, and it now blocks the main road to London. We are in the predicament of having to extend our stay at the inn until they remove the obstruction. My spirits are low with the news. I was looking forward to leaving this place.

The landlady looks up as I approach her whilst sweeping the floor. 'Did you sleep well, miss? It was one of our best rooms in the house, so it should have accommodated you well enough.'

'It was fine ... apart from all the banging in the night. Did it not wake you?'

She continues to sweep the dust into a corner. 'It was a mighty powerful storm, to be sure.'

'But the doors? Did any other guests complain? Someone stood outside my room with a lamp. I thought perhaps they were also troubled by the noise?'

She stops sweeping and looks at me fully, sweat moistening her forehead. 'You were our only guest last night. Those other rooms are usually locked. I'll get my husband, Thomas, to have a look. Maybe a window was open somewhere, and the wind unsettled you.'

I smile and thank her, and then reluctantly head back to my room.

The tree is finally dealt with later in the afternoon, although we continue to fall behind in our progress to London. As we leave the inn, the landlady stands by the carriage talking to the driver. As

I climb into the cab, she gives me a queer look, the kind you would give a child who tells fanciful stories for attention — a mix of pity and distrust.

At the next stop, the carriage begins to fill with more bodies, and I miss my solitude. A family with a young boy squeeze in, bringing with them the smell of bacon fat and stale sweat. The child watches me for the entirety of the next leg of the journey, a most disconcerting experience. His mother has already fallen asleep with the rocking motion, exhaustion cast over her features. The father stares out of the window, adrift in his own world.

I recall the meeting with Miss Earnshaw, who must have travelled this same pitted dirt track. Her words repeat with the movement of the coach: 'You must come, you have a purpose.' All my hopes of a different life filled with my plants and without Mr Whitlock are wrapped in the memory of her soft voice. Any anxiety I feel about leaving the countryside alone falls behind with the passing fields.

The roads are much improved as the carriage edges closer to the city. With fewer potholes and wheels sucked into random mud pits, the journey becomes less of a chore. The sky has altered, too. I had always taken the country's clean air for granted, but now plumes of smoke join the clouds, leaving the forest's freshness far behind. People walk by the roadside, their clothes grubby and soiled by dust.

We stop at another inn outside the city, and two further passengers join the coach. A finely dressed man and a woman dash out of the building on our approach. The man gesticulates with his hands at what appears to be a fine silver timepiece on his breast pocket.

'You are late!' he shouts to the driver. 'We expected you yesterday – we had to stay overnight!'

'Can't be helped … storm, trees in the road.'

'Well, I assume you will make up the time on this last leg.'

They are presumably a married couple or related by birth, as they share the same social standing, clothes, and travel cases, both of high quality. The coach driver alights to assist with their luggage, allowing me a short time to stretch my legs and take a rest stop. I drink in the new travellers with an eagerness to understand London life. They are fascinating to observe. The speed at which they move and speak is much faster than in the countryside, where nature dictates the pace. Here, the clock clearly rules, not the seasons.

'Can you spur on the horses, driver? We are most eager to get going. I must keep an urgent appointment.'

The new stranger directs his demand to both of us standing outside, whilst also hurrying his female companion into the carriage. I return to the coach earlier than planned, feeling pressed by his furtive glances. I am only partially recovered from the time spent being fervently jostled; my nerves have not quite settled. I assume the driver had been driving the horses hard, trying to make up for the lost time on the road.

'Good day for travelling. My name is Miss Granger—'

My introduction is cut short by a curt nod from the pompous man. 'Indeed, I am Mr Henry Griggs, and this is my sister, Miss Amelia Griggs.' His features are sharp, with deep set eyes; there is no kindness in his manner. 'Would you mind telling the driver to make haste? Perhaps he might listen to you since you seem acquainted. This insult of a carriage is as intolerable as I predicted.' He turns to the thin, pale woman sitting mutely beside him. 'I told you we should have taken the train and not this old contraption.'

I lean out the window, about to do as he bids, when I realise I am under no obligation to follow his whim, so instead, I catch the driver's eye on his return to the coach. He silently replies by raising his eyes in apology. I have never encountered such blatant rudeness and wonder if my first impression of London is accurate: that the pace it demands will consume the whole city.

I ask a cabdriver at the train station to take me to a reputable landlady. He drops me off on Elsworthy Terrace, Primrose Hill, and the carriage leaves before I can ask any questions about the accommodation. The house appears expensive, with newly painted cream window frames and an immaculately scrubbed blue and white mosaic front path and black-painted steps. Even the black iron railings separating the house from the street look to have been polished recently. I cannot afford to stay here for long, for I know that the small amount of money I was able to gather before I left will disappear quickly. The net twitches in a bay window on the ground floor. A figure moves within – I am being watched.

After pulling the bell cord, I am swiftly greeted by a middle-aged woman. She observes my clean gloves and, glancing down at the hem of my skirt, I know she is scrutinising every detail and can tell I have not travelled by foot. She is a woman with high standards who is not afraid to conceal her observations. I must pass the test, for her demeanour changes to one more welcoming.

'I am Miss Granger. Do you have a room available for one?'

'Yes, you are in luck,' she replies. 'Normally I am extremely busy, but I had a late cancellation. This way, please.' She opens the door wider and lets me in. 'Have you travelled far?'

'From Surrey, we experienced a fierce storm, and the road became blocked by a fallen tree. I spent the night at an inn.'

'Oh, you poor thing... I am so pleased you made it here in one piece.' She hardly pauses for breath. 'I hear those country roads are notoriously hard to travel on. I prefer the train myself. Please leave your case inside the entrance. My maid will bring it up to the room shortly.'

She seems pleased to see me and I hope I appear normal. I find my face straining to create a constant smile.

'I will give you the room overlooking the garden. One of my best, for it is modest and quiet. I am sure you will be content. I only allow the most reputable company to lodge in this house.'

'Of course,' I agree out of politeness.

'We will go straight to your room so you can recover from your ordeal and warm yourself.'

Floral paper decorates the walls with an overbearing bright-green design. The busy pattern makes the narrow hallway claustrophobic. As we walk up the stairs, she continues to address me over her shoulder.

'How long will you be staying?'

'Only two nights at most.'

'Is that so?' She tuts under her breath. 'Well, here is the door to your room.' She enters before me, checking that everything is to her satisfaction. She must run her help off their feet.

'I plan to visit a friend of my mother's.' The excitement must be prevalent in my face. 'I hope to take up her offer of a brief stay in Kensington.'

Her smile slips a little. She had been hoping for more; perhaps business is slow. Winter always demands additional funds to maintain comfort.

'As you wish.' Her tone has become clipped. She is contrary, but her change of mood does not upset me. 'You are welcome to return if your circumstances change.' Her expression softens again. 'It is so refreshing to welcome ladies like yourself, bringing a little of the clean country air, shall we say?' She laughs at her own joke. 'Anyhow, I will let you rest. The journey must have exhausted you, especially with the drama of the storm. Goodness, wait until I tell Mrs Beechworth. She lodges in the room next to yours. Your misfortune will appal her. How brave you are.'

I hadn't told her of the terrors I suffered in the strange old inn, my mind playing tricks on me in the blackness. The unrest of last night still niggles. Travelling alone without a companion is frightening, but the freedom is exhilarating.

The room is pleasant, though the style differs from that at home. The space is more cluttered; lace and linen cover every surface. The landlady is nice enough, and the house appears reputable and in order. I am sure my mother would approve.

As I unpack my wash bag, I am excited but wary about what tomorrow will bring. Miss Earnshaw's card is in my purse, and I regularly check it, imagining our future conversations. But there is also a slow sense of trepidation building in my chest. An ominous feeling that by coming to London, I have not avoided her strange prediction of dark spirits working against me. I had hoped that by leaving Mr Whitlock and my house full of sadness behind, I would have shaken this foreboding emotion that has hovered over me since the funeral.

Discovering more about who my mother actually was is the only thing that will keep this grief at bay. I need to know about the gaps in time and family she never told me about that led to such secrets being necessary. Perhaps being related, Miss Earnshaw could explain why I behave so differently to everyone else. For the average person does not see and hear things that do not exist.

Was Father right? Is there a history of madness in the family I should know about? I wish to God I might find something. I will take anything, even pouncing on someone else's stories about her – for they might keep her memory alive a little longer.

I slept well for a change, though I was more tired from the stay at the strange inn than I first thought. Thankfully, nothing eventful happened during the night; no strange noises or visions. This is how I imagined my journey to be, waking with the sunrise and the unfamiliar sounds of London. I have left the window open, and the laced nets float in the breeze. It's only first light, too early for the smell of the city to penetrate the room. Yet the streets are already filled with the sounds of people chattering and dogs barking. The clacking of wheels, along with the traders' shouting to each other, is overwhelming. I am more used to birdsong and the maids preparing the rooms, drawing curtains, and sweeping. This is an alien place, and the new sounds intrigue me; it's a different world.

I refresh myself with the cold water left in a porcelain jug positioned by the sink in the corner. I assume the chore of the chamber pot will be the responsibility of the maid. All the same, I cover the bowl with a face towel and nudge it beneath the bed.

I choose one of my favourite dresses: a modest pale-yellow gown with blue embroidered flowers at the waist and matching ivory gloves. Shaking the dress out of the travel case, I lay it across the bed. I pull my long brown hair up and wind the unruly strands the best I can into a simple chignon. Lastly, I secure my navy hat with a turned-up brim and a velvet bow tied at the back with a pin and pull on my black, side-buttoned ankle boots.

I eat a small breakfast of crusty bread left over from the coach journey. I can't leave yet. According to Edith, it's still too early to call upon a house. Ladies do not pay calls until eleven o'clock.

The temptation to explore the city is strong, but I do not want to get lost and miss the correct time, so I sit on the only chair by the bed, with my mother's sketchbook in my hand, watching the clock slowly tick by until it is time to leave.

I cannot fathom the meaning of my mother's drawings or the coded writing. The birds appear to be more significant than the ones we sketched in the garden. These images in charcoal are so real, I could almost believe they might alight from the pages and fly back to the country. I had always preferred watercolour to that of dirty charcoal, but seeing these pictures in my mother's hand inspires me to draw in the same manner.

The dark soot smudges on my finger and won't come off, no matter how much I rub. I will be glad of my gloves. The birds are calling me to draw them, but they must wait.

I finally set out. It is a long carriage ride across London, but the cost is worth it. We must be near the South Kensington Museum, and I fight the urge to change direction.

The carriage comes to a halt outside a tall apartment building painted white. My impression that the lady is wealthy is correct: a small brass plaque shines on the wall, her name engraved in the metal; a pull bell sits beside the number thirty-four. I ring it, and moments later, the door is opened by a middle-aged housekeeper who appraises me with a single glance.

'No callers today, thank you.'

Her abruptness catches me off-guard. 'My apologies for arriving unannounced, but Miss Earnshaw asked me to call upon her. I arrived in London from the country only yesterday. You are the housekeeper, Mrs…?'

'Mrs Forbes. So, you don't have an appointment time?'

'No, not exactly.'

'Then it is as I said. We are not accepting visitors.' She tries to close the door, but I push it back open.

'I am expected. Miss Earnshaw visited me herself. She said I was to come urgently, that we are related in some way?'

'Many people call on this house with different stories, all wanting help. Please be on your way now, Miss, and find it elsewhere.'

Tears intrude into my vision, having come this far. I remain resolutely stuck to the doorstep.

The housekeeper hovers at the entrance. Her black and white uniform is pristine, starched and pressed to perfection, but her eyes are tired and red-rimmed. She seems undecided about what to do with me; to relent and invite me in, or dismiss me outright, causing more of a scene for passers-by.

I gulp nervously. 'Madam was clear I should attend her residence. She said I was in some sort of danger. Did she not leave a note for me?' I reach into my purse and draw out Miss Earnshaw's card with the address and bird emblem as proof. 'Have I called at an inopportune time?'

Her reluctance wavers, and she emits a long sigh. 'You had better come inside. Please, come through to the parlour.'

The house is finely furnished in colours of burgundy, gold, blue and dark green. I am ushered through to the room at the front of the house. Along the windowsill are a line of ceramic pots with similar plants to my own; even a large indoor ivy plant covers part of the wall, all of them stretching up to find any rays of winter sunshine. I cannot wait to see the orangery Miss Earnshaw promised.

'I am afraid the mistress of the house cannot see you now, nor anyone for that matter.'

We both stand in the centre of the room. She does not give me an invitation to sit.

My mouth goes dry. 'Why, is she unwell?'

'Do you not know?' She gawks at me, her eyes forlorn. A lock of brassy hair has fallen from underneath her cap unnoticed. 'Miss Earnshaw has been missing since the 11th. She did not return after her last engagement.'

'She is not here?'

The housekeeper rubs her forehead with one hand as though to comfort herself. 'I'm at a loss as to her whereabouts, as she usually tells me her plans. The police are investigating what happened.'

'What engagement did she have?'

'Her work, of course. My mistress is the most famous spiritualist in London.'

Her words make little sense. Surely, this could not be possible. My fingers rise to my temple as I try to make sense of her words. I had travelled all this way, and we were not destined to meet after all? And a spiritualist, known for their fraudulent behaviour, extorting money from the gullible and vulnerable! Her mention of my fate depicted by the cards suddenly makes sense. I cannot stop my shoulders from sagging.

The housekeeper notes the confusion on my face. 'Did you not read the newspaper?' She walks over to a side table by the large bay window, where a small pile of papers is stacked neatly. She hands me the top one. The front page displays a centre headline:

Mysterious Vanishing

Miss Rosetta Earnshaw, 38, a self-proclaimed clairvoyant and spiritualist, famed in high society, has not been seen since Saturday night, 11th November. Last reported in public at one of her infamous parlour parties on the evening of her disappearance, her case is being treated as suspicious with an official enquiry launched.

The unmarried beauty from Kensington, London, rose to success from the humble foundling house, and was highly sought after in the wealthy social circles, where her 'mediumistic talents' were considered a huge success. Any person with information regarding the case is asked to contact Detective Spencer.

Just seeing the drawing of this woman's face in print brings back stark memories of the funeral. There is no mistake. This Miss Earnshaw, so vibrant in the image, sketched with such detail by the artist, is definitely the person I have travelled to London to find.

'I did not know she was a clairvoyant. I've never met one. I thought they were all actors?'

'Not my Miss Earnshaw. She speaks only the truth.'

The doorbell chimes.

'It must be the detective again.'

The housekeeper quickly leaves, and I am left alone with a brief opportunity to walk about the room. I take the time to examine the photos on the wall, confirming my previous assumption that Miss Earnshaw is indeed a glamorous lady. Even the windows are dressed with lavish burnt-orange curtains, their heavy velvet trimmed with glossy blue tassels. A bronze lamp sits prominently on a small round table next to a day chair. This house is clearly run by a mistress without a husband, for there are no pipes or slippers by the fire.

My eyes dart over to a writing desk tucked into the corner of the room. Still hearing the voices in the doorway, I rush over and appraise the contents. It looks to have been tidied recently. Curious, I try the top drawer and find it crammed with papers and letters. Resting on top is a neat pocket notebook. Made from soft leather with a decorative 'R' monogram, surrounded by gilded roses, it reminds me of my mother's sketchbook. My fingertips caress the raised gold patterns. The object radiates significance, another strange link to my mother – and at that moment I desperately want it; something to make this journey of value. Perhaps this might answer my questions in Miss Earnshaw's absence.

My jaw tightens, acknowledging all the wasted, rehearsed questions. Why had she summoned me here, and what could have happened to cause her strange disappearance? What a poor show I had made of myself, leaving my father upset with me. And for what reason: to stand in this stranger's room, with no future plan and a ridiculous dream of finding a new companion in Miss Earnshaw, a new life in London? I will have to retreat from the city like a wounded animal with my tail between my legs.

Frustration gets the better of me, and with my curiosity unabated, I snatch up the book, quickly pushing the keepsake into my reticule. I look up, and the housekeeper stands in the doorway, eyeing me with what looks like hostility. Perhaps she has seen or does not believe my story and thinks I'm a reporter looking for a newspaper headline. Do I seem like an untrustworthy figure? I suppose my body language, stiff and defensive, could give my curious intentions away. Never have I taken anything belonging to another person. The guilt brings a flash of heat to my cheeks and my mouth dries instantly, palms sweating in my gloves.

She sways on the spot and assesses me further. 'This has been an upsetting time. I'd be grateful to continue with my work now.'

I cradle my bag closer to me. 'It is not my intention to have troubled you. Only, I am not sure what to do next. My sole reason for coming to London was to speak to Miss Earnshaw. Apparently, she is related to my mother. She wanted to help me learn more about my family, and she said something peculiar about danger and fate.'

'Miss Earnshaw knows lots of people.'

'But it was important. She wanted to help me. You honestly don't have any idea where she could be?'

'No, if I did, I would tell the police! As I said, when she returns, you can make an appointment. Plenty of people request her attention.'

'Please.' A sigh escapes my chest. 'I am alone. Might I stay and wait or help look for her?'

She pauses and then says, 'I did not invite you; you cannot wait here. All I can give you is what I gave them.'

Taking a pen and paper out of another drawer of the desk, she jots down a few words. 'This is the address of the house she attended the night she disappeared.'

I read her hastily written words: 'Blackham House, 24 Chester Square, Belgravia.'

She raises an eyebrow. 'If you ask me, they did something to her, but the police won't investigate it properly – too rich and above the law, if you know what I mean.'

She ushers me out of the room with gusto. 'Now, if you don't mind, I have chores to attend to.'

I cast a last glance behind me as I leave the parlour, and am suddenly caught off-guard by an image, an impression... I cannot be certain, but I am certain there is a drawing of my mother on the far wall.

'I wish you good luck, Miss Granger,' she says before firmly closing the door.

On the street, I catch myself, one hand on the iron railing. My dress is uncomfortably tight; the back of my neck prickles with the sense I am being watched.

A man in a long, thick coat turns from me on the opposite side of the road and walks away. But the unease stays with me. Perhaps it is the guilt of stealing that makes me paranoid. This book must be of value.

After taking a few more steps away from the house, I take the book out of my bag. Amidst the gold-embossed flowers on the front cover is the imprint of a bird; the same blackbird on Miss Earnshaw's calling card; the same blackbird on my mother's sketchbook. A rush of excitement pulses through me, proof that they are linked.

Flipping over the first page too eagerly, I almost tear the paper and a pamphlet slips out, a printed advertisement for local suffragette meetings at the Hanover Square Rooms. I tuck it into the back of the book. The handwriting on page one loops in black: 'Observations and Notes'. The pages read like a working diary, complete with hand-drawn illustrations:

> *A first-hand account of my work as a spiritualist. My personal words and thoughts. May God always be with me when I journey beyond the veil of life.*

Hungry to learn more I read on, but I cannot understand the words. They are written in code, a similar type of code used by my mother in her sketchbook, if not the same secret language. In between these strange sentences are loose pages, sketches of patterns, and symbols. Again, they mirror those drawn by my mother's hand.

Frustration is replaced with the creeping realisation that perhaps her disappearance has a deeper meaning. After all, hadn't she mentioned dark spirits and premonitions? I check myself; I have never believed in superstitions or ghosts, and yet I cannot shake the notion that I must help her, that our fates are in some way connected.

My need to find this stranger who is meant to be family is almost unbearable. I look again at the address the housekeeper gave me. Without question, I must go to Blackham House, the last known sighting of Miss Earnshaw.

It is only on my way back to Primrose Hill I remember I don't recall ever telling the housekeeper my name.

Chapter 9 ~ Change of Direction

Ivy ~ London, 20th November.

The train pulls into Victoria Station. The early morning air is dirty already and moist with humidity, adding an unescapable dreariness to the day. I would have preferred a private cab, but I must save money now that my circumstances have changed.

My first trip on a train has left me shaken. The sheer amount of noise and dirt compared to the countryside was overwhelming. The weather doesn't help calm my nerves, only adding to the clamminess under my lace collar and gloved hands. Beneath my cloak, I am wearing a rich dress of navy-blue velvet. Without my maid, Nellie, to help this morning, my fingers are sore from pulling the corset tight and hooking the multitude of tiny buttons from my neck to my waist.

As I walk out of the railway exit onto Buckingham Palace Road, I follow the directions to Belgravia provided by my landlady. I expect to hear thunder. I sense the rain about to fall, casting an unnatural twilight and bringing a chill wind. The clouds are dense, the colour of slate, and droplets of icy dust begin to fall. Pristine ebony carriages pass me by, pulled by beautiful horses, their manes gleaming – not like our country animals, which are bred for their practicality. Inside, I catch glimpses of well-dressed people in furs and lace.

I am becoming colder and am grateful when, after ten minutes of walking, Chester Garden Square, surrounded by tall, wealthy townhouses, comes into view. Searching for number twenty-four, I find the large, gilded brass lettering set on the front door of a house situated further away from the others. The detached three-storey building is surrounded by black iron railings with a well-maintained private courtyard. A church spire looms up not too far behind the property.

The sun appears briefly from behind a cloud and dazzles my vision. It is so bright it is almost painful. A flash of black and white feathers streaks across the sky and then they settle, magpies, four of them chattering together on the tiled roof, looking down at me.

After opening the iron gate and walking along a short path, six stone steps lead up to a double front door. Although smart and well presented, no flowers or plants decorate the porch, unlike other houses in the street. The building looks vacant except for a swift movement behind a window on the first floor.

Hope blossoms that in coming here, I can uncover the truth behind her mysterious disappearance. I only have enough money to cover food and board for a few days, so I pray I'll find her before it runs out. Perhaps I can ask questions that the police have overlooked. I have always been good at finding misplaced belongings. My maid, Nellie, used to call my lucky ability a 'sixth sense'.

I bang the brass knocker on the shiny black door, the sound resonating inside the house. I compose myself by smoothing down my cloak and making sure my hair is neatly tucked under my hat.

There is no response. Where are their servants?

I appreciate eight o'clock in the morning is early to be calling, but I hope if I talk to the butler, he can fit me in with today's appointments for the master and mistress of the house before they become too busy. But knocking again brings no confirmation that anyone will come. It seems most unusual.

I walk briskly around the side of the house and descend some narrow stone steps down to the basement door, which must lead to the servants' quarters. I knock and wait, resisting the urge to shuffle about, trying to bring warmth to my cold feet.

A young girl with a sullen face and long, dirty blonde hair answers. 'Yes?' she snaps.

The girl clearly does not mind showing her annoyance at being disturbed. She appears to be around twelve, but with the cockiness only a gentry house posting could give. I am shocked by her attitude. This would be unacceptable behaviour in our family home, but I am at a disadvantage, out of my depth. This is not the countryside.

'I am here to make an appointment to see the mistress about a private matter.' I wave the paper with the address written in haste by Miss Earnshaw's housekeeper as proof of my eligibility.

She glares at me. 'Wait here.'

With a flurry, she disappears, the door slamming behind her. After several minutes, the door is opened again, this time by a plump, middle-aged woman with a large white apron stretched over her ample body in a simple grey dress. Her tight curly hair struggles to be contained under a starched maid's cap, away from her flushed face. 'Well, it's about time. I was going to give up hope of anyone arriving. Thought they'd be lots of girls queuing up to get a good job in a decent house.'

'I apologise, this is not my—'

The woman cuts me off abruptly and turns her head to speak to someone behind her. 'Lottie, get to the butcher for today's order and be quick about it. And don't let him give you any cheap cuts. Make it clear they are for the master, and I'll be checking closely this time. Tell him I'll buy elsewhere if he tries to swindle me again.'

The young girl appears again a moment later, carrying a basket and a shawl. She narrows her eyes suspiciously as she shoves past me on the doorstep and into the street. Perhaps if I were considered beautiful, she would be more friendly, but I cannot hide my plain features, no matter what Cousin Edith thinks, and would not understand where to begin with the pots of powder and rouge on Mother's dressing table.

The older woman appears tired, with bowed shoulders and dark shadows cast under her eyes. As she rubs her neck, she looks me up and down with an appraising evaluation I am unaccustomed to, her eyes lingering on the black fur trim on my cloak and my newly polished shoes. 'I'd imagine with a generous mistress giving you such fine hand-me-downs, you'd be sorry to leave your current position. Unless there was a scandal, of course... We don't want any nonsense here. We're an honest private house.'

Almost reluctantly, she steps aside and allows me to follow her into the scullery and then through to the warm kitchen. A large wooden dresser lines the wall, filled with white china plates and dishes decorated with a delicate blue floral glaze. Next to the central cast iron range are shelves with a multitude of different sized copper pots and pans, all gleaming in the firelight.

'No, I am afraid you must be mistaken. I wish to speak to the butler...'

The cook ignores my attempt to introduce myself. I fumble in my reticule and try to give her one of my own calling cards, a gift from Edith on my last birthday, but she dismisses it with a wave of her hand. She motions for me to stand by the large wooden table that dominates the room. Beneath it are two long wooden benches for sitting. A single ladder-back chair is tucked in at the head.

'Come over here, so I can get on while we talk. I hoped to 'ave all this done before breakfast started, and this kedgeree won't cook itself.'

She looks to be midway through her morning work. The table is covered with flour, eggs, and meat – not an empty house after all. A woman, perhaps five years younger than me, attends to the fireplace against the opposite wall, kneeling on a large multi-coloured rag rug, adding more wood and stoking the flames. She pays me no attention, not even acknowledging my presence in the room.

'Look, Hannah! At last, we have a response to the advert in the paper,' says the cook.

'Must not be from round here, then,' she mutters in response.

'Well, perhaps that's a good thing.' The cook wipes her hands on her apron whilst studying me with a hungry glimmer of excitement.

'I would like to make an appointment to speak to the mistress or master of the house.' I try to maintain eye contact with her, hoping this time she'll listen. 'There was no one at the front door.'

'Pardon? The front door, you say. Of course, there'd be no answer. Who'd be there to open it for at this hour?' This appears to bemuse her, but she continues talking. 'Anyway, I'm the one doing the hiring this time.'

I seem to have walked into a job interview. I have done myself a disservice as no one of any standing would call before eleven, especially using the servant's entrance.

'You're not from the workhouse, are you?'

'No,' I reply.

'You don't even have a cockney accent – a novelty round here. Mistress might like that.'

She picks up an oval dish from the dresser countertop of what looks to be poached cod and brings it over to the main table, separating the soft white flakes with a fork, and removing any tiny bones with a quick hand onto a small plate. In the centre of the table stands a proud set of scales with brass bell weights. The owners must be wealthy to afford such things.

'I've not even had a moment to myself,' the cook continues. 'This house cannot run on us alone. I am so far behind in the baking, which is nobody's good fortune.' She shakes her head, and I catch the girl by the fireplace, rolling her eyes. 'Go on, show me your hands, Miss... What did you say your name was?'

'Ivy... Miss Ivy Granger,' I mumble.

Setting the dish aside, the cook turns to me and grabs my hands, prising my fingers open without giving me a choice. Something about this woman gives me cause not to argue, and I find myself going along with it. There is a sharp edge. It glints behind her eyes like the polished knives lined up on the wall. The kitchen is well equipped, so the household must be large.

She huffs in begrudged approval. 'They're clean enough, but you don't seem like you've seen much laundry in your time.' She drops my hands and walks over to another side table next to the oven. There, she picks up a large chopping board and chooses a knife from the display hanging on the wall. 'And it's not guaranteed we'll keep you. Although we need help, we do have high standards,' she continues as she makes space on the table between us for the chopping board. 'Maids have arrived and left before their wages barely touched a month's work.' She sizes me up with considered concentration.

'Mind you, we've been employing girls like Hannah over there, not a well-turned-out woman like yourself. Maybe that's where we're going wrong. Maybe you'd last longer, not being so green in the ways of looking after wealthy folk and their particular tastes.'

At the mention of her name, the young woman tuts as she gets up from attending the fireplace, displeased to be discussed so casually with a stranger.

'What experience have you got?' The cook slices a bunch of parsley and begins to peel a handful of small, boiled eggs into a bowl. I'd missed breakfast earlier, and my mouth waters at the aroma of bread in the oven. Last night, the measly amount of food at the guest house had scarcely provided enough sustenance, with taste only an afterthought.

My lack of a reply gets the cook's full attention, and she stops working, moving directly to face me, placing her hands on her hips.

The idea that my visit is the result of a job advert is laughable. My amusement passes when I note the expression on the cook's face turning sour as she sucks in her cheeks.

'Now don't waste my time. Do you hear me? Plenty of things to do without you under my feet in my kitchen, of all places. I don't take pity on bringing in any waif or stray, playing on my Christian sense of goodwill.'

A strange thought arises. Perhaps this is an opportunity to earn a wage and remain in London a little longer, to discover more about the spiritualist and the last place she was seen. I must find her. If her words were true, we are family. I cannot shake the notion that without her, both our futures are ill-fated.

Is this madness what I am about to say? I blurt out the words anyway, despite my hesitation: 'I'm hardworking and honest, and I can turn my hand to most things. Apparently, I show talent for arranging flowers and tending plants.' The lies tumble from my mouth to my own surprise. I had no such knowledge but had seen the work carried out often enough. But the part about the flowers and plants was true; my mother always claimed I had a special gift.

'I see.' The cook shakes her head. 'Flowers … could come in handy, I 'spose, but leave William's garden alone and the more important jobs should be finished first, mind you.' Her eyes flick over to Hannah. 'Quickly girl, get the bread out and start heating up the cold rice you set aside last night in a pan of butter … and remember, no lumps, nothing tastes good with lumps.'

Awkwardly, the girl grabs some oven gloves from the table and bends over in front of the range, removing the tray of freshly cooked bread from the oven, almost dropping the two loaves onto the floor as she glares at me. Banging the tray on the central table, she then turns her attention back to the stove.

A bell starts to tinkle frantically on the wall by the door leading into the rest of the basement. Exasperated, the cook wipes her brow with her apron. 'Fine, you can see I'm in a spot. We lost the housekeeper and parlour maid last week, and the house has run us ragged ever since. I would normally ask for references, but I ain't got time right now... and I pride myself on being an excellent judge of character.'

She says the last comment, more or less to herself, but it grounds me back in reality. Naturally, I would have to present a legitimate background of service, but I hadn't thought so far ahead.

'Yes, yes, I can provide them if you need them. I am sure my current position would recommend me highly.' Of course, I had no existing or previous job, but I would cross that bridge later. Maybe if I write to the cook at home, she might indulge me by saying something kind. Our relationship has always been close, and I'm certain she would undertake my request without telling Father. To say he would be extremely unhappy with this situation would be an understatement. Indeed, his blood would boil at the very scenario.

I squeeze my hands together to steady them, adrenaline pumping through me. Who am I – an imposter servant or a bumbling detective? In truth, I follow no plan and have no comprehension of the path I have steered onto – only the importance of securing this job, so I can remain in London and find Miss Earnshaw. I try not to chew on my lip; 'my nervous tick' as Mother would call it.

The cook nods to herself. 'Fine, I won't complain if this is what the Lord has sent my way.' You look savvy enough to know your way around the pots and pans with only a little direction from me. I need you for at least half a year. I haven't time to train you, but we'll keep a close eye on you for the first couple of months to check if you're suitable.' She pauses, a strange look passing over her face, her eyes glazing over. 'We'd normally know by then.'

My back twitches with a cold shiver. The bell rings again and the cook chats on as if the unsettling moment never happened: '... which would be a blessing, as many a word I've wasted on Hannah, repeating myself until I'm blue in the face and still no better off.'

Again, the girl glances up from stirring a steaming saucepan, flinching at the open rebuke. I can sense her already hardening against me, intruding on her space.

'Can you start this afternoon? I need a maid of all work. The wage will be seven pounds for half a year, half a day off every other week. You can call me Mrs Higgins, and this is Hannah, who you'll work with. I need the washing organised, the delicates separated, and the vegetables prepared for the soup tomorrow.' She rolls up her sleeves. 'I must get started on the jelly, so she'll help you find everything you need. You can share the same sleeping quarters next to the kitchen to keep an eye on the silver and be on hand if you're needed.' She narrows her eyes at me. 'Oh and keep out of sight of the master. For your own sake, we want no more trouble.'

I have no idea what she means by no more trouble, but I am relieved. Whatever the forces that have brought me to this house, I have a compulsion to stay. I will tell Edith and Father I have found a temporary position as a governess. The alternative of returning home to marry my life away, or Edith's choice of asylum cannot happen. I must have hope that my fate can be changed.

My father's anger at my becoming a servant would be hard to endure, but he will never find out about my new lowly station. And surely, he cannot argue with a brief period of work to help ease my grief? I won't be missed before the marriage is supposed to take place. Anything might happen between now and then. After all, the proud Mr Whitlock might fall off his horse and break his neck. I'm sure his burial casket would even outshine the one he provided for Mother.

'Yes, I accept. I am most grateful. Thank you, Mrs Higgins. You won't regret your decision.'

And with a wave of her hand, she motions me over to Hannah's care. 'Get the last maid's uniform; I expect it will fit her.' She glances back in my direction. 'Start when you return with your belongings.'

The rain comes down heavily as I leave Blackham House. I hurry through Chester Garden Square, back towards the train station. The lack of sleep from the night at the inn, combined with the strain of the impromptu interview, has caught up with me. I need sustenance and a strong cup of tea. The small birds, finches and blackbirds, are seeking shelter from the unfolding storm, shrieking warnings to each other from the trees. A sense of loneliness washes over me, bringing an old tune from memory.

'We are unalike, the doves and I, for I will never sing again.

I have lost my wings and am without song, cast forever to the ground.

If ye should ever find me hidden in the meadow spring,

a kind smile or touch I seek, for I struggle without sound.'

Mother sang the sad melody, often gazing out of her bedroom window that overlooked the forest. Losing her weighs heavily on me once more, along with the concern about Miss Earnshaw's disappearance. Finding employment within the house where she was last seen is a start to understanding what happened to her, but would it be enough? Could I survive in London on my own wits? Surely, I must have more ability and prospects than to be bartered off into marriage as a silent wife.

Despite the uncertainty, part of me deep inside relishes this new challenge and a sense of independence not yet experienced. The train takes me back to the lodgings to give notice, settle my account, and collect my luggage.

I leave a letter with the landlady, addressed to Edith. With polite wording, I inform her that I am following her advice to better myself, thus taking a role as a governess. I have kept the boarding house in Primrose Hill as the place of my residence. Edith will read that my new position resides within a high-status residence, where the proprietors would not take kindly to personal mail. I do not want her to turn up at Blackham House and find me dressed in a maid's uniform. I hope the letter will be enough to stop them from looking for me. This new turn of events might even work in my favour; an opportunity where Father's lack of affection for me might be a blessing. If I am no longer a burden to him, he might call off the wedding and let me stay in London without a backward glance.

I dispatched the landlady with a modest sum from my remaining coins to act as keeper of my correspondence, but no doubt I will find any letters already opened when I call to collect them.

❖

My first afternoon of work passes in a blur, with most of my effort spent in the kitchen scouring and polishing the pans and then scrubbing the floor. I don't even leave the basement. Supper at nine o'clock is bread with cold cuts of meat and cheese. I eat heartily, famished from the exertion of the day, and then attempt to find some comfort on the dingy pallet besides Hannah's in the small servant's room next to the kitchen. I leave a candle burning on the floor by my bed to keep my melancholy at bay. My nightmares are lessened when there is a light shining at night, no matter how weak the flame.

When a service bell rings in the kitchen, we hear it loudly. Hannah disappears to the upper floors of the house and must have returned after I fell asleep around eleven. I dream of home, sleeping beside my mother in her bedroom scented with violets.

My duties start at five the next morning, and it's still dark outside. I rub my eyes, having slept fitfully on the hard and uninviting straw mattress. My arms and back still ache from all the scrubbing and cleaning, unused as I am to such exhausting tasks. I can barely face more of the same.

Seeing me still laying under the covers, Hannah moves around the room noisily; she bangs her boots on the floor as she sits on her bed to put them on. 'Come on then, up you get, no sleeping at this hour. Those who would thrive must rise by five,' she laughs. 'Endless jobs to do today. They don't let us sleep in until six until January, and then only for a couple of months during winter. This house will chew you up and spit you out.'

She is already dressed and nudges me from her bed with her black laced-up boot, and I sit up, drawing the rough grey blanket around me, indignant at being addressed so familiarly by a servant. I realise, though, that I will have to be a convincing addition to the household; otherwise, I will be ousted without money or a roof over my head and be unable to discover if Miss Earnshaw's disappearance is linked to this house. I will endeavour to ask Hannah questions about any unusual occurrences on the night of the parlour game. Maybe she witnessed her leave with someone, which could be a clue to where she is now.

The last thing I want to do is return home, having failed in my quest. The more time I spend away from my father's estate, the more desperate I am to stay in London. Don't go back – the words curdle my thoughts. Licking my lips, I taste blood. I have bitten through the skin again.

I splash my face with water from a bowl sitting on an old side table and dress quickly in a uniform begrudgingly provided by Hannah from the laundry cupboard in the hallway: a simple black dress with a white linen collar and cuffs. The white apron is also large, covering the front of my outfit; the bib shoulder straps cross over my back and tie around my waist and into a bow. I am relieved to find the uniform fits me well enough, but I can't help pondering who wore it last and where they are now. I look to Hannah for guidance and tie my hair back in the same style of bun with my own pins, positioning the little white cap similarly trimmed with lace to hers. Catching sight of myself in the small, tarnished mirror hanging on the wall above the table, I believe I look the part.

Mrs Higgins yawns loudly from the housekeepers' bedroom adjacent to ours, but there is no noise from the third bedroom in the basement on the opposite side of the corridor, which I assume belongs to the butler.

Hannah shuts the servants' door, which is concealed under a marble staircase. The ground floor is a huge contrast to the simple basement, with its whitewashed walls and rusty nails protruding from the old wooden stairs in need of repair. This level reveals luxury tapestries and gilded gold picture frames. Along the wall are glass cabinets displaying weapons from all countries and eras. Some look to be African hunting artefacts. Others are polished spearheads with Chinese writing sweeping across the metal; they range from the basic slingshot and coloured-tip arrows to magnificent heavy shields and polished guns. I am not sure whether to be comforted or afraid of the small armoury.

The hallway continues to our left, but we turn and enter the grand entrance hall facing the front door, where I had called only yesterday. We are greeted by a large, dominating painting of an old man. The artwork depicts him standing regally, holding a hunting gun with a foxhound at his side, his shrewd eyes following our every move. An embroidered rug of red, orange, and blue is the centrepiece of the polished mosaic floor. To our right, opposite the painting, towers an elaborately engraved, silent grandfather clock and a mahogany side table. Two doors stand facing each other in the entrance, each one solid oak with a large brass handle.

'The grandfather clock has stopped. Should we wind it?'

'No,' she snaps, 'leave it alone; all the clocks were stopped at the time Lord Blackham died.'

The silence is heavy between us.

'What's up there?' I crane my head back to see further as the top of the marble staircase reaches up out of view.

'The first floor, where they all sleep, of course. Also the drawing room and a locked storage room.' She hands me her box of brushes as she takes out a large bunch of keys from her apron pocket. 'Second floor has more bedrooms, and the third is the attic. Unless instructed, it is forbidden to go to the top of the house. We will be cleaning two rooms on this floor.' She speaks quickly. I assume we are already behind on the chores. 'The parlour and the library.' She motions to the two doors nearest to us. 'Down the hallway towards the garden is the dining, morning, and another room, but that is forbidden to us.'

A forbidden room? Already my interest is piqued. I nod, taking in the vast space of the house.

'Right, first things first. We sweep up the dust from the fireplace in each room. You can work with me to clear out the grates, blacken the ranges, light the fires, and top up the coal if the basket is low. Then from tomorrow, they are your jobs.' She nods. 'Mind, 'tis dirty work, so be careful with your whites. You don't want to upset Mrs Higgins on day one by looking like a chimney sweep when it's time to serve breakfast.' She laughs to herself, but no warmth is directed at me. 'You must also shake out the rugs. Start with the heavy woollen ones. You should eat breakfast in the kitchen before anyone upstairs wakes … and from now on, it's your job to scrub the front steps of the house. Use the carbolic soap in the pantry.'

I inhale sharply. 'What will you be doing?'

'I have the master's room to clean and tidy, his coat and hat to brush, and then I'll polish the furniture.'

That seems like the easier task. I think Hannah is taking advantage of her experience over me. A foul smell drifts into the hall, a dank sweetness of decay. Searching the hallway for the source, I see a solitary vase of wilting white lilies on the hallway side table. The water must have turned stagnant overnight. From my mother's name, Lillian, I know they symbolise purity and a rejuvenation of the soul. The unexpected reminder of her is like a blow to my chest. I hope she is at peace, and I wonder whose memory they might represent here.

'We'll prepare the library first.'

She carefully scrutinises which is the correct key from her huge jangling bundle and pushes it into the lock, twisting with a flick of her wrist to the right. She shows me the bundle. 'The key with the bay leaf is for the morning room door, out into the garden.' Looking me up and down, she turns her nose up slightly. 'Master always keeps this room locked away from those who are not to be trusted. He uses this as his study.'

'Does he not have his own study, separate from the library?'

'No, there's another locked room overlooking the garden. And as I said, it's forbidden to us. It's full of the old man's books and the rest of his things. Nobody's touched them since Lord Blackham died a year ago. We don't light fires in there; it's too dangerous for the artefacts.'

'Who is Lord Blackham?' I ask.

She points to the imposing painting with the foxhound and then to the panelled door further away towards the garden, which has a large brass plate engraved with the words: 'The Collection'. 'The master's father, Lord Blackham, He started it all.' Her face clouds over. 'You are never to go in there without express permission from the master himself. It's what the Blackhams are famous for: they collect things.'

'What kind of things?'

'Old curiosities and the like.' She nods, her expression solemn.

This house is strange indeed. I already want to find a way to explore everywhere. 'What about the flowers?' I ask.

'What about them?' Hannah's tone is dismissive.

'The water needs changing... Can't you smell them?' I cover my nose with my hand, the repulsive scent growing stronger.

'Probably just the damp of the house, which will disappear when the fires warm up – which won't get done if we stand around nattering about nothing.' She turns the handle and pushes the door open. 'You can sort out those flowers if you fancy.' She shrugs. 'The mistress insists on them, but I think they make no difference in brightening up the house.'

As we enter the library, I notice it is very much like my father's, although at least three times the size. Shelves line the entire length of the far wall, books crammed into every space. A stuffed fox baring its teeth sits on the rug near the door, greeting us with a foreboding sense of attack. A guardian, perhaps, for the books? By the window stands a large desk, with piles of folders and letters stacked haphazardly. Papers have fallen onto the floor, scattered everywhere.

I place the box of brushes next to the fireplace. Beside the mantel sits a fawn leather padded chair, shabby with regular use. Alongside is a small teak table with an engraved decanter and crystal glasses on a silver tray. A set of keys rest on a corner of the table, the wood scratched underneath where they have been carelessly discarded too many times. A bottle of red wine is half empty. Someone has knocked a glass over and spilt its dark liquid across the table. It's clear this is a favoured room where a great deal of time is spent, but by the sight of the mess, the owner has left in haste with little care for his belongings. I suddenly notice a small portrait lying abandoned under the chair.

'Who is this?' I stoop down to pick it up and show Hannah. The woman is strikingly beautiful, with hair the colour of harvest wheat, high cheekbones, and a full mouth, but her captivating hazel eyes portray a flicker of sadness.

'Oh, that's his dead wife.'

Her bluntness is shocking. 'So, he's been married before?'

'Yes, but he didn't love her.' She snatches it out of my hand and finds the nearest drawer in the desk to push it into.

I stand motionless, stunned by her action. 'How did she die?'

'She killed herself in the back room upstairs. It's locked now, so don't go poking your nose around. Anyway, we must get on; the master will stir soon. Once he's awake, he doesn't like to be disturbed.' Hannah pulls back the heavy velvet drapes. The trees in the square at the front of the house stand starkly bare, with the glistening of early winter frost.

'I shall sort out his fire. I know how he prefers it.' She kneels by the fireplace and sweeps out the ash from the night before with one of the brushes we brought with us. 'You can tidy the room as best you can without looking like you've been prying.'

I am still reeling from her talk of Master Blackham's wife's suicide. Here, in this house? She must be lying, trying to challenge me to argue, knowing I would fail. Regardless of how she treats me as a subordinate, I am here to work, and I can bear this arrangement for a short time until I decide what to do next.

I collect all the loose papers scattered on the rug and place them into piles. Glancing at them, the handwriting is barely legible, so I cannot decipher their contents. I remember seeing some wine bottles in the basement, so I use a cleaning rag to clean up the mess, gather the empty glasses, and go back downstairs to the kitchen to fill up the decanter.

When I return, the library fire is crackling, with small flames dancing over the lumps of coal, disturbing the morning quiet, and Hannah has already left to prepare the dining room. I reprimand myself for taking so long in the kitchen and not watching to see how Hannah got the fire going. I place the filled decanter and clean glasses on the table and then look at the rows of beautifully bound books. They speak to me, touching me somewhere deep within. Running my fingers along their spines, my heart gladdens at the fine covers. Removing one at random, I am surprised to see a worn volume tucked behind – a botanical dictionary, Species Plantarum, the cover soft with use. I have read many titles on botanica, but I have not seen this one before.

The sound of a door closing startles me, and I quickly replace the book in its hidden spot, determined to return and look again.

I leave the library and walk across the hallway, opening the parlour room door. My skin prickles with excitement; Miss Earnshaw had been inside this room. The space is cloaked in mystery by the thick velvet curtains. After drawing them open, I look around for anything that might be out of the ordinary, but all is in order and appears normal. Disappointed, I make a start on the hearth. Kneeling, I sweep up the ash and soot and clumsily spill some cinders, smudging my hands and apron. I attempt to light the fire but use up all the kindling. Reluctantly, I have no choice but to go into the dining room and ask Hannah for help.

'I knew you'd never done this before,' she answers curtly, with a steely glare whilst dusting the scenic countryside paintings. 'A good housemaid can light a fire in minutes. You failed the test. 'God only knows what Mrs. Higgins was thinking when she hired you.' She sighs with irritation. 'Expecting me to train you? That's not part of my wages.'

She stuffs her cloth inside her apron and pushes past me roughly, snatching at more kindling from a nearby basket beside the fireplace, thrusting them roughly into my hands. I don't stop her. She understands she has the upper hand and my heart races. How might she use her new knowledge of me? She could get me dismissed before the sun has even fully risen.

'I don't know why you're here.' I can tell by her eyes widening and the flush in her cheeks that she is enjoying the sound of her own voice. 'You are not a maid as far as I can see. I know more than that old cook, I can tell you. The things I know about this house... I'm clever, you understand. And no one expects it of me, but I am.'

She stops speaking and looks up, clearly listening to something I cannot hear. A strange expression flitters across her face. 'What I want to know is why are you in this house and are you going to make my job harder? My life is tough enough here as it is!'

I shake my head, at a loss for a reply. I don't want to confirm her suspicions outright, but I need her if I'm to remain here and discover what happened to Miss Earnshaw.

'We don't have time for this,' she sighs dramatically, straightening up each dining room chair under the long, polished table. 'It takes two maids to make the house ready in the morning, and I've been struggling too long on my own. It's been hellish this month.' She breathes out, exasperated.

'I am from the countryside. Perhaps things are a little different there … but I am here to help,' I mumble.

Hannah rolls her eyes. 'I suppose a little help would suffice in the absence of nothing. Look, that should be enough kindling and then add the coal. When you're done, polish the mantelpiece and anything that looks dirty. I can't be holding your hand all day.' She resumes fixing the furniture. 'I'm off to start on the grates upstairs on the first floor, so be quick about your work and join me when you're done.'

I deliberately stay mute, grateful for her charitable gesture and not wanting to antagonise her again. After I finish cleaning the parlour room, lighting the fire to the best of my ability, I take the sorry-looking flowers from the hallway table to dispose of them in the scullery.

The clang of saucepans banging about on the stove indicates that Mrs Higgins is preparing breakfast, and the loud clatter from the dustcarts outside declares the street is waking up. There is also birdsong in the courtyard trees, but inside the house, it's unnaturally quiet.

As I run back up the servant's stairway, I become lightheaded. There's a faint sense of being unwelcome. I shrug it off, knowing Hannah will be waiting for me. But the impression stays, settling on me like a fine layer of dust. I wait to catch my breath and place my hand on the cold brick wall, reminding myself that I came here for a reason. This is the last place Miss Earnshaw was seen – there must be a link to her disappearance. I have always been the observer, hiding behind curtains, listening to servants' conversations, a spectator on life. Perhaps these habits frowned upon by Edith and Father will be useful. I can delve deeper than the police. There is something amiss about this house; an unusual atmosphere that goes beyond the dark furnishings; a story waiting to be told, but instinctively, I already sense it does not have a happy ending.

Hannah meets me at the top of the servant stairs on the first floor. 'There you are. I'd wondered if Mrs Higgins might have you on one of her errands. So much to do around here, you'd be chasing your tail half the day and still receive no thanks for it.' She affirms with a gesturing glance towards the six doors on either side of the long hallway. 'We only need to clean the master and mistress's rooms on this floor, since no guests are staying. We can do the drawing room later if we have time, as they barely use it.'

'Where are all the other servants ... the butler and the other maids?' I ask.

Mrs. Higgins mentioned that two had recently left, but I would expect more for a building of this size. The lack of staff is dawning on me: Mrs Higgins, Hannah, Lottie, the young girl who opened the door when I first arrived, and now myself. 'This house cannot be run properly by us alone?'

'There used to be others, but now it's just us. They're sacked on the spot if the master doesn't like them, or if they can't keep up with the work.'

'So, there are no others? What about when the house holds a party?'

The question causes her to give me a sideways glance. 'Parties? What a funny thing to ask?'

'Well, with so little help, it would be hard for the house to cater for such an occasion, wouldn't it? How do you manage?'

'Why, did your last posh mistress always do that? Did she teach you to speak with a plum in your mouth to impress the guests, too?'

'Yes, she did, actually.' The dry humour of my answer makes her smirk.

'We do have the occasional party, and we cope well enough. Staff come and go as we need them.' She hesitates. 'But I always stay. Do you understand me? I am a favourite. Do not assume that you will be treated the same.'

For a moment, Hannah drops her disconcerting gaze, unable to look me in the eye. 'Anyway, that's enough idle chat,' she blusters. 'The master always sleeps in on account of working late in the library, so I always do the mistress's room first.'

'They don't share a room?'

Hannah lowers her voice. 'They have an adjoining door, but they never use it. The master is a private man and likes to be on his own.' She then nods, suggesting this is perfectly normal. 'Her highness has her own tastes. Not English, you know. Master brought her back from Italy; didn't even warn us.' She looks at me as though to confirm that this fact alone would merit individual rooms and a reason to dislike her. It seems she has little loyalty towards the mistress.

The question follows me as we walk along the hallway: Is it usual for servants to leave so often? In our country house, I had grown up with the same familiar faces, and it was rare if anyone left by choice.

There was something guarded about Hannah. It would take time to gain her trust, but perhaps friendship might evolve in time. I have never really had a friend other than my mother and our servants. In a week or two, I should know if there is a compelling reason to stay and form a plan for what to do next. If Miss Earnshaw should return, I could lodge at her apartment for the next few months and laugh this job off as an eccentric adventure.

Hannah stops abruptly in front of a glass cabinet mounted on the wall. She rubs it with her dusting cloth, giving it a thorough polish until it gleams.

'What's this?' I ask, pointing to a life-sized wax doll of a young girl behind the glass. The presence of the figure unsettles me. The painted face appears almost real; strands of soft blonde hair frame its face, but the glass azure eyes depict an unnerving sense of sadness.

'I clean her case every day. It's my most important task.'

'Who is she?'

'Master's infant daughter died in the winter, almost two years ago. He had this grave doll made from her real hair to remember her just as she was. It must have cost a small fortune. She had his same piercing blue eyes … couldn't help but love her.'

She continues to polish the glass with such gentle strokes, it is hard to believe this is the same maid. 'It's the least I can do for her.'

'Such a young age,' I remark. I try not to recoil at the notion of a grave doll. 'What was it, the pox?'

'Something much worse than that—'

A loud crash interrupts her from the room next door, sounding as though a heavy book has fallen off a shelf.

'It's the master. I will let him settle before cleaning his room. Best he stays resting. It's easier that way.'

As we enter the neighbouring mistress's room, it's clear she is still asleep, with everything still shrouded in shadows.

'What was it then?' I whisper, curiosity tugging at me. 'What could be worse than the pox?'

Hannah turns away, her face in silhouette in the half-light. 'It wasn't illness that took her. She died by her own mother's hands.'

I shudder, my mouth gaping open. 'Why would she do such a thing, murder her own child? Was she unwell?' I look at the person in bed.

'Not her, you fool, his first wife.' She almost spits the words at me.

'The woman in the library portrait?'

She nods slowly. 'But we're forbidden to talk about it.'

'But…?'

'Shhh, do you want to cause trouble?'

Her reaction is so loud, I am concerned she will wake up the mistress. Seemingly reading my mind, Hannah motions over to the figure in the lavish four-poster bed covered in a rose-pink eiderdown quilt. 'She's a deep sleeper, never wakes before nine – such is the life of the spoilt and lazy. Open the curtains, I need to get some fresh water.'

She leaves me alone. I am shocked at her rudeness and without concern of being caught or reprimanded. But it is true. The woman remains a frozen figure in the dimly lit room.

As I pull back the heavy navy curtains, I can finally see the ornate wallpaper decorated with flowers and birds, along with threads of silver and blue hues. The bedroom appears recently decorated, a welcome contrast to the dated décor in the rest of the house. A small yellow canary flitters in a cage hung from the ceiling. The dressing table stands next to the bed with all the trappings you would expect of a lady: a bristle hairbrush, pins, ribbons and lace, several bottles of expensive perfume, a collection of blue-bottled apothecary tonics, and gold necklaces that spill out of an engraved wooden box.

The sight immediately returns me to my mother's room and the medicine she took daily for her nerves. I wonder what ails the mistress to have such an assortment of remedies by her bedside. I walk quietly towards it. A framed photo of their wedding day is set back against the wall, my fingers gently touching the makeup pots and powders: charcoal to darken the eyebrows, along with skin-coloured dusting powders. I open a jar out of curiosity; the cold cream greets me with the scent of summer roses. Foreign words adorn them; the glass jars in myriad colours are as pretty as the promises they give. I, like my mother, prefer the subtlety of violets.

On a separate dresser sits a bowl next to a small bar of soap and a flannel – all that is needed for a morning wash. Hannah returns with a jug of warm water to the washing stand. She sloshes its contents, the water spilling over as she detects my interest in the mistress's beautifying potions.

'Don't go touching her things. No amount of powders will help you,' she whispers to me, finding her own joke amusing.

I glance at her over my shoulder. The need to shame her for her cruel words is tempting, but the confrontation is too much effort, and besides, I cannot reply with a retort fast enough. I remember Cousin Edith's words: that a woman's function is to make the best of her appearance, so she can raise the spirits of all the men she meets. I must fail terribly at this.

'The mistress must be a real beauty with all these fine things,' I mumble, just loud enough to be heard.

Hannah screws up her face. 'More like putting butter on bacon. That's what I think – far too fancy for me.' She works methodically and quietly, tidying the room and folding clothes. She points her finger at the fire grate, and I kneel in front of it, beginning the tedious job of sweeping the soot and preparing the kindling again. This time, I am determined to use less and be faster, just like Hannah. My white apron is still smeared with dust, and I'm worried about marking such a lovely room. I try to make myself more presentable by dabbing at the spots with a handkerchief from my apron pocket.

'Make sure you change the pitcher of water in each room. They become filthy once they've absorbed all the soot-filled air from outside and the fires. I don't suppose you have that problem in the countryside?' She rolls her eyes, sniggering at her own joke.

Despite our chatter, the mistress remains sound asleep under the embroidered eiderdown. It hides her face, but I imagine her to be perfectly charming with her long black hair, spilling over the pillowcase and the array of silk ribbons nestled with a golden hairbrush on the mahogany dresser top. The woman begins to stir, and this is our sign to leave, as Hannah pushes me out of the room in haste.

'If they wake, they don't like to see us or hear us - otherwise, we are in trouble,' she says as she quietly closes the door behind us. 'We have to be quick with our work. You don't want to draw attention to yourself in this place, believe me.'

A dull thud comes from the hallway ceiling above, followed sharply by two more.

'There she goes already.' Hannah winces and flicks her eyes upwards.

I follow her gaze to the ceiling above us. 'Someone is up there?' I ask.

'Her upstairs is what we call her. The master's mother … Lady Blackham. She's bedridden, prefers the chamber pot to the privy and to bang her stick, as well as the bell cord to summon us on account of being deaf too.'

Two more thuds resonate from above in quick succession.

'And she rarely moves to use the metal speaking tube on her wall to talk to us in the kitchen. But the effort she puts into banging that stick of wood beggars belief for a frail old woman her age.'

Hannah stands beside the next door, trying to smooth down her hair and apron. I picture a little old lady struggling alone in such a big house, unable to move from her room.

'She has the whole of the second floor to herself. You can attend to her. Use the servants' stairwell, which goes further up into the house. You will find her well enough.'

She notices the apprehension on my face at being sent off alone and smiles. 'Off you go,' she says. 'She doesn't bite and will be grateful for a friendly face, I'm sure.'

My stomach twists at the unknown.

Two thuds bang again.

They sound closer this time, almost as if she is aware that we are listening.

Hannah motions for me to leave, waving her hands for me to hurry. 'By the way, don't get any ideas that you can enter the master's bedroom. He only likes me doing things for him.'

With her curt remark, she slips inside his darkened room and shuts the door in my face.

Chapter 10 ~ The Old Lady

Ivy ~ Blackham House, 21st November.

I access the staff stairwell behind a heavy plum velvet curtain at the end of the corridor. Once inside, the steps continue to spiral upwards to the top floor. The staircase appears to get darker and more claustrophobic with every step, as I try to avoid the cobwebs hanging against the brickwork. I make a note to clean this area if my visits to the old lady become regular; it would not create a good impression to arrive with spiders nesting in my hair. The very thought makes my skin crawl.

The sense of being uninvited surfaces again, which is foolish since the woman has evidently called for a servant's attention. But I am grateful to Hannah for giving me a more comforting role. I'd much prefer to visit an old lady than enter the master's dark room alone, and as I emerge through the doorway, I am ever so slightly bolder.

The thuds continue, seemingly from the last door along the hallway. As I enter, it takes a moment for my eyes to adjust to the dimness of the room, and then I almost gag with the stench of human waste mingled with the scent of dried lavender. I rush in to open a window and refresh the stuffy air.

The room is large but crammed full of clutter and furniture. I stumble, wary of knocking anything over, pulling the dark drapes aside to get to the sash windows, which to my surprise, are already slightly open.

On my right, there is a muttering sound from the elderly woman slumped against the headboard of a large oak bed. She is gripping a walking cane in her right hand, which she waves in my direction.

'Don't close the window… There is no oxygen in this room, and I refuse to die in my sleep!'

'Good morning, Lady Blackham,' I reply. 'Please do not upset yourself. I'm only trying to open them a little more.'

I stretch up, lifting the windows as far as they'll go, glimpsing a costermonger selling warm gingerbread in the street below. The cold air rushes in and dust flies everywhere, particles dancing in the sunlight.

I jolt as two orange eyes greet me from a large shelf above the fireplace: another stuffed fox. This one is larger than the one in the library. It could be its mother; fiercer and more dangerous if the poor soul was still alive. The irony is not wasted on me; Lady Blackham must have been a formidable character in her youth.

I glance around the room. The furnishings all reveal evidence of fine quality, but time has stood still in this room, and it is now shabby and dated. At least ten clocks of different sizes sit on top of intricately laced white tablecloths, resting on a row of oak dressers lining the walls. The timepieces are all stopped at five minutes before eleven, just like the grandfather clock downstairs.

A large portrait of a handsome young man hangs above the fireplace, yet there is a callousness about his features, a sharpness to his cheekbones, and a malevolence captured in his malachite green eyes. He could indeed be the hunter for the queer assembly of creatures stuffed in cabinets around the room.

One corner cabinet, nearest the window overlooking the street, showcases a family of mice all dressed in miniature clothes. Another, in the opposite corner, displays an owl frozen in mid-flight, its wings stretched out, positioned next to a field mouse; the terror on the rodent's face depicted with uncanny realism. Droplets of dried blood stain the fur, depicting the two animals forever suspended as predator and prey. An atmosphere of death weighs heavily and a cold chill settles on the back of my neck. Why would Lady Blackham enjoy looking at such a cruel spectacle of nature? Hannah's motive for directing me here is revealing itself to be a horrid joke at my expense.

The old lady sits hunched and small, using cushions to prop herself up. Although somewhere in her eighties, she is clearly alert, but her lined face is dour, with a mean, pursed mouth. 'At last, come here, girl, at once. I have been calling you for some time. The standards of this house have dropped to an unsuitably poor standard. Your tardiness will be reported to my son if you are not careful.'

I am reluctant to approach her, for the white china chamber pot, positioned beside her bed, is almost to the brim of overflowing. Repressing the urge to gag again, I take a small step forward to appease her.

'I see you have been looking after her first! Downstairs, in all her wanton luxury, with all her expensive Italian fancies. Purchased at an absurd fortune to me and my son. But this is my house... Do not neglect me, girl. It will be at your own cost.'

Cold eyes appraise me, and I am conscious of the smudge marks on my apron. She drops her cane onto the floor and her bony hands, adorned with rings, wring together in agitation. Dressed in a white nightgown with a cream knitted shawl draped around her shoulders; her hair is hidden under a simple white bonnet. Despite her age, her eyes are bright – but full of malice.

She reminds me of a strange woman I grew up fearing who lived on the outskirts of Fernecome. There were rumours she was a witch, so bitter was her repulsion of people. If a child were to go missing or a much-loved pet was found dead, it was she who received the blame, for she showed no compassion. I saw her once when I was no older than eight, after taking a shortcut through the forest while running an errand for Mother. She emerged through the trees, her face haggard, her eyes fierce as she rushed towards me and pinched my arm hard. She stared so intensely into my eyes that I imagined she was able to steal my very soul. 'You cannot fight the spirits, child,' she'd muttered, and I tore myself away from her grip, her fingernails drawing blood from my skin.

Fleeing, I ran all the way home without stopping for breath. I told no one about the encounter. Yet the experience still follows me in dreams, and I never took the same pathway again. The more I recall the memory, the more I am convinced it was the same woman who appeared in front of the carriage on the way to my mother's funeral.

Yes, I see it now. There is a similarity between that crone and this one before me now. I find myself reverting back to childhood once more, and I want to run downstairs and out into the street, away from this place, where I can get some fresh air. But where can I go? I have no means to afford further lodging in London, and I would rather die than return home. I owe it to Mother to stay and find the only member of her family that I know of that still exists. To lose them both would break me.

'Can I be of help to you, Lady Blackham?' I force myself to be polite, despite the unpleasantness emanating from the woman.

'Who are you, anyway? I don't remember you. Where is that other one with the sullen face?'

Perhaps she means Hannah; her face does have a somewhat sulky characteristic.

'My name is Ivy. I'm new here. Today is my second day.'

'Do not whisper, girl. It is such a nuisance. Are you a mouse? Speak eloquently and loudly, so I can hear you without struggle.' She reaches for a trumpet on her bedside cabinet and holds it to the side of her face.

'I'm Ivy. I work with Hannah,' I almost shout, making an effort to speak louder, but she interrupts me, anyway.

'No matter who you are … you are here, at least. Fetch me the black leather book over there by the table.'

I scurry over to the other side of the room where she's pointing and bring her a small bound book with a silver inscription. She snatches it from my grasp, and I note the gold rings on her fingers. All of them have silver hair woven into the designs, just like my mourning ring, fashioned from the lock of my mother's auburn hair. Covered with remnants of the dead; perhaps she sleeps in her ornaments from grief or fear of theft.

'Now you may assist with my ablutions. I require fresh warm water and, of course, that thing needs to be disposed with.' She glances down at the direction of the chamber pot but briefly closes her eyes, the acknowledgement of such an act beneath her. 'I have decided to have breakfast in my room today. You will bring me two boiled eggs with bread and butter and some hot tea.'

I nod at the instructions, desperate to leave. I hold my breath and tread around the bed to the source of the foul stench. Covering the pot with a piece of cream muslin lying on the floor, I carry it carefully out of the room, almost knocking into a dusty piano positioned flush against the wall, just inside the door. How I managed not to spill anything in my haste to leave, I do not know, but I make my way along the hallway where I dispose of the contents into the second-floor water closet and rinse out the china pot.

I am so nauseous from the task that I do not return to my chores. Instead, I run down the servants' stairwell, down to the basement, and out into the garden, making sure Mrs Higgins does not see me going through the kitchen. There, I take my time regaining my composure and breathing in the outdoor air, a welcome relief from the odour of the old lady's room, even if it's filled with the haze of London chimney smoke.

In contrast to the small courtyard at the front of the house, the back garden is wild and unkempt. The thin grass covered in russet leaves is overgrown in places, and the soil beds are empty apart from the occasional planting of an unusual prickly looking shrub. If I had time now, I would examine it further for my studies.

A gravel path leads to the back, where there's a cluster of old, dead-looking yew trees and rose bushes have taken over, creating a dense climbing wall of thorns. In the centre, presides a large gnarly tree – bare of leaves and sinister in its presence as it towers over the grounds with long, twisted, outstretched branches. My heart aches for the possibilities this bleak garden could possess if tended by the right hand. I want to investigate the prickly shrubs in the flower beds, but a rustling noise catches my attention. A grey cat brushes up beside me, causing me to jump. I have always liked cats, and this one seems amiable enough – perhaps an unexpected ally in this unfriendly house. It mews softly at me, looking decidedly in need of nourishment.

'Searching for food? I shall see what I can find. Let's see, what will I call you? Mr Grey seems to fit.' I smile. His new name suits him. Bending over to stroke him, he purrs in response and nuzzles against my legs.

I dart towards the kitchen to get him a saucer of milk before anyone notices. I quickly place it in a gap in the hedge, lest the cook catch me and complain about wasting good food. Mr. Grey appreciates my gesture and rushes over to enjoy it without hesitation.

Heading back into the house, I pass on Lady Blackham's breakfast request to Mrs Higgins, prepare a jug with warm water, and make my way back to the second-floor bedroom. I am still apprehensive about returning to the oppressive room, but I push my reluctance to the back of my mind. Tapping twice when I arrive, I nudge the door open and find the old lady now sitting on the edge of her bed.

'There you are. I thought you might have gotten lost in the house or have your hackles up like the last one and left. It is so hard to find loyal servants these days … ones that don't argue and simply do as they're told.'

Her statement addresses the room and not me, so I remain silent and adjust the covers around her and then straighten up the pillows as my maid, Nellie, had done for me in what feels like a lifetime ago.

'I will wear the lavender outfit today.' Lady Blackham gestures with one hand towards the tall oak wardrobe in the corner of the room. 'I expect you to lay it out for me when I am ready, once you have returned with my breakfast.' She gives me a hard stare. 'And no dilly-dallying with the butler.'

'The butler?' I cannot suppress my surprise at her assumption.

'Yes, you silly child. I will not tolerate inappropriate behaviour between servants in this house.'

'I was not aware there was one working here.'

'Nonsense, of course we have a butler. What fine house would be without one? I only trust a man in a freshly pressed uniform. Discipline is the only way to manage people.' Her lips pucker with irritation. 'He must be on one of my errands and will return soon. He will bring order back to this household quick smart.' She dismisses me with a curt wave. 'You may go. I do not wish to have hard-boiled eggs due to your slack attitude.'

I rush out of the door with relief and meet Hannah in the stairwell, already travelling upwards, carrying the silver tray laden with eggs, bread, and tea. Taking the tray from her in the small space, I underestimate how heavy it is, and now find it difficult to negotiate the narrow stairs. As she turns from me to go back down, a defiant smugness spreads across her lips at my discomfort. I glare at her, frustrated that she gave me no warning. She is still neat and

fresh. I, on the other hand, am already dirty from the soot and hot
and sweaty from climbing the stairs over and over again, with my
uniform sticking to my skin.

Instinctively, I fear that no bond of friendship can ever
develop between us, and she will never take me into her
confidence; like others before who have pretended to befriend me
for sport, only to hear them secretly laughing at my gullibility. It
would be best to treat any so-called kind moments as empty
gestures. Perhaps Mrs Higgins, the cook, would be a better source
of information. As soon as I am able, I will ask her what she knows
of Miss Earnshaw and Saturday the 11th of November.

I am tidying up my nightdress the next morning in our servants'
bedroom, when I see a small wooden trunk tucked onto a low
shelf. I have been so dog-tired I must have missed seeing it before.
The wood has been delicately carved with small leaves. I run my
hand over the design. Undoubtably, this would be someone's
treasured possession and is out of place in the basement.

'Hannah, what is this?' I turn to her as she pins up her hair
under her white cap.

'Nothing … just stuff without owners.'

'Can I open it?'

She shrugs.

I lean down and lift the lid to discover a hoard of
belongings inside: a polished pair of black patent boots, a
hairbrush, a miniature brass candelabra, a small round mirror with
a silver lid, as well as an unopened box of scented lavender soap. I
keep looking. There are so many things that I lose count. At the
bottom is a small doll dressed as a soldier. Its army uniform has
been handmade with great care, with so many little stitches edging
the jacket and trousers.

'Why is this all here?'

Hannah walks towards me and talks over my shoulder. 'It's
what previous staff left behind. If I find anything, I put them in
there for safekeeping. Seems a shame to throw them away. Might
come in handy or be worth something.' She eyes me with a

territorial glance. 'I keep meaning to take them to the pawnbroker. By right, I found them, so they're mine.'

'Well, it's a strange collection, and no doubt they must have sentimental value to someone.'

'Not as strange as the Blackham collection. I stay clear of their things, and so should you, unless they give permission. Antique relics are everywhere in the house, but the most precious items are locked away in the old master's collection room.'

'Why, are they valuable?'

'The family spent more money than you'd ever imagine, on all manner of queer things from their trips abroad. It's taken years to curate and people have even died in the process,' she lowers her voice, 'even the master's very own brother. I warn you ... do not touch them.'

I want to ask about the brother, but Hannah's dark expression challenges me not to, so I look again at the contents of the trunk. Even examining them without permission, I feel like I'm trespassing on another's property. 'Why would people leave behind their belongings? They would need them in their new place of work.'

'People go in a hurry or just forget things,' Hannah says vaguely.

'But why would they be leaving so fast that they didn't have time to pack a few simple items?'

'How should I know?' she huffs.

'Can you remember their names? Perhaps we could try to find them?'

'I can't remember their faces, let alone their names. You are full of questions this morning. I would save your energy for the fireplaces. You need to do a better job of them today.'

I take an uneasy breath. Would I leave my things if I felt frightened enough to never come back for them? I move the objects about lightly with the tips of my fingers. A pretty comb is at the bottom of the pile. Next to it is a small brooch of a blackbird, clearly valuable. Then a thought strikes me... Could any of these belong to Miss Earnshaw?

I glance at Hannah. 'Are any of these new to the trunk?'

'No,' she replies sharply, barely taking a breath, 'in fact, they've been there so long I'd forgotten about them myself.'

'And you don't want any of these? Some of the things are so pretty.'

'I don't need to forage for gifts. My man buys me presents simply to make me happy.'

'Is that so?'

'An Irish policeman, no less.' She stands straighter and smiles, proud of the statement. 'Yes, Frank calls me his girl. Although I have many offers, I am considering him now. He has a good job and promises me a comfortable life.'

'Who else are you thinking about?'

'Never you mind.' She looks up. It's a subtle gesture, but it doesn't go unnoticed.

I am still interested in the trunk, and I try to poke again for answers. 'So ... where did everyone go? Did they stay in London? Or did they disappear like Miss Earnshaw?'

Hannah's face flushes red. 'You ask too many questions. Have you been reading the papers? We can't talk about the spiritualist.' She brings her voice down to a hush. 'It's forbidden.'

'It seems lots of things in this house are forbidden.' A rush of adrenaline flows through me. 'Apparently, Miss Earnshaw's disappearance is being investigated. Although I doubt anyone would report much, wary of scandal and gossip?'

Hannah turns abruptly and peers at me. 'All I know is that the local police take everything seriously in a posh area like this. They like to keep the rich happy. Servants steal stuff all the time and get fired. Any crime against this house would be foolish. Once you're disloyal to the family, you're not welcome back, or anywhere else, for that matter. You might as well be dead.'

Her comment is final. She steps towards me, bends over, snapping the lid shut in front of my face. 'There's still room in there for more things,' she sucks at her cheeks. 'I'd be careful if I were you. All this prying is dangerous ... and you're making us late.'

Chapter 11 ~ First Meetings

Ivy ~ Blackham House, 22nd November.

It is late morning when I find myself alone with Mrs Higgins.

'You need to clean and chop the vegetables for the meat and potato pie for tonight's meal!' she calls to me as I walk past, tutting at my apron, already dirty from cleaning the fireplaces.

I start sorting through the vegetables at the scullery sink. I am surprised to find that half of them have already softened due to mould. Putting them aside for scraps, I scrub some firmer carrots and potatoes, my hands stinging in the icy water.

'Where's Hannah?' I ask, bringing the clean vegetables to the table.

'They've sent her to the apothecary for the mistress.'

I nod in response, and we prepare food together, with only the chopping of knives and the crackling flames of the fire punctuating the silence between us. 'Mrs Higgins?'

'Yes?' she replies as she stands in front of the kitchen table mixing the meat filling in a ceramic bowl with her hands, adding seasoning and flour to thicken.

Mrs Beeton's Book of Household Management sits open on the table in front of her, the pages creased and covered with small food stains. Mrs Higgins takes her role as cook seriously.

'You must know about everything that goes on in this house...' I leave the sentence open, encouraging her to talk.

'Yes, nothing gets past me. Even though I'm down here slaving away.'

'Then would you know about a woman called Miss Earnshaw? I understand she came to a parlour party here last month.'

She glances at me sternly. 'Now what are you enquiring about her for? What business is it of yours?'

The atmosphere in the room is suddenly heavy. Was she protecting the reputation of the house or someone within it? I'm reminded of Hannah's instruction not to speak of the spiritualist.

Mrs Higgins shifts her weight from one foot to the other.

'It's just that I saw an article in the paper and it mentioned this house, along with her disappearance. The house is so quiet, I can't imagine many social gatherings would be held here.'

'You'd be mistaken. Occasionally, we throw a fine party. But they have become less frequent of late.'

Flour spills onto the worktop as she mixes the filling too vigorously. 'I don't understand what got into the mistress thinking of hosting such a night. We got quite excited, I can tell you. Expecting to help with a night of charades and games, but ... we discovered otherwise.'

'Really?' This is the most I'd heard her speak, other than gripes about previous rotten food from the market and recent lapses of standards in cleaning. But she pauses, scraping the flour and meat mixture off her fingers.

'I want no part in all that speaking to the dead nonsense. Don't know who they're dealing with ... all that table knocking and asking questions to the air. They could be demons or anything else they conjure up. Hannah was white as a sheet at the end of the night.' She made the sign of the cross over her large bosom. 'Now fetch me a big pie dish. We've baking to do and no good will come of talking about this any further.'

I pluck a large rectangular dish from the shelf in front of me and pass it to her, desperate to hear more. 'But what went on that night? They say no one has heard of Miss Earnshaw since?'

Mrs Higgins places some rolled pastry into the dish, pressing it down into the corners firmly with her fingers. 'Well, everyone got themselves all whipped up, claiming they spoke to the dead, and with St John's so close... I mean, what would the vicar say, such a godly man?' She shook her head dismissively. 'Mark my words, I'd like to tell the mistress those kinds of parties won't ever bring happiness into this house. I'm not surprised the spiritualist disappeared – probably carried off by the Devil himself!'

She turns to look at me, wiping her fingers on her apron. 'Enough of that talk now. This new menu has me flummoxed. Mistress says a man called Banting knows the best diet for keeping slim, but she needs fattening up if she wants to keep the next baby. My food is better than a trip to the countryside.' She stops abruptly, dabbing her face with her apron. 'Just forget I said that last bit, Ivy. I'm worried about her, that's all.'

The cook looks genuinely concerned, and I nod in reply, noticing it is almost time for midday luncheon.

A lost baby? My thoughts move away from Miss Earnshaw. The revelation stuns me. I am sorry for the mistress. This house has had its fair share of sadness.

'Now take this food up.' I watch as she then serves up a meal of broiled cod gently onto a silver tray, along with some cutlery and a white linen napkin pushed into a silver napkin ring. She adds a glass bowl of what looks like pale brown mush. 'Tell me what she thinks of the fish and pureed fruit.' Her voice rises an octave with false cheer. 'And make a pot of tea – she likes it with no milk or sugar, but I'll add a bowl of sugar cubes anyway. I'll rest easier, knowing my mistress has had a decent sweet brew after all those concoctions she takes.'

There's a nervous flutter in my stomach. 'Should I wait for Hannah to return? I've not been formally introduced to the mistress yet.'

'Formally introduced?' she guffaws. 'There's no need for formalities, lass. Just get on with it.'

Plodding up the servant's stairway with the heavy tray, I am out of breath and grateful to stop on the first floor rather than stagger up another flight to the old lady's room. Already, I know each morning will be the same. I will dread taking old Lady Blackham her breakfast and cleaning out her chamber pot.

'Si?'

The voice is faint as I nudge open the door with my back to bring the tray in last. Turning around, I appraise the room in the afternoon light. It is even nicer than I remembered on my last visit – a pretty room with cerulean and yellow flowered wallpaper, along with matching blue drapes and bedspread.

She is standing up and gazing out at the garden, her hand resting on the sash windowpane. 'Grazie, you can set the food down over there.'

Her hand waves towards her bedside table, and I step towards it, bend my knees, and carefully place down the heavy tray, sensing she will be less work than the confrontational woman upstairs.

Situated at the back of the house, the room is much quieter away from the street noise of horses' hooves and chattering ladies of leisure. Only the chiming of the church bell disturbs the peace.

'The dead leaves have almost covered the grass,' she murmurs. 'So many trees. They will ruin the lawn unless the gardener clears them up. A bonfire is what's needed. Is that not what winter is for? Tell him, would you?'

She turns and I see her clearly. The light from the window almost gives her a luminous glow in her white dress. I note the pale blue tones under her eyes and the way her shoulder-length ebony hair hangs free and loosely around her shoulders. She seems fragile, undone.

The mistress notices I am observing, for she self-consciously composes herself, standing straighter and touching her face. She doesn't acknowledge I am a stranger, but only points towards the food.

'I am sure Mrs Higgins has done herself proud. Unfortunately, I had a restless night and find my appetite somewhat diminished. Please tell her I was content with the meal. No doubt she will be waiting to hear.'

I nod in response, unsure of what to do with my hands. Her demeanour is kind and her Italian accent charming. She has been through so much recently; I do not understand why Hannah spites her so.

'I have no appointments today, so I will read in my room. Tell Hannah I will not require her help with dressing today.' She moves towards the pot of tea. 'I will take a light supper after six. I may feel nourished by the rest and manage a little food by then.'

The fire we lit earlier in the morning is dwindling. If the mistress notices the drop in temperature, she doesn't show it. Kneeling in front of the hearth, I attempt to rekindle the flames and give some warmth to the room. I then make the bed, gaining confidence in my new role as a maid. I believe I've passed as an acceptable imposter and congratulate myself on the progress made from being merely a disappointing daughter.

She watches me at work, following me around the room with her eyes. 'That will be all, thank you,' she says softly, her accent pulling at each syllable.

Perhaps she is lonely. I can identify, and I pity her. It appears that most of the time, everyone stays in their own rooms, hidden from the outside world and from each other.

I wish her a good day and close the door gently behind me.

'The mistress is suffering,' I state to Hannah as we eat our lunch of bread and cheese at the long oak table in the kitchen.

'It is her way,' she replies. 'Her moods are up and down. Heaven knows why she doesn't sleep.'

'You purchased some new tonics for her, didn't you?' Mrs Higgins says, eyeing Hannah from the other end of the table.

'Yes, I had the bottle added to the account like the others.'

'Maybe this one will do her some good, but I'd never touch the stuff myself. A disgusting thick brown concoction but needs must.'

The lamplighter whistles a tune as he walks down the path, lighting the streetlamps. It must already be four o'clock and almost dusk. The simple melody is the only sound apart from the scrubbing brush on the floor.

My back aches, stiff from bending, and I get up slowly, stretching it out with a long sigh. Standing against the landing banister, I appraise my work. The wooden floorboards of the first-floor corridor glimmer with new life.

It's a shame no children play here. I glance around; it is a lonely place. There should be a family bringing life into the rooms. I recall the encased memorial doll, an eerie statement, proof that she once existed. No one apart from Hannah has spoken of her. I cannot believe she was murdered by her own mother; a woeful accident must have occurred.

The lamplighter appears to have gone and now the house is silent. The grandfather clock in the entry hall is still, as if the single heartbeat of the building has stopped. Something interrupts my thoughts – that familiar sense of being watched.

Without moving, I let my eyes roam the two floors, searching for another person. Then I see him on the ground floor, leaning against the parlour doorframe. I shudder, not knowing how long he has been there. His face lifts and he looks directly at me through the staircase railings, an aura of torment surrounding him. Dressed in a pressed evening suit, he is clearly an upper-class gentleman, but something about his thick, unkempt beard and the way his copper-brown hair falls messily over his brow undermines the wealth of his clothes. His face could be handsome if not for his dishevelled state.

His height takes up most of the doorframe, but as he holds a large glass brimming with red wine in his hand, he remains perfectly still, his eyes solely focused on mine. The intensity of his penetrating gaze is shocking. Slowly, he brings the glass to his lips and takes a sip. He takes his time. Finally, he looks away, steps back into the room and shuts the door. In a moment, an oil lamp shines light from under the wooden door, spilling out onto the floor. The temperature has dropped, and goosebumps appear on my arms, although my face remains flushed.

So that was the master? He must know what really happened the night Miss Earnshaw disappeared. What secrets might he hide? Flustered, I bend down to pick up the bucket of water and the scrubbing brush. Twilight has now descended. I must get back to the kitchen and light the lamps. I hurry, almost spilling the dirty water, my thoughts full of the mysterious, troubled man behind the parlour room door.

Chapter 12 ~ After the Lights Went Out

Master Blackham ~ Blackham House, 11th November.

'Ha! You've seen a ghost! Are they in this room with us?' asks Captain Lynch, with an uneasy grin on his chiselled face. He shuffles, crunching his shoes on the broken glass, glancing over at his wife nervously. 'Why, this is the most frightening game I've played for a while.'

The rest of the group remain silent, waiting with apprehension as to what the spiritualist will say next.

'This is not a game, I assure you,' Miss Earnshaw retorts. The moonlight shines through the glass window, illuminating her face in an eerie half-light.

'Hannah, find another lamp at once,' Mr Bancroft orders the young maid as he turns towards her.

Master Blackham steps forward; his arms folded defensively across his chest. 'This is my house. I demand to know what is going on?'

'You are Alexander Blackham?'

'Of course,' he replies, straightening his back.

The spiritualist flinches. 'Something dark happened in this room.' She shakes her head, a flash of recognition across her face. 'I thought the curse on this family could not get any worse, but I was wrong.'

'Stop, now!' Master Blackham shouts. 'What in God's name have you got to do with this family, this room? Who have you been talking to?'

'I can assure you,' she continued, glaring at him, 'God does not look favourably on this house. I do not need to speak to anyone. To my detriment, I have been involved with the Blackhams before. If I could, I would banish you all from this earth and cleanse the very ground you walked on.'

'I say, that's not very polite. You are only an entertainer, after all.' The captain's voice cracks with nerves as the tension in the room heightens.

'Hush!' Miss Earnshaw casts him a scathing look as he withdraws to the outskirts of the room, ushering his wife with him.

'But I booked you in the name of another. You could not possibly have known it was for my husband?' said Mistress Angelica, her eyes widening as she clenches her hands together.

'I know this address well. I have waited until summoned as the cards demanded. And now, here I am.'

A bird flutters close to the window, squawking loudly, sounding in pain. Angelica jolts, startled at the abrupt noise.

'How dare you! I don't understand what business my family is to you?' Master Blackham anxiously scrapes his hair off his face with his fingers.

'Where is your mother?'

'Upstairs… Why?'

'I must speak with her at once.' Miss Earnshaw strides out of the room, disappearing down the corridor.

'You cannot disturb her… This is an outrage!'

'Looks like the party's over,' laughs the captain as he pulls out a cigar from his jacket pocket, attempting to lighten the mood. 'I suggest we all make a quick exit and allow the Blackham's to sort this debacle out in peace.'

'Yes, let's escort the women home before the winter fog becomes all encompassing,' Mr Ashcroft quickly replies, as he guides their wives back down to the ground floor.

Master Blackham moves to follow behind the spiritualist, his breath shortening as he calls out to his wife. 'Angelica, what kind of misfit did you bring into this house?'

'I'm so very sorry,' Angelica answers as she tries to catch up with him, her rich purple dress rustling with every step. 'Sorry, darling. I only had the best intentions.'

With a flick of his wrist, the master motions her away. He spits out his words through gritted teeth, 'Go downstairs woman – you have done enough, this is no longer your business.'

Master Blackham is rarely invited into his mother's personal space. No one hears when he knocks. The two female voices within the bedroom are talking so vehemently over each other, he is able to enter unnoticed. Unsure of where to stand, he takes a spot by the window, eyeing the two outraged women with caution.

His mother remains seated at her desk, her face puce red with rage as she scrawls words on white Blackham House stationery. She folds the letter and seals the envelope.

Master Blackham glances back at the door as Mr Bancroft finally entered. His servant skirts the edge of the walls to stand beside Lady Blackham, never taking his eyes off the stranger standing in the centre of the room, commanding all their attention.

'You cannot keep this a secret. They need to know!' The spiritualist shouts, her eyes blazing.

'Mother, what is all this?'

Miss Earnshaw turns to look at him. 'Dear Victor, how you remind me of him,' she says sarcastically, pointing to the portrait of a young man above the fireplace.

'My brother … but he died at sea. You knew him?'

Her lips curl back into a sneer, her eyes black as ink. 'I had the great misfortune of keeping his company. I am not sorry to hear that he's dead. After what he did... I pray his death was not an easy one.'

'What a dreadful thing to say. You must be confused or quite clearly mad!'

'This is your mother?' She points to the old woman, her tone slick with irony.

'Yes, but what is your point?' He shakes his head.

'You have changed much since you were a boy. Back then, you were always bedridden with an illness of some sort. You don't remember me, but I assure you, our paths have crossed.'

He raises his hands as though quietening a young child. 'You've clearly done some in-depth research for tonight, but now the game is over, and we can all calm down.'

His mother stands up, grabbing her stick for balance. 'Get away from me and my son! I won't tolerate you a moment longer. Leave my house at once.' She sways about, spittle forming at the corners of her mouth. 'How dare you come here and threaten me and my family! You have never been welcome. And now, I will ensure you are finished, once and for all.' Her eyes darken as she glares at the spiritualist. 'How easily you forget who we are and what we are capable of. Leave now, before—'

'I have connections.' Miss Earnshaw interrupts, her face flushed with anger. 'I am not the weak young girl I once was. You will find my power has grown.' She points a finger at the old woman. 'There is a curse on you and this house. I am not afraid of you anymore.'

'Bancroft!' Lady Blackham barks, cutting her off. 'Take this letter at once, deliver it personally. There is not a moment to lose.'

'Yes, of course,' replies Mr Bancroft with a benign smile, as he takes the letter and rushes out of the room.

His mother turns again to the spiritualist standing before her, owning the space as though it were her own. 'Get out of my house. I will not warn you again. My son will ensure your filthy lies are extinguished for good this time.'

Master Blackham's eyes widen as he finally finds his voice. 'You truly know her? Mother, how on earth is that possible?'

'Do as I order, Alexander. This is no business of yours.'

Miss Earnshaw narrows her eyes, her jaw tightening. 'No matter, I am leaving, but I will return. The dead will not rest in peace as long as your evil goes unpunished.'

Lady Blackham leans forward, balancing against her cane, her face tightening into a sneer. 'Alexander, escort this woman off the premises at once! She has gone raving mad, making no sense whatsoever. And make sure she does not reappear ... ever!'

The spiritualist turns to Master Blackham, still hovering several feet away. 'I believe you do believe in ghosts, sir. You are aware that the dead never leave us? They will always seek vengeance for sins committed. I know the truth of this house. This family has always been haunted – but, I suppose, you must already know that you are never alone!'

Master Blackham's mouth gaped open in shock. 'What on God's earth?'

'There is no God in this house,' she mutters, her eyes full of sadness.

Turning on her heels, she strides towards the door, her long ankle-length dress knocking over a small table, smashing a clock to the floor. As she exits, she glances back over her shoulder at Master Blackham to confirm her warning.

He hesitates, unsure of whether to stay or go, and then takes a cautious step towards his mother.

'Stop fussing,' she hisses. 'When will you stop disappointing me? Your brother wouldn't have let her within a hair's breadth of our home!'

'I don't even know who she is! How am I to act on your wishes if you won't confide in me?'

'Weak willed and whinging again ... and still here, I note.' She fixes her steel-blue eyes on him and sinks back down into her chair, waving her hand, dismissing anything further he might say.

Striding past the broken time pieces on the floor, Master Blackham slams the bedroom door behind him, and something finally snaps inside his chest – he can barely breathe, as colours of red and orange flash like fireworks before his eyes.

Chapter 13 ~ Screams

Ivy ~ Blackham House, 23rd November.

It is the middle of the night, and I wake abruptly to the sound of screaming from upstairs. Hannah also sits up, rubbing her eyes with the palm of her hands. I light a candle to brighten the room, struggling with the match.

'It's the mistress. You go to her; I'll wake up Mrs Higgins. But give me that!' She snatches the small candle from my hand. 'I'd better guard the silver.'

Her excuse to remain in the basement seems weak, but I can see unease in her eyes. I pull on my shawl and take another candle from the shelf nearest the door, dashing up the servants' stairs and across the landing to the mistress's bedroom. The shrieking continues from inside.

I try to open the heavy wooden door but am astonished to find it locked. Mrs Higgins rushes up behind me, still foggy from sleep, fumbling with a key.

'Allontanati da me creature malvagie!' The mistress cries from behind the door.

'Why is the room locked?' I demand.

Mrs Higgins breathes heavily. 'Master's orders. He has his own set of keys and usually deals with bad nights like this, but if this noise hasn't woken him, then he hasn't returned home yet. She normally sleeps through, once the tonic kicks in.'

The door finally clicks open, and the cook runs into the darkened room. 'What is it, mistress?'

I am shocked to witness this woman, seemingly so calm earlier, now wild with distress. Sprawled out in her bed, her hair hangs in a matted mess, sweat and tears mix on her face, as her eyes wide and unfocused eyes search the other side of the room.

'L'ho avvertito. I warned him!' She shouts, looking wildly around. 'He was just there.'

I shiver as I follow her gaze, searching the shadows.

'I'm sure you did.' The cook sits beside her and strokes her hair, guiding her to lie back down.

'I would kill the harlot if he betrayed me,' she continues to shout. 'Why doesn't he touch me since the accident? He blames me. I know he does!'

She is clearly beyond reason. Trapped in a nightmare, she is speaking with voices beyond this reality. Mrs Higgins appears unintimidated, suggesting this is a familiar occurrence, and I grasp at that small comfort.

'I saw the way he looked at her,' Mistress Angelica spits with venom as she attempts to clamber out of bed.

'Hold her while I get her to drink some more tonic – it's on the bedside table!' shouts Mrs Higgins.

I move quickly, grabbing her arms and securing her to the bed, but the mistress resists, her strength difficult to control, only yielding when Mrs. Higgins leans over and pushes the spoonful of dark medicine through her tightly pressed lips. Thankfully, she welcomes the bitter liquid, throwing her head back and relaxing just a little. Her white nightdress is tangled around her body, exposing her arms and legs where long red scratches, some raw and weeping, resemble a network of barbed branches. 'Her skin!' I gasp, my hand over my mouth. Mrs Higgins casts me a sharp look, instructing me to compose myself.

'The black and white demons peck at me! They won't leave me alone. Why didn't they touch her? He won't want me now,' she wails as tears stream down her face.

'It's only a dream. You will wake up the rest of the house, and we don't want that now, do we?' The cook smooths her hair, gathering the loose strands up in handfuls away from her damp face as she gives her another spoonful of tonic. 'It's all over now. Go back to sleep.'

Something is tapping loudly outside. I rush to pull down the window and quiet the noise. Moving the curtain aside, moonlight shines on a single magpie perched on the outside sill. Its dull red eyes are not frightened by me. But as I get closer to pull down the sash, it lurches up, feathers splayed, and crashes into the pane, its sharp beak almost tearing at my cheek. I stifle a scream as I slam the window shut and pull the curtains tight. My fingers tremble as I touch my skin, looking for a wound I don't have, expecting to find blood on my fingertips.

My ordeal has gone unnoticed, but I am shaken to the core. Within a few moments, the cook's softly spoken words coax the mistress to lie back down, and she tucks her under the covers as though she were a young child.

The cook glances over at me. 'You can go now, Ivy. I'll sit with her until she falls asleep.'

The front door slams shut as a muffled voice rises from the entrance hall below. The master has returned.

Grateful to leave the mistress's room, I make my way along the corridor, looking over the stairway bannister, squinting with the dim light of the hallway chandelier, where only a few candles remain lit.

Oblivious to the noise he is making, I watch as the master stumbles into the mahogany hallway table, knocking the vase of flowers over with a crash, spilling water onto the floor, clearly blind drunk. As the master glances up at me, he loses his balance again, colliding with the grandfather clock. He staggers, regaining his composure, and waves at me, a friendly gesture that seems strangely out of place. I find my hand waving slowly back and immediately regret my action.

This man drinks and is evidently a womaniser – a beast of a husband. Yet in the entrance hall, as I watch him struggle, I see a man troubled with sadness. Much like myself, he is clearly haunted by his inner demons. I wait until I hear the library door close, and then I go down to clean up his mess.

Chapter 14 ~ The Secret Door

Ivy ~ Blackham House, 24th November.

Through the morning room window, I watch an old man with silver-grey hair walking about the garden. The sun has risen, although the day still feels overcast with the remnants of night. Slim and wiry with a black flat cap and a white beard, his scruffy grey coat is hanging open, revealing a faded, red-chequered neckerchief, an oversized brown waistcoat and baggy trousers. He slumps down onto a small wooden bench under the sorry-looking, gnarled chestnut tree.

I cannot help but notice the absence of plants in the beds of soil again. Only a few groupings of the unusual thick-bodied shrub exist; I do not recognise their long, narrow blue-green leaves with their stems full of orange thorns. My interest is piqued by their marble-sized green fruit. I have never seen a singular species dominate a garden with such vigour; already I want to examine the plant with my hand lens. Even in winter, there should be more clues as to what else will be budding in spring. A garden of this size should be bursting with foliage.

The elderly man pulls out a paper bag from his trouser pocket and, extending his hand, throws a cloud of crumbs onto the ground. From nowhere, a myriad of birds instantly swoop down, surrounding him – magpies, crows, jays. All are members of the corvidae family but the majority are magpies. Their black and white bodies are everywhere.

My mouth stings as I remember the frenzied bird at the mistress's window, and as I touch my lip a drop of blood smears on my fingertip from biting through the skin. There are no signs of any pretty blue tits or finches. What small bird would be brave enough to approach these creatures, the most ruthless and intelligent of their kind, preying on the weakest?

Despite my creeping unease, my fingers itch to draw them, to depict the motion of their fluttering wings, their elegant flights to the ground, revealing their iridescent colours. Charcoal would be the best medium to capture the depth of their darkest feathers; I will purchase some from the apothecary, although I will probably never use them with so many chores taking all my time. I now understand my mother's choice; watercolours alone are not distinctive enough for these powerful creatures.

This house appears to be both a sanctuary and a mausoleum for these corvids, part of the strange Blackham collection. From the stuffed birds on shelves and in display cabinets that fill the many rooms, these ominous creatures appear to be watching everything. They are nothing like the delicate blackbirds depicted in both my mother's artwork and Miss Earnshaw's diary.

I need to understand more about the symbols – the sun, arrows, and bird patterns that Mother drew. The Latin volume in the library might help. It is funny how I have never seen these symbols before, but now they feel almost as familiar as my own language.

The gardener seems to keep busy. After feeding the birds, he stands up from the bench and begins raking the empty flower beds until he gets to the occasional blue-green shrub, which he carefully navigates around. These areas of the garden seem to be the only areas that are well maintained, for he appears to ignore the dead leaves scattered in heaps decaying across the lawn. Even the rambling rose bushes growing amongst a row of towering yew trees at the back of the garden look wild and forgotten.

Some birds peck at the freshly turned soil, finding treats of unearthed worms. He looks to be their guardian, talking to them, stopping now and then to throw more crumbs, encouraging them to stay. I open the window to hear what he's saying, but he stops and turns to look in my direction.

The birds scatter and I know I have ruined the moment. His unfriendly expression takes me by surprise, his scowl displaying an obvious displeasure with the interruption. His rheumy grey eyes fix on mine, assessing me.

Pulling the sash window down abruptly, I leave the old man in peace and head upstairs to join Hannah, where she's making a start cleaning in the mistress's room. We have a little time whilst the mistress reads in the drawing room.

'Who is it that feeds the magpies?' I ask as I grab a duster from our bucket of cloths and brushes by the door. Walking over to the fireplace, I begin to clean the marble mantel before Hannah reprimands me for my idle hands.

'You mean William?' Hannah remakes the four-poster bed with the top sheet and blankets. 'He's the gardener. Best to leave him alone.'

'He didn't look kindly on me.'

Hannah looks up from straightening the covers. 'Don't go upsetting him; that's the last thing we need. Why are you so interested in what's out there? Inside is where your attention should be.'

'Has he been here long?' I wipe the black marble until it shines.

She huffs as she throws another blanket across the bed. 'More than any of the staff. But he doesn't like to talk and gets angry if he feels intruded on. 'He probably thinks the grounds belong to him.'

'Why are they so neglected, then?'

'What do you mean?' Her words are sharper than usual.

'The lawn is untidy, and there are no designs of plants in the flower beds.'

'Well, it is winter – what do you expect?' She rolls her eyes. 'He does what he needs to. Nobody manages him, he looks after himself.' Hannah sounds almost defensive.

Curious, I continue to polish. 'It is just that I haven't seen him before, and he only fed the birds and raked the soil. The garden has so much potential. It's a shame.'

She stands up straight, adjusting the corset under her uniform. 'I guess he's old. The master won't dismiss him... Besides, where would he go? Only the poorhouse at his age.'

'Does he ever talk to anyone?'

'Mrs Higgins knows how to handle him. He mostly takes his food outside, although sometimes when it's bitter, he eats in the kitchen.'

'Where does he sleep? I haven't come across a bed for him anywhere in the house.'

'I don't hold all the answers!' she retorts, glaring at me. 'This talk is no business of mine or yours. Come on, help me with the rest of the bed.'

I bang the two frilled pillows together, standing them upright against the headboard. 'Seems strange, that's all.'

'Why should I care? One thing he does is whittle – makes things out of wood from the old, crooked tree.' Hannah motions with her head to the window that looks out onto the garden, but I know what she means: the strangely dead-looking chestnut tree with twisted branches.

To finish, we spread the satin eiderdown quilt out between us over the two blankets, smoothing out the goose feather creases with our palms.

'If you're lucky, he might make you a present.'

'A present? Why would he do that?'

She erupts into laughter. 'A romantic gesture! I would accept them myself if I didn't have my copper ... but you've got no one?'

I bite down on my lip, hard. The notion is not amusing, and I want no gifts, certainly not from a surly old man. Something isn't right about the garden or him – like everything else in this house.

Over several days, there is an endless downpour, and the hours pass in the monotony of cleaning. When the weather finally clears on Tuesday morning, Mrs Higgins instructs me to visit the local market, giving me a large wicker basket and a few pennies to buy fresh ingredients for the evening meal. The stored vegetables in the pantry had become mouldy again, even though they were expected to last another week.

Standing on the path outside the scullery, I'm relieved I brought my winter cloak and gloves from home; the rain has been replaced by an icy wind that stings my cheeks. With the basket hanging on my arm, I draw the thick velvet closer around me and then recheck the shopping list, not wanting to make a mistake with the order: carrots, parsnips, turnips, and some new potatoes. My ability to think clearly is impaired by another night of broken sleep with the mistress crying from her nightmares.

I jolt when I hear a catlike wail and tuck the paper list into my cloak pocket. Walking round to the back of the house, I listen out, wondering if it's the cat, Mr Grey. Another yowl comes from the direction of the yew trees. Amongst the rose bushes at the back of the house, I see my newfound ally. He is indeed caught between a cluster of sharp rose bushes and a brick wall.

'What are you doing here?' My tone is soft, and he responds by answering with a louder cry.

'There now... shh,' I say softly, as I put down my basket and pull back the prickly stems. These are particularly sharp rose bushes, and as I reach to pick him up, despite my gloves, the thorns scratch my skin through the material.

'Hello there, Mr Grey.'

He responds in gratitude with a low purr as he nestles in close to my neck. As I survey the grounds, there are no signs of the gardener, and again my attention is drawn to the unusual shrubs that surround the lawn. This close, I can see the exotic orange thorns which adorn the stems and surround the green berries like protective jewels. Next time I will bring a knife and take a cutting.

Yew trees cluster together above me, their branches woven together like old spidery hands. The rose bushes and trees are stark, their former beauty diminished by the early December frost – or something else, as the plants are not just devoid of foliage, but appear to be ailing, for what leaves are left are covered in dark blotches of black and red. The trees are similar in their poor health, with brittle bark and discoloured trunks. In the midst of these branches, I notice a well-hidden door among the ivy-covered bricks. If not for the tarnished brass latch catching my eye, I would have missed it entirely.

To my sadness, Mr Grey jumps out of my arms and races off towards the house, but despite my impending errands, curiosity fuels me. Picking up my basket, I use it to force my way through the brambles until I reach the door. I attempt to twist the brass handle, but it remains stuck, perhaps with age.

After trying again whilst leaning on the door with my full weight, it finally gives under the pressure and I emerge into another garden crowded with the same yew trees, but these are healthy and strong. A narrow path stretches out before me, overgrown with moss and weeds, and I wonder if this might be an alternative way to the market. I could still buy the vegetables in good time, so I close the secret door behind me.

The footpath takes me around a bend. A hedge shields my view until I come to the edge of a graveyard. I glance behind me: the trail almost disappears, blending in with endless headstones. I have had my fill of churches and start to retrace my steps back when the snap of twigs stops me.

'Good morning!' I am surprised to see a vicar waving. Wearing a white cassock, he wanders over towards me.

'A fine day – I didn't mean to startle you. It is a pleasant time to take a walk, is it not?'

'Yes, it is sir. Good morning.'

'What brings you to God's garden?' He waves his hand as if all the graves were flowers to behold.

'I seem to have lost my way; I took a different path and was just leaving.'

I fidget with the basket, worried he might reprimand me for trespassing, for I have no family buried here.

'Many who have lost their way find that their feet bring them here to St. John's.'

He smiles at me with genuine interest. He seems older than I first thought, perhaps in his seventies.

'Have you seen a black rabbit?' He laughs, looking across the gravestones. 'I often find him in this part of the grounds.'

'Sorry, I haven't seen anything,' I reply, shaking my head at the strange request.

'No matter, he'll turn up – he always does. I bring him these, you see.'

He takes a couple of carrots from his pocket. He then motions towards my wrist where blood has trickled through my glove. 'Oh dear, you're hurt?'

'It's nothing, only the thorns from a rosebush.' I try to rub the blood away, but the stain remains.

'Ah, they are deadly when provoked.'

His humour is endearing. The tension in my shoulders eases with his kind words.

'Which direction did you come from? You seemed to come out of nowhere,' he says with a benign smile.

'I came from the townhouse garden behind us.'

The smile falls from his face. 'The building behind the trees... You came from Blackham House?'

'Yes,' I say with a nod. 'I found a door concealed in the garden and it led me here.'

'I see.' He looks back towards the house, but I sense a shift in his opinion of me, for his eyes darken and he steps back. 'I'm surprised. The church hasn't been visited by that household for many a year.'

Heat flushes my cheeks at his subtle scrutiny. 'I am only visiting for a short time. It's my first time in London.'

'Well, please ensure your visit takes in some other parts of the city too. 'St. Paul's or the South Kensington Museum is an interesting afternoon well spent.'

I don't believe he considers me a servant; such is the quality of my cloak, and now that I have implied I am only a temporary guest, his face brightens.

'You have a concern about the inhabitants of Blackham House?' I cannot miss this opportunity to learn more about the Blackhams. He has an obvious disapproval of the place, and I need to know why.

'No, my dear. It merely holds a sad past. Nothing to do with you, and certainly not a matter to be concerned with.' He smiles again, but this time it seems forced.

'I am intrigued. History has always been a personal interest of mine,' I reply.

He sighs. 'It is not a joyful story. I am sure it would not be to your taste.'

I lean forward slightly, keen to know more. 'On the contrary, sir. I would be most grateful to know the story.'

His reluctance is clear, as deep frown lines crease his forehead, but with a tilt of his head, he seems to surrender to the idea.

'Come then, if you can spare the time. It is too cold to talk here. The black rabbit can find me another day.'

He leaves the carrots next to a nearby headstone and points to the church along the path and a small cottage next door with smoke billowing from the chimney. 'My housekeeper at the vicarage can make us some hot tea and attend to your hand. If you still wish to know, we can discuss it over the freshly cooked biscuits. I smelt them being baked as I came out for my walk... They should sweeten the tale.'

'Thank you,' I agree immediately, the trip to the market slipping further back into my mind.

Chapter 15 ~ History

Ivy ~ The Vicarage, 28th November.

On approach, the vicarage cottage is cosy and inviting. The red-brick building is set within a neat box hedge. All the windows glitter, with their polished lines of individual, small squares of glass in each lead frame. A large chimney dominates the side of the home, puffing smoke into the air. Glossy, pointed green leaves cover the front with splashes of red holly berries. The vicar pushes through a small wooden gate. A grey-haired woman watches us through the front window and the door opens.

'Mrs Guilden, we have company for morning tea. I found this dear girl in the grounds, shivering in the cold, and she needs to warm up and sample some of your renowned baking.' He ushers me in. 'This is my wonderful housekeeper; she has been the keeper of this house and my stomach for the past ten years.'

The woman steps aside with a smile as we enter. 'Indeed, I have. And you're here in good time. I've only just taken some shortbread out of the oven.'

'Good, good,' the vicar replies. He turns to me in the small hallway. 'I don't believe I asked your name?'

'Miss Ivy Granger, Sir,' I answer.

'Come in then, Ivy, and make yourself at home. My name is Vicar Evans. Norman is my Christian name. This is a house of God, and as such, you are always welcome.'

The hallway leads us past a kitchen and into a small parlour. The inside is as tidy as the front of the house, full of knitted blankets, folded on the backs of chairs and on the sofa.

Every belonging has an organised place; the smell of warm biscuits fills the room and wraps itself around me like one of the knitted blankets. Mrs Higgins doesn't do much cake baking on account of the mistress's dietary menu, but this aroma takes me back to my childhood memories. My eyes well up as I remember enjoying sweetmeats with Mother when she was still in good health.

'I don't know what I would do without dear Mrs Guilden,' the vicar says.

'Probably be surviving off bread and cheese, I would expect.' She laughs and pats his shoulder like a beloved child. 'Did you find that black rabbit of yours today?'

'No, alas, he remained quite the elusive fellow on this occasion.' The vicar settles into a straight-backed chair next to the fire and nods for me to do the same on a small floral sofa placed opposite. Slumped with fatigue from the walk, the small measure of exercise must have tired him more than he cares to admit.

'So, he found you instead?' She passes a plate in front of me. 'Can I tempt you with some of my biscuits, dear?' Thick cream-coloured disks, dusted with sugar, fill the plate in her hand.

'Yes, lovely, thank you.' I say, taking the nearest biscuit. 'I won't trouble you for long. I am on my way to visit the market.' The shortbread crumbles and melts on my tongue, my eyes closing briefly as I savour the sweetness.

'It's no trouble, dear. What would you be after at the market?'

'Just some carrots, new potatoes, and parsnips; they've been difficult to store without turning.'

'Surely the cold weather would preserve them. Perhaps the house has damp?' Her forehead creases in puzzlement.

'That is possible.' I think of the soft vegetables, already going putrid in the basement kitchen, and the flowers which never stay fresh for long.

'Have you tried Old Man Tim, on the corner of the market? His fruit and vegetables are always good quality.'

'The proof is Mrs Guilden's apple cake she makes on a Sunday,' the vicar interjects, 'the finest there is.'

Mrs Guilden fusses around him, placing a blanket over his knees and stoking the fire. She makes a steaming pot of tea and sets it down next to the plate of shortbread on the narrow oak table between us. As the china clinks, the flames crackle in the fireplace. I cannot remember the last time I felt so truly cared for. It is very much in contrast to the house I have just left. It is funny how two worlds can coexist in such close proximity yet be so vastly different.

'Now then,' he says, stirring his cup, watching the liquid swirl around. 'You are interested in the Blackham residence, is that correct?'

I nod in agreement.

'And what is your connection with the family again?'

I dislike lying, especially to a vicar, but if he thinks I am nothing but a prying servant, he may not entrust his story to me. 'I am a friend of his wife.'

'He has married again?' He raises his eyebrows.

'Yes, within the last year. They met in Italy – Angelica is Italian and does not know many people, so I am a new companion to her.' There is a veil of truth in my deception, and I breathe easier for it.

'Of course, and you have concerns about her?'

'Only the house is ... shall we say, a little different from any other I have visited? There are lots of strange artefacts in cabinets and … and I have heard unsettling stories.'

'Hmm, quite,' he interrupts. 'I hear their collection is most peculiar. That house seems to attract problems. And you would like to know more to give you peace of mind?'

'Yes, if you please, I would be grateful, for it might explain some strange occurrences which have taken place recently.'

'Tell me, is the young master still a troubled soul?'

The tremor in my hand at the mention of his name is almost visible as I replace my cup on the saucer. 'I believe so, sir.'

'That does not surprise me – not at all,' the vicar replies, and then tuts to himself.

He pauses before continuing, taking a mouthful of tea and considering his words. Putting down his cup, he reclines back into his armchair. His hands come together, the fingertips forming a steeple in front of his chest.

'I am afraid what I am about to say will not bring you comfort. But perhaps you might take the story as a warning to be on your guard and take extra care of the new mistress. The house has an unhappy past, one that happened a long time ago, when I was first training as a vicar. I found God in my forties, older than most, but He has always guided me.' He raises his eyes to the ceiling with a wry smile. 'The Reverend before me was undone by love. Perhaps if he had not strayed away from God's path, he would have lived his days out here, instead of...' His sentence trails off.

'Isn't that rather unusual for a man of the church?' I ask.

'I believe she was no ordinary woman, for she captivated you with her kind heart and angelic face.' He shifts in his chair, reaching for his tobacco on the table next to him. 'I must say, I became quite taken with her myself. No wonder Reverend Geffrey abided by her every whim.' He glances at his housekeeper walking through the kitchen doorway as though his admission might cause mischief.

Lighting his pipe and taking a long draw, he reclines back into the fireside chair and continues. Mirroring him, I also relax. The market can wait. My mother often warned me that history repeats itself if a sin is evil enough and never absolved.

'So, the Reverend Geffrey and his wife disregarded this humble cottage and took the plot next to the church instead. It contained an old building which had been empty for some time, and they built it into the large house you now know as Blackham House and turned it into the new vicarage for St John's. They created the private pathway from their garden to the graveyard, which you discovered today. The arrangement worked well for a time.' He nods in agreement with himself. 'I would often visit and take lessons with Reverend Geffrey in his study, keen to advance my knowledge of the Bible. I never dreamt circumstances would lead me to take over from him, and still reside as the parish vicar, nearly twenty-five years later.' His eyes begin to glaze over with decades of memories.

'What happened next?' I press gently.

'At first, his wife made a valiant effort to decorate the new vicarage with pretty rugs and pictures. The female touch she brought to the place was impressive. Many visitors came and made their own judgements on his recent marriage and the wealthier lifestyle he had chosen. One by one, they, too, fell under her spell, and they welcomed the married couple and the house as an addition to the church vicarage.' He clears his throat; the words have become stuck. 'Then, after a year, their son, Jeremiah, was born.'

My mind flicks to the toy soldier in the box of forgotten belongings.

'You couldn't quite put your finger on it, but during this usual happy period, there was a dark cloud hovering.' His expression becomes pained. 'They appointed a nanny, and little Jeremiah thrived; he was bright and healthy. I often saw him playing in the grounds, but as he grew, his mother went into decline.'

'Where did the nanny stay?' I ask, already knowing the answer.

'I believe she took a room in the attic. I recall her as a quiet woman who was also extremely fastidious and religious. I hoped her presence would be a blessing to the family.'

At once, I can imagine a nanny in a small bed under the eaves of Blackham House.

'Gradually, Mrs. Geffrey stopped leaving the house and attending the weekly Sunday service. On the rare occasions we saw her out in public, the beauty she had effortlessly possessed had vanished. It was most distressing to see her weakening, and in view of what eventually happened, I regret that we let her down in a time of need and vulnerability. We should have been on guard, protecting her from herself or whatever else plagued her.'

An outburst of commotion beyond the window startles me. The knifelike chatter of the magpies has followed me, intruding on our conversation with their hostile racket, but the vicar does not appear to hear.

'It was a matter of course that such a lady of stature would find the burden of parenting a hardship. The nanny continued to help, and they consulted a physician who prescribed leeches and various tonics, but alas, she deteriorated faster than his ability to assist. The lady's maid, on listening at her mistress's door, often heard her talking to someone, but when she entered her bedroom, she found no one – only the mistress watching out the window over the garden, fascinated by the birds.' He shrugs his shoulders as if the memory still confuses him now.

'As men of God, naturally, we dismissed the notion of any mental aberration and prayed for the good fortune of the parish to continue. However, it did not escape our attention that something was not right within the house.'

I lean forward in my chair, absorbing every word, encouraging him with a tentative smile to continue.

'Two years went by, and it became increasingly hard to ignore, especially when the servants left, white-faced and tight-lipped. Eventually, after most of the servants had gone, they could not find replacements as rumours spread throughout the city.' His voice lowered to almost a whisper. 'There were stories ... of people witnessing a ghostly white figure with a lamp standing at the windows moving from room to room. The air in the house became stifling and heavy. Once or twice, I would see a shadow move out of the room or hear the sound of footsteps following me into the hallway, but no one would appear. It put me most on edge within those walls.'

He takes a breath, sucking his teeth.

'One night at dusk, I was alone in the entrance hall, preparing to leave. I sensed I was being observed and turned to find the mistress barefoot on the stairs in her nightclothes. Her hair hung loosely over her shoulders. Her face was blank and her eyes vacant. She did not move, but looked straight ahead, almost through me. It was by far the most unnerving sight I had ever experienced.'

He rubs his eyes, as though wiping away tears shed long ago.

'I no longer felt obliged to pay calls on the vicarage and preferred to stay in this much smaller residence, taking my Bible reading and studying amongst the gravestones. Even then, the sensation of being watched followed me to the outside grounds. I never believed...'

'Now then, Vicar Evans, you don't want to scare the young lady now, do you? On account of her staying in the house of which you speak?'

I jump at the interruption of the housekeeper. So absorbed by the vicar's story, I had been quite transported to another time. I easily imagined the family existing in the same rooms inside the house I now clean; the hallways the wife and I had both wandered alone, with the lack of staff, a repeat occurrence.

The housekeeper nudges her way into the snug nook by the fire with a fresh pot of tea. 'You don't want to excite yourself, either. I don't want to rush down to the doctor at an ungodly hour because you take a funny turn, what with the weather changing and all looking like an early winter. Besides, I don't enjoy hearing about that house. It still gives me the shivers even when the sun shines.'

'Ah, Mrs Guilden, you needn't scold me or concern yourself with weak dispositions.' Shaking his head and waving his pipe to make his point, he continues: 'Ivy has taken a special interest in the house and has asked specifically to hear about its history. See how contented she is, sitting in our home, eating your fine baking with gusto. And who knows, this might be the last opportunity I have to tell it! We simply must learn from our history.'

I nod in unison, and he smiles at the housekeeper as if no further argument exists. In exasperation, she returns to the kitchen, banging pans about in mild protest as he continues.

'Of course, common sense prevailed. They sent the nanny with the boy to the countryside to give the vicar and his wife time to focus on their wellbeing and on his job in the vicarage. The parish was growing, and they needed him for all the numerous christenings and marriages.'

'Unfortunately, events took a sombre turn.' He folds an arm over his chest, hand over heart. 'The mistress succumbed to long episodes of sobbing and hysteria and was often found sleepwalking, searching for her child. The night she died, she stood on the windowsill of an open window, facing this same building. I don't recall the reason I took a late evening walk past the house, but I remember thinking it was a bad dream or some frightful vision, seeing her nightdress fluttering in the night breeze. I could not see her face well, but I knew in my heart it would be void of any expression, like the time I saw her on the stairwell.' He swallows hard. 'She seemed to remain on the edge for a long time, although it must have only been a matter of minutes. One moment she was standing in the moonlight, and the next, she had stepped off the ledge.' His voice cracks. 'Within moments, her body was lying broken on the ground.'

He closes his eyes briefly, overcome by emotion. 'I believe I was the only one to witness her fall. As I ran down the path, I shouted out in panic, alerting everyone, but it was too late. It was a heart-wrenching night; we could do nothing to save her.'

'How terrible,' I exclaim, palm to my mouth. Shocked by his revelation.

'The Reverend renounced his position and abandoned the house, overwhelmed with grief. He journeyed to the countryside to collect his child from the nanny's care, but another tragic part of the story is that he could not find them.'

'The boy … he went missing?' My voice falters, as I somehow know the answer again before he says it.

'It was as if they had both simply disappeared. They never arrived at the place where they had been expected. This last news broke him. For years, he searched everywhere for them, desperately roaming the country, but nothing. There was no trace of the child. Now he lives on the outskirts of London, half-mad in his own world of loneliness. A horrible ending.'

'That's awful.' I shudder at the immense tragedy the poor man must have suffered. My heart aches in my own recognition of my own grief. Is that why the rooms feel so tragically sorrowful?

'And then, curious things began to happen.' He watches my reaction as the story takes a change of direction. 'The house remained empty for a few months before a wealthy family took ownership. But there was talk that another inhabited the house whilst it was empty, for occasionally a flicker of light was witnessed during the evening. Tales abounded in the local taverns of men on their way home after an evening of drinking, observing a glow moving about the floors. Tales spread of this poor woman still trapped in the house, her spirit roaming the rooms. Of course, these stories could merely have been the silly fancies of drunken men, but still, it came to pass that people avoided the house, particularly when it was a moonless night.'

He draws on his pipe slowly, letting the flavour linger in his mouth before exhaling.

'The new owner was the late Lord Blackham, the father of Alexander, the current Master Blackham. He was wealthy, and it was a prime location. He was not put off by the history of the property or the vicinity to the graveyard. In fact, it went well for him, as he ran for politics, and was seen to be somehow connected to the church. I believe there may have been some trouble or scandal with his eldest son. He had quite a flamboyant lifestyle in the city, but the property improved his social standing; money has all sorts of power.' He shakes his head. 'Disaster struck again. He lost Victor, his oldest son and Alexander's only sibling, on a ship sailing back to England from Egypt. There was also the matter of what happened to Alexander's first wife and child – a devastating business.'

'A most tragic set of circumstances,' Mrs Guilden muttered. 'Fancy a mother and child not being buried together? A travesty it was.'

'Why was that the case?' I am so absorbed by the calamity of the story that I can barely refrain from taking my gloves off and biting my nails.

The vicar cuts in: 'Unfortunately, the late Mrs Blackham is buried in the north corner of the cemetery, which is no place for an innocent child.'

'The north?'

'It is the plot for murders and suicides, and sadly, in the end, she committed both.'

Silence fills the pause in conversation as the full impact of his words settles over me. Hannah was telling the truth.

'Enough, now. It is time you took some rest,' says the housekeeper. 'All this dramatic talk has worn you out.' She turns to me. 'And if you want to make the market, you better hurry. Nothing worth buying is there after midday.'

He looks deep in thought. 'Ivy, please take heed. I would recommend the mistress takes a new home. A fresh start for the young Blackhams would be best. We are only human and can be weak against the influence of evil. There is something about that house which makes my spirit uneasy. You must come to us if you ever feel the need. We must remain strong against the Devil and the wicked tricks he uses to turn us from God.'

Chapter 16 ~ Memories

Master Blackham ~ Blackham House, 29th November.

Master Blackham hesitates before edging the door open. The collection room remains untouched. Even though his father had been dead for the last year, he could still smell the tobacco in the dust covering his precious artefacts. They are his now, a responsibility he unwillingly accepts, another burden to think about. He sits behind his father's desk and stares at the stuffed animals and clay statues until a gentle rap at the door behind him breaks his concentration.

'Yes?'

'I presumed you might prefer a stronger drink than tea.' The butler enters with a tray of white sandwiches and red wine. He places the food on the desk, warily noting the dark expression on his master's features.

'Thank you, Bancroft. I'm afraid you find me feeling morose again.'

'I'm sorry to hear that, sir.' He answers gently and places a full glass of red wine in front of him. 'Is there anything else I can help with?'

The master sighs, but then looks around as if there are others in the room he doesn't want listening. 'Tell me, do you remember my brother?' He asks, his voice lowered.

The butler is almost successful in hiding his surprise at the question. 'Yes, sir, although I was only a boy.' He clears his throat delicately to change the conversation, but the master looks beyond him, seemingly engrossed in the large magpie above the door.

'Those days have been playing on my mind again.' He is almost muttering to himself. 'I have one vivid memory – Victor's excitement on the day of the voyage to Egypt. He was so sure of himself. It left quite an impression on me.'

He reaches for the wine glass and takes a generous gulp. Then his lips turn down into a sneer, his voice turning rough like gravel. 'I was nineteen but still wet behind the ears according to him. Did you know, if I hadn't been ill with whooping cough and been forced to stay here with my mother like a child, I might have gone with them? I could have proven myself somehow. At seventeen, Victor had the run of London, but I was constantly kept on a tight leash.' He turns to face the butler again, now raising his voice. 'Still, what good did it do him in the end? My perfect brother only lasted until twenty-seven. I have surpassed him, but still Mother isn't satisfied. The day he went missing changed everything.' His expression becomes puzzled. 'Surely, you must have come to the memorial?'

'No, sir. Staff were not allowed to discuss the trip … after what happened.'

'Of course, the aftermath.' He gives a hollow laugh. 'My father never recovered from the loss of his favourite son. And Mother never forgave me for remaining alive.'

The butler wipes the desk with a cloth from his pocket. Drops of wine have been spilt across the varnished wood like pools of blood, but Master Blackham is unaware. 'Lady Blackham has her ways, sir, but I am sure she means well.'

He takes another slug of alcohol. 'You gloss over the truth, and you should know my mother better than most! My own mother hates me. She cannot even bear the sight of her only living son, and my father preferred to be with these stuffed creatures. To be in the company of the dead rather than his real family. I always thought there was something sinister about these artefacts; they completely consumed his attention and stole any relationship we might have had.'

'They are just old, sir.' He swallows, licking his lips where they have become dry. 'This room is a little cold. Perhaps you would prefer to take a rest elsewhere in the house. Your library is warm?'

He waves him away, almost spilling his wine again. 'No, I am fine, Bancroft. As I said, I'm merely in a melancholy mood.' He takes a deep breath. 'The time has come to auction a couple of artefacts to keep the house running. No doubt you are aware, the bills have been high this year.'

'Yes, sir.' He paused, as if choosing his words carefully. 'Winter is an expensive time.'

'What would you sell?' He points his hand towards the door. 'How about the ugly giant magpie? I could certainly live without its silent judgement.'

'May I suggest that it would not be wise to remove that particular piece from the house? That was a favourite of Lord Blackham's... Lady Blackham might have an opinion.'

The bird, in all its winged glory, overshadowed them, along with the rest of the objects in the room.

'Hmm, perhaps not.' The master turns his back on the black and white creature. 'I do not share the same passion for this strange hobby, but my father always insisted that a man needs to collect things to prove his existence in the world.'

'Must you sell anything, sir?' The butler hesitates. 'It is not my place to say, but surely there are other options to review?'

'No, I'm afraid the time has come.'

'It's only…'

Master Blackham puts his drink down and rests his elbows on the desk, running his hands through his hair. 'Lord, I cannot think straight with all this dust. Get one of the maids to get rid of this filth.'

'Are you sure, sir? The servants are not normally allowed in this room.'

He folds his arms. 'Have I not made myself clear? This is my collection now. Order a maid to clean it or do the task yourself.'

The butler gives a low bow. 'As you wish, sir.'

'Angelica is not well. I surmise the musty odour from these creations might be the cause.'

'The mistress will recover soon, no doubt.'

'She gets worse by the day.' The master lets out another long sigh. 'I don't know why I hoped it would be different this time.' He lowers his voice dramatically. 'Is it me or this place that changes these women for the worst? Are they such weak creatures that the London air affects them so badly? I had hoped I could forget, but there are times when I feel she never left this house.'

His eyes well up as he looks out of the window. 'Do you ever see her?'

'Who, sir?'

'You know perfectly well who I mean!' The master slams his hand on the table. 'Miranda is still here with us!' He looks around the room. 'She is constantly in my dreams, and when I wake, I catch a fleeting glimpse of her standing by my bedside. I know her spirit still blames me for what happened.'

The butler takes a step back. 'You mustn't blame yourself, sir.'

The master rakes his fingers through his hair. 'Then who should I blame? This house? I was fooling myself that Angelica could even come close to replacing what we had. I have made a dire mistake, and now my legacy is reduced to this.' He motions to the preserved animals and birds mounted on blocks of wood. 'For a moment, I had it all.' His breath shudders. 'My wife, my daughter.'

The butler lowers his head. 'Grief takes time, sir. I have no doubt your decisions will give you peace soon enough.'

'No ... we should never have returned from Italy but continued to live in a make-believe world. Being here is nothing but a punishment. We should have left this house to rot along with the stuffed animals and dust. The beasts and ghosts of the past are the true inhabitants of this house now, not us.'

Chapter 17 ~ Mentors

Ivy ~ Primrose Hill, 30th November.

It is Thursday, and Mrs Higgins has given me my first afternoon off. Perhaps she can see that my many chores are taking their toll and is worried that I will leave like other servants before me. Although I need to rest, I want to use the time wisely.

After I had paid a visit to my old lodgings in Primrose Hill to collect any post, I sit on a bench in the nearest park reading the single reply from Edith on behalf of my father. As I had hoped, I am one less burden for them to consider. It seems that they trust this brief period of work will ensure I return ready for marriage. Even my assertion to remain away over Christmas has not been questioned, confirming that my company will not be missed, and that I'm only required for my impending nuptials.

Edith intends to visit next month in the new year after her son, Timothy, has recovered from his recent illness. Her attention to him, even now as a grown man, borders on obsession. But then I am not a mother, so perhaps I do not understand. Fortunately, her reluctance to be away from him will be to my advantage, for I am sure she will only meet me for afternoon tea at a hotel, and my absence from the lodging house will not be noted.

I wonder what to do with the rest of the afternoon. I'm toying with the idea of revisiting Miss Earnshaw's housekeeper again or the vicarage, but my mind is too tired to decide. The vicar's story weighs heavily on my mind. Sudden deaths and people missing: an innocent child and a nurse; the boy would be around my age now if he had survived. And the master's first wife and young child? Such a waste of life. Surely, the events can't all be linked to the house? Yet, I have an eerie sense that somehow, they are.

The Blackham residence is becoming more unsettling by the day, but nevertheless, I can't leave without finding out the truth about what happened on the night of the parlour games. Something awful must have happened, for Miss Earnshaw was adamant that we should meet. Did they release something evil from the other side in their seance? I have never given much credit to spiritualism, but I continue to see and hear things that are not physically there. My father would say my nerves are frayed, but I feel close to uncovering a huge secret. My body is almost vibrating with anticipation.

It is almost three o'clock. I have become frozen with cold and need to warm up quickly. I suddenly recall that the suffrage meeting mentioned in Miss Earnshaw's pamphlet occurs every other Thursday afternoon, so I set off to find the Hanover Square rooms, hopeful. There could be someone there, a friend or acquaintance of hers to speak to.

I am in luck: a meeting is taking place. Entering from the cold into the hot, stuffy room, I flitter in the doorway, unsure of what to do, until I catch the eye of the nearest lady. She gives me a small nod and ushers me in. Lavender and lemon oils scent the charged atmosphere as women of all ages fill the room.

'Welcome! I am Mrs Jones.' She shakes my hand with gusto and then passes me a pamphlet from a nearby table.

She is round-faced with strawberry-blonde hair styled under her sage green bonnet. The lemon ribbon wrapped around her hat matched her silk scarf. A nice touch, I notice, wishing I could carry off this London fashion with its vibrant colours and pretty details.

'Thank you. Am I not too late?'

'No, we are just about to start. This is only the warm-up.' She motions to the loud conversation.

This is a world apart from any meeting I have attended before, even church at Christmas. Another woman leans in, her hazel eyes wide with excitement. 'Every person makes a difference.' There are no more seats free, so she stands against the wall to let me squeeze in beside her at the back.

There's a hush as a svelte figure steps up onto a small stage at the front of the room. The woman next to me exclaims, 'It's Mrs Finch!' and strains to stand taller, at once becoming enraptured by the new arrival.

Mrs Finch stands confidently, dressed in a finely tailored azure velvet dress with gold buttons down the centre, white lace frills at the neck and wrists, and a matching blue hat with peacock feather. She speaks clearly, pronouncing every word with the authority of pure conviction, and I listen avidly.

'We are talking about why, after all these years, it is the right time for women to take their place in politics and have a voice. Thank you for turning out today in your numbers. It is a joy to witness so many passionate faces. We must use our position here in London wisely to our advantage. The country is modernising, changing dramatically with new transport such as trains and new factories. Are we not also part of that change?'

Her eyes sweep over the audience, ensuring she addresses everyone, as eager faces watch on with bated breath. 'Do women not contribute to society? Should they not have the right to say how their country is governed? We are integral to the running of Britain and should not be ignored!'

The crowd ripples with claps of appreciation and murmurs of agreement.

'Our husbands and fathers may believe they are indulging us, humouring our female notions. But they will find our brains are as capable, if not more so, than theirs. We will march, taking strength in our numbers and show the government we will have a voice!'

I am inspired by her words. The message is similar to what Mother frequently said, but she was only one person. Perhaps, together, times might change; women might finally have a vote. I am heartened to have discovered this movement. My mother would have loved it.

I see her then, sitting amongst the crowd in the third row from the front. Or could the figure be Miss Earnshaw? In my memory, the two women are blending into one. My heart falters as the woman turns, but her profile is different. The disappointment is a kick to the stomach.

As the speech finishes, I absorb the words and the female camaraderie, my shoulders relaxing for the first time in an age.

I smile at Mrs Jones, who welcomed me. She is brimming with enthusiasm, as though she is a child on an outing. 'How long has this been going on for?' I ask.

'Oh, this work has been happening in the background for years, but recently we have really started to make progress.' Mrs Jones leans across me to gesture to the speaker. 'Let me introduce you to our inspiring leader.'

She waves the woman in blue over as the crowd parts towards us. 'Good afternoon, Mrs Finch. We have an excellent turnout today, with some fresh faces.'

Mrs Jones beams as though she had found me herself. They both look at me, and my skin flushes under their appraisal.

Mrs Finch touches my arm briefly. 'We are always delighted to find new support. Can we rely on your presence in our next march?'

Her eyes are sharp and intelligent, the same deep blue as her dress. I can see that more women are waiting to talk to her, and I am dazzled by her presence and conviction.

'Yes,' I blurt out.

'Wonderful.' She nods as she proceeds onward to greet others, waiting impatiently.

I am left with Mrs Jones. We are like sunflowers, straining our faces towards her for the last rays of warmth as she leaves us. There is an awkward pause in the conversation that I want to fill before she walks away too. 'What type of people come here?'

'Oh, from all walks of life, but we also represent those who cannot be here. We are a voice for all women.'

I think again of the spiritualist and the real reason why I chose to come here. 'Is anyone famous here?'

'Like whom?'

'Miss Earnshaw, the spiritualist?' I can't help but search for her again in the crowd.

'Ah yes, the glamorous Miss Earnshaw. She's been here; she's a prominent voice. Such an inspiration to us all.'

'Really?' I watch her lips move, and the rest of the room becomes a blur.

'Sadly, she's missed the last few meetings.'

'Would say she is a committed attendee then, having never disappeared before?'

'No, she was always here, as regular as clockwork. I read about her in the newspaper. I do hope her situation is resolved, and she returns soon.'

I look around the room at the animated faces of the ladies talking loudly. 'Does she have a particular friend or anyone close to that I could speak to?'

She hesitates. 'No, not really. But she was amiable with all the ladies. We are all a little in awe of her, to be honest.'

She carries on talking about the women's movement. Although disappointed not to find out anything else about Miss Earnshaw, I hang on to her every word.

'But we are stronger together; they cannot ignore our voices forever.'

'And what happens if nothing changes?'

'Well, we will get louder, demanding their attention until they do acknowledge us.'

My mind wanders. It has been so long since I had a conversation with a woman that was not about chores. Her words remind me of the faceless words I hear at night. Perhaps they will also get louder if I continue to ignore them.

'Do you believe it is possible for voices to speak from the other side?'

Her forehead crumples. 'The other side? I am confused.'

I grip the pamphlet tightly, almost crumpling the paper, already knowing my mistake. 'Nothing... Please excuse me, I'm tired and rambling.'

'Ah, you are thinking of all the women who are not here, the ones trapped by this society? We represent them all, dear. This cause unites us. That is why our work is so important.'

It dawns on me I have been here longer than I planned, and I must leave at once. 'Thank you, I have enjoyed this immensely,' I say, as I prepare myself for the cold weather.

She shakes my hand firmly. 'I hope we will see you again.'

'Yes, I am sure you will.' I search for a clock on the wall but cannot see one. 'Do you have the time?'

The woman looks at her own timepiece. 'Just turned five o'clock.'

It is as I feared. Almost two hours have gone by, far longer than I had intended to stay and panic quivers in my chest. I bid her good evening and hurry outside. Blackham House is a long walk, at least forty minutes. I do not have enough in my purse for a train fare, and Mrs Higgins will be expecting me to help with the evening meal.

I walk fast, as it is already dark. This constant demand on my time is exhausting; my lower back is aching again from rushing around in a corset, and my hands are chapped inside my gloves from scrubbing the front steps. I try to summon memories of my life when my mother was alive. When I used to have the freedom to indulge in planting and drawing, but those are nothing but faint dreams now.

I do not want to return to the pallet in the basement bedroom, but my feet turn in the direction of Hyde Park, anyway. There's a sharp tug, an unseen force pulling me back. All the hopes of a new life and understanding my mother's history are woven into the mystery of the vanished spiritualist, a missing part of my family.

The fierce cry of a nearby crow startles me, its black silhouette illuminated in the lamplight. I will find you, Miss Earnshaw, I say to myself, promising with all my heart. Picking up my pace towards Blackham House, my pledge spurs me on, even though every instinct warns me to turn back.

Chapter 18 ~ Footsteps

The Nightwatchman ~ Eaton Square, 30th November.

The torches flicker as the night watchman walks through Eaton Square. It is not yet six o'clock and frost already glistens on the ground. His hands turn numb with cold, and his feet grow increasingly uncomfortable in his battered old boots. But his breath, steaming up the night air, gives him a strange sense of comfort and relief that his lungs still worked after hearing of another outbreak of tuberculosis near his rented room down by the docks.

His thoughts escape to a rum nightcap and perhaps the company of a woman, if he has enough coin at the end of his shift. The maid will pass along through Eccleston Street, and he wants to make sure he reaches the corner with enough time to be ready for her. He is used to waiting and biding his time.

In the distance, he sees something burning – a house or yard fire. Then the faint sound of whistles. The watchman tries not to conjure up a memory of flames licking at timber beams … and stifled screams.

He doesn't allow himself to reflect much on the past or his work. He only lives for the moment, motivated by money and his bodily desires. Payment is always given under the anonymity of rough pubs in dingy corners. A man for hire, he will take any job, but he likes these jobs the best – an easy target to follow and a handsome reward. But this is personal and without payment; he would gladly forfeit his usual Friday night arrangement with Mrs Braddon for this.

His mind wanders to the homely widow who takes him into her bedroom each week in exchange for food on the table. She prefers to look away from his scarred face, but he will take the fleeting warmth of her body in the absence of a real relationship, for any scrap of affection helps to dull the pain of his loneliness.

As he stands in the unseen coverage of a small passageway, he hears her footsteps light and quick before she walks past. She looks innocent. Her expression takes him by surprise; her eyes are determined, only looking ahead. She fails to understand that she's in danger, too lost in whatever occupies her mind. He follows, keeping her in his sights.

His instructions were to remain anonymous, but she soon notices he is only a few steps behind. When she turns and sees him, he gets a thrill. He should be disappointed he wasn't hidden as well as he was warned to be, but he relishes that feeling. He is no longer invisible.

Her pace has quickened; he can see her body tensing more with each step. She fascinates him – she's not the usual maid he sees about London, scurrying from one chore to the next, face pinched with exhaustion. This one walks with the mannerisms of a society lady, head held high.

He will gladly do this particular job for free; this is the most excitement he's had in a while. It beats being down on the docks. And he prefers this area of London. He may not be a part of the wealthy set, but he enjoys dreaming what life is like behind the curtains of fine houses, fantasising about sitting next to a warm fireplace with his pipe and slippers and a pretty wife beside him.

The maid runs over to the house as he knew she would. He has gotten too close. She disappears down to the basement, fast as a whippet, and is gone.

He is engulfed by desperation; the void of his loneliness encircles him again, as if the dim streetlamps have all been extinguished. He comforts himself. It won't be long before he finds her again. It is his job after all, and he is the watchman.

Chapter 19 ~ Enough

Ivy ~ Blackham House, 30th November.

I arrive back inside the safety of the kitchen, my heart still pounding from being followed. Paranoia wraps its arms around me in the absence of human company. I need to confide in someone, but whom? I have cut myself off from everyone.

The smell of warm yeast fills the room, ready for the morning's baking. I call out further into the basement, but no one replies. My life is as lonely as before I came to London. To keep myself busy, I make a pot of tea and start washing the dirty dishes by the sink.

The country house is no longer my home, despite all of my beloved plants. If I return, my fate will belong to Mr Whitlock; he of the lingering gaze, puffy face and wet lips. My life would be over, as I'd be moulded into a subservient creature: the ideal wife. My body is restless as I consider surrendering all my decisions, my money, and my body into the hands of someone I cannot abide. There was violence in his eyes when he tried to force himself on me; he is a cruel man beneath the illusion of charm.

The rest of the evening chores pass by in a blur, my thoughts occupied with my outing. When Mrs Higgins and Hannah appear as if from nowhere, no one asks where I have been; perhaps no one really cares as long as the house keeps running and the tasks are all completed each day to the master's satisfaction.

Outside the bedroom window, caught on the ledge, a small blue feather dances in the night breeze, perhaps from a swallow. I try to reach out and press its softness between my fingers, but it drifts off into the night.

Mrs Higgins is asleep now in her own room along the hallway, and Hannah has gone out somewhere with her policeman, preferring to exchange rest for another type of physical comfort. I shut the window and turn away from the cold draft, which continues to seep into the room. Already, I can sense the voices from my dreams calling to me. I am not free to let my mind rest, even in sleep.

Mrs Finch, who spoke at the meeting, looked unburdened. What would she do if she were me? Closing my eyes, I try to imagine myself at the front of the crowd talking, inspiring others. The image fails and dissipates within a second. I am despondent and lost.

This house is a frightening, eerie place. Even inside, away from the shadows that prowl the streets at night, I am afraid. Does history repeat itself? I can almost sense the tormented ghosts, the wives of the last vicar, and the master walking the corridors upstairs. Did they know they would perish? There is a chance that I too could be cutting my own life short by being here. What use is freedom if you are dead? I need to find a solid clue soon, and then I can leave. Whatever my future holds, I don't want to die under this roof.

I open my eyes and it is morning, although my body aches as though I haven't slept. I am still fully clothed from the night before. My mouth is dry, and my feet are numb with cold from being exposed in the night without the warmth of a blanket. Hannah lies asleep across the room. She did not even have the care to cover me.

For a moment, despair crashes over me, followed by grief for my mother. What is the point of this? Then a quiet thought slips past, like the blue feather on the night breeze. If I have no more strength to continue ... then what? The idea spins round and unending.

What would Miss Earnshaw do? What would she do? My family? My blood? The mantra becomes my heartbeat, the solution I need to survive. And then, I seize upon the answer like a famished animal in need of meat: she would take charge of her path and find the strength to face the situation alone.

Everything the vicar said about the building is true. Death roams this place like a beast unleashed. It prowls at every door, in every macabre ornament and relic of death, stalking, hunting. But I will not be its next victim. I will find out the secrets of this house. Whoever is responsible for Miss Earnshaw's disappearance has underestimated the tenacity that runs in the blood of our family.

Chapter 20 ~ Unanswered Questions

Ivy ~ Blackham House, 1st December.

The evening is almost finished, and I mentally run through the list of outstanding chores: cleaning the footwear is next. The jobs I am taking over from Hannah are increasing. With each day, it seems she unburdens her workload a little more. I have never properly cleaned shoes in my life. In the country, Thomas the houseboy always had this task. I would leave my shoes outside my bedroom door and, just like magic, they would be ready to wear the next morning. The previous mud or dust from the garden was carefully brushed off, and the leather buffed to a shine.

Hannah finds me with my thoughts in the basement hallway. She is carrying a heavy tray laden with a pot of tea, three slices of buttered bread, a hunk of cheese, and some cold slices of ham. It was her turn to look after the old lady's supper, but I heard her arguing with Mrs Higgins that the work for Lady Blackham should now be mine.

'You won't find all the shoes standing there like a pudding,' Hannah mutters to me, and then throws her eyes up, supposedly seeking guidance from Heaven. 'You need to go to each room and see if they've been put outside for their nightly clean. Take them down by the scullery sink where the polish and brush are. Clean off any dirt on them outside, otherwise Mrs Higgins will have your hide.'

'Thank you,' I reply with only a touch of sarcasm, as I stretch out my already aching back. I want to say more, but I bite my tongue as the words will not be kind and part of me still wants her as a friend. 'Hannah?'

'Yes, what now?' she snaps, shifting the tray in her hands.

'Have you ever been followed back to the house?'

'What do you mean?' She is impatient, but at least I have her attention.

'There's a man I've seen a few times. I am not convinced it's a coincidence.'

She contorts her face into a leer. 'You caught the fancy of someone?'

'I hope not. A stranger following me in the dark is not what I hoped for.'

'Then, perhaps, you should think twice about running around on your own at night. Some men can't help themselves.'

'I just wondered if he knew who worked here. Is there a chance he thought I was you?'

'Hardly,' she scoffs. 'Plenty of men used to follow me … but now, I got my policeman, they know to keep their distance.'

'So, you don't know a nightwatchman?'

'A nightwatchman? No, don't be daft!' She gawks at me. 'Let me get on. My arms are aching something rotten from holding this.'

She struts off down the corridor with the heavy tray, and I follow a few paces behind, looking for grubby shoes to clean. I can tell she is pleased to have the upper hand again, to have the favour of a man in uniform when I only have men in shadows and women in dreams for companions.

I find two pairs of shoes upstairs to clean for the master and none for the mistress or Lady Blackham. They both stay inside more often than not, and their shoes have stayed pristine, untouched by the filthy streets. I pull the curtain away from under the scullery sink and find the black polish, brushes, and cloths. Besides the products are another pair of men's shoes, almost the same quality as the master's, but larger. The leather was so soft that when the owner walked, it would barely creak. It must be hard to keep them waterproof outside.

'Mrs Higgins, who do these belong to?' I shout out into the kitchen.

'What are you talking about, Ivy?'

She walks past the scullery door and glances in, her face tinged with a pink hue; my suspicion raised that she's made an early start on the sherry.

'Why, they belong to the master. You know that, you daft girl. You must have collected them yourself.'

'No, these.' I reach in and pull out the left shoe.

'Oh, they're William's.' She stumbles slightly, resting her hand on the whitewashed wall. 'Put them back or else there will be murder if he can't find them.'

'William – the gardener? Why would he have shoes as nice as these when the rest of his clothes are so threadbare?'

My question is harmless enough, but the air simmers with expectation. I know she is lying. The shoes have become objects of incrimination, evidence of something that does not ring true.

She gazes at the empty shoe dangling in my hand. Her face is paler now, losing the flush of alcohol as her eyes flash with sombre recognition. The response is fast replaced with a smile as false as I have ever seen, for the truth does not reach her eyes.

She focuses on a handkerchief taken from her pocket. 'Yes, William, the gardener, Ivy. Honestly, don't go poking your nose into the cupboards and corners of this house. You never know what you might find.'

She returns to the kitchen, and I hear her fussing over the floor, which has not been swept yet. 'And where is Hannah?' she asks, raising her voice. 'I expect she is with that chap of hers again. Look at that … it's almost ten o'clock.'

She returns to the scullery. 'Finish up the kitchen and lock up the rest of the house now, will you?'

I nod, listening to her rambling words, wondering why she doesn't look at me in the eye. She dries her hands on a dishrag.

'This day feels like an age and I'm going to my bed now; no more questions for me. Make sure you heat the stove early tomorrow; it's baking day. Get a good fire burning by six at the latest. I can rely on you, Ivy, can't I?'

She pauses on her way out, not turning back but clearly wanting an answer. It's quiet; only the sound of the last embers of coal popping can be heard, as the kitchen fire slowly dies.

'Yes, Mrs Higgins.'

She looks over her shoulder at me, one hand on the door frame. She's trying to tell me something, I am sure: a crumb of a secret, but I lose it in the cracks of silence.

Then she sucks at her cheeks, shaking her head. 'That girl, she should be here with you. Whatever next? She will imagine she is the lady of the house before we know it. Sometimes Hannah goes too far.' She pauses. 'She doesn't know her place, and we all have a part to play, Ivy.'

Then she does look me straight in the eye, with the most sombre of looks, and a chill touches the back of my bare neck.

'Don't fight it Ivy – trouble comes when we don't accept our role.'

The fire cracks again, and the strange moment is broken.

'Well then, let's pray the mistress sleeps well enough tonight. God knows we could all do with some rest.' She smiles at me, her expression completely changed from the one before. 'Sleep well, Ivy.'

'Goodnight, Mrs Higgins,' I call out as she shuffles away. I try not to read much into her words. The effects of the sherry are obvious.

After all the chores are done, I try to get comfortable on the straw pallet. My heart pines for the comfort of home when my mother was alive and well. I never truly appreciated all the work entailed in keeping house. But now, I find myself on the other side, my feet silently padding behind the steps of others.

What was the greater meaning of all this effort? As servants, we are kept busy, with no time for anything but work. Our lives, along with our meagre desires, become buried under the needs of the wealthy. Whilst I find some satisfaction in a job well done, I am already struggling against the boundaries of this role.

Perhaps I am a selfish person at my core. I assumed, in only the way a child can, that the servants in my family home were content with work; that everyone had been born into the job they were most at peace with, perfectly able to fulfil their own dreams and personal lives. And if they decided on a different path, they had the power to change their own destiny.

Now my eyes are open wide, and I see how naïve I was to believe the world worked this way. We are all trapped by some means, but daily struggles affect staff and upper-class alike. We are all the same, chasing something, the elusive thread of happiness or just being able to make it to the next day, avoiding the black hole that threatens to consume us with the fear of the unknown. The demon drink is what Master Blackham turns to; the mistress, her laudanum; and the vicar, his faith. My escape is botany, but how long can a simple passion keep the troublesome thoughts at bay? What is strong enough to keep the darkness from our minds?

Without the company of Hannah, my thoughts spiral, past decisions and regrets circle around in my head – until I hear movement. Someone is in the corridor outside my room. I cannot explain why, but suddenly I am alert. The sound is out of place, my melancholy forgotten.

Steeling myself, I open the door a crack, holding the small candlestick out into the hallway. I call out softly: 'Hannah?' But no one is there.

I expect to find Hannah or Mrs Higgins in the kitchen. Perhaps they have drunk too much and are stumbling in the dark, but I find the room is also empty except for the dying embers of the fire.

My bare feet are cold. I linger until the hairs on my arms prick with unease. A faint whisper of my name curls about my ears; my stomach plummets. I almost drop the candlestick as I scurry back to my bedroom, but with each step I take, I hear a different one approaching behind me, heavier, firmer. As I turn to slam the door, I see nothing but a small mouse scurrying along the edge of the stone floor.

There is a sadness at the core of this house that tugs at me, an insidious energy which creeps closer each day. No matter if I sleep or lie awake, I can sense it wrapping itself around me, and the voices I once heard as a child are getting louder. They call my name. The other words are indistinct, formed from a mix of anger and longing. I yearn for my mother who chased them away with her songs and warm smiles. Now, I have no one, and I worry Cousin Edith's opinion of me was true, that I lack the strength of character to face them alone.

❖

The day passes much the same as yesterday, although my nerves are jittery and Hannah is miserable, declining to go out. She lights a candle inside our meagre bedroom. Neither of us wishes the night to descend on us just yet, and I try not to dwell on the footsteps I heard last night.

We get onto our pallets, pulling the blanket tight under our chins. I can tell from the way she lays glowering at the small flame flickering that she is sulking. But she has no one to blame but herself. I saw her making doe eyes at the master again at dinner. The mistress might be in ill health, but she is not blind. It will be less time in the warm parts of the house for her, away from the master for her punishment.

'Are you going to the apothecary tomorrow?' she mutters.

'Yes, in the afternoon, for more tonic to calm the mistress's nerves.'

'Get more poison too, then … those rats are multiplying. God knows what they are feeding on. William needs more to keep them at bay, but the cupboard is empty.'

My hackles rise at the mention of William. Something about him still doesn't seem right to me.

Hannah's fingers slip under her neckline and pull out a gold chain. The small links glimmer in the candlelight.

'What's that you're wearing?' I ask, surprised at the jewellery. Maybe she has started using the belongings left behind by the previous servants.

'Oh, this?' She feigns surprise at my interest. 'A token from Frank.'

'The policeman?'

'Of course… He is a man who knows which side of his bread is buttered.' She nods with a sly smile. 'He says he loves me, but they all say that when they want something.'

'Well, it's very pretty. What does he want?' I ask, intrigued by her new openness towards me.

She rolls onto her back, looking up at the ceiling. 'A tussle in the dark, Ivy. Like they all want. But what I'd like to know is … what makes a man fall in love with a woman?'

I feel my face flush red. 'I'm not the best person to ask on the subject.'

'Haven't you been with a man?' She shoots me a mischievous glance.

'No...'

I hesitate, pulling the blanket further up around my face and pushing the vile memories of Mr Whitlock out of my mind. She is clearly enjoying a topic of conversation she has more experience in than me.

Her mouth turns downwards. 'He says he loves me, but it's all a lie, isn't it, to get what he fancies? How do you know who to trust to keep a roof over your head and food in your belly?'

I touch my wrists together, the soft skin a reminder of the bruises from Mr Whitlock. 'I have always believed what my mother told me: that love already exists; you just have to discover it. If they force it on you ... well then, that's not love.'

She sniffs, wiping her nose on the back of her sleeve. 'I reckon you must look after yourself as no one else will. I have youth on my side now, but that won't keep a man happy for long.' She tuts, scrunching up her face. 'And I won't hand my wages over to my husband for him to spend on drink or pox-ridden strumpets. I don't want to be stuck in a slum with three screaming brats willing each day to end. No, I've seen it all before and I've had enough of being used.'

My entire body stiffens. 'Who has used you?'

I think some brandy must have loosened her lips. 'You know ... him up there. He's had his fun, and now see how he treats his new wife, coming in at all hours, locking her up. Who knows where he's been?'

I can tell his actions hurt her, and for the briefest of moments, I glimpse her vulnerability.

'Do you consider the master to be a bad man?' I ask.

'He is good when he wants to be,' her smile is coy. 'But only when he picks and chooses. You are jealous, but I am his favourite. I've seen the way you watch him.'

'What?' I am so shocked that I sit back up. 'I have no interest in him, Hannah. I would rather keep to myself.'

She laughs at my discomfort, but I hate to admit it, she is right. There is something magnetic about him, like a hypnotic trance drawing you in. I do not feel like Hannah, but I can see how a person could fall under his charms and become manipulated to their detriment.

'Don't worry,' she remarks curtly, 'he is like that with everyone, even that spiritualist you keep asking about.' She rolls her body away from me, so I can't see her face, but I still hear the disappointment in her voice. 'He couldn't stop gazing at her all night ... men are all the same.'

'Did you see anything else happen between them?' I can almost hear my heart beating as I listen for a response.

Hannah doesn't reply – this is what I have been waiting for. Could he be capable of an act worse than philandering? Attraction has been known to drive people to madness; passion replaced with violence, jealousy with murder.

But still, Hannah is silent. I resign myself to the fact our conversation is over. But just as I am succumbing to the pull of sleep, she mutters quietly.

'He was running down the main stairs, didn't even see me standing in the hallway. He was too intent on following her out into the night. I will never forget. His eyes had the look of a madman.'

Chapter 21 ~ Secrets

Ivy ~ The Apothecary, 3rd December.

Winter brings the sky closer, overcast and brooding. Armed with an umbrella to protect against the impending storm, I am sent to the apothecary on St. James Street in the late afternoon.

I use the opportunity away from work to return to Miss Earnshaw's apartment. I want to ask the housekeeper more questions about any prior links between Master Blackham and Miss Earnshaw before the night she was employed. And there is something bothering me about Mrs Forbes herself. But despite seeing movement at the ground floor window when I knock, and waiting an age for her to answer, the door remains closed, and I am forced to abandon my quest. I manage to make it to the apothecary five minutes before it closes.

'My last customer of the day. Welcome!' exclaims the shop owner, eyeing my empty basket with expectation.

The tall man beckons me inside; he is older than me, but I'm certain not by much. The stubble across his jaw only gives the illusion of age.

The shop smells of camphor, a pleasant aroma, especially after the stagnant miasma of the house. It reminds me of the medicated chest rubs I had as a child. Perhaps I can purchase something to remedy the airs too.

The shelves are filled with blue and green bottles, and I spy an old-fashioned jar of leeches in the far corner, the black blobs wriggling ever so slightly against the glass. I had heard they used to be a popular practice. My breath slows; everything looks to be categorised and in order – this is my kind of world.

'You find me holding the fort at my uncle's fine apothecary. But I can assure you, I am suitably trained in the art of medicine and am able to assist you.'

I suddenly find myself awkward, unused to talking with men in general. 'I would like to collect a prescription in the name of Mrs Angelica Blackham.'

'Certainly, please, bear with me for one moment. The remedy for Mrs Blackham is close at hand.'

He disappears into a back room and returns with a large blue bottle and three smaller ones. 'Here are the magic potions,' he says with a smile.

He decants the liquid into smaller ones; these are the bottles I am familiar with from Mistress Blackham's room.

'Why do you not give the remedy in the original bottle? Would that not be easier and save time?'

He grins, showing dimples on either side of his cheeks. 'Do you think it would impress the ladies to be seen with a laudanum label on their dressing tables? No, we need to ensure the medicine looks far prettier. I do not touch the stuff myself. Mine is more of a discerning palate.'

I do not know what he means or if he is referring to another drug. He smiles to himself, realising the comment is lost on me. 'I like your innocence – a rose among thorns. I can tell you're not from around here with your country accent and fresh face.'

'You are correct, it has not been long since I arrived in the city,' I admit.

He lowers his head, as if to tell me a secret. 'I hope that the ways of London will not corrupt you. But if you ever need a guide, I am here. A beautiful girl like you deserves to be treated well.'

His words are hard to believe. I have never been complimented by a man before, other than the deceptive words of Mr Whitlock.

'The medicine order is the same as last time, and will be the same next time, no doubt.' He wraps them in brown paper and hands me the trio of blue bottles.

'Thank you, kindly,' I say as I put them gently into my basket. 'Also, do you have anything to freshen the air in a room?'

A smile plays at the corner of his mouth. 'It depends on what you are trying to hide?'

'It is an old house... For the damp and the like.'

'I am sure I can find something. I like a challenge.'

He stoops down as he browses through the many shelves at the back of the shop and returns with a bowl of what appears to be crushed herbs and rose petals, sliding the scented object between us. 'Now, this is deliciously pleasant. My own mixture if I dare to be so bold. Leave the remedy in a room and the air should smell as sweet as fresh flowers.'

I smile, relieved to have something to alter the unpleasant atmosphere, and only pray it will work. Then, I remember the raw scratches on the mistress's skin. I doubt Hannah would have attended to them or called a doctor.

'And also, I need a balm made of honey and some lavender water to soothe a wound, and ... some poison.'

'Poison?'

'For the rats.'

'You must have quite a rat infestation!'

'No more than usual in a city, I suppose.'

He runs his finger down a ledger on the countertop. 'Only last week, a purchase was made on the Blackham House account for two bottles of arsenic.'

'Really? I see, well, I am not wise in the world of pest control. I only ask for what is requested by Mrs Higgins, the cook. She is the current housekeeper in the absence of one.'

'Only it is a little unusual to need more so soon, that is all. Perhaps a bottle got spilt.'

He steps over to a large glass-fronted cabinet and unlocks the door with a key from a chain at his waist, humming to himself while he picks out my request. He brings back a jar of balm, lavender water, and another blue bottle, which I assume holds the arsenic. Without the label, it looks exactly like the others in his shop.

'Can you please sign here?' He points to a space in his leather-bound book. I can't make sense of the previous signature in the book for Blackham House. It is only a scrawl of a mark.

'Goodness, it could be easy to confuse the bottles?'

My voice catches as I sign my name in black ink. I suddenly feel accountable for this poison. The dead rats will be my responsibility, as will anything else that consumes it.

'You are astute. But see here, there are patterns on the poison bottles as a warning, so even without light you can touch the difference. But I always add a label, just in case.'

He potters, creating a small white note and affixing it to the glass.

A memory flashes before me of the way Hannah looks at the mistress – in such a way, she would wish her dead. And then there's Miss Earnshaw... How easy would it be to murder someone? My throat constricts at the notion. I must have paused too long, for he coughs politely to get my attention, passing me the wrapped items.

'Oh, forgive me. I have unsettled you. Please take this.' He passes me a silk handkerchief from his breast pocket, embroidered with the motif 'W.T.' The fabric smells of oranges: a sharp, clean scent. After dabbing my face, I try to hand it back to him.

'No, keep it, please... I insist.'

He pauses and takes a breath, his arms stretched out on the counter. He is perfectly comfortable commanding the desk and what is stored beneath it. 'And what can I get for yourself? What ails you? There is something you need, isn't there?'

His powers of perception are sharp. He must see it all within these walls. All kinds of bodily illnesses and minds to purge. I am a little embarrassed to admit my weaknesses, so I blurt out the words before I regret the decision. 'I would like some charcoal to draw with and ... I have disrupted sleep; I am a little jumpy of late.'

He gives me an encouraging smile. 'You might say you are easily startled?'

I glance down at my gloved hands, briefly avoiding his gaze. 'Yes, maybe ... because I am so tired.' I laugh nervously. 'You will think me foolish.'

'No, please indulge me.'

'I sometimes hear and see things which are not there.'

'You are dreaming during the day?' he asks, scrutinising my face kindly.

'No, I am awake. I mean, it would be impossible for these things to be real, but they continue to happen.'

'Do you entertain a wild imagination?'

'I would not consider myself out of the ordinary, nor a person with a nervous disposition.'

'I have just the thing.'

He reaches down under the counter and produces another small blue bottle.

'This is a nightly tonic. Do not worry, it is only a mild solution of chloral sedative, not like the one for your mistress. You will wake up refreshed and ready to take on the day. But hopefully, this should ease your mind enough to get some proper rest and calm your thoughts. Come back if you need something stronger.'

I release a long breath I didn't know I'd been holding onto. If I can sleep better, then perhaps the voices will disappear too. 'How much do I owe you?'

'Nothing, madam. Consider these as a welcome gift to London. I shall add your mistress's bill to the usual account.'

He winks at me, wraps the small bottle, and gathers some pieces of charcoal in a separate package of brown paper with a string and hands it to me. My hands tremble a little as our fingers graze each other's. I have never received a lovers' present. Is this what it feels like?

He seems bright and optimistic, the opposite of Master Blackham, and I want to stay in his company, but I normally avoid people without even trying. It is my way; perhaps I would rather be alone and have no man than risk the consequences of false charm again.

'Thank you for your time.' My response is curt. My guard has returned. 'I am much obliged,' I nod goodbye, looking past him at the many remedies, all with a specific purpose. I would love to learn more, but I force myself to leave.

'As you wish, I am here to serve.' He bends forward, giving me a mock bow.

But as the door jingles shut behind me, it is only his smile that lingers in my mind, and I forget about the rest of the shop.

My steps are lighter as I return to Blackham House. It is only five o'clock, yet the lamplighters are already igniting the streetlamps. Two watchmen, walking side by side, make their rounds, and my shoulders instinctively stiffen with unease. One stops and glances at me. I am unsure if the man is the same watchman as before, but it cannot be, for surely there are many who patrol the streets in London. Shaking off the apprehension, I put it down to the nervousness of being out alone again at night and Hannah's warning of safety. I rush back and manage to arrive at the house within a half hour.

As I approach, I see Hannah standing close to a man on the corner of Chester Square. Even in the mist, I can tell he is a policeman by the glinting pair of brass lion's heads on the cape chain across his chest. She must have sneaked out again, for we still have work to do. They huddle together, almost creating one silhouette, their breaths fogging the night air. He whistles a lilting tune, and the sound carries through the crisp air, echoing eerily. My mother always told me it was bad luck to whistle at night – it attracts the bad spirits, so I can't help but recoil from the sound. Hannah pretends not to notice me as I stride past, but I sense the man watching me as I quicken my pace to the servant's entrance.

As I enter the kitchen, hot steam immediately hits me in the face. There are at least four pans of bubbling water. Mrs Higgins is preparing a hearty pie.

'You took your time – have you seen Hannah?'

I hesitate. A sense of new loyalty since her revelation about Master Blackham stops me. 'No … it's pitch black out there already.'

Mrs Higgins sighs loudly, wiping her hands on her apron. 'Where is she when I need her?' She motions to my basket. 'Did you get the mistress's potions?' Both hands go to her hips as she looks at me with expectation.

'Yes,' I reply, setting down my umbrella and basket, and then taking off my cloak.

'Then, quickly get upstairs with them. And what about the rat poison?'

'It's here.' I remove the brown paper and feel the glass ridges of the poison bottle slip through my fingers as I pass it to her.

'Good. Put it in the pantry cupboard up high. I'll get it to William later. He hates those dratted rats in his precious garden.'

Stretching up to the top shelf of the cupboard, I see many bottles and place the poison within easy reach. Most of the glass containers are empty or dusty, but there is one right at the back that is spotless and half full of liquid. I bring it down. Inside is a thick green cordial, the smell of which is pungent and sickly sweet. Perhaps it is also for the garden, but I have never needed such a remedy for my plants. I put it back before I am seen.

The mistress is grateful for her tonic, but grimaces at the bitter taste. I don't imagine she knows what she consumes; I doubt the doctor told her the details of the laudanum prescription, her special tincture of opium and morphine. Now I understand the reason she sleeps so deeply at night and yet she does not wake refreshed. Her health appears to be deteriorating by the day. Often, she gets dressed but changes her mind, appearing to suffer at the thought of leaving her room, preferring solitude to company.

She will be expected to play hostess for the party they are throwing tomorrow. It will be their first gathering since November 11th, and my first in the house. The master has surrendered to his friend's whims when they requested a winter soirée.

Perhaps the guests, like me, also want to return to the place where Miss Earnshaw was last seen. I heard the master and mistress arguing about it. That they do not wish to host another party, but appearances are everything. For the mistress's sake, I hope she can summon the strength to entertain. After their fight, he threatened to keep her bedroom door locked until her hysteria subsided.

The tonics only take the edge off; they don't remedy the cause. The vicar's words intrude in my mind again: the tale of the poor, deranged wife of the Reverend Geffrey, along with the master's first wife; how they all lost their grip on the world. The parallels between the three women could just be a tragic coincidence, but they all seemed to enter this house healthy, and now only one of them is left alive.

Chapter 22 ~ Charades

Ivy ~ Blackham House, 4th December.

Everyone cheers in the drawing room as the sound of a shotgun pop erupts from uncorking a champagne bottle. I jump from the noise. Two couples and a young man have arrived tonight: Mr and Mrs Ashdown; Captain Lynch and his wife; and Mr. Taylor, her cousin, visiting from Bath. They must all be in their thirties and shimmer with the beauty of privilege and wealth. I believe they might be the same guests from the night of the parlour game. The air is charged with a hum of anticipation.

'Whose turn is it next for charades?' Captain Lynch shouts.

'You know, I can never guess your idiotic messages!' replies his wife.

She sits perched on the edge of the red velvet sofa next to her cousin. Her blonde curls framing her petite face, and her corset tight, showing a tiny waist in a damsel-blue dress. Mrs Ashdown balances on a neighbouring chair, her russet red hair pinned up, revealing a black choker with a female cream cameo, framed in jet around her swan-like neck.

They all laugh in high spirits.

Opposite sit Captain Lynch and Mistress Angelica. She is wearing a yellow silk gown that I helped tie her into, the vibrant colour giving me hope her moods have improved, although her eyes never quite leave her husband as she watches him from across the room.

Hannah and I serve the drinks. Mr Ashdown and the master are talking politics beside the mantel piece, above a roaring fire.

'What do you make of it?' Mr Ashdown looks around the room. 'Do you mind if I smoke ladies?' he asks as he lights a cigar, his heavy moustache framing his lips as he smiles.

'Not at all,' the mistress replies, after he has lit up. She nods at me to open the sash window, which I do gratefully; the air is becoming heady with the heat from the fireplace.

'Some political leaflet about wasting taxpayer's money,' the master states, swishing a shot of amber whisky around in his cut crystal glass.

'Another reason women should not get the vote,' Ashdown's brusque voice interrupts. 'What a farce this all is! All they are doing is getting under our feet. Can't they leave us to get on with the job of running the country without interruption?'

The women smile politely, not taking the bait. The conversation lulls.

'Are you part of these women's rights?' Mr Ashdown changes his attention to the mistress. 'I hear the movement is gaining popularity in Italy.' His polite tone defuses any possible tension, leaving only a hint that he disapproves of the subject.

She is about to answer when the master cuts in, 'My wife is far too busy to be involved in political antics.' The drink seems to have lessened the master's patience; he adjusts his stance. The colour red blossoms in the apples of his wife's cheeks.

'You attend the suffragette meetings don't you, Christine?' The mistress asks the captain's wife, leaning forward, revealing more of her décolletage. I note the subtle provocation to her husband.

'Yes, I believe they are important,' her eyes flicker across to the men. 'You might like to join me on occasion, Angelica?' Her blonde ringlets swing like miniature church bells, as she talks with enthusiasm.

Might I see them both at the next meeting at Hanover Square? The notion of socially crossing paths with them is almost absurd.

The mistress glances at her husband, whose eyes betray no trace of affection. 'Perhaps I...' she begins, and then I see the subtle shake of his head and the slight inclination of his chin. Such a small detail, and I doubt the rest of the room noticed, but she does. 'Thank you. I will consider the invitation.' She sits back in her chair with a tight smile.

'We shall see. My wife will be busy dealing with the collection. We have much work to do with auditing all the pieces.' The master has the final word on the subject as he motions to Hannah for another drink refill.

'Are you having an exhibition?' Mr Taylor chirps up, unaware of the surrounding tension.

'Have you not heard of the infamous Blackham House collection?' Mr Ashdown exclaims. 'You must see it all in detail. The items are the most extraordinary things; some of them are quite macabre. Alexander's family is obsessed with shiny objects.' He guffaws, almost spilling his drink, 'Are you by chance related to the magpies outside, old boy?'

Master Blackham smirks at the retort and then focuses on his whisky, returning to swirling the now full amber liquid around in his glass.

'I would love to; it all sounds intriguing. From all over the world?' Mr Taylor uncrosses his legs, making ready to leave straight away, his toothy smile beaming.

'My family has travelled far and wide to bring back the most interesting of objects. Of course, I will give you a personal tour, but perhaps another time.'

I watch from the edge of the room as the master struggles to remain polite, his jawline flexing from the effort. He catches my eye, as if he knows I understand him and his need for privacy. A flicker of disappointment crosses her cousin's face before he composes himself.

'Apparently, it's full of stuffed animals, strange pieces of pottery, and the odd ancient weapon or two. We passed a little of it in the hallway,' Mrs Lynch proclaims.

'We have a few items of that nature on display,' the master retorts.

'Ahhhh, but what are you keeping hidden away?' Captain Lynch interjects. 'I heard your father had some extremely private things.' The fire burns as the coal snaps and pops. Silhouettes of farmers and milkmaids from the brass hearth ornaments dance together on the floral wallpaper.

'That is no secret. Some things are sensitive to daylight and must be kept away from dust and the fading of the sun. They are incredibly old.'

'And valuable, no doubt?' Captain Lynch raises his glass in a mock toast.

'Quite.'

'I was told your father's last expedition was extremely successful. Shame about your brother. What a ghastly time your family went through. What, fifteen years ago? Your mother must have been devastated; first born and all that.'

'Yes, she was ... still is.' He glances up at the ceiling. I half expect to hear the banging of Lady Blackham's stick.

The atmosphere is no longer lively, and I can't help thinking that all the guests are together, that someone in this room must know more about what happened the night Miss Earnshaw was here. The silence is awkward until one of the guests coughs delicately.

'Anyone else notice that the house feels odd since the last time?' Mrs Ashdown speaks through smiling lips, but her almond-shaped eyes are serious.

'What are you inferring to?' her husband replies, stepping away from the fireplace, too hot but unwilling to move far from the flames.

'You know, after all the spiritual stuff with that strange woman... As I sit here, I have the oddest sensation I am being watched. I haven't slept well since.'

The candles by the window suddenly extinguish, and I stumble as I move to relight them; my attention is torn between watching their expressions and striking a match. My face must be a picture as Hannah peers at me strangely.

'Is that why we are upstairs tonight and not in the parlour room?' Captain Lynch throws the question to the master. 'And you managed to get that spiritualist to leave after she started raving about your family?'

'I personally prefer this room, further away from the street noise. And yes,' he pauses, 'everything was taken care of. Every word that woman said was nonsense. In fact, the whole night was a total farce.' He forces a thin smile. 'I have a good mind to report her for being a time waster and a fraudster.'

'But I can't help but wonder what happened later that night. Detective Spencer said she completely disappeared.' Captain Lynch leans back on the sofa, raising his eyebrows and crossing his legs.

Mr Ashdown strides over to an empty chair next to his wife, his face flushed. 'So, he came to visit you too, as well as us?'

'A detective?' The master almost drops his glass.

'I believe his name was Percival. Just imagine, we might be the last people who saw her alive!' Mrs Lynch cools her face with a teal silk satin fan from her reticule, the carved bovine bone sticks glowing as they move. The fire is getting hotter.

'He came to my office to ask some questions, and then to the house, a persistent fellow, I thought.' Mr Ashdown blows the cigar smoke into the air above him. 'Of course, I told him it was an evening of great entertainment, and that unhinged woman fulfilled her job of giving us something to talk about.'

'And was that sufficient to halt his curiosity?' I watch the master's knuckles go white as he tightens his grip on the glass.

'Quite enough; I had nothing of significance to tell him. We saw nothing; we know nothing. I don't know about you, but even if I did have any clue what happened after she left, I wouldn't say anything. I don't want my good family name ruined in the papers, especially so close to the election. The opposition would have a field day.'

'Did you happen to mention the back room?' The master's voice deepens.

'No, but I did say the spiritualist asked an awful lot of questions about you, that she stepped out of line with her dramatics.' He blows a perfect ring of smoke into the air above him. 'Did I speak out of turn? I hope I haven't caused you any trouble.'

The master clears his throat. 'Not at all. I just don't want the detective to come back to snoop throughout the house. You can't even trust the police, lots of pocket-sized valuable things, if you know what I mean.'

'We can solve the mystery ourselves!' Mr Taylor announces, and his cousin, Mrs Lynch laughs louder than necessary to break the tension.

'What were you doing at the exact time the mysterious spiritualist was seen?' He directs his question to the master, who does not return the humour.

Captain Lynch also laughs with forced effort. 'Did you witness her disappearing into a cloud of mystic smoke? Did the Devil come to collect her? Come on, tell us – you must know something. We had all left before she did.'

The master surveys his drink a moment too long, and the joke loses its edge. 'Damn you, Lynch. You found me out – I'm guilty.' The master's sarcasm is dry, a scowl quickly consuming his features, a hostile glint appearing in his eyes. Even I suck in my breath at the sudden change in his demeanour.

'Shut up, you fool. You're upsetting our host,' Mr Ashdown interjects to the captain.

'Not at all.' The master's reply is functional and polite, as he gulps down the last of his whisky.

'But it's all a bit melodramatic, don't you agree?' As Mr Ashdown waves his arm, I notice the tiny embers from his cigar landing on the rug.

'Not if it turns into a murder case,' Mrs Lynch squeaks, her eyes wide, her fan snapping shut. 'Do you think we are to blame for what happened to her?' She leans over to touch her husband's arm.

'What on earth are you getting at?' Captain Lynch splutters, aghast.

'Well, if we hadn't been at the party, perhaps her circumstances might have been different,' she replies, frowning at her husband.

'I think if she goes around claiming to talk to the dead, she's asking for trouble,' he blusters, rubbing beads of moisture off his forehead with a handkerchief.

'But I can't help still being unnerved by it all…' Mrs Lynch mutters, more to herself than anyone else.

The mistress stays mute, her eyes lowered to the floor. Looking about the room, my instinct tells me someone must be lying. The master does not respond. Instead, he watches the bright golden flames licking at the bricks, reaching ever higher into the chimney. Droplets of sweat trickle down my skin inside my chemise held tight by the corset; the open window is not helping with the rising temperature.

Mrs Lynch resumes her fanning. I watch the unfolded butterflies sway back and forth as I try not to feel faint. I sense Hannah standing beside me is also struggling, as she huffs and fidgets with her dress. The atmosphere is tense, perhaps from distress or guilt. I am hungry for every drop of information as I strain not to miss a word or furtive glance thrown away during the conversation. I know better than most, from years of watching people unnoticed, that the body can give away far more secrets than words ever can.

'It's the change in the weather.' The mistress finally offers her excuse. 'The cold can change a house. Maybe the air is bad... English winters can be hard to endure.'

'Yes, you are quite right my dear, the fog has been awful recently.' Mr Ashdown finishes his cigar and takes out another and a small silver knife from his suit jacket, searching for an ashtray as he slices off the end. 'Apparently, snow is forecast soon. Winter is always freezing in London.' Hannah dashes forward to provide a glass dish, smiling coyly at him as she puts it on the nearest side table.

The master motions me over. 'Ivy, will you get some more of the champagne for the guests?' Gone is the dark temper; his blue eyes are bright again.

'Now then, we need to discuss the next group outing for the ladies...' I hear Mrs Ashdown regaining control of the conversation as I leave.

The evening of charades is over; I can hardly remember getting ready for bed. My mind returns to the golden-thorned plants in the garden; the urge to take a sample and analyse their origins grows stronger. My interest is more than just a hobby. It has become a physical need to unravel their mystery. I will not listen to the scorn of my father's words. I believe the plants have some significance; they can tell me more, for they are intrinsic to this ungodly house.

Sleep pulls at my conscience until I succumb to the dream invading my thoughts. It is still the dead of night, but I find myself standing outside barefoot in nothing but my nightgown. Before me looms Blackham House, taller than before. There are no other houses in the street, but the certainty pulses through me that Miss Earnshaw is here, somewhere within these walls.

I enter through the front door and rush down the hallway, trying all the doors. They are locked, all seemingly bolted from the inside. I turn to go back outside, but the entrance is now also barred.

Panic bubbles up into my throat, making it hard to breathe. I am close, but she is still out of reach. 'Miss Earnshaw!' I cry out, but this weak voice is not my own. My legs weigh heavy, as though I am wading through water.

Despite all the stopped clocks, somewhere, one is ticking loudly. The mechanical swish of a metal pendulum swinging back and forth, each beat echoing off the cabinets of strange artefacts. I am running out of time. I pinch the skin on my arm. This is a nightmare I want to wake up from. The ticktock sound gets closer, pulsating, mirroring my heartbeat, pumping in my ears. I follow the noise all the way up to the attic. A grandfather clock stands before me; the hands have also stopped at five minutes to midnight.

A scream curdles from somewhere on the floors below. Is it too late? Backing away, I turn down the servants' stairs, but they continue on endlessly. The steps become uneven, soft, and covered in filth – human waste. The stench of sewers is overwhelming, and my feet keep slipping into the muck. My hands slide down the brick walls as I try but keep failing to get a grip.

'Ivy!' a desperate woman's voice shouts out.

Finally, the staircase ends, and I find myself standing before the collection room door.

'Miss Earnshaw?' I bang on the locked door. 'Is that you?'

There is a pause and one soft knock answers.

A strange feeling washes over me, somewhere between uncertainty and acceptance. 'Are you trapped?' I press my body up against the wood to hear better.

Another faint knock responds.

'Are you alive?' I wait and listen, and then two solid strikes knock on the door with such violence I am thrown to the floor.

I wake up.

Part Three

Chapter 23 ~ Rising up

Ivy ~ Blackham House, 5th December.

The hot coffee pot slips from my hand and the brown stain bleeds across the crisp white tablecloth. Breakfast is not going well.

'Are you ill, Ivy?' asks the mistress, watching as I try to dab the coffee away with a napkin, making it worse.

'I am so, so terribly sorry,' I stammer. 'I will clean this up right away.'

'Leave it!' The master holds up his hand, his voice curt. 'Cleaning can wait until after we have left the table.'

I am torn between loathing him and something else. What is the opposite of hate? Pity? Sometimes my instinct is to fear him, repulsed by his controlling behaviour towards his wife and his late-night drunken arrivals. I dread what he might be capable of. But as he raises his head and meets my gaze, I see a man at odds with himself: an innocent boy trapped within, vulnerable and scared like myself. He is clean-shaven and immaculately dressed this morning in a pressed suit, such a contrast to his appearance after he has been drinking. Part of me wants to help him, aid in his suffering. But then, as I watch his gaze return to his newspaper, I wonder if you can ever really save someone from themselves.

'I can tidy it up nice and fast, sir.' Hannah steps forward to take over from me. Her voice is sickly sweet.

'It is fine, there is no need. Thank you, Hannah.' He dismisses her without looking up as he puts the paper down and starts to tap his boiled eggs with a spoon, crushing their shells repeatedly.

'We are all a little tired this morning. I, for one, have another awful headache.' Mistress Blackham offers me a small smile, to forgive my clumsiness. She does not acknowledge Hannah in any way.

Hannah and I return to standing by the far wall.

'What is wrong with you?' Hannah spits at me through her teeth, low enough for the rest of the room not to hear. Your clumsiness will mean an extra load on wash day. I'm not taking on your mistakes.'

I cannot shake the impression from my dream that Miss Earnshaw is dead. That someone in this house could have murdered her. The thoughts I previously kept at bay, too dreadful to comprehend, now strike me as obvious. My legs are restless. I want to explore the house more than ever, delve into all the locked cupboards and its strange collections, revealing every secret.

The scene of the mistress and master sitting calmly together at the table puzzles me. Could they be responsible for such an act? How well they hide the truth if they are.

'The evening turned out well, but I believe your friends were a little disappointed,' Mistress Blackham says with a sigh.

'What do you mean?' asks Master Blackham.

'After the excitement of the last spiritualist gathering, I rather think we have set the bar too high regarding all future soirées. Perhaps last night was a tad dull compared to their previous evening with us.'

He pauses, remembering something; I scrutinise his features. Will he show any emotion now that Miss Earnshaw is the topic? A flick of his wrist beckons me over to bring more toast. I note he still does not make eye contact with Hannah, who is standing closest to him, waiting for instructions. I collect another silver rack from the side table, which is laden with enough food to feed at least three families. When I lean over with the toast, I catch his scent of musk and spice oil.

'I hardly think our responsibility is to frighten them out of their wits every time they visit.' He appears relaxed, with no signs of his usual hunched shoulders, but the muscles in his face tighten and there is a slight twitch in his right eye; almost imperceptible, but I can clearly see it.

He spreads the creamy butter, thick and generous. I watch as the gold nuggets melt and drizzle over the edges of the toast. My stomach rumbles in protest; I missed breakfast this morning.

'If they want that type of entertainment, I know plenty of backstreets in the city that would suffice.' He adds, before taking a large bite. He eats quickly, almost swallowing the food whole. 'I don't want you to overexert yourself at the expense of trying to please the whims of my friends. They are a fickle bunch. The likelihood is that next month something else will take their fancy.'

'That's nice, dear.' She acts as though he is a coiled snake, ready to strike, chewing her food in small movements, assessing her words carefully, avoiding provocation. 'Well, I have already agreed we should host another séance.'

He straightens his silver egg cups, but the action is clumsy, knocking the knife off his plate and onto the floor. He glances at me to pick it up, which I do at once and I see his hand is trembling.

'It is not a good idea,' he retorts. 'In fact, I must insist that we never indulge in any of that nonsense in my house again. Let me make it perfectly clear, I do not wish to discuss this further. The matter is closed.'

The mistress glances down, stung by his rebuke. After a few moments, she speaks again, softly. 'In any event, I felt the wives had some interesting thoughts.'

'Yes darling, fun memories indeed.' He flicks his ironed newspaper open again with a flourish of a point well made. The comment is dry and without feeling. Silence pervades the conversation until he suddenly laughs out loud. 'Ha! See here!' He opens the pages wide onto the table, covering his plate. 'Here is an article on precisely what bothers me about the whole thing: Another blasted spiritualist, Madame d'Esperance has been publicly denounced by Hereward Carrington. They maintain that scientific proof shows the business of talking with the dead is utter nonsense. What else do they need? We have confirmation in black and white,' he scoffs. 'These spiritualists should all be locked up!'

The mistress continues to butter her toast, the scrape of the knife filling the pregnant pause. 'Calm down, dear, you are getting worked up.'

'I am perfectly calm.' He drops the newspaper, the thick folds landing heavily on the table.

She sips her coffee before speaking again. 'It is not possible to know everything on God's earth. There are still things we don't understand. In my country, we also have many wise women. Not everyone can be a fraud, can they?'

'You are naïve in your understanding of how the world works, dear. Your aunt protected you in Italy.'

Mistress Blackham holds her cup, her hand revealing the weakest of tremors, but she continues unfazed by his response. 'I only wish to get to know your friends, to be social. It is a wife's duty after all, is it not?'

'What are you getting at?' He casts a furtive glance at me and Hannah. 'You are both dismissed. Leave at once!'

Hannah and I scurry out into the corridor, but Hannah hangs back, loitering by the door. She wants to eavesdrop on the rest of their conversation, as do I, so I join her in silent conspiracy.

'Do you love me, Alex? Why did you bring me here to this strange house? You wanted to come to England. You convinced me I would enjoy London, but this is not what I believed our life would be like. Your mother is…' Her words falter. 'And you are different, more distant. I know I keep seeing that shadow. It is not I, who is going mad; I am still the same woman you married.'

Hannah tenses up beside me, her hands tugging at her apron with such force it might tear.

'Shh, you're imagining things. Have you taken your medicine this morning?'

'Of course, I have.' The mistress's voice rises again, gaining in confidence. 'But I wonder at times if I am nothing more than a mere ornament to display in front of your friends. Or am I here just to upset your mother, a pawn in your game of control over this house? In Italy, you showed a very different version of yourself. You charmed me and I fell for it. But now, I don't believe you truly care for me at all.'

'You are being ridiculous.'

'And I know how you look at other women. I'm not stupid.'

'Don't be absurd.'

The sharp sound of falling silver on crockery startles us. Hannah tenses beside me.

'Just like that spiritualist, you couldn't keep your eyes off. Your friends watched to see how I would react. I feel like a fool. I'm glad she's gone. One less to fight off for your attention.'

'I will not dignify your remark with a response. I have never given you a reason not to trust me. Like the doctor said, this is all in your imagination. We must ensure it doesn't turn into hysteria; Mother wouldn't be sympathetic if anyone found out. Besides, you seemed more than happy babbling on with the other women last night.'

'Your friend's wives do not view me as hysterical. For some reason, they find my life before we married beyond interesting. Our supposed great love story. They want to know what brought me from Italy to London.'

'What else do they ask you?' He snaps.

'Oh, you know - how we met, the proposal.'

'It's none of their damn business.'

Hannah looks at me, raising her eyebrows at his strong language.

The mistress clears her throat, as if the action might be enough to rid the room of his words. 'Anyway, the ladies are planning a trip together. Wouldn't it be wise for me to become more acquainted with the wives of your peers, so I can fit in? That's what you want? Isn't it? For me to slot in with everything your life consisted of before? Some might say a replacement for—'

'I am unsure where this is leading?' He cuts in. 'I sense you are goading me into some kind of argument?' His voice is sharp.

A strained silence follows as Hannah and I exchange a confused expression as to what will happen next.

'But, I agree, a trip to the theatre would be nice for you.' He continues, suddenly sounding calmer, as though he is unaffected by the previous conversation.

The mistress coughs delicately again. 'Oh, it is not the theatre. The outing is something much more interesting.' She pauses. 'Have you heard of slumming? Apparently, we dress simply and walk around to experience the poverty first hand. It's all the fashion and an excellent way to help and understand the poor.'

There is a clatter of more cutlery on a china plate. 'What? I would never allow that!'

'What is it that concerns you?'

'Frankly, your health. You know how weak you are. The doctor said you needed rest. Gallivanting around the filthy streets of the city does not sound like the best idea.'

The tension prickles from outside the room, and I am glad not to be a part of it. Is he losing control of her? Is her health that bad?

'Are you not the one with the poor conditions, dear? Your mother tells me you have quite the history.'

There is a long pause.

'I am only concerned that you do not have the strength to be in the carriage alone. The streets are dangerous, darling. I would hate to call the doctor late at night, at such a cost and inconvenience to us all.'

'Well, your concerns are easily remedied. I can take Ivy. I am sure she will be a great comfort in case my nerves are not strong enough, and an excellent travelling companion.'

Hannah pouts with disapproval.

It is unclear who is indulging whom. Now I am involved, and I am not happy about this decision being made on my behalf. What if the area is where the strange nightwatchman lives? It is an irrational fear, but there may be a good chance of him following me again. And if he did, would he tell the mistress he had seen me at Miss Earnshaw's house?

'You win the argument, dear.' He laughs, but the sound is hollow. 'Not my idea of fun, but you will have your way. At least you can say you are not controlled by your husband; perhaps guided on occasion, but not guarded.'

I think of her locked door at night. Is he so unaware of his actions?

We hear a chair being scraped back.

'Why don't we sell it all, move abroad and start again? Besides, I told you I don't feel right since living in this house. Especially after...' She lets the rest of the sentence go, allowing the words to fade away. 'I did see a man, Alex... I still do. Why won't anyone believe me?'

'Let's resolve this once and for all.' His voice is harsh, cutting through her soft Italian melody of an accent.

The dining room bell rings, calling Hannah and me back into the room. My palms are sweating from the threat of being discovered. We wait a couple of seconds to compose ourselves and pretend we are not walking into the heat of an argument. We motion to clean up the crockery, but he shakes his head to stop us.

'Tell me. Have either of you noticed anything out of the ordinary? Any men to account for in the house?'

'What do you mean, sir?' Hannah curtseys.

'Have you seen any strange men who do not belong in our household roaming the corridors?'

Hannah bats her eyes at him, doe-eyed. 'You are the only man I see in the house, sir.'

He coughs, and I am aghast at Hannah's brazen words in front of his wife. The mistress ignores her contribution to the conversation.

He turns to his wife. 'You know what the doctor said: it was only a fall. There is no need to blame anyone.' He pauses and peers at her, tilting his head. 'Shall I call for him again? It seems you are still obsessed with seeing things which are not there.'

She looks down at the floor, plucking at the folds of her skirt with her fingers.

He continues, oblivious to her inner torment, now unconcerned with us being in the room. But I notice a shift in his demeanour: his chest protrudes as his back becomes straighter.

'It is not possible to leave. The collection is my responsibility, my duty. I have spent my whole life taking care of the artefacts.' He stands and throws his white napkin onto the table. 'This house is mine now, and I have had enough of being dictated to by bloody women.'

His eyes are jet black and defensive. Unease flutters in my gut like a frantic insect trapped in a bell jar.

After breakfast, the mistress summons me to help with her wardrobe. A sweet song drifts from a cage hanging from the ceiling, holding a solitary canary. She has undressed from her morning attire and sits in only her corset and petticoat with an open cream silk dressing gown over her shoulders.

'I am cold. This British climate does not agree with me.' I sympathise as she already looks tired, both of us drained from the drama at breakfast.

'So many lights!' I blurt out as I walk across the room, as indeed, new gas lamps and candles have appeared, balancing on every available surface.

'It's… How do you say in English?' She struggles to find the right word. 'Ironic,' she says at last, a weak smile on her face. 'I do not enjoy the dark, so I need the room to be light, but then the task of sleeping is difficult with them lit.'

We are more similar than she realises. I lean towards her with concern, remembering the master's words about the doctor at breakfast. 'Are you unwell?'

'I am well enough. There is a small issue with some of my dresses that require being taken in. They have become loose and quite unseemly. I need to make myself more presentable... It might help matters.'

An awkward silence prevails, which is broken by the loud, urgent squawking of birds outside. Perhaps William is feeding them again. She stands up and we appraise the contents of her wardrobe together. The mahogany structure is a handsome piece of furniture, and the odour of lavender and mothballs lingers within. A selection of sumptuous clothes hangs waiting to be brought to life.

'This one is lovely.' I say, gently touching the satin of a beautiful dusky pink dress.

I would not have the confidence to wear the bright yellow and green silks, but encased in this outfit with the layered skirt, trimmed with lace on the sleeves, I would feel like a duchess. If I wore some of her other velvet dresses, who would I be? What character would I play? Certainly not myself.

'See here.' She points to the waist of the pink satin dress. 'This only needs a few stitches, and the fit will be perfect again, especially after my corset is cinched in a little tighter.' She looks at me. 'You must help me with my wardrobe, under my supervision. Talk with the family tailor: Mr Gilbert, I believe, is his name. The fashion in this country is confusing. If this goes well, Ivy, I shall consider making this relationship between us more of a permanent one.'

She imagines she is doing me a favour. How funny, only a few months ago, I had a similar conversation with my own maid. I wonder what happened to Nellie. Did she stay on at the house? I still miss her company and the daily routine.

My cheeks blush under her attention. 'What about Hannah?'

'I am sure she would understand, or maybe not. It does not matter. You have more experience of what a lady needs, do you not?'

'I suppose.'

'So, we agree I need someone I can trust.' She rests her hand on my shoulder as though we have created a pact together.

I am about to ask her why when she swiftly steps back and almost deliberately changes the conversation.

'Mr Gilbert should alter the blue and green silk; the embroidery could do with a refresh too … but I am not sure about this one.' She points to a deep apricot-coloured outfit. 'Will you help me try it on again?'

She slips off her dressing gown, wincing as the material falls from her skin. I reel in shock. Fresh red scratches run across her shoulders and back. An animal with sharp claws could make the same injuries. The raw edges carry a fine crust of blood. She catches my quick intake of breath. Is it her husband? Is he the one abusing the mistress at night? I note that although the hallway door is locked, he can still come and go through the interconnecting door unnoticed.

I touch my wrists; they are no longer tender, but I remember the bruises. We have both suffered at the hands of men. Their natures, behind closed doors and hidden garden paths are all the same.

'Don't be alarmed.' She is embarrassed, mistaking my expression for concern, but in truth, it is pity and disappointment in the prospect of marriage. 'Apparently, I sleepwalk. I get myself into all kinds of mischief.'

I have an uncomfortable lump in my throat. The bad things happening within these walls have not stopped with the disappearance of Miss Earnshaw. 'Is that why the door is locked sometimes?'

'What door?' She glances between the internal door and the hallway entrance.

I look away, awkward in the moment. 'I find some doors bolted at night.'

'Occasionally, they take action for my safety. This is not the type of house to wander around at night; it is too dangerous with the valuable Blackham collection everywhere.' She holds her hand to the pale skin of her throat. Sometimes I wake up in different rooms, and my dreams and wakings merge - it's a symptom of my condition.' She sighs and then strokes her stomach unconsciously.

Who are they, who act on her behalf? The question is silent but resonates loudly in my head.

'This is the reason I need my maidservant to be discreet.'

I bite my lip, summoning the courage to ask about Miss Earnshaw. 'Was your door locked the night the spiritualist disappeared?'

Her head jerks in my direction. 'Who?'

'The spiritualist who came to your last night of parlour games.' My voice becomes strained as my fortitude wavers.

Her expression narrows. 'What makes you ask that?'

I understand I am crossing a line, but I must press for more while she's gaining confidence in me. 'I heard rumours and read a newspaper article. They even mentioned murder…' My sentence trails off as her eyes bulge wide.

'Murder? Who said it was murder?' She exclaims. 'How absurd – of course, I don't know anything. The indignity of it all. That party was a success... All the guests thought so, except my husband.' Her voice falters. 'He does not like theatrics. But what happened after she left is nobody's business but her own.' Her fingers fidget as she tucks an escaped strand of hair behind her ear.

'Did you hear anything to wake you? Did you try to leave your room that night?' I am overstepping my position; maids have been let go for much smaller displays of impertinence. My face prickles with fine beads of sweat. But I'm sure she's concealing something.

She touches her cheek. 'I have no recollection... I assume I slept. This is a private house with its own rules. I have learnt not to question.' She raises a perfectly arched eyebrow at me.

The birds outside start chattering loudly. There must be many, each clamouring to be heard, creating a raucous racket in the garden. A strange atmosphere lingers between us.

'Perhaps you might like to use a salve for your cuts; the marks would heal faster.'

'You know of such a balm?'

'My mother used to make an excellent ointment for soothing ailments. I have such a jar with me, just in case.'

I rush downstairs to my belongings in the basement and return only a few minutes later, out of breath. She is still sitting poised in the same position, like I had never left. I take out the small glass jar I bought from the apothecary and gently dab the mixture over the raw cuts. She winces but does not stop my work.

'Good, they feel much better already. See? I knew I was right in asking for your service.'

I help her put the apricot dress on and we both review her reflection in the mirror. The fabric hangs loosely on her hips without form or structure. 'This one should be altered, too.'

'But is it wise to take them all in? You might need them.' I glance at her stomach.

She is quick to understand my meaning. For a second, her face is sad until it reforms into the polite mask she normally wears. 'It is not necessary at the moment, but who knows what next year will bring?' She smiles. 'Mrs Higgins says I could be like Queen Victoria and have the same treatment to make the birth an easy one.'

'Treatment?' I ask.

'Chloroform à la reine,' she says. 'Apparently, all I will smell is lemons and then the pain disappears until the baby is born. I know Lady Blackham would approve of my following in the behaviour of the royal family.'

It must be public knowledge, but I am stunned that Mrs Higgins would know so much about the drug. I am aware I have led a sheltered life and understand little about children or the fashions of Queen Victoria, but surely a cook should not be so involved?

'Talking about lemons,' she laughs, 'what do you think about a new yellow dress for spring and what should I wear on this day out with the ladies of the club? I will need a suitable outfit. Can you ask the tailor to prepare something simple?'

I nod, noting her mood has improved; she even has colour in her cheeks.

'So, three dresses for Mr Gilbert to alter, and an order for two new outfits. A productive morning, don't you agree?' I am about to say yes, but she continues speaking. 'Alex has warned me that if I don't keep my dresses up to date, I might look like a servant walking around in hand-me-downs.' She huffs. 'Of course, he just doesn't want to upset his mother. Heaven forbid! The great name of Blackham has to be protected at all costs, even with appearances.' She laughs at the folly of this notion. 'You have done well, sweet Ivy.'

I glimpse her character as she must have been before she came to England, when, I assume, she had friends and family surrounding her. My mood has also improved. I am surprised to have enjoyed spending time with her, a refreshing change from all the other duties. Hannah will not be happy, but I will deal with that issue later. Just as I am leaving the room, she calls out.

'Can you refill my blue bottle? I seem to have run out of my tonic already.'

Chapter 24 ~ The Attic

Ivy ~ Blackham House, 6th December.

'You'd better move your things up to the attic. From now on, you will work in the main house.' Mrs Higgins beckons with her finger pointed towards the roof. The late afternoon sun is barely shining through the narrow kitchen windows, down into the basement. The lamps are already lit, casting shadows in the corners. She picks up the vegetable knife with gusto, peeling the potatoes with speed for the evening meal. I cannot tell if her manner shows disappointment or concern.

'The attic?' I ask.

'Yes, that's the new place for you, dear, third floor, on mistress's orders.'

Hannah interrupts, 'The master will not be happy about it. He took against any staff moving around the upper floors at night.'

'Ivy shall assist the mistress if she is needed at night.' Mrs Higgins continues, ignoring Hannah's remark. 'There is an earpiece in the wall, and it still works well enough. William has tested it. In fact, Ivy, we also have ones here that connect upstairs.' She motions to three metal pipe openings in the kitchen wall.

Hannah tuts and screws up her face.

'I'm sorry, I'm confused,' I add. 'Am I to sleep in the attic? But no one goes up there. Isn't it forbidden?'

'After the incident at the end of summer, it's been empty. The mistress must have talked him round. It is quite safe.' She doesn't look at me, continuing to prepare the vegetables.

I step closer to her. 'What incident? What happened?' I come over slightly nauseous. 'I am fine down here. Surely, there is no need to move anywhere else?'

Even Hannah would agree that despite our differences the current arrangement works for us. That begrudgingly, we have started to rely on each other's company as a form of simple comfort. I seek her support, but she busies herself stirring a pot, her back rigid. The statement hangs in the air. The excitement of my promotion is fast draining away, replaced with apprehension. What would I be agreeing to? I'd only seen the attic room from the street, and the small window looked dispiriting. How did someone even reach it?

Putting down the knife on the oak table, Mrs Higgins wipes her hands on her apron and pats my shoulder. 'Ah, there is nothing to worry yourself with. Just remember that the master is a man who switches day for night, coming back from his business all hours in the morning. He likes his privacy, simple in his ways. He complained that the last maid intruded on his space.' She shrugs. 'The girl said there were noises that woke her; but she was young with a head filled with silly tales and fancies. I told her he is sometimes loud in his library and the noise travels up, but—'

The cook stops short, checking herself, and changes the tone to one of forced joviality. 'There now, we shall say no more. You will like the attic. It has a set of drawers and its own window over the street. Who wouldn't enjoy such a view all to themselves? Count yourself lucky they have given you this favourable opportunity.' I note she does not look me directly in the eye as she speaks. 'After all,' she continues, 'we all have a purpose, and you have been chosen. Don't be ungrateful.'

I pull at the hem of my apron. 'I appreciate the new role. It's only the attic might be small, and I dislike cramped spaces.' I watch as her expression becomes impatient. 'But if you say it is good, I will accept the change. Thank you.'

My mind flashes to the shed in my family's garden house. My half-brother, David, had locked me in there as a child for his own amusement, an act which quickly turned sour. To this day, I dread the walls enclosing me; being trapped, unable to move. I can feel the same sensation of suffocation rising in my chest at the memory. I chide myself for my childish response. When was the last time I panicked? Before my mother died, but not since. I must be becoming better at controlling the anxiety.

Nodding in agreement with my acceptance, the cook focuses back on the potatoes, slicing them into thin pieces for the leek pie. 'Don't go upsetting the mistress now. She is a delicate creature, and you may do a sufficient job yet of soothing her nerves.'

'Of course, Mrs Higgins. I will do my best; it must be lonely for her all day on her own. Has she no friends?'

'You can see for yourself that she rarely leaves the house anymore. Such a shame. I remember when she arrived … so exotic with that accent.'

My thoughts and questions are jumping from subject-to-subject. Cousin Edith always said I struggled with polite conversation. 'Will I have to polish the child doll in the cabinet?'

'No, Hannah can keep doing that.'

I hesitate, remembering the glass blue eyes and real hair. 'What happened to the master's child? How did she die?'

'What, dear?' she says, turning to face me, almost stuttering at my question. This time, her eyes drill into mine without hesitation. My resolve to continue talking nearly crumples under her harsh scrutiny.

I lower my voice to a whisper, barely audible even to my ear. 'I heard it was his first wife who killed her, but that cannot be true?'

The cook holds the knife in mid-air and then looks in the direction of Hannah, who is oblivious to my last question. In a heartbeat, her face loses colour, turning as white as her apron.

'We do not mention the child. Master Blackham requests the cabinet be polished every day, that is all.'

'But…'

'Stop this talking. All this gossip will do us no good. Your job is now upstairs and anything else the mistress requests. It's enough to keep you occupied. It's not our business to ask questions about our betters. We are here to serve and work well, lest we find ourselves out on the street – and I do not relish seeking other employment.'

Hannah glances at me. 'I shan't be missing you … and I'll not be calling you Miss, now you're upstairs. I'll be glad to get more space. You won't be here long,' she shrugs. 'Girls normally leave after a promotion, after they go up to the attic - they get airs and graces, onto a better job, more money. Doesn't bother me I've not been chosen again. I don't like the attic anyway; it's too close to all those shrieking birds.' Her expression changes from petulance to contempt. 'I bet the mistress had some say in them overlooking me all the time, jealous she is.'

'That's enough.' The cook snaps at Hannah. 'We are only the servants, and don't think I've not noticed that you purchased the same bonnet as the mistress and then paraded it about along the street. Remember your place.'

Hannah stirs the pot with a final flourish and then moves it away from the fire, her chin jutting out, displaying a sharp silhouette. Yet I would rather face the scorn of Hannah than venture further up into the house, such is my lack of courage. But I am determined to prove myself stronger than the meek, irrelevant daughter my father assumes me to be.

'I just remembered I am expected elsewhere,' Hannah states, as she strides out of the kitchen on a mission of her own, leaving the room with an air of disquieting silence.

In her absence, I decide to brace a subject which has been niggling at my conscience since the trip to the apothecary. 'Mrs Higgins, before I go, something has been on my mind.'

She wipes over the kitchen table. 'Yes?'

I lower my voice again. 'Would Hannah ever do anything that could be considered a danger to others?'

She twists her head in my direction, her eyes flashing. 'Whatever do you mean?'

'Only that she asked me to buy more arsenic from the apothecary.'

'Yes, I'm aware of that. What are you getting at?' She looks me dead in the eye.

'Their ledger said the household had recently bought a large amount. The shopkeeper seemed surprised.'

Mrs Higgins wipes her forehead with her hand. 'Well, we do have a problem with rats in the garden. They are the bane of William's life.'

'But, as I signed for more, could you give me assurance that it wouldn't be used for anything else? Only I have read tales of people being poisoned, and the mistress... Isn't her poor health a little surprising for her age?'

She gasps, her chin disappearing into the folds of her face. 'What are you implying? Not my Hannah. Although she's had a hard childhood, and she might have taken against the new mistress.' She pauses, deep in thought. 'She would never do what you're suggesting.'

'But—'

'It goes without saying that she loves Master Blackham.' She cuts in. 'Once, he showed her a scrap of affection in his male weakness, and she holds on to that. I don't believe she would ever leave him, only if death grabbed her by her heels and took her away himself.' She grimaces. 'Even entertaining her policeman friend is her poor attempt at getting attention from him. But she wouldn't have such bitter thoughts or risk anything to jeopardise her position here.'

I bite my lip, trying to think. 'Something just doesn't appear right about the order.'

Mrs Higgins walks into the scullery and washes her hands over the sink. 'Ivy, you are mistaken – your imagination will get you into trouble. Now, stop nosing around and be grateful you have errands to run at all. Do not query the running of this house.' She waves me away, out of the kitchen. The conversation is over, and I go to gather my belongings. Maybe I am wrong then, but it begs the question: why are there still so many rats?

Despite being a bright winter day, the atmosphere inside the house is solemn. I make my way slowly along the basement corridor and up the back stairs into the eaves. I hold my carpet bag close under one arm and with my other I carry my leather case, but it is cumbersome knocking against my legs.

The attic room is down a short hallway on the left, situated in its own recess, tucked away out of sight in the shadows. The rest of the space must be for storage. A small door stands above three steps, trying, but failing, to impose itself on anyone who approaches. My heart sinks. I can almost taste the unhappiness rising from the lower floors, accumulating in the eaves. As I walk in, the room is just as I had imagined it would be when the vicar was telling the story of the nanny and the missing child. Probably because I know of the sad history, there is a strange ambience, as if the room does not wish to be disturbed. A musty smell lingers, so I open the window, watching as the sun is slowly eclipsed by grey clouds and then become mesmerised by the dust motes dancing in the breeze around me. At least I have privacy now. The contents are simple: a single wrought-iron bed, a bedpan, and a modest chest of drawers. An old, embroidered wall-hanging of a garden with two small figures hangs above the mantelpiece. The grate is dirty and empty. I make a mental note to bring up some kindling before the evening. There are scuff marks on the wooden floor and a meagre rag rug.

I test out the bed, the mattress sags in the middle. It's clear that this room was occupied in the past. I wonder what happened to the last maid and the one before that?

The absence of a lace net gives the window little privacy except for a thin curtain. Although at this height, I doubt anyone can see me from the street. Facing the front, the room overlooks Chester Garden Square.

Edging up on the tips of my toes, I spy Hyde Park nestled amongst the houses in the distance. It is a pleasant scene. I leave the door open to get a couple of cleaning rags and kindling.

When I return, both the door and the window are closed again. They could not have shut by accident. The room feels different, and even more stuffy than before. My leather case has fallen off the bed with my clothes strewn over the wooden floor, an act of defiance to my arrival. Thankfully, my carpet bag is untouched.

Although there is no immediate audience, I am reluctant to react and show my displeasure. I persuade myself it must be Hannah. She will be nearby, listening. Her jealousy of the rise in my position is driving her to play mind games with me.

As I reopen the window, making sure the catch is secure, an ice-cold draught blows over my ankles. A low cupboard I had not seen before, the size of a small child, catches my eye in the corner next to the fireplace. I touch along the edges and confirm a chilled breeze is easing its way into the room. A small brass handle glints near the floorboards. With a hard tug, I am able to prise the door open.

The hidden space is only slightly bigger than my travel bag. It is full of spiderwebs but a perfect place to keep things out of sight. Pushing the webs aside I manage to fit all my belongings inside. Then turning my attention to the fireplace I use all the kindling to create a small fire, hoping it will lift my spirits. Having my own room does not give me the peace I had hoped it would. I am uneasy and realise I am more vulnerable at the top of the house – for there is no easy way out.

Chapter 25 ~ Wild Eyes

Ivy ~ Blackham House, 7th December.

A scream wakes me from the depths of sleep. My eyes are open, but I am unaware of my whereabouts. Then, I discover, with delight, that I am at home, with my mother in the bed beside me. I can hear her breathing, her heart beating rhythmically, the edges of the walls blending into the darkness.

'Mother?'

My voice is a stranger to me, like a child's calling out, expecting her to soothe me with sweet words. I always leave a lamp or candle on the bedside table next to my bed, letting the flame burn low throughout the night. Where has the light gone?

I search around the bed-covers to take my mother's hand, which is always a comfort. But I find nothing, and although the blankets are weighted, they are not the soft materials I expect to feel. Woollen and scratchy, they nudge my recollection to a different place.

I call out 'Mother?' again. But there is no response, and the sound of my mother's breathing has stopped.

There's another piercing scream, closer, sounding female. My blood runs cold. Is the noise human or something else unearthly?

My eyes slowly make out the furniture in the room. The attic, I am back at Blackham House. My stomach sinks as I absorb the reality that my mother will never answer me again. Now I recall, I took the tonic from the apothecarist for the first time tonight. I had high hopes of a restful sleep in this new room, but my senses are jumbled.

The noises must be coming from the speaking tube, the mistress must need me.

I stumble across the room, putting my ear against the cold metal mouthpiece by the fireplace. I listen, but I hear nothing except my own breathing. Once again, a high-pitched sound slices through the quiet of the night. Nothing would make such a distressing call unless driven to do so by anguish or pain.

I pad over to the window and open it. The bare wooden floor is cold against my feet, and my nightdress provides no protection against the winter draughts blowing down from the chimney.

The sound echoes from behind the house, and something primal compels me to help. I have heard many sounds at night in the countryside, but this is different. I could not stop my mother from dying, but there might be a chance I could save this woman. Someone still needs me. In my sleepy state, I wonder if it could be Miss Earnshaw? There are noises up here near the roof I could have missed whilst being in the depths of the basement.

I manage to light my room lamp by fumbling with the matches on my bedside table and then find my winter shawl. I sense there is not a moment to lose, almost as though I'm being summoned. I open the door with one hand and carry the lamp with the other. I descend quickly down the servant stairs, running through the shadows as I hold the weak flame before me, my nightgown blooming around my legs.

Could this be madness, a dangerous journey into the night? Am I still dreaming? For I have the strongest sensation of not being entirely in this world.

No one else appears to be disturbed by the noises, as everyone still seems to be asleep. The moon is barely visible as I let myself out of the scullery back door and onto the path that runs along the side of the house. In my rush, I have forgotten my shoes and am barefoot, with the crisp ground frost biting at my toes.

The cry shoots through the air again, startling me with its urgency, breaking out from the shadows of the trees at the foot of the garden. I stand on the edge of the lawn alone, but for my feeble excuse of a light, common sense returning, and all dreams of rest banished.

For what reason had I left the warmth of my bed to come outside in the middle of a winter's night? Would my screams blend with the other and my fate also be doomed? My teeth chatter. I am terrified of what lurks in the dark. The Devil takes on many forms.

I hesitate and take a step back towards the scullery. If I fetch the cook, she will alert the authorities. I know tales of a monster in London who preys on people in alleyways and unlit courtyards; or the street vendors who plunder gardens at night scrounging for holly to sell at Christmas. My slight build would be no match for such men.

And it is clear at once: this garden is not a happy place. For what reason was it kept like this by the gardener? The flower beds are full of nothing but thorny plants and soil.

A glimpse of moonlight illuminates the unusual shrubs that I yearn to study closer. They are raising each of their long narrow blue-green leaves upwards towards the stars, but I can still clearly see the orange spikes, dotting each stem like constellations. I bend down to the nearest flowerbed and trace one golden thorn gently with my finger, and a sliver of sharp pain shoots through my hand like a bee sting. I wince as an undercurrent of danger moves with the wind around me, rippling through the branches of the chestnut tree.

The whine comes softer, almost a whimper, and my plan to exit fades. Maybe the mistress was sleepwalking and woke up calling for help. Besides, I am here now.

In the centre of the garden, an obscure form gradually appears, with two eyes glinting directly at me. What spirit have I found? With the graveyard nearby, anything might have escaped, the walls are only an illusion of a boundary. My imagination is vivid, already forming the shadow of a demon waiting for me.

The shape moves, slinks forward; only a little, but enough for me to make out the body of an animal, not a spirit. It is a scrawny looking vixen, not filled out like the animals in the countryside. But it is the colour of its coat that steals my breath: a splash of ink, a sleek silhouette cutting a thin outline hardly visible in the gloom. I have only heard tales of black foxes; they warn of bad luck. I shake the thought away. In the countryside, many vixens cry at night, but nothing has affected me so deeply as this one.

The black fox now stands on the lawn beneath the back-room window on the first floor, a wildness in her eyes as she looks in my direction, startled at the sight of me. She opens her jaws wide and screeches again. The harsh sound, jagged and violent, shatters the silence of the night with desperation; it is such a mournful noise. This creature emanates a warning, resonating deep within me. Its infectious fear, unguarded and raw, spreads through my veins, creeping heavily into every limb until my legs lock and my feet sink into the cold, damp grass, unable to move.

Could it be that the fox is standing on the very spot where the vicar described the woman falling to her death so many years before? Was she pushed or did she jump, her blood running into the soil, staining the earth with a memory only the animals can sense?

The notion of being watched surrounds me from the building and the secrecy of the trees. Is the gardener out here? I tighten the shawl around my shoulders for the animal has seen something that I cannot.

The fox sits back on her hind legs as her orange eyes observe the house. She whimpers and whines. I follow her gaze to what appears to be the cause of her distress. There, at the back-room window, a candle gently glows behind the glass, and someone stands unmoving, watching us.

The fox barks again and bolts into the hedge, her black coat melding with the night, leaving me with only the ghostly figure. The pain from my finger spreads to my whole hand as it throbs by my side.

A lonely church bell strikes once, echoing across the houses. A queer time for it to ring. I blink, and the apparition in the window has vanished.

In my new role, I am on call for the mistress between eight and ten in the morning to aid with dressing and her daily errands. I plan to apportion the hours over the rest of the day for other jobs in the house. We are still low on staff and my chores are endless. I have not seen Lottie, the young girl, since my first day; apparently her mother has just had her fifth baby and needs her at home, and Mrs Higgins is reluctant to ask her for help. So, it is only three of us who carry out the brunt of the housework. William, the gardener, is like a ghost who comes and goes with little proof of his existence to show for his efforts on the grounds.

It is only 9 o'clock in the morning, and I already wish I could sleep again. I edge the mistress slowly out of her white nightdress and into a cotton chemise, for my hand is still tender from touching the orange thorn. Perhaps it was her I saw at the window? I want to ask if she noticed me in the garden, but the fragments of the night piece together like a bad dream that I don't wish to reconstruct.

Mistress Angelica sits before the dressing table. 'I am tired today, Ivy. Look at my skin, the colour is so pale.' She touches the blue half-moons beneath her eyes. 'What will people think? I need some lemons to scrub my face with … to brighten and also get rid of this mark.' She exposes her neck.

It is true, there is a new red mark spreading up from her back and across her collarbone. It will be difficult to hide with the dusting powder. This is my chance to gain her confidence.

'Yes, I will prepare a lemon, but the lotion might sting, so just in case, let's put on some more balm to reduce the redness.'

I pick up the jar from the apothecary, which has found a permanent place on her dressing table. She needs it almost daily now. She winces as I dab it onto her tender skin. I check her nails. Perhaps they are too sharp, harming her in her sleep, but I see they are all bitten back to the quick.

'Thank you.' Her reply is half-hearted as she continues to appraise her reflection.

Brushing her thick, soft hair, I start to tease it up into a bun high on her head, sweeping all the loose strands up with a small toothbrush dipped in bandoline. Her ebony hair smells of the lavender oil on her pillow. Now her neck is visibly elegant, as fashion dictates, but she looks so fragile and exposed. More scratches, more unexplained wounds. Could she have fallen amongst the plants in the garden? The thought is hardly likely.

'I suggest a nice high-neck dress to protect you from draughts today.'

She nods, her attention far away. Her skin is so pale, her eyes glazed, the sapphire blue startlingly bright. Without intending to, she has almost captured the bony consumptive appearance so popular in London. A fashionable hollow-cheeked look that many women emulate, trying to capture a rare type of fleeting beauty before death.

'Did you hear the noise last night? It was quite a commotion outside.' I want the words to sound casual, but I know there is a note of desperation in my tone.

'I heard some sounds, but then again – I always do. The garden wildlife can be noisy at night.'

I finish her hair and take a step back. 'It was a black fox; I have never seen one that colour before. Vixens normally make such a disturbance with their cries, but I've only ever heard them in the countryside.'

The mistress looks up at me through her reflection in the mirror. 'A black fox? That is peculiar and in our garden too. William will be unhappy. How close did you see it?'

'Well, the animal was crying, and I wanted to help.'

'You ventured outside … alone?'

'Only for a short while.'

'But is that not dangerous at night? Surely, you read the news about the madman who attacks people in the street?' She covers her mouth with the palm of her hand.

'The thought had crossed my mind.'

'But you and the fox were well in the end?' She looks away and starts to move the glass bottles and pots around on her dressing table, seemingly separating the medical cures from the beauty.

'Yes, but weren't you at the window watching?' I ask, as I prepare a blue dress on the bed with a neckline high enough to cover most of the scratches.

'Me?' she asks. 'You must be mistaken.'

'Are you certain it was not you?'

She turns towards me on her stool, her eyes watering. 'You doubt me too? No one seems to believe me anymore. I know I fell asleep straight after taking my medicine and I have no recollection of waking.' She stifles a yawn. 'Was it a dream, Ivy? Perhaps it's this house, the move to the attic and your new roles are straining you?'

I smooth out the creases in the blue dress. 'My apologies, I must have been confused. Only, I was convinced a woman stood at the window in the back room wearing a white nightgown just like your own. She held a candle.'

'Did you see her face?' Her eyes widen.

'No – unfortunately, there was not enough light.'

'What was she doing?'

'She simply watched me, nothing more, and then she disappeared.'

'That image is most disconcerting.' She picks up a small silver-gilt, cut glass bottle of perfume and dabs a little onto a handkerchief; the scents of bergamot and lemon oil fill the air. 'Could the woman not have been Hannah or Mrs Higgins?'

'I don't believe so. The lady had ebony hair; it looked almost black, like yours. I really thought it was you.'

She furrows her brow in concentration. 'That is not possible. Hannah unlocked my door only minutes before you arrived.'

There must be a rational explanation. *Was I hallucinating?* Did I sleepwalk or dream of myself in the garden – suffering the effects of my sleeping tonic? The idea is ridiculous, but my head is spinning with possibilities. I remember the vicar's story: the woman at the same window. The comparison is eerie, a sick joke. Is someone deliberately trying to scare me away?

'Yes, probably a trick of the light.' I say with more conviction than I have. 'Perhaps it was Hannah. I am still learning the rooms in the house. There may be more servant corridors hidden that I do not know of, and she used one.' This would be a logical reason, and I almost succeed in convincing myself.

The mistress discards the suggestion with a shrug. 'I have not heard of such places.' She lifts her head and fixes me with her eyes. 'I would be careful, Ivy; this house is not ordinary. It has a way of playing tricks with your mind.'

She gets up and walks over to the dress on the bed. 'Only trouble will come of curiosity; even I know the English rhyme about what killed the cat.'

Chapter 26 ~ Slumming

Ivy ~ Blackham House, 9th December.

Master Blackham paces up and down the first-floor landing. Breathing hard, his fingers flex and clench constantly. I dart past him carrying a dress box, trying to avoid his attention. It is not usual to see him this animated before midday. His expression is thunderous, today is the morning of the ladies' outing. I knock on the mistress's bedroom door.

'Ivy, is that you? Come in.'

I open the door and see her perched on the chair by the window. 'What do you think?' She enquires with a smile.

Her face is flawless; her hair is still in place, pinned up high on her head from my earlier work this morning. If I did not know she had been up in the night again with more bad dreams, I wouldn't have noticed the traces of grey shadows beneath her powdered skin. This time she was crying out about protecting her songbird from the magpies in the garden.

'Very good, madam. I have your dress ready. The packages with the alterations and new dresses have also just arrived from the tailor.'

I take the box to the bed and unpack the contents for her. It is a plain outfit, simple but still made of quality material. There is no chance that the mistress would blend in with the poor. Not quite the slumming experience, but probably as close as you could get from a proud high-street tailor. I doubt he could bring himself to make anything less.

As she steps into the dress, the grey fabric somehow makes her look frailer and yet brings a fragile elegance to her features. You cannot tone down her beauty; perhaps that is why the master is so anxious.

'Are you sure you wish to attend today? I could pass on your apologies?' I say, as I help her change.

She is still not eating well. The signs of pregnancy are all there. I have heard of women who get so sick that they never gain any weight but waste away until the baby is born. But when could she have conceived? The couple are rarely together?

Once dressed, she returns to her seat. The door bursts open, and Master Blackham strides into the bedroom.

'Hannah tells me you are not well.'

Hannah shuffles inside the doorway behind him and gloats at me.

'La tua puttana di una cameriera dovrebbe badare ai fatti suoi,' the mistress mutters to herself.

The master exhales. 'Please speak English, my darling. Otherwise, how will we know what you are thinking?'

'Of course.' Her smile is thin, but her eyes flash briefly with annoyance. 'Thank you for your efforts, Hannah.' The tone of sarcasm is barely concealed.

'I have considered the subject of this ladies' outing more thoroughly this morning,' Master Blackham continues. 'Your health is a huge concern to me. How should I know if something untoward happens?'

She touches her hair, checking it remains in place. 'I will be with the wives of your closest friends. Is that not enough to reassure you?'

He paces the room with his hands folded behind his back and then fixes his eyes on the picture above the fireplace. 'Mother is also unhappy. The Blackhams do not make a habit of visiting the slums.'

The mistress flicks her attention towards her husband as she puts on her travelling gloves. 'My dear, you cannot prevent me from going. What would they say, knowing you lock me up during the day as well?'

'Your comment is uncalled for,' Master Blackham blusters, his pupils darkening. 'Perhaps taking in the foul air of London will make you appreciate how well you are looked after in this house.'

Hannah grunts from the corner.

'We can help the unfortunates if we are able to understand them better. Charity serves both the giver and receiver.' The mistress lifts her chin, exposing her neck and I catch a glimpse of one of the fading red scratches. 'Surely you cannot protest this? I saw the benefits of helping an orphanage in Italy. The girls' lives and prospects were greatly improved. I think we may even have saved some from the workhouse. Our contributions go towards teaching them domestic skills which will serve them well.'

'This is absolute folly – entertainment at the sake of the poor. I absolutely forbid this outing.' He strides towards her. 'Look at your face! It is positively feverish. 'I heard you screamed the house down again in your sleep last night.'

'I have no such fever and how would you know about my sleeping habits? You are barely here,' she retorts, her eyes flashing with defiance.

'And all these lights?' He points to the multitude of lamps and candles sitting on nearly every surface. 'Are you trying to burn us down? This behaviour is not normal and simply can't go on. I won't allow it!'

I see Hannah's smirk twist as she gloats over her small victory.

The master leans down, bringing his face down to the mistress's cheek, so close they are almost touching. 'You will stay inside this house until you are better. I shall dine with you later, and if these whims of yours continue to stress your nerves, I will notify the doctor to be ready for a call.' He swivels sharply on his heels and stalks out of the room.

The mistress slumps on the seat, visibly deflated. All her bravado has vanished. 'I hoped a change of scenery and some charity work might have helped my nerves.'

No longer with her husband as an audience, I wonder who she is talking to?

The canary chirps loudly from the cage, mirroring the need to escape.

She turns to look at me, eyebrows raised. 'Ivy?' A glimpse of a conspiratorial exchange, perhaps prompting me to persuade her to act.

I go to the window. 'A carriage is waiting in the street,' I reply. I am about to say more, gathering the nerve to suggest that we should go anyway, quickly taking our leave, when Hannah interrupts.

'I shall tell the driver you feel unwell, and you will be staying at home, as the master requested,' Hannah states, barely hiding the glee in her voice, as she almost skips out of the room.

Watching as the mistress slowly removes her gloves, the despondence in the air is suffocating. I regret at once not taking her by the hand and dragging her outside into the frost bound street.

Chapter 27 ~ Detecting

Ivy ~ Blackham House, 10th December.

A short man in uniform is standing in the master's library. I hover by the open doorway, polishing the woodwork in the hallway in the weak afternoon sun, listening to their serious tones.

'I am still investigating the disappearance of Miss Earnshaw. After questioning all the people of interest in the case, it has become clear your party were probably among the last to see her.' His voice is low and calm, unflustered by the authority of Blackham House. 'As you will be aware, she has now been missing for some time. I'm afraid the search has turned into a possible murder hunt, and we need to make sure we have not missed any vital clues.'

'Murder hunt? How can you be so confident?' The master replies. My chest becomes tight at the mention of murder. I edge closer.

'We have found her coat. Her housekeeper confirmed it belonged to Miss Earnshaw.' The detective clears his throat. 'There are traces of blood on the wool.'

'I don't understand why I am still involved in all of this?' The master's voice rises. 'I told you everything we knew at the time. All this from a foolish night of games my wife organised. Blood? This is totally absurd.'

'Clearly, this is a delicate situation, but all lines of interest must be fully reviewed.' The detective continues, his voice remaining matter of fact. 'This would be much easier if you were to cooperate and then we could both get on with our work. I appreciate you are a busy man, Mr Blackham.'

'Naturally, I will help.' The master's abrupt tone changes to something more polite and calmer. 'Of course, you are welcome to talk to any of my staff. I am sure they will be just as obliging. They have nothing to hide.'

'Of course. Now, if you could just run through what happened at the end of the night again.' The detective waits patiently for an answer, and I hear the chink of glass. I imagine the master is pouring himself a generous shot of whisky from the crystal decanter.

'Well, there were the usual theatrics - the excitement of talking with spirits, along with many glasses of wine ... all the expected drama you'd conjure for a séance.'

'You are mocking me, Mr Blackham?'

'On the contrary, I tell you the truth; the party was a most eventful evening. This house appeared to come alive with the dead. Pardon my pun. They are superb, these charlatans.' He laughs. 'Did you read that recent article in The Morning Herald?'

'Which article are you referring to?'

'About a spiritualist who the police caught red-handed using trickery in her séance – making things disappear and reappear. Maybe Miss Earnshaw did an experiment and evaporated herself!'

The voices become muffled as a street seller passes, shouting his wares loudly. I must know more; I take a gamble and peer through the crack in the door. The detective seems unamused. He holds a pencil tightly. He notes the throwaway comment down with a sigh. I am surprised the lead tip does not snap under the pressure.

'Come on, you are not writing that down as well?'

I wonder if he records that it is still only mid-afternoon and how heavily the master is drinking, his speech already slurring.

'All information is important, sir.'

'We also have the local policeman and nightwatchman. This street is a popular round on their beat and I will interview them again too.' He replies confidently.

'What do the police believe to have happened?' Master Blackham pours himself another measure of whisky and offers the detective a drink, but he declines. 'The papers are full of this killer stalking the streets of London. Do you suppose this incident involves this madman? I mean, who is to say where Miss Earnshaw went after she left here?' He takes a large mouthful from his glass.

'Unless we find the body, we cannot be certain it links the case in any way to the same person. This killer's style is, shall we say, quite unique. If it was him, I am sure more evidence would have been found by now.'

Master Blackham shakes his head. He almost catches a glimpse of me, so I quickly recoil into the corridor.

'Chances are, the longer time goes on, the less chance we have of finding her alive.'

'Such a shame. What a waste of life.' The master replies.

'At present, we can only conclude she must have taken a disreputable cab back to her apartment and never returned. Her coat was found in a nearby street.'

'Perhaps the police should look down by the docks? I hear that is where the most disreputable people conduct their business.'

'Well, yes.' His voice sounds strained. 'But that is not my area to direct. I am tasked with speaking to everyone she was close to or saw in the week before she disappeared.'

'Who else are you interviewing then, apart from my guests that night?' The master's voice is curt again.

'I am not at liberty to say, sir. But I would like to confirm the description we have of what she was wearing?'

'Surely you have all that trivial information already?'

'I am only following procedure. Sometimes details that were missed come back to one's memory on second reflection.'

'I have no idea.'

'Can I speak to your wife?'

'I am afraid she is indisposed. Her health is weak with the smog and filth in the air. As you would understand, the news of the missing woman has hit her badly.'

'I am sorry Mrs Blackham is unwell. Perhaps if I made an appointment to visit her at a more convenient time?'

'She feels responsible, as this was the last house where Miss Earnshaw was seen. I do not wish her to be more distressed than she is already.'

'That is understandable, sir.'

'Besides, I am sure we were not the only people to have seen her that night.'

'Well then, how about your staff? Could I have a word with them now?'

'Perhaps one of our maids could oblige you? Clothes and accessories are the fancies of women. But I am unsure if they'd even remember the colour of her lace gloves. They are paid to work, not observe us.'

'The lady was wearing lace gloves?'

'How should I know?' The master barks. 'Shall we not waste any more of each other's time? What would your superiors say if they were to hear that you had been bothering law-abiding residents of one of the wealthiest houses in London?' The chair scrapes, as I imagine him taking a seat by the fireplace. 'My father had quite the influence within the constabulary. I am sure the name Blackham would still hold reverence.'

'I am only doing my job, sir.' The detective pauses. 'You have not answered my question. Do you prefer not to answer?'

'There you go again, putting words into my mouth. Of course, she must have been wearing damn gloves, lace or no lace. Don't all women at this time of the year? I am simply reminding you that the residents of the esteemed Blackham House should not have to go to such efforts to prove their innocence.'

'No one is above the law, Mr Blackham. All questions must be followed through.'

'Have you seen the Blackham collection of valuable artefacts?'

'The collection, yes. It has been noted.'

I look again through the crack and watch as the detective thumbs through the pages of his notebook.

'I would be more concerned that she might have been here with the ambition to steal my precious artefacts. Perhaps one is missing, and she sold it and left the country?'

'That is possible. I will write that down. But I hardly think—'

'You dare to imply I am lying?' Master Blackham's voice snaps. 'To doubt my morals over those of a con artist. No better than an actress on the stage?'

'Of course not, sir, only that she was rich in her own right. I have visited her home. And we have no complaints of theft filed after any of her other visits to wealthy establishments. So, I see no other reason to explore the idea.'

Master Blackham sighs. 'Just get on with what you need to do and leave. You will find you have wasted all our time, and your own, soon enough.'

I back away down the corridor and hurry downstairs, stopping halfway to compose myself from the reality of their conversation. Murder ... the detective's theory confirms everything I feared most. Balling my fists at my temples, I could weep with the agony of never seeing her again, but the tears do not come. Instead, I am consumed by the desperate need for truth. This cannot be the end of my search.

If I were alone with the detective, could I reveal I was also looking for her? And I am coming to the tragic conclusion that the Blackhams have committed the worst crime. We could conspire and solve this together, sending Master Blackham to prison, but then I would have to confess everything. No policeman would believe a maid who is overwhelmed by her own imagination over a rich gentleman, and certainly not trust me after stealing Miss Earnshaw's diary and working here under false pretences. My morals are now questionable, whereas once they were impeccable. Murders, theft, fraud in London are not unusual. The city must be quick to change a person.

In the basement, I find the detective already talking to Mrs Higgins in the kitchen. I am relieved to see Lottie has arrived and has been helping to scrub the potatoes. I know my promotion has increased the workload of downstairs, but Hannah will never admit it.

'Here she is - you can ask her yourself.' Mrs Higgins glances at me, but I cannot read her expression.

'Good afternoon. Your name is Miss Ivy Granger?'

'Yes,' I reply.

The detective records my name in his notepad. My top lip beads in perspiration, battling the despondency that finding Miss Earnshaw alive is becoming more unlikely by the day.

'My name is Detective Spencer. I am working on a special case, which unfortunately involves this house and its residents.'

His smile urges me to confide in him. 'Can you remember what Miss Earnshaw was wearing on the night of the 11th of November? She was a guest at the party held on that particular night.'

I stall; my nerves are unravelling. My mouth is suddenly dry with all the attention.

'Answer his question!' The sharp tone from Mrs Higgins makes me jump.

'I wasn't here. I only worked here after the 20th of November, five days after the party.'

'Oh, is that right?' Mrs Higgins rubs her forehead. 'I must have been thinking of another maid we had helping... Well, Lottie, it's your turn.' She glances at the young girl and then turns to Detective Spencer. 'Lottie is only twelve. She cannot be of much help, surely? She is barely here. And I would appreciate it if you didn't bring her to the attention of the master. I haven't mentioned that I've hired her on occasion.'

'I need to question every person who was present on the night of the party.'

Lottie pouts and folds her arms, petulantly. Mrs Higgins reaches out a plump arm and gently touches the girl's dirty blonde hair. 'There's no reason to be frightened. Answer the nice man, and after you'd better get home, your chores are done.'

The young girl, normally full of attitude, becomes shy under the scrutiny of everyone in the room. 'I was mostly in the kitchen helping you.' She looks up at the cook, who responds with a tight-lipped smile.

'Lottie, did you at any time see the woman known as Miss Earnshaw?' Detective Spencer keeps his voice low but takes a step forward towards her, stooping down to her height.

'Well, there was one time … when she came in. I hid in the servant's entrance near the hallway. I wanted to watch the guests and I saw her take off her coat.'

'What was she wearing, Lottie? Anything distinguishable?'

Mrs Higgins gives her a nod, giving her the permission to continue speaking.

Detective Spencer writes something in his notepad again. There's a gold ring on his wedding finger, and I imagine his wife; what she'd serve for tea, knowing he'd be home soon. She would be normal, stable – not like us, the women who live in Blackham House.

Lottie bites at her nails. 'A bird brooch, sir. I remember because the jewellery was made of black gems. I've always been fond of birds, and it took my fancy.'

'A bird brooch?' Echoes the detective. 'How interesting. And was she wearing lace gloves?'

'Yes, I think so. They were a pretty purple,' she mumbles.

'This is good, Lottie. Thank you. I shall pass this on to my superior. He might have heard some noise about such a brooch being sold down by the docks.' He writes the description in his notepad.

My insides lurch at the prospect of what could have happened under the cover of nightfall at the docks. It is a rough place. Against my will, I conjure the picture of Miss Earnshaw's lifeless body, angry bruises about her neck and the gems still glistening in the murky water.

Then another thought strikes: could this be the same brooch I had seen in the trunk of forgotten things? I glance at Hannah and expect her to come forward, to provide the evidence which might hold important clues to this case, but she just stands there looking blankly straight ahead. I remember the same bird motif on my mother's book and on Miss Earnshaw's calling card and diary. The burden of truth constricts my throat. Should I say something?

'Thank you, miss, although such a nice piece of jewellery would be long gone by now. But you never know, the mention of such an unusual piece might jog someone's memory.'

Detective Spencer can read Lottie's unease and smiles, trying to comfort her. He is kind to people, empathetic. Is he loyal to his wife? I imagine he is. Does his wife know how lucky she is to fall asleep next to such a gentleman? I am sure he would keep the nightmares at bay.

I don't want the detective to leave. He is a positive presence in the house: solid and reassuring. Time is running out, but the words won't come. I can sense Mrs Higgins getting restless, wanting to continue the preparations for dinner without further interruptions. As if sensing my need to talk, he gives me his calling card.

Finally, my voice finds itself. 'Has anyone else offered information?'

'Miss Earnshaw was last seen leaving her home after returning from the party here.' He thumbs through his notepad to an earlier entry.

'Who said that?' I ask.

'A nightwatchman confirmed these facts, but the weather was bad with fog, and he wasn't sure. You can be certain I will interview him again now that the case looks more serious than a missing person enquiry. We have, however, discovered evidence to imply that something more sinister may have occurred: an item of her clothing has been found with blood on it.'

His words shock us all into silence. Could it be the same nightwatchman who watches me? There are so many of them in London, but alarm beats inside my chest nonetheless. Where would a lady travel again at such a late hour?

'Didn't her housekeeper say she never returned?'

'How do you know?' His eyes narrow at me in concentration.

I stutter, almost giving myself away. 'I must have read it in the papers. What reason would she have to lie?'

I am confused. Possibly I was wrong to believe her, and all this time she had directed me here as a diversion.

'Ah! She is after her money. I've heard this all before; a wealthy woman with no husband leaves it all to her housekeeper. She probably did away with her.'

'We cannot assume anything without the facts Mrs…?' He searches through his writing trying to find her name.

'Mrs Higgins.' She flushes red from the attention and the subtle reprimand.

'I commend your detective skills. And on this occasion, the housekeeper does, in fact, look to inherit the house; unless we can find a signed will, but we know of no other relatives to follow this up with.'

A wave of unease washes over me. Am I not related to her? Could my name be mentioned in the will?

'See! A motive right there.' Mrs Higgins is triumphant in her discovery. Her lips pucker together in confirmation of her statement.

'We'll continue to explore all options until we discover the truth.' Detective Spencer tucks his notepad and pencil into his coat pocket, bids us good day, and walks out of the scullery door.

The tension in the basement swiftly dissolves from the questioning. But I am even worse for his absence.

It is dusk before I am in the kitchen alone. I slip unnoticed into the servants' bedroom and pull out the small trunk full of anonymous items from the low shelf. This time, I'm not afraid to touch them. I know what I'm searching for. I reach around at the bottom, and everything is as it was before – except the bird brooch has gone.

Chapter 28 ~ Black Ink

Ivy ~ Kensington, 11th December.

It is late in the evening; the church bells have just struck nine. I use the excuse that the mistress needs something personal. In my new role as her lady's maid, I am harder to ignore. Mrs Higgins reluctantly allows me to leave.

'Don't be long!' Hannah calls out after me. 'I'll be locking up at ten and I won't wait for you. You won't be any good to the mistress if your bed is on the street!' She is still angry at me for becoming the mistress's favourite.

I waste no time in hailing a passing hansom cab and heading straight to Kensington, to Miss Earnshaw's house. The lights are on. I pray desperately that her disappearance is all a mistake, and I will find her inside.

The housekeeper thankfully opens the door this time. She appears tired, as before.

'Good evening, Mrs Forbes. I am Miss Ivy Granger – we spoke before. I need to talk about Miss Earnshaw again.'

She clenches her hands together. 'They found her?'

I feel bad for raising her hopes. 'Not as far as I know, but I must speak with you.'

Her eyes glisten with unshed tears. 'You had better come inside. Will you take some tea?'

'Yes, that would be kind of you. Thank you.' I am surprised at her kindness compared to the last time I came here.

I remember where the parlour is, although she gestures the way as a formality as she goes off to the kitchen.

Sitting down in a red velvet chair, I notice that everything seems the same; no dust has settled, and the many plants along the windowsill are still alive. The housekeeper, it seems, has been biding her time, rattling around the house until her mistress returns.

My eyes follow the pictures on the wall, drawings of different types of birds. The style is a mix of familiarity and something else. There is a harshness in the lines, which contrasts with my mother's more subtle artwork. And these are drawn in black ink, not charcoal. Even so, the images are beautiful. The graceful motion of flight is created in a single brush stroke. The artist must have spent considerable time observing the creatures to capture them so well. There is a permanence to drawing with ink; a display of courage, for it cannot be blurred or smudged.

I remember the image I thought I'd seen of my mother. I stand up and head to the corner of the room, searching for her face, but there is no picture. Yet I distinctively recall it was here. Continuing to scan the drawings on each wall in turn, there is nothing that looks like the black and white profile I saw. But then I observe an anomaly: a gap in the frames I had missed. Only a faint outline remains where the sun has bleached the wallpaper pattern. The clink of china rattling on a tray gives notice of the housekeeper's return.

'Mrs Forbes, is there a picture missing?' I point to the vacant space on the wall. 'Last time I was here, a drawing of a woman was displayed.'

She sucks in her cheeks before placing the tray on a round oak table. 'You must be mistaken.'

Did I detect a change in her manner? A slight shake of the teapot sends the liquid spilling over the cup's edge and into the saucer. Her eyes avoid contact with me; she is not a good liar.

I don't want to push further and spoil the delicate truce we seem to have formed, in contrast to my last visit. Perhaps if I can gain her trust, she will tell me more. But it is another oddity which sits uneasily. What is she hiding?

We sit opposite each other, drinking our tea in silence. The sounds from outside are muffled by the heavy velvet curtains, creating a cocooned calm a world away from the city. The quality of the furniture is luxurious, and I remember Miss Earnshaw's will. What motive does the housekeeper have to keep secrets? I want to ask her directly and tell her I am staying at Blackham House. That I know the pain and darkness in the building, and the Blackham family must be linked to her disappearance. She knows it too, otherwise she would not have sent me to the address. But I am still not sure I can trust her.

'The weather is better today,' I eventually say, breaking the silence.

How long before we can talk properly, unravel the tension between us? Presumably, we both want the same thing.

'I attended a recent women's suffrage meeting at the Hanover Square rooms. They mentioned Miss Earnshaw had visited them regularly.'

Mrs Forbes does not look at ease. And I am not surprised when she gets up from the couch and stands by the desk, leaving her teacup on the table.

'Did you attend together?' I continue. I have so many questions, but I am worried that she will become irritable and send me away.

'Yes, she was quite passionate about a woman's right to vote. I don't have the energy to go to them now.'

A burst of confidence arises from her answer, and I press on. 'Did she disagree with anyone ... any politicians she might have angered with her point of view?'

She examines the tips of her fingers. 'It is possible. My mistress is outspoken and fortunate that a husband doesn't censor her actions.'

'Mrs Forbes...' I pause. 'Do you believe she is still alive?'

She wobbles a little on her feet. 'Why do you say that?'

'It is just that everyone I talk to refers to her in the past tense and you do not.'

'No, if she had died,' she says, folding her arms defensively, 'with no parents, and the rest of her family dead, I would be informed as her next-of-kin.'

Again, I consider the possibility that I am Miss Earnshaw's next of kin. It is strange that the housekeeper has no knowledge of this but knew my name on my first visit?

'And I am still very much expecting her return,' she continues. 'It is only a matter of time; she just needs to find her way home. She said she would come back...' The housekeeper gulps and shifts from one foot to another. 'I had never seen her so distressed.'

'You saw her again? On the night she went missing?' I lean forward, absorbing every word, every detail on her face.

Her fingers pick up a loose thread on her skirt and pull on it; the whole seam begins to unravel.

'You didn't tell the police this?'

'No, she made me promise.'

'What happened?'

'She was only here briefly.' Her eyes flicker from me to the hallway. 'She was flustered, kept talking about redemption. She took something from her desk and left.'

'What did she make you promise?'

'That if someone asked, I hadn't seen her since she attended Blackham House. I couldn't tell if she was frightened or angry. She didn't want anyone to know of her actions, that's for sure.'

'Can you work out if anything is missing?' I hope she doesn't mention the diary I took.

'No, whatever it was, she hid it from me too. Nothing looks out of order.'

My heart pumps harder in my chest. 'Did you argue?'

'No!' Her answer is strained, her eyes watering again at the memory. A solitary tear runs down her cheek. 'She is my world … everything to me. I would do anything to protect her, even if it means protecting her from herself.'

I fidget in my seat, undecided about what to believe. Something still rings false about her words.

'Did she have a special companion? I understand this is a personal question.'

She dabs at her face with a handkerchief from her apron pocket. 'Men are interested, of course. They come and go, trying their luck. You always get moths around light, and she presents a challenge to be conquered. But she is too strong for them – and does not love or trust easily. I would say Mr Witherfield is her only long-standing male acquaintance.'

I jolt at the mention of this new contact, of someone else I can ask. 'Mr Witherfield? Would you give me his address?'

The housekeeper hesitates. 'This is the only calling card she has not thrown away. Miss Earnshaw keeps it in her important papers, so I know it means something.'

She moves and takes out a small ivory box from a drawer in the desk and copies the details onto a piece of notepaper. She hands it to me, and I put it into my reticule before she changes her mind.

'He lives in Camden. I'm not sure what help he might be to you. He's getting on in years now – knew Miss Earnshaw from when she was a young 'un.'

'Have any men called here since her disappearance?'

'I've not seen her last companion. He must be keeping a low profile; the attention would not be good for his career.'

'So, there is a lover?' A question such as this would have embarrassed me not so long ago.

'Naturally, but they inevitably end. I am the only real constant in her life.'

'Did anybody else visit?'

'A few reporters, they delight in any potential scandal. So far, they have nothing and leave disappointed.' She shifts again, her body language stiff and awkward. I sense a spring ready to uncoil in anger, or perchance, it is another emotion entirely that simmers. 'I don't wish Miss Earnshaw's good name to be dragged through the mud anymore.' She wrings the handkerchief still balled up in her hand. 'And I will do my utmost to ensure the papers stop tarnishing her reputation with gossip and lies.'

I nod in understanding, urging her on. There is a sadness, a notion of regret about her I hadn't noticed before.

'The detective in charge is nice, but a little naïve. I'm not sure if they put their top people on the case. I only want to do the best by Miss Earnshaw – she is like my own family.'

I instantly recall the detective with the kind face and wedding band. His possible lack of experience masked by his eagerness to solve a mystery.

Then she brings her hand to her mouth, her eyes closing briefly. 'Ah yes, I do recall another visitor. Not a reporter, but a well-dressed older man. He didn't leave his name.'

The description could fit anyone, even my own father.

Chapter 29 ~ Lost and Found

Ivy ~ Blackham House, 12th December.

Laughter erupts from the kitchen as I approach with the breakfast dishes from the dining room. It is Mrs Higgins. I know her voice well now, but I have never heard her laugh. This is new. I assume it's Hannah she is talking to, but as I enter quietly, I am surprised that a stranger answers. He is a tall man, with deep brown hair slicked into a sharp side parting. His pale complexion illuminates his eyes, making them appear a bright jade green, piercing and alert in the dim morning light.

'I told you not to trust that thief.' The stranger's accent sounds local. 'He gets his produce half-price round the back of the docks... No wonder you've been getting dodgy food, turning rotten.'

'Yes, but they were good enough for a while, and the extra bob or two came in handy.' Mrs Higgins replies.

'Nah, best leave him be. He's a scoundrel through and through. Not worth saving the money. Pay the full amount, then you don't have to worry about upsetting them upstairs.'

'Thank you, James. You always know what's right.'

When she sees me, Mrs Higgins quickly takes her hand away from the man's arm: a tender gesture. Usually, she is a force to be reckoned with, but I sense I am intruding on a private moment.

Flustered, she busies herself with straightening up the utensils on the table. 'Now, Mr Bancroft, I must find my turtle-soup recipe; I will be needing it soon. Christmas will be here before you know it.' She starts rifling through a drawer, but the man stays still, taking me in.

When I give him a polite smile, I suddenly have a feeling that I have met him before, but the moment quickly passes for it cannot be - I have never left Sussex. We are about the same age by a few years. He looks to be in his late twenties and is dressed in the crisp black and white uniform of a butler. He certainly seems at home in the kitchen and has the assurance of someone much older.

'There you are, Ivy. How are you getting on with the morning chores – all done? Are both Lady and Mistress Blackham looked after?' Mrs Higgins asks.

'Yes, Lady Blackham is settled.' I try to ignore the scrutiny of the stranger. 'I aired her room again, but it's still stuffy. She requested poached fish for her lunch … and when I checked on the mistress, she said she would like some tea sent up with some rusks in an hour.'

Mrs Higgins sighs as she looks at the full plate of bacon and eggs that I've brought back down, now solidified, on the china plate. 'Oh dear, I see the young mistress is still off her food. I don't know why she won't take a Beecham pill; they've always worked for me.'

I wait, expecting an introduction to this new man, but nothing is forthcoming.

'What are you gawping at? Best be getting on. Chop-chop,' she says, shooing me off.

'Good morning, Ivy. All well with you today?' The man asks me.

He speaks as though we know each other, but I still have no memory of him or can recall him being spoken of, other than the ramblings of Lady Blackham mentioning a butler.

I falter, gauging that all is not what it should be. 'Where is the butter? Perhaps I could make the mistress some simple toast.' Is all I can think of to say.

'What a daft question.' Mrs Higgins raises her eyes in mock disbelief. 'It's in the blue and cream pot in the pantry. But don't waste your time; the Mistress won't eat it either.' She looks to the man. 'Honestly, a brain like a sieve this one. We should keep an eye on her.'

He looks like he might. His smile disappears, replaced with an alertness in his features – a quiet intelligence. I know have seen this look before. I am almost able to place it when the expression vanishes under a perfect mask of composure. The arrival of another servant to help should make me feel relieved, but I am not.

Hannah walks in behind me carrying a silver tray, with empty egg cups and breadbasket.

I watch her, interested in judging her response to this new man in the house.

'Morning, James,' she says with a nod.

She does not seem the least bit surprised. But underneath her normal bravado, her step quickens and her shoulders tense at his appraisal. He strikes an imposing figure, taking up much of the kitchen space, his confidence even more so than his physique.

'Don't you mean Mr Bancroft, Hannah?' He snaps. 'And I notice the rugs haven't been beaten yet. Is it not usual for us to do this on a Saturday?'

She does not answer his question. Instead, she puts the tray on the table and looks down, scuffing her feet on the stone-tile floor. 'I'm glad to hear Ivy moved up to the attic, Mr Bancroft.' Her manner is submissive, but there is a defiance in her tone.

'Don't be disappointed, Hannah.' He straightens his white cuffs. 'It will be your turn one day. Until then, Cook needs you down here. You do need her, don't you, Mrs Higgins?' He asks.

'I certainly do,' she replies, nodding in earnest.

I leave them to it. Slipping out into the scullery, I hear Hannah continue the conversation with minimal words, which is unlike her. Peering behind the curtain under the sink, the pair of shoes I asked Mrs Higgins about, which she claimed belonged to William are no longer there. Where has Mr Bancroft been until now, and did he disappear around the time Miss Earnshaw went missing?

I go upstairs to the entrance hall and rearrange the fresh flowers I had brought yesterday, but I am disappointed to find the stems are going brown and the petals are wilting already.

Hannah passes behind me on her way to the library. I try to make eye contact, but instead, she looks through me as if I don't exist. 'Hannah?'

She cocks her chin towards me. 'It won't be long until you leave too. Whether you want to or not, you'll be gone soon.' She draws up close to my face. I think she is about to apologise, but her eyes darken. 'Just keep the mistress's dresses in good order, for they will be handed down to me when you're nowhere to be seen.'

The next day, I am scrubbing the tiles of the entrance hall when screams erupt from the basement. The noise splinters through the silent house, interrupting the sound of the rhythmic rough bristles, working back and forth on the mosaic patterns. I drop the brush beside the bucket of water and rush downstairs. Mrs Higgins is in the centre of the kitchen, shouting at something in the corner.

A cat slinks low, sprinting across the room. It crouches down under the table, a deep rumbling growl emanating from its throat to ward off Mrs Higgins. In its mouth is a mass of black and white feathers. The crushed magpie moves, trying to flex its wings within the grasp of strong teeth. The animal makes another guttural sound, unwilling to part with its prize, and darts under a cupboard.

I recognise Mr Grey instantly. 'Hello, puss, what do you have there?' I crouch down, attempting to coax the cat towards me.

'Get that creature out of here!' Mrs Higgins spits.

'It is only a gift for you, Mrs Higgins.'

'Don't be deceived, Ivy … this is no present.'

I stand back up. 'But that's what cats do; it's a form of affection. Or else he is hungry. Must only live off scraps, poor thing.'

Mr Grey has become slimmer since I last saw him, his ribs now poking through his fur. Winter is unforgiving to us all. I bend down again, clicking my fingers, clucking with my tongue, anything to cajole the cat out and away from the cook, who is getting more distressed by the minute.

'I don't want that thing in my kitchen. If Mr Bancroft finds out about all this, there will be hell to pay.'

The cat tentatively walks towards me but then slinks away when Mrs Higgins shouts again.

'Get the broom, Ivy!'

I reach for the broom when the bird is dropped next to my feet, expectation in the cat's amber eyes. 'A gift for me?' I exclaim. I would laugh if it were not for the angry expression on Mrs Higgins's face.

The gesture is touching, but I am also horrified. The bird has one eye missing and a red-stained belly; all the soft white feathers are covered in blood. It isn't dead yet and the small body twitches on the stone floor, clinging cruelly on to life.

'Can you save the magpie?' Mrs Higgins edges forward.

The question is strange. Usually, a cook wouldn't have cared for something as trivial as a half-eaten bird, especially when she serves up plenty of pigeon pies for dinner.

'Why, do you want it for a pie?' It is the only reason I can think of.

'Of course not.' She widens her eyes at me in disgust. 'I just don't want any trouble.'

'It would be kinder for the cat to finish it off. It's almost dead already.'

Hannah enters the kitchen carrying a bundle of bedsheets. She screams at the sight, and in one fluid motion, the cat snaps the bird back up in its mouth again and scurries out through the open scullery door and into the garden, leaving behind specks of blood and a single ink-black feather.

'Clean up your gift, Ivy, and the mess it made. Make sure you use plenty of carbolic acid,' barks Mrs Higgins with her arms folded. 'I want no trace of this, and next time you see a cat, for God's sake, chase the creature away from the house. No more feeding it, do you hear? We have enough to worry about without upsetting him out there.'

'Who, William?' I ask, puzzled. 'I know he looks after the magpies, but I'm sure he would understand. The cat is only hungry – he can't help himself. It's only one bird after all and there are so many in the garden.'

Mrs Higgins's face is flushed. She dabs her apron against her forehead, removing the copious beads of sweat created from the ordeal. 'Don't think I don't know about you leaving saucers of milk out. Nothing good came out of trying to tame anything wild.'

I step outside in case the cat is waiting for me, but there is no sign of him. Only the distressed screeches of the birds, crying out to each other in the trees.

It is Thursday night, and I am restless, pacing the wooden boards of the attic. The days' activities, although tiring, have left me het up, especially with the appearance of Mr Bancroft. I am sure Mrs Higgins and Hannah didn't mention him before, but even after a couple of days, it is hard to imagine the house without him. My mind must be playing tricks on me again. Was he here from the beginning, but I missed him in passing? As I pull on my nightdress, my skin is itchy from where I have perspired under my simple cotton shift during the heavy chores. I long for the soft cotton chemises I left behind in my countryside home. This is the first time I have ever felt exhaustion like this, but still my thoughts race.

I couldn't eat much of dinner. Instead, I've brought an apple up with me in case my appetite returns. Sitting down on the bed, I dread falling asleep, yet I also fear to stay awake. The attic is not a comforting space. I would rather let tiredness wash over me than wait for the voices or the dreams to come. They follow me wherever I sleep.

My dreams about Miss Earnshaw keep tormenting me. Could she be dead? As well as the unthinkable of what may have happened, disappointment rises. The finality of never seeing her again means that unless I forge a different plan to stay in London, my time has run out. With no money, I would be forced to return home, to an asylum, or to the grip of Mr Whitlock. My hopes of finding my mother's family and becoming a botanist would be nothing but a childish escapade. If I stay, I could permanently become like Hannah, lost in a life of service, always one step from poverty. Either option leaves me cold, but I will do anything not to return home.

I'm being selfish. I have made a promise to discover the truth about Miss Earnshaw and my mother and shouldn't falter in that task, yet the tangled web I find myself in is becoming harder to understand. If she has passed over, could she be using her spiritual powers to contact me? Despite my usual logic I am starting to believe she is haunting my dreams and this house, returning from the afterlife to avenge her death.

I entertain playing the knocking game that I've heard spiritualists use to speak to the dead, but if the prospect is real, I am frightened by the consequences. My mother always said ghosts do not exist, so I have never considered that the strange occurrences that happen when I am alone are linked to the afterlife. Neither have I confronted or asked anything of them. But if I did validate them, would they be free and develop greater in their substance?

Taking my sketchbook from the cupboard, the need for a distraction from these troubling thoughts spurs me to draw. Not my usual plants, but birds. To release my unease and frustration onto the pages, to purge myself of these negative emotions. I turn the gas lamp up higher and choose a suitable piece of charcoal. The creative process takes over, a welcome respite from my torrent of worries. The movements come with ease, turning the page from white to a pattern of black marks. I work until the light dims; this is what I've missed. This connection to letting go, becoming totally consumed, immersed in the action of creating something out of nothing.

I sit back. I hadn't decided what to draw before I started, but now the subject is obvious. Black and white, black and white; the pattern repeated until the whole page is full of miniature birds, all magpies, each one with a single black eye peering back at me. Like the one the cat dropped at my feet.

Flicking back through my sketches since arriving in London, all the illustrations start to merge. Apart from the drawings of the orange-thorned plants in the garden, they are all birds: grey, black, and white. They all belong to the crow family. *Corvids.*

Is it any wonder they invade my thoughts, for they surround the house day and night. I put the sketchbook down. The realisation is unsettling: how much my art has changed from the light botanicals to these dark illustrations. How did I not see the progression? But it is these images that exist inside me now; these are the ones I need to express and release.

Finally, the exhaustion of the day washes over me, and I crawl into bed as sleep calls. The slow breath of relief comes easily. My mind is quiet; I have escaped the voices. But then they come, slowly, softly at first, but getting louder as I hover between consciousness and sleep. This time, murmurs from a man and a woman. These sounds must be real and not just in my mind.

I turn my head in the dim light. The noise seems to travel up through the fireplace, the voices rising and falling, agitated. The wind howls in the chimney, but the cover has fallen away from the earpiece – a direct link to the mistress's room. I get out of bed and press my ear against it, a female gasp and a moan. Instinctively, I am relieved to hear that these are not the voices that usually seek me out at night. But my blood still runs cold. They are primal, private sounds like an animal makes in heat; the master must be a brute indeed.

The open grate looks ominous, but I am too unnerved to light a fire. I quickly close the cap and return to the bed, covering my ears to block it all out, but the muffled groans remain. And as I chase sleep again, my mind wanders … and it is my bare neck that the master grazes with his lips, the moans slipping out of my mouth as I abandon myself in his embrace.

I sit up, startled, in the middle of the night. Shocked at my vivid dream, for I certainly do not desire the master like Hannah does. My mind is not my own, either waking or asleep. I berate myself in the freezing room for losing control of my thoughts and for not lighting a fire. The curtains are blowing, and I struggle to remember why I would have opened the window. I get up and close the sash firmly shut. Through the water-streaked glass, lightning flashes, slicing across the sky, and the nearby branches thrash about in the wind. I stumble back to bed, disgruntled and tired.

When I wake, I can tell by the weak sunlight that it is morning. My body is drained and exhausted from the disturbed night. The room feels off, somehow – dampness lingers in the air, and the sound of birds cawing in the garden is louder than usual. I roll over to face the window with apprehension. The sash has opened again, revealing the storm still raging outside; the curtains hang heavy, sodden with water; pools of liquid seep onto the wooden floor. A single magpie perches on the windowsill, as large as a crow. It opens its beak and cries out a harsh, sharp call before flying off into the slate-grey sky.

One for sorrow.

My stomach aches with hunger. I reach for the apple on my bedside table from the night before and my body recoils. The red skin is rotten: frantic spores of mould cover one side; and on the other gapes a hole the colour of a ripe bruise, a mix of purple and green, where something has eaten the flesh from the inside. Creamy maggots wriggle out of the soft pulp and fall onto the wood. Bile rises in my throat, and I retch over the bed.

Chapter 30 ~ Thorns

Ivy ~ Blackham Garden, 15th December.

Beneath the large, ugly chestnut tree in the garden, an odd assembly of dead leaves has appeared overnight: clumps of holly and twigs are woven together like funeral wreaths. There are even a few sprigs of rosemary, traditional for remembrance. They pile up near the remains of a magpie, which is slowly decomposing. I assume it's the same bird that the cat, Mr Grey, had run off with. I had only come out to calm my stomach after seeing the rotten apple, but now I am feeling even worse.

William comes to stand quietly beside me, looking at the strange scene. 'What is all this? Did you do it?' I ask, turning to face him, but he keeps his eyes on the ground.

'It's the birds. They are grieving the loss of one of their own.'

Disbelief flares up inside my chest. 'Don't be so ridiculous. Are you saying that birds created these patterns themselves? They are not capable of such an act.' I count at least six magpies watching me with interest from the lowest tree branch above me. I doubt my question already.

'It's a mark of respect. Birds can grieve too,' he mutters.

'Then why don't you clean up the bird or bury it?'

'I wouldn't dare – not my business. When the magpies group like this, 'tis their own parliament they are holding. The garden has its own rules.'

I am about to walk away when I get the courage to ask more: 'Is that why this garden is left to its own devices without a nurturing hand to guide it? There is nothing but thorny plants and diseased trees?' I point to the yews and the shrubs with the blue-green long, narrow leaves, remembering the sharp pain of a bright orange thorn on my fingertip.

He looks around the garden, taking out his pipe and filling it with tobacco from a small wooden box. He strikes a match and pulls on the pipe to make it take light. After he finally exhales, he clears his throat but still does not speak.

'They are most certainly not native to this area.' My voice sounds shrill in the early morning quiet. 'You're the gardener here. Surely, at least you must know where they came from?' I push again for any answer that might be useful in some way.

'Only planted what Lord Blackham brought back with him from Egypt.' He motions his pipe towards the shrubs. 'They were wrapped in damp sacking from the boat; if the garden wants it, it grows.'

A rush of adrenaline quickens my heartbeat. 'They have settled here from another country?' I ask, forgetting all else in the moment. 'It cannot be possible. Do you know its proper name?' I desperately want to examine the jagged leaves again, but not in front of William. Such a study might aid my application to the Royal College of Science.

'Nope,' he replies, shaking his head, as he looks at me slowly, 'I don't concern myself with names.'

A chill brushes my neck and slips down between my shoulder blades. I shake it off, wishing I had brought my shawl outside. 'How has it survived in this climate? Surely it is tropical and unnatural for such a species to grow within British soil and in winter without a glass house?'

'True, they don't care for the company of others.' He takes another drag on the pipe, the small puffs of smoke he exhales rise above him.

'Whatever do you mean – what are they?'

'Nothing survives around them, but they seem happy enough. Lord Blackham called them Victory plants, after Master Victor. They grow in strength in all weathers, and no weeds go near them, so they live up to their name.'

'But why are they here? There are no other exotic plants, or much else apart from the roses.'

He coughs and clears his throat again. 'Protection. These grounds are valuable, both above and below. We don't like intruders. So, what's the reason you're here, is more the question?' He turns on his heel, his milky grey eyes roaming my face; there is little kindness behind the pale irises.

The wind picks up, reminding me of the time. Someone will be searching for me, unhappy with my absence.

'I came out hoping to find a few snowdrops for Mistress Blackham. She is unwell, and I hoped they might give more cheer to her room.' It is true in a sense; snowdrops represent the ability to overcome challenges in life, but I instantly regret my flimsy excuse. Of course, I had already admitted there was no such thing out here. I do not mention my gut reaction to the rotten apple. My weakness is my own burden I do not wish to share.

'Flowers?' he mutters. 'Best get them elsewhere, nothing much else is alive in this garden.'

'So, what is your purpose then?' The words are out of my mouth before I can catch them.

He pauses and notes the lack of colour and design as if noticing for the first time. 'I have my jobs to do, but growing flowers is not one of them.'

'But even the roses, don't they need cutting back?'

A firm shake of his head is my reply. 'The roses live on without my hand. The rain kills off what insects it needs to. It's the acid from the smog. Nature always finds a way to protect what's precious.'

'What about the door behind them?'

He furrows his thick eyebrows together. 'I wouldn't go poking about in them thorns. As I said, the garden does not like to be intruded on.'

'What a funny thing to say,' I reply, but he remains unaffected by my comment.

'Best you get along now. I believe Mistress Blackham needs you.'

Something about the way he looks at me. It is a considered gaze, how a tailor might measure a customer for a new dress.

'Mistress Angelica?'

'No, the real mistress – Lady Blackham, upstairs.'

William's attention is drawn to the second-floor windows before he turns without saying goodbye, his shoulders hunched as he limps away towards the scullery door, trailing a thin line of vapour in his wake.

'I best attend to her, then,' I say, more to myself as he is already out of earshot.

I leave the dead bird along with the wreaths and hurry back into the house, following in his footsteps. I am hardly a moment behind him, but I find the kitchen empty.

Knocking on Lady Blackham's door, I steel myself for the foul and stagnant room.

'Enter!' Shouts a voice from within. Lady Blackham is sitting in her chair by the fireplace, counting the items from her jewellery collection on a tray. There are at least thirty different rings and pendants; gold, silver, and sparkling jewels; a small fortune. I try not to inhale; noticing for the first time the stench of the chamber pot is almost bearable. I had discreetly left a bowl of the crushed herbs and rose petals I had collected from the apothecary on a side table, and their scent was working hard against the odour.

'Ivy, I was just thinking about you.'

She pushes a ruby ring over her knuckle above her gold marriage band and admires it. 'I need you to collect a package from the jeweller's shop at once – it should be ready by now. I expect my new brooch this same evening, no matter what. It is most urgent, and I will be extremely displeased if you fail me.' She scrutinises my face. 'You don't want to displease me, do you?'

I find I am cocking my head, as I consider what would happen if she was vexed and the memory of Edith's criticisms return. I correct my posture as her steely eyes narrow in concentration on me. 'No, Lady Blackham, I will leave now.'

'Do not disappoint me, Ivy.' She points at me with a single bony finger. 'This brooch is to be my newest treasured possession.'

I run down the servant stairs and stop outside the kitchen, to catch my breath. I see Mr Bancroft sitting at the table cleaning the silver: expensive items I am not allowed to touch. He is so much a part of the house that it is difficult to imagine the place without him. All those days when he was absent seem to have never existed. No one commented on it, not even the mistress. It was like he had been forgotten and then remembered. At least I think that's the case. I am doubting myself more and more.

The sensation of unravelling pulls at my mind, and my reasons for staying are becoming confused. First, it was Miss Earnshaw, but now I also struggle with the need to take care of Mistress Blackham, for who else would perform that duty if I left? My mother had brought me up to be a companion for her. It was a natural role for me, and one I missed, but my gut warns me to be wary.

Everywhere I look, the laws of nature seem to be off balance; decay has become accelerated. My revulsion of the maggots in the rotting apple still holds the power to make me gag. The fruit, the flowers – life does not last long in this house.

I should head to the sanctity of the vicarage, but I have become part of something larger than myself, and the thrill of the danger that stalks this place numbs my grief. If I go now, I shall have failed to find any connection to my lost relative. I will have nothing, no answers, no life of my own to return to and Mother will be even further out of my reach, with no one to tell me of her past and keep her memories alive; the pain would swallow me whole.

Mr Bancroft looks up and sees me loitering in the corridor, a questioning look in his green eyes.

'I have to go to the market square right away,' I say, entering the kitchen. 'Lady Blackham has a package that needs picking up from the jeweller, and I am sure the mistress would appreciate more flowers to brighten her room.'

'A kind thought,' he answers. 'You appear to have the ability to read minds. Would you like me to accompany you? I've some business of my own to attend to.'

'No, I am quite fine, thank you.' I am about to fetch my cloak when he clears his throat.

'It was not a suggestion, Ivy. We will go together in fifteen minutes. Why don't you run along and ask your mistress if there is anything else she needs? You wouldn't want to waste time going backwards and forwards with all the chores still to do.'

He watches me as he continues to polish the tarnished silver with a rag, his hands working the candlesticks with a practised rhythm. His tone is friendly enough, and to an outsider, nothing would have been amiss, but something queer vibrates under the surface of our conversation.

'As you please, Mr Bancroft.' My weak attempt to stay confident with my head held high almost falters as I exit the kitchen.

I find the mistress sitting up in bed looking pale, with shadows under her eyes. She looks worse than usual, shedding the persona of a popular socialite and becoming fragile, like a cast-off, forgotten doll.

'I am getting some fresh flowers.' I point to the existing display by her bedside. I had expected they might survive at least the day, but they stand limp already. 'Unfortunately, there is nothing in the garden I can use. Is there anything else you would like from the market?' My voice is unnaturally cheerful. It sounds false, even to me.

'Thank you, Ivy. I don't seem to be myself these last few days. Would you cancel any commitments this afternoon?'

'There are no appointments today,' I reply.

She places a hand to her head. 'Oh, I am confused. I didn't sleep well again, and I cannot face the food from the kitchen.' She points to the plate of bread and cheese on the bedside table.

The loneliness emanating from her resonates with me, but her unwell appearance is worrying. 'Is it possible you might be with child? It is not unusual to have sickness during the early months.' I am hesitant with the question, but the reason for her illness could make sense.

She laughs, but the sound is hollow. 'Don't be absurd, Ivy. I would know, and besides … I can't be, much to the disappointment of Lady Blackham.' She raises her eyes to the ceiling as if even speaking the old woman's name might summon her. 'No doubt she would like nothing more than to add another Blackham to this sad house.' She sighs. 'But you must excuse me, Ivy. I am out of sorts.'

Her delicate fingers wave me away, as if our conversation is too hard. 'Please get some more resilient blooms. This house seems to kill everything off.'

Mr Bancroft is waiting by the back door. He is a clean-cut man, and no doubt uses his looks to his advantage. Hannah watches with her arms folded. If only she knew this was not my doing and that I would swap places with her if I could. I will, of course, pay for this unwanted attention later with her small acts of petty revenge.

Three days ago, she had left the scullery door open with one of Mrs Higgins's rabbit pies uncovered on the table waiting to be cooked. A couple of brave magpies had ventured inside and hacked into the pastry with their sharp beaks until the kitchen was covered in crumbs and raw, half-eaten flesh. Mrs Higgins was livid and blamed me for being careless, but I knew the act was deliberate on Hannah's part. The possibility for friendship is fading.

As I close the door behind us, she looks in our direction, but I realise she is not looking at me with venom but instead staring past me, outside beyond the threshold, her shoulders hunched as if all the pressures of the world weighed on her. I get a glimpse of what she might look like as an old woman, wizened and frail.

Mr Bancroft and I turn away from Blackham House and begin to walk along the street side by side, awkwardly. I carry my shopping basket to me, unsure if I should start the conversation with a trivial comment about the weather or housekeeping chores.

'I am glad you came to join the staff.'

His smooth voice interrupts my thoughts, deciding for me, and his compliment takes me by surprise.

'As you are probably aware, some of the staff left, and we were struggling to cope without the help of extra hands.'

He doesn't mention his own absence, which is interesting. It is peculiar how everyone acts as though he has been in the house the entire time. But where had he been?

'I hear you make a fair effort at your work, and it's good for Hannah to have other company besides Mrs Higgins.' He laughs. 'My mother isn't always the easiest to get along with.'

I stop mid-step. 'Your mother? You are her son?' My voice creeps an octave higher. How could I have missed this connection?

'Yes, are you shocked?' He stands by my side, a half-smile playing on his lips, clearly enjoying my discomfort.

'A little,' I answer. But now it makes perfect sense. How she quietly dotes on him, using his first name. I consider the idea: perhaps they do share similarities, the same sharp eyes and dry wit. 'But you have different surnames?'

He puffs out his chest proudly. 'The butler before me was called Bancroft. It is somewhat of a tradition left over from the late Lord Blackham. The name comes with the uniform.'

'You grew up in the house?'

'Yes, for a time ... and also overseas.' He motions for us to cross the street towards Regent's Park. 'My mother is loyal to the family and will follow them anywhere. Grateful, I think, for letting me stay, when other people would have sent her to the poorhouse without hesitation.'

'Your father?'

'That is an indelicate question, Ivy, even for you.' He clears his throat before continuing to speak. 'He was not around; my mother was never married.' He flicks an imaginary speck of lint from his black woollen coat. 'Perhaps now you might understand why we take our roles so seriously. The people of Blackham House are no ordinary family. I will go to the greatest lengths to ensure I serve them well.'

I examine his profile as we walk together. He is a hard man to read. I have another sense of déjà vu about his features, similar to when I first set eyes on him. But he does not notice. He is looking off into the distance, carried away with his words, his memories.

'And since the incident of the woman who unfortunately went missing, deciding who to trust can be a difficult task.' He turns his head, his sombre eyes meeting mine.

Now I know where this is leading. My dress dampens under my arms even in the cold weather, like a child who learns they have been discovered stealing and awaits the punishment to come.

His measured footsteps slow down. We are getting to the heart of the reason for this walk.

'I understand you have been asking questions about Miss Earnshaw?'

My breathing quickens. He tips his hat to another servant striding past from a neighbouring house. To a passing observer, our stroll might appear innocent, as if we are stepping out together.

He moves closer, still with the acceptable distance of a gentleman, but his words invade my space.

'Why do you want to find out so much about Miss Earnshaw? Do we have an amateur sleuth in the house? Do you work for the papers?'

He is mocking me. Has he discovered who I am, trying to uncover something the police have missed? How arrogant I must seem, or perhaps merely naïve.

'There was an article about her in the newspaper.' I try to conceal the slight tremor in my voice.

'I heard you could read,' he snorts. 'Her disappearance is deeply sad and a mystery to everyone. It is such a shame the detective dropped the case.'

'He has?'

'Yes, didn't you know?' I see the faint trace of a smirk on his lips? 'He called round yesterday. They have dismissed their line of questioning. It was only ever Detective Spencer who was pursuing the enquiry, wasting everyone's time. The police now believe she ran away and doesn't wish to be found, or she succumbed to an unfortunate event after the party. Either way, without the identification of a body – alive or dead – they are no longer continuing with the investigation. Not enough evidence or funds, apparently.'

I am disappointed and he knows it. I had imagined the detective solving the mystery with my help, me playing a small role in the success. But I didn't even have the courage to tell him about the bird brooch Hannah had hidden away. How do I dare imagine I can succeed where others more qualified than me have failed? But my instinct continues to insist this is not the end of the matter. Besides, without enough money for a deposit for bed and board, I cannot leave. I would still rather work as a maid than marry Mr Whitlock, and I have yet to take a cutting from the Victory plant for my studies.

But still, I am sick to my stomach with this new information. What if I am making one mistake on top of another, and how can Miss Earnshaw's housekeeper be so positive she is alive when I fear she's dead? My mind spins round and round like the painted horses on a carousel.

'Does that upset you, Ivy? Were you hoping she would turn up? Would you still work in our house without a mystery to solve?'

His voice, deep and clipped, draws me out of my private thoughts. He has no patience, or is he teasing me? Again, his mannerisms give nothing away. He tilts his head to one side. This time his closed smile appears genuine, but I know it could be a deception, just as false as his detachable shirt cuffs.

The threads of despair pull tighter. I had not acknowledged the hope I had put in the detective to uncover something new. Can I still leave if there are more secrets to unravel, if I know in my gut that they are responsible? The certainty flows through me. It is in my blood, every heartbeat. Miss Earnshaw is my family; I cannot abandon her. How much evidence do I need before they reopen the case?

He continues to stride forward confidently, shoulders back. We fall into step, our rhythm the same, mirroring each other. 'Anyway, Ivy, let's not dwell on such sad stories. We must enjoy our time out together; who knows when we will next get the chance?'

He offers the crook of his elbow for me to take. His eyes bore into mine again, and again something familiar shifts inside of me. The action would be unmannerly to refuse in public and would cause more problems if I did, so I reluctantly place my hand around his arm. A small gesture, but we both know it's compliant, submissive. He brings his other palm across as if to lock me close into his body and strokes my glove gently with the tips of his fingers as we walk. My skin crawls and I suffer in silence, just as I did the first time a man touched me.

Chapter 31 ~ The Jewellery Shop

Ivy ~ Bond Street, 15th December.

'Make sure you pick up the package for Lady Blackham. Ask for Mr Richmond himself. She will be upset if we do not present it to her today.' Mr Bancroft passes me a coin. 'And get a cab home.' Is he concerned about my safety or the value of the parcel for the old lady?

We arrive outside the jewellery shop on Bond Street. I bought the flowers on the way; a mixture of pink and white heather nestled together safely inside my basket.

'Tell my mother to keep my dinner warm. I may be some time,' he says, striding off.

I watch him disappear down a side street. Where does he go? The mystery bothers me. So far, I have discovered nothing but a strange house and staff who keep leaving.

The smell of the flowers brings me back to the present moment; fresh and delicate. They are pretty, and despite the strained walk with Mr Bancroft, I am in a much better mood, especially now he has left.

The jeweller's window display is filled with an assortment of gold and silver rings, necklaces, and bracelets. I will purchase something to complement my mourning ring, but then I remember I am living off a maid's wage, and these items are now beyond my reach.

The bell rings as the door opens. Inside are three ladies, all in velvet and silk, taking their time perusing the cabinets. A portly man with a shiny black waxed moustache stands behind the counter. Dressed in a rich blush-pink jacket complete with a shimmering blue waistcoat trimmed with black velvet, he reminds me of the woodland jay bird, colourful and astute. Surrounded all day by magpies I have corvids on my mind, and I reprimand myself for the ridiculous notion.

He gives me a quick cursory glance and at once dismisses me as someone who can wait and returns his attention to the wealthier customers. I stand for what seems an age listening to him explaining that the inscription of the word 'Beloved' inside a gold ring refers to the first letter of each gemstone set around the outside. At last, after he explains that the high cost is because the letter d is a diamond, the proprietor looks at me long enough to question my reason for being in the shop.

'Yes?'

'May I speak to Mr Richmond? I believe there should be a package ready for Lady Blackham.'

He leaves his customers discussing the ring and shuffles out of the back doorway, only to return empty handed a moment later. 'I regret that particular piece has not been delivered yet.'

Beyond him, there is a small room filled with a narrow table and two men hunched over working quietly.

'How long will it take? Should I wait?' I wave to an empty corner where I could stand. 'I assumed they made it here in your workshop?' I say puzzled.

'I'm afraid it all depends on the particular goldsmith. My hands are tied.' He makes a theatrical motion of uniting his wrists together in bondage.

My heart skips a beat as I imagine Lady Blackham's cruel eyes fuelled by disappointment. 'I have strict instructions to collect the parcel now. Surely you are the person commissioned to work on the piece?' My patience is already wearing thin.

'Shall we say your mistress took advantage of a unique service we offer only to our most esteemed customers? The Blackhams partake in special requirements, which are unfortunately beyond the realm of this humble shop. We create beauty, but not miracles.' He coughs discreetly into an embroidered handkerchief. 'But naturally, we were able to assist … to marry the process of perfect design and creation. It takes time to achieve perfection. Tell your mistress it will be here tomorrow.'

Already I sense I bore him, and he wants me gone, but I know I must do her bidding or be in trouble. 'Lady Blackham asked specifically for it today. I am not to return without it.'

He emits a long sigh, aware that I'm making a scene. 'I am sure the piece will please her. High quality craftsmanship is our promise. You may wait outside, but I cannot assure you of a time. You would be better off coming back tomorrow.'

Mr Richmond refuses to give any further information and returns to his other customers with a dismissive air.

I catch the eye of his assistant, a tall young man with a sandy mop of curly hair and a plain grey waistcoat, who has appeared from the back room and observed the interaction between us. He waits until the owner is consumed by his conversation before approaching me.

'Can I help you?'

I lower my voice. 'Maybe you heard my predicament? I am at a loss whether to wait or return empty handed.'

He bows his head in conspiracy. 'Well, you could pick it up directly from this shop.' He passes me a thick calling card with the name *Godwin* embossed in gold swirling letters, with the address printed smaller beneath. 'It is not far on foot if you know where you're walking.' His eyes flick across to the front window, 'but it might be better to get a cab, before it gets too murky outside.'

'Thank you, I am much obliged.'

He smiles at me; I assume out of pity. 'Take care, the back streets are not a place to lose your way.'

'Come over here, John, and assist this good woman.' Mr Richmond's voice cuts in. 'She needs a hand mirror at once.'

With an apologetic look, the assistant bids me farewell.

If I leave now, I have just enough time to return before I am needed to serve dinner. It is the master's birthday, and we have polished the silverware especially.

Outside the shop, I call for a hansom cab. 'Drury Lane, please.'

'Sorry, miss, that's not on my route,' states the driver gruffly.

'Why not?' I ask, conscious of the time passing.

'Not a place for a respectful carriage like this. I might lose my wheels or worse!'

He splutters out a laugh with a pipe still suspended between his lips, but he is serious. He calls over to a young boy, perhaps ten years of age. 'The nipper will take you for a small fee. He's fast, so don't take your eyes off him or else you'll find yourself lost.'

The child's face is grimy but eager to help, with only a scarf and no coat, his trousers revealing his pale, thin ankles exposed to the cold.

The address is down a warren of backstreets. I follow the street boy obediently as he swiftly leads me through a maze of narrow passageways and cobbled lanes. I almost lose him and begin to doubt if I have made the right decision. Perhaps returning with nothing would be better than taking my chance on a dreary winter day in a rough part of London.

A distant church chimes three o'clock. The sky is fading to a dull grey; the afternoon is already succumbing to an early dusk. Straining my eyes, I note there are too few streetlamps placed down the street for my liking. With even less light as I venture further on, I pass hunched strangers seeking shelter and entertainment in the narrow pathways. This is a cold, cruel place to be without money, the comfort of a fire, and the safety of a locked door.

Once I've paid him, the young boy motions for me to proceed alone to my destination. He points towards the right side of a narrow passageway. I turn to confirm his instructions, but he has already bolted in the opposite direction, like a rabbit escaping a fox.

The shop has no obvious window display, and I am underwhelmed by its humble presence tucked between two non-salubrious looking establishments. Set back from the street, the building blends into the other worn facades with its peeling black paint and unobtrusive decor.

Checking the address on the calling card once again, this is most definitely not the place one would imagine producing expensive jewels. The window is covered in a thick layer of grime, and I can barely see the outline of furniture inside.

Am I about to become undone by my stubborn nature to admit defeat?

The bell above the door rings with a single chime as I enter. The workshop is tiny compared to the garish decor of the first shop, where there were chairs lining the walls for customers to rest and peruse the jewellery with ease. Here, there are no such seats, only a large workbench occupying most of the space alongside the far room; in contrast to the outside, everything is polished and well kept. To my left, there is a modest mantelpiece with a fire blazing underneath it, and in the corner stands a small display cabinet next to a rhythmically ticking grandfather clock.

Facing me sits a man surrounded by metal tools and a multitude of different sized magnifying glasses, each their silver handles engraved with ornate swirling patterns. My eyes, accustomed to the fading light in the street, now ache inside this bright room where many candles dazzle, burning together in unity. Some are almost melted down to the wick, others look to have been lit within the hour. They cast shadows over the walls, the wax pooling in random shapes on the surfaces.

The jeweller is of slight build, perhaps in his forties, with chestnut-brown hair slicked back and neat mutton-chop whiskers hiding most of his face. He assesses me with intelligent eyes behind a pair of steel-rimmed spectacles and then resumes his position, leaning over what looks like a metal press. His appearance is impeccable; his understated grey tweed suit is finely tailored. This man is misplaced in this area of London, more suited to a gentlemen's club discussing the news with a whisky and a cigar than these backstreets with such abject poverty.

'Good afternoon, sir.' I project my voice with command, hopeful of fulfilling my quest within a matter of minutes. The door closes softly behind me, the dancing flames settling back into their wax creators.

The man is neither friendly nor rude, indifferent to the interruption I bring to his work. A small wooden box next to a sheet of brown wrapping paper sits on the counter. I hope it contains the jewellery for Lady Blackham.

Clearing my throat, I prompt him again to acknowledge me. 'Sir, my name is Miss Granger. I wish to pick up a package which was due for collection at Mr Richmond's shop.

Unfortunately, the parcel had not arrived. The assistant was most helpful in providing your address.' I am still holding the gold-embossed card in my gloved hands. I wave the card at him in the hope of a reciprocal response.

'Indeed,' he replies without looking up.

'You are Mr Godwin, I presume? Is the package ready for Lady Blackham? She is most eager to receive the brooch today.'

He glances up briefly and picks up a different tool before returning to his work. A light tapping noise begins as he crafts a small shape of gold before him. 'The delivery is not scheduled until later … a boy takes them on my behalf. He is fast and able to navigate these back streets with nimble ease, more so than I.' He leans in closer to his work. 'I am he that you seek – but if you will just oblige me one more minute.'

A flurry of tapping occurs before he abruptly stops. Finally, he stands up straight, stretching his back. 'There, it is done – this has been a good day's effort. And now, what else do I have before me?' Taking in my appearance for the first time, he pauses. 'Don't tell me you made the journey here by yourself?'

'A greater inconvenience if I return without the commission.' My response is curt.

He nods again. 'Yes, I am aware that Lady Blackham is exacting in her impatience, but good things come to those who wait, or so they say.'

He puts his tool down and adjusts his spectacles to appraise me further, as he would an unpolished stone. 'I seldom ever receive visitors. Forgive me if I am unpractised in the art of conversation. Would you like some tea?' He smiles. 'I have no housekeeper, but it is a good time for afternoon refreshment. Don't you agree?'

'No, thank you,' I say, taking a step closer to his bench. 'I will not trouble you any more than I must. I mean to return to Blackham House as soon as time permits.'

'As you wish.' He shrugs. 'You are fortunate today. The work is complete. I shall wrap the brooch for you now, a most splendid piece.' He exaggerates his words, raising his thick eyebrows. 'I am sure Lady Blackham will be impressed by your endeavour to unite her with this special creation.'

He senses my agitation to be on my way and motions to the windowpane. 'People rush past my window. What are they rushing for, I ask myself each day? Surely it is an early meaningless death for so many of them.'

His humour is dry and wry, amusing only to himself. I imagine he must lead quite a solitary life. As if reading my mind, he tugs at his embroidered waistcoat, pulling the hem down further.

'Yes, I spend a lot of time here, but I am never alone, not really.' He splays out his hands, indicating the creations across his table.

Looking closer, I comprehend this is no ordinary workshop – the tools differ from the usual workbench. There are no simple hammers and pliers, but metal utensils shaped in an ornate fashion, with spirals and spokes, their handles decorated like carriage wheels. A small crimson velvet wall hanging is displayed behind him with Egyptian hieroglyphics embroidered with gold and silver thread. Beautiful lines of strange shapes surrounded by birds, feathers, and people.

'Mr Godwin, what does your work involve that Mr Richmond cannot accomplish in his?'

He motions for me to come even closer, drawing me in further away from the door. The gold and silver objects lie on a narrow midnight-blue velvet drape, along with an array of colourful gems amidst the black onyx and enamel.

'You are a bright girl. I can see that. There's a fire in your belly; otherwise, you would not be here now, would you? So, what is the answer?'

'I mean to say, there is something unusual about your shop.'

His face lights up. 'Honesty is a trait I respect in a character, along with curiosity. It's what excites me the most. Look around. What do you think is so different?'

A fine breeze traces the nape of my neck, running down between my shoulder blades. I shiver despite the warmth of the fire. 'I see nothing to give a reason why a jeweller would send out for your work and not use his own workshop?'

'Ah, but is it not just about the things you observe…' His eyes widen; the whites of his pupils are startlingly bright, almost feverish. 'It is about what is invisible to most but demands our attention, nonetheless!'

He opens the small wooden box. Inside is a beautiful brooch with many jewels set in a figure of eight; rows of different coloured gemstones are entwined in the unbroken shape, making them stand out against the black enamel. A single lock of silver hair is woven in the centre between the two circles. 'This is the infinity sign.' He traces the figure of eight with his fingertip. 'On and on, with no end. You must ensure this is well looked after – it is a precious piece of mastery.'

'No doubt it is beautiful and will bring comfort to Lady Blackham.' I reply politely.

His expression drops in disappointment. 'The meaning is lost on you. It is not your fault; it is complex.'

His comment irks me. 'Please, enlighten me. What is it I fail to understand?'

Again, a look of mania returns to his eyes. 'Now you raise an excellent point. Maybe, the best question for a person to consider is: what is all around us but not visible?'

'I am not good with riddles. Are you toying with me?' The conversation with this stranger makes me suddenly uncomfortable. 'I should be on my way; I would be grateful for the package if you please.'

He peers at me for a moment in contemplation. 'I've upset you. Again, my apologies; this was not my intention. I forget how much I enjoy the stimulation of youth. But I am afraid I cannot answer your question without a cost, even though I am the keeper of this shop.'

He wraps the wooden box in paper, tying it with string, and then finishes with thick red sealing wax. The image of a bird in flight is imprinted clearly in the centre.

'I propose an exchange if you like. A fair price for knowledge, a sacrifice for the truth.'

The statement hangs in the air between us. The candles create a glow around him. Despite wanting to leave, I am intrigued to understand what he is trying to convey. His voice is gentle, compared to the yelling of people in the street. 'I can tell you my secret in exchange for one of yours.'

'I have no secrets,' I answer at once.

'Everyone does.' He shakes his head, dismissing my answer. 'Besides, I am sure you will want to embrace my jewel of a secret, for it will no doubt change you forever, and that demands a trade of sorts.'

'Nothing you could say would alter me to such an extent. You go beyond yourself, sir.'

His eyes narrow, fixed on me. Still, I am none the wiser as to whether he might be teasing or priming me for something worse.

'But you are wrong. My knowledge has a permanent, irreversible effect. For when you gain wisdom in the face of uncertainty, are you not surrendering?' He hands me the wrapped box. 'Would it not be good to allow a new seed of intelligence to enter your mind?'

Clutching the parcel like a fragile flower, the exchange is not quite over yet. I hold firm. 'I have given you my answer. I have no desire to indulge in your nonsensical games.'

'I am sure your mind will change. You will never be able to return to the ignorant state you inhabited before truth arrived.' He holds his palms up in the air, as if he is a priest giving a sermon. 'The version of you before you walked through my door will be lost forever.'

I wonder if this man is slightly mad, but he continues to talk at me, relishing his single audience of one. His voice becoming louder and more animated, transforming him into a completely different character than the one he projected only moments before. 'See through the window? Do you think they notice me sitting in this building? Do they have the faintest idea of the power they could hold, if only they would step inside my doorway? But they will not look up from their path. They will not see past the dirt on the glass, beyond the humdrum of their lives. No! They fix their eyes on the ground, fear of knowledge holding them back in their comfortable, safe prisons.'

'Very well, tell me, so I can be on my way.' I sigh, but part of me is becoming curious about his strange ramblings. 'Do you claim to hold some sort of magic?'

'Not magic – common tricks are only an illusion. I speak of the ability to travel beyond and return again, to manifest the unthinkable, the previously unattainable, but now possible thanks to my research and skill. Take this mourning piece, for example.'

He picks up a ring with two birds engraved in the gold. 'You are aware that the symbolism in design is not accidental?'

I nod. I already know the meaning of the design I had requested in honour of my mother.

'Here we have the swallows – bonded for life with the wish, just like the birds they will unite again. And note here...' He picks up another piece, a delicate gold chain with a heavy pendant. 'I weave the hair into the design with just the right amount of care and precision. This lock of curls is surrounded by fern under the protection of glass' He continues. 'I am a fan of the botanical, but it is the setting of the jewels that is of utmost importance.'

I almost mention that I too am enchanted by plants, but I don't want to encourage him.

'Once word spreads of my work, my pieces will gain in popularity. It won't be long, I am sure of it, and then I shall move to a more prominent location fit for my status in society.' He replaces the ring and gold chain on the bench and takes out an oval brooch from his waistcoat pocket, cradling it gently in his hand. 'This is one of my new favourites, I carry it with me everywhere. The arrangement of gems framing the woven-hair centrepiece is just like the infinity design for your Lady Blackham.' He pauses for effect, ensuring I am listening. 'This is an extremely special pattern: pearls, opals, rubies, topaz, amethyst, and lapis lazuli. Together, they unite to dazzle and create the most fitting tribute to a loved one who has passed on.'

'It is beautiful,' I admit; despite his eccentricities, his work is talented and divine.

'Thank you. It has a deep meaning and power; a true token of love for its owner.' He returns it carefully to his waistcoat pocket. 'I have applied the knowledge I gained from studying unique, ancient texts about life after death. The type of old, dusty books you will not find in the London library.'

'Not even the museum?'

'Oh no, these are extremely rare and precious. I had the lucky fortune of purchasing them from Lord Blackham when he returned from his last trip to Egypt fifteen years ago. And have not stopped working on their secrets since the day he placed them gently in my hands.' He holds his empty palms towards me as if they are a wonder to behold. At the mention of Lord Blackham, I become rooted to the spot. 'The doomed voyage,' he continues, 'and the loss of a first born. Some might say it was a tragic shame, but their sacrifice was not in vain. The artefacts still arrived in port and were delivered in excellent condition.'

'So, you are the same as Lord Blackham – a collector?' I am shocked by his lack of sympathy. 'But you dismiss the loss of life on the ship with ease. Does the tragedy not affect you or your conscience – benefiting from the cost of others?' I ask sharply.

'Life, death …. it is all one journey. It does not trouble me, I assure you. I collect, but I also set people free. Where are you now on your path?' He taps his chin as if in thought. 'Do you know yourself? The beginning, middle, or perhaps near the end, if there is an end.'

'What is this book called that Lord Blackham brought back?'

'A most valuable piece from the collection of manuscripts with the catchy title: Book of the Dead. The Egyptians far exceed us in their knowledge of the afterlife. The secrets of the hieroglyphics and their magic spells bring my jewellery to life, or should I say, death? They become like cogs in a machine to open up possibilities you can only dream of.'

'Surely, the artefact should be in a museum if the writing is so old and precious and not be used for personal experiments?'

'They are, mostly… Mr Samuel Birch, an Egyptologist of the British Museum, conducted a most splendid translation of what they possessed into English only a few years ago. I enjoyed the exhibition a great deal. But the manuscripts I have in my possession are, well…' He pauses, sucking air through his teeth. 'They are very rare indeed, and only known to a handful; and unfortunately, for Mr Birch, he is not one of them.'

I click my tongue in disgust, for this man is immoral. 'You do not seem to have many scruples regarding the important business of the museum, Mr Godwin.'

'On the contrary. I only deem that my work of creating a more enlightened future is vastly more important than the museums job of preserving the past. I am in the unique position to explore new possibilities and delve into the once closed void of the afterlife, using the spells as they were intended hundreds of years ago. Do you believe in life after death, Miss Granger?'

'Yes, naturally,' I correct my posture, standing taller. 'I am well versed in the Bible and entrust that Heaven waits for those who repent.'

'Ah, but what about the spaces in between? The small fractures that exist between this world and the next ... passageways connecting those who linger? They, the spirits, can return if we help them. With my jewels, we can forge a pathway to the dead, prise open the little cracks and allow them to escape.'

'Do you mean there are spirits trapped in purgatory between Heaven and Earth that are able to come back?'

'Some might refer to it as such a world. The place has been called a multitude of names. I prefer to address it as *beyond the bridge*. They are waiting, so many with no direction. The poor souls cry out to us, but we ignore them, unable to listen, except for a special few.'

My throat constricts. Is this what I hear at night, their voices escaping from my mind? Is it the undead, desperate to continue their journey, trapped without hope, without peace?

'You are playing God – it's blasphemy, the Devil's work. No one is meant to return.' I move to leave, putting the box into my basket beside the heather.

'Wait! Is there no one you would like to reach out to, Miss Granger? A dear one lost forever? There is a sadness about you. I am never wrong about these things.'

My feet hesitate at the door, and I touch my gloved finger automatically, missing the ring that is carefully hidden away in the attic. I cannot wear it during my chores.

He watches, his eyes drinking in the smallest details of my movement.

'Do you own a beloved piece, something containing the hair of the loved one? If you could separate yourself from it for a small amount of time, in exchange, I could give you so much more.'

'My mother...' I murmur.

He exhales loudly, and then steeples his fingers together. 'I am so sorry for your loss, my dear. Death can be so terribly cruel.' His words are sympathetic, genuine. 'What if I told you she's waiting for you? So close to us, that the possibility of reaching out to her will soon exist?'

I snap back to reality, my hand already on the door handle. 'I cannot believe my mother would be anywhere but in Heaven, where she belongs. When it is my time to die, I will reunite with her. It is simply not possible before.' My voice is strong but inside, I am unravelling, the conversation gnawing at me. Layers of grief I had pushed deep down threaten to resurface.

'Quite right. Insufferable loss is a heavy burden to carry. Time will tell, Miss Granger. I do hope you will change your mind. My offer still stands, and I am sure I would not disappoint you with my work. We are almost finished...'

'We?'

'There is a small select group who meet for a common goal.' He places a finger to his lips. 'But I must say no more. Do not let money hinder your decision. It is not fortune I seek, but the surrendering of treasured secrets. I sense you possess more than you know. I am most astute in these matters.'

My mother's woven hair is my only keepsake of her. Could I contemplate handing it to him? Nothing is ever free in this city. What does he presume I have? Can he tell by my face that I hear voices? Can one mad person recognise insanity in another?

'I give you permission to reach for your deepest desire.'

'I do not recall asking you for your permission,' I answer, perplexed at his motive and his sudden closeness.

'Don't forget me. I can take away the loneliness.' He nods low, bending almost to a bow.

'I bid you a good day, Mr Godwin.'

Frowning at his strange suggestion, I open the door. Cold air blasts in from outside, and the candle flames waver in protest. Stepping into the street, I pull the door firmly closed behind me. As I had hoped, the guide boy appears, waiting for another halfpenny tip. As I follow briskly after him, I cannot help but think of Mr Godwin's unusual proposition and a small seed of hope takes root. *What if I could talk to Mother again?* The possibility is madness, and surely against the will of God. And would it truly be her or something else entirely?

Chapter 32 ~ The Trance

Master Blackham ~ Blackham House, 15th December.

Sitting opposite his wife in the dining room, Master Blackham is taken aback by her decline since their arrival in England. Although she is wearing new clothes, dressed in a dusky pink, her collarbone and ribs are clearly outlined through the silk material. He preferred her as she was in Italy: slim but curvaceous. Her once naturally pretty face now reveals smudges of blue under her eyes, and her olive skin has turned a sickly yellow. Surely, he thinks this dire transformation cannot be his fault? After all, he had followed all of the doctor's recommendations and kept her safe from the city's miasma; safe at home ... but perhaps that is the problem.

The sound of shuffling and a hard stick banging on the wooden floor alerts him to their extra guest – his mother's arrival for dinner. He can't help but sigh, not feeling up to her usual critical remarks. He draws a deep breath and forces a thin smile onto his lips as he stands to greet her. 'Mother. How delightful you can join us.'

Lady Blackham raises an eyebrow as the butler pulls out a chair for her and slowly sinks down into her seat at the table. Dressed completely in black taffeta, wearing a single brooch at her throat, she is a sombre contrast to his wife. 'You seem surprised to see me, Alexander. You didn't imagine you could keep me in my room forever? This is my house; you would benefit from remembering that.'

'I do remember, Mother, all the time,' he answers softly.

She straightens out the silver cutlery before her. 'And, I have heard you have been talking to a museum curator?'

Angelica picks up her glass. 'Should we not wish Alex a happy birthday first, before we begin dinner, perhaps with a toast?'

His mother purses her lips. 'I, of all people, do not need reminding that Alexander was born on today's date. I gave birth to him.' She turns her attention back to her son, whilst his wife returns her wine glass to the table, her eyes downcast from the reprimand. 'Now, what is this curator nonsense concerning? Surely you don't believe you have the power to separate the collection?' She scoffs: 'Certainly not while I am alive.'

'Mother, I would never wish to upset you, but you must remember that when Father died, he handed the house over to me, to take care of everything as I deem fit.'

Lady Blackham rolls her eyes. 'And what a disappointment that turned out to be.'

'There is no need to be so—' Angelica interjects.

'Hold your foreign tongue, girl,' snaps Lady Blackham as she glares her into silence. 'You are no more a Blackham than that servant standing in the corner.' She casts her hand towards Hannah. 'And, may I add, this is no business of yours.'

Master Blackham's eyes flash with anger. 'Excuse me, Mother, but Angelica is my wife! As you requested, I remarried, but nothing is ever good enough for you. Must you insult everyone you speak to?'

'Oh, do shut your mouth,' she mutters as she reaches for her wine glass. 'Nothing is ever good enough … because you are not good enough—'

'I have no peace,' bellows a deep, gravelly voice.

The master recoils in his chair as a new voice booms out from somewhere in the room, interrupting the conversation. Hannah clinks the decanter down heavily on the table, abandoning her serving of drinks, and takes a shaky step back.

The master looks aghast at his wife and then at his mother, whose mouth is gaping open in shock. Standing against the wall, Ivy twists her apron string.

'Set me free.' Angelica's lips twitch but the guttural words are not her own.

The master watches in horror as his wife slumps forward onto the table, her arms falling limp by her side. In a sharp spasm of movement, she suddenly throws her head back so violently she could have snapped her own neck. Her expression is vacant, her eyes fixed on the ceiling. The eerie, deep voice returns from her throat. It is not female, but crackles and gasps like the death rattle of a dying patient.

'I am here. I have always been here. I wait whilst the seasons change as people wither and die.'

No one in the room dares to move, their eyes all locked on Angelica's moving lips.

'The innocent birds you believe fly so freely, they speak my language, do my bidding. They bring you all to me, eventually.' The unearthly sound continues. 'This is my house, and my earth. I watch you tread on my soil, walk over my bones, breathe in my air. There is a cost; you must pay for trespassing on my grave; a sacrifice to quench the thirst of the dead.'

His wife growls another horrific noise and then moans, her eyes wide but unseeing before she slumps forward, her limp body falling from the chair and onto the floor.

The doctor, so urgently summoned, is at the front door, handing his coat to the butler as Master Blackham rushes to greet him. He's been waiting for him to arrive, pacing the corridors like a trapped animal.

The two men walk together side by side, muttering in hushed voices as they head to the next floor. Entering his wife's bedroom, Master Blackham notes the look of concern on the face of their maid, Ivy, as she stands beside the bed. Angelica appears to be exhausted after the strain of the dinner only an hour ago. Her complexion, waxy and pale, her hair pulled back in her own half-hearted effort to make herself presentable. Leaning on large plumped up pillows which consume her slender frame, she could pass for a child.

She acknowledges the doctor with a mix of politeness and uncertainty. 'Good evening, Doctor Sheppard. I do not remember complaining about an illness which would warrant such swift attention.'

'My dear, I hear you took a turn during dinner.' The doctor approaches the bed slowly with a forced smile across his lips. He moves a small vase of heather from her bedside table, replacing it with his black leather doctor's bag. Snapping it open with a loud click.

'A turn...?' She looks towards the master who stands by the window, running his hand through his hair.

'Darling, you know what happened.' He responds. 'Clearly you are not well.'

'I remember feeling faint, but I was sitting too near to the fire, and the heat was unbearably hot.' She touches the nape of her neck.

The doctor nods. 'It is possible that could have had an influence – but is it true that you have no recollection of what happened next?'

Her face crumples in confusion as her gaze flitters between the doctor and her husband. 'No, you are scaring me. What happened? I thought the dinner with your mother went well, although the details are a little blurred. I don't remember eating much, could that have played a part?'

Doctor Sheppard leans over, picks up her slender wrist, and checks her pulse. Then, removing a silver-handled stethoscope from his bag, he takes his time listening to the mistress's heart and lungs.

'You took on the pretence of another character entirely,' the master adds. 'The whole scene was most unusual.'

'What did I say? Did I speak Italian? I know you prefer English, but when I'm tired...'

'No,' he shakes his head. 'The manner in which you spoke was the most alarming thing I have ever heard.'

'In what way, Alex? I don't like how you are looking at me.'

'My dear, you were no longer my wife. Your voice...' He speaks slowly. 'It was the mad raving of a man. Or worse ... some sort of demonic creation. It was upsetting for Mother; she took to her bed again.'

She gasps and covers her face with her hands. 'I don't remember any of it!'

The doctor stands back up and tuts. 'This is most unfortunate but can easily happen when nerves are pushed to their limit – a young wife, a new country.' He pats her arm and packs up his bag. 'Extreme hallucinations followed by full amnesia of the event.'

'Does she need to return to the countryside?' The master is abrupt, almost rude. 'What are the options?'

'I recommend complete bed rest and a stronger, more suitable tonic for this diagnosis. She can leave the city – but I am not sure she is well enough to travel. We shall see how she is after Christmas; it would be timely then to move her somewhere less stressful, away from unnecessary stimulation.'

The doctor raises his eyes briefly to the ceiling above and then takes his notepad from his bag, scrawling a few words across the page.

'See to it this prescription is arranged first thing in the morning. I must admit, it disturbs me how much she has declined since her return from the countryside. Is there anything else I should know about?' He tears the note off and hands it to the master.

'Her scratches – they are worse recently,' mumbles Ivy.

The doctor turns to her. 'Scratches?'

'On her back, sir.'

The master sighs. 'She sometimes harms herself in the night, from unbearable nightmares, and she sleepwalks, so we lock her in.' He waves his hand towards the door. 'For her own safety, of course.'

'Yes, of course.' The doctor nods at the master's words. 'May I?' He leans over the mistress again, delicately moving her nightdress to examine her back. He sucks the air in between his teeth. 'There are marks that have healed, but many of these are new. This will require immediate treatment with a balm. Do you have such a remedy?'

'Yes, sir, we have treated them, but new welts keep appearing,' Ivy replies.

'Keep applying it until they go away.' He eases the mistress back onto the pillow. She winces at the movement. 'Most women's ailments can be put down to hysteria, but this could be more complicated. She must have rest and not be disturbed.'

Angelica sits forward. 'I don't want to be alone … I want to be with you, Alex.'

'Ivy, you will look in on her every hour.' The master throws the command across the room.

'If this continues,' says the doctor, 'I may be forced to recommend a psychiatrist.'

'That sounds extreme and expensive,' Master Blackham says, hastily.

'Naturally, the weather doesn't help.' The doctor breaks into a weak attempt at a smile. 'Winter always brings on melancholy for those of a sensitive nature. Any other symptoms … anxiety, poor appetite?'

'Yes, she fits all of those descriptions,' the master replies.

'Are you sure she wasn't suffering before you married? Was there any trauma she experienced when arriving in England? Moving can be a big transition.'

'Apart from the fall? And maintaining she saw some sort of ghost who pushed her,' he scoffs.

'Alex, you make it all sound so childish!' His wife cries from her bed.

'Well, yes, the fall could have had an impact,' the doctor continues, 'along with the loss of the early preg—'

'Doctor Sheppard!' The master interrupts sharply. 'I insist you concentrate solely on what she needs to become well, as she was when I met her in Italy.'

'Does she have any family? Any new friends?' The doctor huffs, exasperated.

'No, only one relative. My wife was her aunt's travelling companion. They lived in Tuscany together before she came here. I believe they write to each other occasionally.'

'There is no one she sees regularly. Recently, she has preferred to stay in her room.'

His wife looks up to interject, but changes her mind, remaining silent.

'Could this change in behaviour be linked to this house? A building full of unusual artefacts could spark the weakest imagination into sleep terrors, hearing noises in the night and such like. You remember, I have treated you and your family for years. This type of behaviour must not be allowed to get out of hand.' The doctor snaps his bag shut and casts the master a private glance.

The colour bleeds from the master's face. He knows they are both thinking of his late wife, Miranda. 'Perhaps,' he replies, folding his arms, 'but I am sure Angelica is fine in this room.' He pauses. 'It is at the front of the house, away from the windows overlooking the garden.' But even to himself, his words lack confidence.

Chapter 33 ~ Rapping

Ivy ~ Blackham House, 18th December.

This morning's work is a welcome escape from the worries on my mind. The second Monday of the month is laundry day, a big event with much organising and preparation. Hannah and I started this morning alongside each other, separating the coloured clothes from the whites. I catch her smelling one of the master's shirts. I try to start a little conversation about the coldness of the weather, to find a sense of normalcy, and share the struggles of the day. But her mood has soured. She throws down the shirt and stalks off, leaving me alone to sort out the washing.

Curiosity wins, and I also inhale the linen shirt that had been worn next to the master's body. I catch the musk and spice oil, but alongside it is a different, more feminine fragrance; not lavender like Hannah's, but it could be a new perfume worn by the mistress, one I had yet to discover on her dressing table. Or maybe, as Hannah's behaviour suggests, the scent belongs to a new mystery woman.

The prescription has not improved the mistress; instead over the past couple of days, she seems to have become more of a recluse, taking to sleeping during the day and eating even less. I keep ruminating about the unnatural voice that erupted from her mouth. That could not be her. She looked to be truly possessed, which means my mother lied to me; bad spirits do exist. To speak in another's tongue – for skin to be scratched and bloodied without knowledge, can only be the work of the Devil.

A gurgle of laughter had almost escaped from my throat when talking to the doctor about the absurdity of his cure. How can a balm stop the Devil? I know I am bordering on hysteria myself. The veil between what I perceive as reality and what is surely madness is slipping.

After several hours of turning the wooden dolly handle in the boiling cauldron, another woman joins us. She reminds me of an old workhorse on a farm – blinkered, strong, plodding through the workload. Any distractions due to the strangeness of the house, she hides well and does not react. If a garment is ripped or has blood stains, she puts it to one side to be given extra care later. No questions asked. It is likely that she knows better than to look deeper than the shallow water sloshing in her bucket. Even the mistress's underarm dress protectors require soaking in carbolic acid; no amount of scented starch can conceal the smell of stale sweat. The mistress hardly moves, and the rooms are not warm enough to produce such an effect. Only anguish would cause such a primal bodily response.

My fingers are red and chapped from pushing the sheets through the mangle and rubbing the clothes clean. The pale softness of my skin has been lost and lines cover my hands like cracks in a vase. Does my face also appear haggard too? Have I aged so much in the last month?

The washerwoman kindly gives me a wax balm unlike one I have seen before. She slips the small pot into my uniform pocket and motions for me to apply the ointment over my fingers and wrists. It smells terrible, it must be made from animal fat but thankfully, once absorbed the greasy mixture takes the soreness away. She holds her own hands in front of me, and they are thick with calluses but not raw. For a moment, her tender eyes pity me, but then she glances upwards towards the ceiling, and at once her focus is back on her work. Our exchange abruptly ended.

She doesn't seem to speak; Hannah says she is mute. I think her absence of voice is the reason they employ her. Any secrets she uncovers stay hidden. Yet, the undercurrent of danger increases every day. The fresh scratches on the mistress and my dreams becoming more terrifying only seem to heighten the impression on my senses. I cannot touch or name the threat directly, but I know it resides here in this building, for when I leave the house, the pressure lifts like dawn rising.

It isn't until much later, when my thoughts have become nothing but those of wringing and rinsing the fabric before me, that another possibility arises: that the scent on the master's shirt could be that of Miss Earnshaw. I'm not sure if this is a good thing or not, but it leaves me quite unsettled.

At the end of the day, I return to the attic. My lower back aches from hunching over the mangle. Even untying my garters is an effort. The pain does not ease much as I lie on the bed. Such is the life of a maid. A new understanding resonates with me – that I have become nothing but a faceless cog behind the facade of this house. If I am worn out or damaged, no doubt someone will replace me, ensuring that the regime continues.

The energy it takes for me to appear socially acceptable is draining. I preferred it when I didn't have to speak very much, and I watched life happen from the distance of my garden. I still believe myself to be cowardly. I find it hard enough to talk to people who are alive. Perhaps Hannah and I are forming the beginning of a friendship, it is hard to tell, I have never had a friend before. I might find it easier to connect with people if they were departed; they might judge me less from the afterlife.

Mr. Godwin claims he can bring souls back from purgatory, releasing them from their spiritual prison - but would the dead then walk the Earth? The possible truth of this is a story of nightmares. To go against nature, God's will, is absurd. Once our souls pass through purgatory, there is only Heaven or Hell.

The sound of rapping interrupts my thoughts. They come from the chest of drawers containing my clothes, sounding soft, like the gentle wings of an insect trapped inside a box, a fluttering distress. Dragging myself up from the mattress, I pull open all the drawers. The knocking stops. Under my belongings, there is no sign of anything moving around. There is only the leather diary, the treasure I had taken from Miss Earnshaw's house. I can imagine her sitting at the desk in her parlour, taking care to record her sentiments in small, formed letters and quick sketches. I have no guilt in borrowing the book. On the contrary, holding it feels right, like I am meant to have the diary in my possession. Somehow, we are connected.

I turn up the gas lamp. Reading the suffragette pamphlet tucked into the back page, I marvel at this elusive woman. She is unmarried, with only her own work to support her, and fights for the cause of women's rights. I am in awe of her bravery but again I worry that I am too late, that she might already be dead.

My own harrowing dreams are becoming worse; each morning I wake in a damp sweat despite the frosty chill. I am struggling to maintain the effort of dismissing these nightly terrors and ignoring the voices emanating from nothing, from no one. I must be losing my battle with sanity, for I am certain that within this empty room, I am not alone.

The rapping starts again, louder this time and more urgent, moving from the drawers over to the picture above the fireplace. My imagination races despite my usual logic. I had believed the existence of the supernatural to be false, but the unnatural voice I heard from the mistress's own lips is pulling my argument apart.

The repeated taps sound like a question. What would a spiritualist do with this situation? *What would Miss Earnshaw have me do?*

'Is anybody there?' My voice is feeble and lost in the room. I am silly. The notion of talking to something that does not exist is absurd, but the rapping increases, moving to the cupboard in the corner. Again, I ask: 'Is there someone here? Has God sent you?'

Pure stubbornness not to be weak and the yearning that this could possibly work drives me forward. Did they murder Miss Earnshaw and bury her body nearby or even somewhere in the house? The idea forms and becomes tangible. Is her spirit trapped within the walls, trying to communicate with me?

Perhaps she can reach out because her soul is not at peace. God has allowed it. Could I succeed where the detective failed? As if reading my mind in acknowledgement, the tapping becomes louder and more erratic. I kneel on the bed – I'm desperate, but I cannot be frightened. Not now, not after I've worked so hard to be here. The room drops in temperature. My breath fogs before me.

'Please, if you wish to talk, answer one knock for yes.' I am almost faint with expectation. Dear God, I pray, let it not be the voice that possessed the mistress. A part of me hopes it was just a cruel joke; perhaps the mistress was trying to frighten Lady Blackham. Her increased tonic dosage could have caused confusion and unhinged her sense of humour.

A solitary hollow thud resounds from the wall above my pillow.

'Do you want me to leave?' I ask under my breath.

Two hard thuds in reply.

'Miss Earnshaw is that you?'

For a moment, silence is my only company, then I am overwhelmed by noise. The sound of rapid knocking breaks out from all over the room. Even the windowpane rattles, like a trapped bird trying to escape, beating its wings furiously against the glass. But then it suddenly stops.

I glance at the door handle, expecting it to turn, and Mr Bancroft to arrive, charging in and demanding to know the nature of the disturbance, but all is quiet. I hold my breath, but still nothing. The room has returned to how it was before. Eventually, I let out a sigh, and then a fraction of a moment later, something else near me also exhales.

I jump up, fling open the door and run.

The light is better in the kitchen. I have almost recovered from the strange noises in the attic; I will not think about them. Doing so gives them power and makes them real. To distract myself, on my way down to the basement, I took some paper from the library and borrowed the well-used botanical dictionary, Species Plantarum. I am writing a letter to Mr Witherfield, the acquaintance Miss Earnshaw's housekeeper told me about, requesting a visit. I have left it too long already and have so many questions. Writing is a good distraction to draw out the evening, delaying the moment I must return to the eaves to sleep.

I slip the finished letter into my apron to post in the morning and turn my attention to the dictionary. Flicking through the native English categories, I cannot find any drawings that look similar to the Victory plants in the garden. My fingertip is still sore to the touch from the prick of the orange thorn, and on intuition, I turn to the familiar solanum genus section - the deadly nightshades. There are many, but I continue to peer closer at each picture in the dim light until finally I come across a page which is more dog-eared than the others, and in the centre is an illustration of the perfect match. The blue-green jagged leaves and berries are drawn with a flourish; even the orange thorns are painted with care, each tip ending in a crisp point.

I nearly jump out of my seat when the scullery door bangs shut and Hannah storms into the kitchen, bringing the winter weather with her. Her face is pale and blotchy from crying, and as she removes her coat, I notice her necklace, normally on prominent display when she is out, is gone.

'What's that?' she demands, looking at the book before me. 'Master won't take too kindly to thieves.'

'It's about plants,' I retort as I quickly turn the page, not wanting to share my discovery.

She steps closer. 'Makes no sense to me, doesn't even look English,' she says, pointing to the words.

'The plants also have Latin names. Do not concern yourself, they are difficult to pronounce. I will return the book tonight before he notices.'

'You and your fancy words – you are no maid, that's for sure. Making fun of me cause I don't talk like you.' She fusses with her hair, damp from the cold.

'It is not my intention to make fun of you. For what it is worth I cannot speak Latin either.' I want to wrong-foot her, to show her in some ways we are alike.

She pauses, surprised by my admission. 'But you can read normal words?'

'Yes.'

'My brother once tried to learn. He managed enough to write his name, but I always had too much work to do.'

There is a new, fragile air between us, a break in the usual tension. The lonely discerning the pain of dejection in another.

'Do you have a big family?' I ask tentatively.

'Five sisters and one brother.' She lingers by my side, a new curiosity in her eyes. 'What about you, you've never mentioned your family either?'

'A half-brother, but I recently found out I might have more family in the city.'

'Old or young?'

'An older woman, but younger than my mother. That's why I came to London, to find her.'

'Any luck so far?' Her face seems to soften in sympathy.

'I have spent some time asking about her. I hoped I might have some free time to—'

Hannah's features harden again, her hands resting on the bones of her hips. 'These fantasies are dangerous,' she interrupts, 'and can be a waste of time, stealing you from your chores and adding to mine.'

'Anyway, it seems she's gone.' I stop myself before I say anything more. 'So, I'm still looking. It must be nice to have a brother and sisters?'

Her shoulders slump. 'He was all right, I suppose, in his own way. But reading did him no good in the end.' She looks downcast, and I almost touch her arm as I sense the sadness under the surface of her words.

'Why? What happened to him?'

'Got into a fight coming home from the pub; he must have hit his head on the cobbles. We found him stone-cold dead in the morning, lying in the alley next to our house.'

As she talks, a flicker of anguish passes over her face, which she composes almost instantly. She leans forward again, examining the contents of the book. 'The flowers are pretty, I suppose.'

The way she hovers over the page, gently tracing the drawings and print, is so in awe, an idea comes to mind: 'I could teach you to read if you like?'

'Who, me?' She stands up straight. 'I'd never be clever enough. You're making jokes at my expense again.'

But I feel her guard is down, and she is softening. The gas lamp flickers, and she shuffles her feet. I sense a hesitancy in leaving. We all have secrets and burdens, but in this moment, there is a spark of hope, a change between us. I cannot continue to disconnect myself from others as I did in the countryside. For the first time in my life, I want a real friendship to happen, to not face everything alone.

'We could start at the beginning with your name. You could practise the letters with me in the evening.' I take out another piece of paper and spell "Hannah" out slowly. She takes the page from me in wonder.

'You would do that for me?' She smiles in disbelief.

'Of course. It's a much better way to pass what spare time we have before bed than sitting in silence with nothing but our prayers to do.'

'I will think about it.' Her expression has hardened again, but still, she doesn't go. I want her to stay. I wrack my brain, trying to say anything to make the conversation continue, and then I remember her bare neck.

'Have you lost your necklace?'

Her fingers fly to her throat. 'Frank asked for it back to help pay for his mother's treatment in the hospital.'

'I'm sorry.'

'Well, I'm not. Doesn't change anything,' she snaps. 'He said it's only pawned, and I will have it again by the end of the month. It was his own fault. He spent too much on me. He knows I can choose anyone and didn't want my head to be turned by the affections of another.' She smooths down her skirt. 'He has mentioned marriage.'

'That is good news, is it not?'

'I am considering it. In fact, he said, if we could get enough money together, we could start afresh back in Ireland. The air would be better for his mother. I don't suppose she would live much longer, and then I would be the lady of our house.'

I study her with interest. 'Would that make you happy?'

'What has happiness got to do with it? I've had a gut full of being on my own. We all make sacrifices to survive.'

'So, will you leave Blackham House?' I am surprised that, despite our disagreements, I've grown accustomed to her abrupt demeanour and would miss her; yet another person to mourn.

She sighs. 'I've stayed in London long enough, slogging away for nothing. Thought I'd found a scrap of comfort here, a place where I belonged. But it seems my affections—' she cuts herself short. 'I mean, despite my hard work and loyalty, my efforts are not to be rewarded after all.'

For the briefest of moments, her eyes are blank, lost in a memory, her face twisting as if she's in pain. A single service bell rings abruptly on the kitchen wall. We both turn to the source of the vibrating noise, breaking the spell between us. The shrill sound continues, demanding service to the master's bedroom, and I know she has left to attend before I have even turned back.

I return to the dictionary and find the matching drawing again amongst the deadly nightshades. I can hardly absorb the information as I skip to the section that states the plant will die if exposed to icy temperatures. It only grows in tropical conditions on the islands of the western Indian Ocean. My assumption is correct: the plants should not survive here, and for the first time in an age, real joy ignites in my chest at the thought of the research prospects this creates.

As I reread the text more slowly, it comes as no revelation that, like many members of the solanum genus, the leaves, flowers, and fruit of the plant are all poisonous, containing highly toxic tropane alkaloids. In small amounts, they can cause hallucinations and delirium, but in larger doses they are deadly. I search for its true Latin name, but then a hard lump forms in my throat as I take in the words: Solanum pyracanthos – the Devil's Thorn.

Chapter 34 ~ Realisations

Ivy ~ Blackham House, 19th December.

I wake up to the curtains blowing wildly for the second night in a row. Frustrated with the faulty panes disturbing my rest, I stumble over groggy and tired, only to find that the window is shut, and the weather is calm outside. Confused, I climb back into bed. I had taken the sleeping tonic again, but it does not seem to have helped this time either. Whispers fade in and out of earshot. They could be the wind or inside my own head. It is difficult to tell.

    I take another sip of the tonic hoping it will start to work soon. I lie motionless, listening to the creaking sounds of the walls and reflect again on the deadly nightshades and the ways they can be used. The dangerous plants are within reach again, but this time, I find myself pushing away the thoughts of poison I had before. They hold a different power over me now: curiosity. I am not ready to leave this world just yet. I want to learn more about them and why they are here, of all places. Is it a coincidence that the name "Devil's Thorn" suits the tone of this house, and why would they grow that plant above all others?

    The mattress seems to shift beneath me, disturbing my thoughts. I open my eyes wide, straining in the dim light. The candle I had left burning has almost burnt down to the quick, but the sickening sensation that the attic is moving about me remains.

    Desperate for a distraction, I focus on the embroidered tapestry hanging above the fireplace. The colours have faded with age, but the scene depicts two figures in a garden, much like the one attached to Blackham House, but this lawn is healthy with greenery and coloured blooms. As the candle flame dances, the image ripples, and the couple seem to come alive, dancing hand in hand, flittering around the flowers and trees. They move faster until the woman falls onto the ground and all the plants wither and die. The man stands still, turning his face out into the room. My heart falters as his eyes find mine, his features becoming disfigured in anguish until he is nothing but a mass of blurred shapes.

Nausea rises as the room spins. I grab the mattress tightly, feeling the floor tilt. The angles of the walls are all wrong; the mantelpiece distorted and crooked. A strong breeze whips around my body, pulling at my hair. Then the movement halts, and the room appears to have resumed its shape. Confusion fights with the certainty of what is real. Is this just a hallucination from the sleeping tonic?

I recline back onto the pillow when the sound of rapping comes from the chest of drawers, as before. My mouth becomes dry. Perhaps the spiritualist never left Blackham House; her soul trapped like all the stuffed animals in their glass cages.

'Miss Earnshaw?' I lick my lips, and the question is feeble, strained. I try using the same words as before: 'Knock once for yes and twice for no.'

I wait.

The rapping stops – the silence is a comfort.

Then a muffled bang comes from the fireplace. I jolt, my heart racing. 'You're a spirit?'

A soft tap follows in quick succession to my question. 'Do you need me?'

Then, one solitary thump answers, above my head and louder than all the rest, leaving me in no doubt that I am not alone.

The following morning, in the kitchen, Mrs Higgins passes me a loaf of stale bread. 'Give this to the magpies outside. Keep them happy.'

I find this request most strange. Was it our responsibility to manage the birds' mood? The creatures in this garden always appear to be lacking the joy that country birds express. Perhaps the city wildlife is burdened by the soot and the overcrowding with fewer trees.

The early morning is bitter, so I take my shawl outside with me. Although the sun has risen, it sheds no warmth on the ground, and most of the twigs and dead leaves show signs of frost. Maybe the birds will be grateful for the food. I see them perched on the branches, and I sense somehow that they are expecting me. Only magpies now, no jays, crows, or any other type of bird. They gather in twos and threes as if they have increased in number, eyeing me greedily.

I don't approach them. Instead, I pick at the loaf until it is gone, throwing the crumbs as far as I can across the grass. I expect them to flock down to feast, but they do not move. Instead, they sit motionless, watching me. I want to make them fly off, but my instinct warns me to retreat. Do not antagonise them, I tell myself. Their beaks are sharp.

I turn to another cluster of magpies on the ground in the far corner near the secret gate. These are not interested in my offering either, but hop around on the soil, pecking in unison at something at their centre. Through a gap in the feathers, there's a glimpse of grey fur.

Time stops.

Instantly, I know it is the cat. They have my only true friend in this place.

'Get away... Leave him alone!' I run over, waving my arms, but the earth is unsteady underfoot as I get closer.

The birds fly up to the treetops to sit with the others, their black and white bodies melding together. On the ground is the small, ravaged body of Mr Grey. Bile rises to the back of my throat, and my hands cover my mouth. The scene before me is horrific. The magpies have destroyed him; even his beautiful eyes are gone.

This cruelty is mixed with guilt and disgust. This was my fault – I did not take care of him. I think of his innocent gift at my feet only a few days ago. Surely this is not revenge for killing a magpie? It is in the same place as the birds had arranged the strange wreaths. Through the numbness, a grating sound surrounds me, getting louder, the jagged chatter cutting through the air and biting at my nerves. The magpies are laughing at me.

My fists curl as I dig my fingertips into my palms. It is all I can do to distract myself from the familiar pain of grief; I would rather embrace the heat of anger and hatred. I detest those birds, those evil, red-eyed devils. I will find out the truth of this house fast and never return. The coward I was when I arrived has vanished; I have grown up.

I sense someone standing next to me. From the corner of my eye, I observe William's boots and dirty grey trousers. Being so close to him makes me wince with repulsion, but I want him to bear witness to the horrendous scene. 'Look at what they did.' The statement slips through my gritted teeth. I am somewhere between weeping and rage.

The birds seem to be listening now, their cries of glee have quietened with the man's arrival. He glances up at the magpies, his face is impassive, showing a calm detachment from the situation. 'I told you, girly, the garden has its own rules.'

'We should bury the poor cat.'

He shakes his head. 'Leave it be and don't go running to that vicar again. The birds told me this won't be the last death if you get any clever ideas about bringing outsiders into the house.'

He limps away, leaving me in stunned silence.

Anger still pulses hot through my veins. I need to increase my efforts to find out what really happened to Miss Earnshaw. The collection room must contain answers to why this house is Godless and at the Devil's mercy. I am sure I can find something to give to the detective to ease Miss Earnshaw's restless spirit. And now Mr Grey is dead, her prediction of forces working against us feels even stronger. As I try to erase the image of the cat's lifeless body from my mind, I finally understand her warning was never about Mr Whitlock or life in an asylum. It was about this house.

I hide behind the grandfather clock in the hallway and watch Hannah finish an errand in the collection room. I will her to forget to lock the room when she leaves, and as Hannah takes out her set of keys, she suddenly appears distracted. To my good fortune, she turns her face, confused, as if she hears a voice calling her away, and in the blink of an eye, she runs down the servants' staircase without a second glance to the unlocked door behind her.

Inside the collection room, the air has a strange atmosphere. The solemn face of Lord Blackham in the hallway portrait is so lifelike, his image is imprinted on my mind, and I can almost see him sitting at the mahogany desk set in front of the window.

I am taken aback by the sheer quantity of artefacts in this room. There are tables, shelves, and cabinets filling every space. To my right, the walls are covered with a multitude of preserved butterflies and insects, silver pins holding their tiny bodies to black cards, glinting in the weak winter sunlight. All the stuffed animals in their own glass cabinets appear to regard me with disdain, as if they know I have trespassed into their world. They should be polished daily, for the city smoke creates a perpetual layer of dust which blankets every item in the house, even if the doors are closed, but I see this room has not been cleaned in a long time.

I understand the attraction of collecting, capturing a piece of life to preserve it for knowledge and science. My sketchbook full of pressed plants and flowers is testament to this, but I am at a loss to comprehend the grim interest in these lifeless bodies. As a child in a museum, I would find fascination in examining the lifelike fur and posture, but the creatures surrounding me have an expression of terror, as if captured at the point of death – all except for a large magpie, which is poised on a branch above the doorway. It reminds me of the bird that perched on my windowsill. I have never seen such a dominating magpie, even in the countryside. It sits almost regally, smug in its solitary position, overlooking the rest of the room.

Along the left wall is a long table with a selection of bizarre silver medical instruments. Next to it is a whole cabinet devoted to what looks like shrunken heads. Some are contained within bell jars, others are propped up on sticks, all with tufts of realistic hair emanating from their strange little skulls. With their contorted leather faces, I cannot entertain the idea they were once alive.

A display to my right is dedicated to bones and teeth, all shapes and sizes, both animal and human – a miniature graveyard. Next to the bones is an enormous egg. "Taken from a dragon's nest" is handwritten in spidery looping letters below it. Another note: "Fiji mermaid" describes what looks to be the head and torso of a young monkey crudely sewn to a scaley fish tail preserved in papier mâché. A monstrous concoction and for what function?

But by far the most grotesque are the specimen jars. They make me uneasy. All lined up on a wide wooden shelf near the window, they contain freak occurrences of nature: twin baby mice joined together, their spines fused above the tail; a small six-fingered hand; an embryo that looks still alive. In summer, the amber preservation liquid must become warm through the glass.

I hasten to the prominent desk. I do not have long before Hannah might return. Opening drawers and rifling through pages of documents, nothing relevant catches my attention. Most of the papers come from the British museum requesting further information about which artefacts they might consider selling if they are provided with their true history. My mind whirls. Many of the letters include returned arguments from the master, protesting they are not stolen.

More papers are layered in the next drawer down. These are in a different handwriting, instructions about taxidermy, pictures and detailed drawings of animals, their insides depicted in skin-crawling detail, their eyes locked onto the observer, black pools of ink. I turn the images over. I cannot abide them; they make me sick.

Under the ledge of the desk is a floral decorative panel, much like my father's own desk. He always teased me about his disguised hiding place when I was a young child. It fascinates me how secrets can be hidden in plain sight.

As I find the lip of the wood, I hold my breath as it slides across as I hoped it would, revealing a small hidden drawer also covered in swirls and flower decorations. Crouching down to see better, a tiny keyhole in the middle of the patterns becomes visible. Rummaging in the other drawers for a key that fits proves to be a fruitless endeavour. I am replacing the panel when male voices come from the hallway. The adrenaline that drove me to this room has petered out. Now I am only tired and drained. Abandoning my search, I hide behind the thick velvet curtains before the sound of footsteps enter the room – more than one person.

The cool glass of the window presses up against my cheek. I watch my breath fog against the reflective surface as I wait and listen.

'There is the indelicate matter of requesting more money, sir.' Mr Bancroft speaks and then stops. Is he nervous? His voice is clipped, more strained than usual. 'I wouldn't bring it up,' he continues, 'but time has passed, and they want another payment. I told them I would deal with it, but the guard is a slippery character and mentioned his brother-in-law, who works at the local paper.'

'My father still owns some stocks; I can sell them if I must.' The master replies, sighing loudly, 'I am waiting for the museum to come through with a sale or two, but they are dragging their heels.'

A drawer opens and closes, and I hear the scratch of an ink nib on paper, so near to me I hold my breath. Would he notice anything is different? Have I moved too many papers?

'Take this to my lawyer with this letter and settle the cursed bill once and for all.'

'Yes, sir.'

'Ensure I am not bothered by this matter again. What costs could they possibly be incurring? This price is utter extortion!'

'I don't know … food? I wouldn't expect charity stretches very far in that place.'

No one speaks, and the air is heavy with tension.

'Do you think she was real?' Mr Bancroft's tentative voice interrupts the silence. 'Could she really speak to the spirits? You know what she said, about what will happen to us…'

I am surprised by his words. This is the only time I've heard him openly doubt anything.

'If she was legitimate, would she come to this house willingly if she possessed any kind of ability?'

'You are correct, sir. Please forgive my bluntness. I only want everything to continue as planned.'

'Bancroft, you are a loyal servant and in goodtime you will be rewarded well for your efforts. But do not let the ravings of a mad woman distract you from your work.'

They leave the room and move out of earshot. I try to piece together their words. They must be discussing Miss Earnshaw and the revelation penetrates like a shot of warmth in my chest. The bloom of possibility, for if the spiritualist is not dead, a chance to find her still exists.

As I wait for the footsteps to fade away, the excitement ebbs and a horrible sinking sensation replaces it. A hideous understanding transpires. My unravelling thoughts feel like pouring salt onto a festering wound. The truth comes fast and painful. If I haven't been communicating with Miss Earnshaw, then who or what is it? The same spirit that bedevilled the mistress – could it have also possessed my thoughts too? I had believed the voices were only a warped creation from my imagination.

The wall above me knocks heavily, a deep resounding noise from inside it. The sound shakes me to my core, for I know it is not created by man or nature. I close my eyes.

'You are not Miss Earnshaw?' I whisper.

And then, a single thump strikes next to my head.

The violence is startling; the wood vibrates against my body.

And then another forceful thud.

Two, the answer is no.

A new noise emanates in the room: a raw, strangled laugh, eerie and cutting. God help me, I thought I lost him in childhood. Has he been with me all along, haunting my dreams, whispering to me in different tongues? I questioned my own sanity, but my mother must have known. Her drawings of the beast are proof of it. Evil takes on many forms. The Devil is amongst us.

Part Four

Chapter 35 ~ Old Friend

Ivy ~ Blackham House, 21st December.

I wait for the church bells to chime at ten to pull on my cloak. They are a lonely, solitary sound at night. I have visited the lodging house for my post and there has been no answer from my letter to Mr Witherfield, so I will have to pay him a visit without an invitation. Unfortunately, this late hour is my only opportunity, but I cannot waiver in my decision. After the conversation I heard in the collection room, I must seek help to understand Miss Earnshaw better and fathom why the Blackhams would take her?

My feet pad through the hallways, each floorboard protesting at my movement. Everyone is in bed, but I still sense I am being watched – that the house somehow knows what I am doing. As I step into the kitchen, a heady, fruity aroma stirs my appetite and my mouth waters. Mrs Higgins has been busy preparing the Christmas pudding mixture for boiling.

The room is dim, lit only by the streetlamp shining down through the basement windows. From memory, I move to where the knives are kept. I take a small one, sharp for vegetables, the weight is comfortable in my hand. It might be of use. I am no longer naïve to the dangers lurking in the shadows. I look over my shoulder. Is there a spirit with me now?

Nudging the scullery key off the wall hook, I unlock the door. The cold air blasts against my face as I step out into the night. Winter has claimed the season and is unforgiving in its hold. Slipping the metal key alongside the knife in my cloak pocket. The solid feeling of metal reminds me of my garden secateurs, and my mind returns to the Devil's Thorn in the garden. This might be my only opportunity. It is a poor choice of name, but I need it for my future, to be able to stay and study in London – a possible gateway into the Royal College of Science.

I run along the side of the house and into the back garden. The golden thorns of the shrubs glow in the rays of the moon. Taking out my knife in one hand and wrapping my cloak around the fingers of the other, I carefully take two swift cuttings laden with the green berries at the stems. My gloves offer no protection against the spiky armour of the orange thorns, but the cloak helps. I wrap everything inside my handkerchief and place the small bundle into my reticule.

The thudding of my heart keeps me company as I make my way out of Chester Gardens, through Eaton Square towards Hyde Park. Carriages should still run even at this late hour, but the light from the streetlamps becomes dimmer, as they are spaced less often. I walk faster. Master Blackham is out; I might witness him in the city. What would he conclude if he saw me hurrying alone at night, free from the confinement of the attic room? Would he notice me?

I pull the hood tighter around my face. Knowing the precious cuttings are in my purse, my mood is buoyant. Despite the cold, the street has a few huddled figures in the rising fog. I am conscious I am a woman travelling without a companion, so I clutch the wooden knife handle close.

The nightsoil men pass me with their cart, carrying their long-handled shovels and buckets towards the next outhouse and cesspit. Even the cover of nightfall cannot hide their stench. I take no comfort from seeing the night watchmen on their rounds, although when one man steps out of a side street, I am relieved to see he is not the same person who has followed me on previous evenings. This man has a friendly face and appraises me as one would a lost child.

'Evening, Miss.' He tips his hat and nods in my direction.

I involuntarily slow down, hoping not to engage in conversation. I pull my hood down further, an urge to conceal my identity.

'Are you all right there? Are you lost?' He steps in front of me, stopping me abruptly.

'No, I am quite fine, thank you. I am on an urgent errand for my mistress.'

'An errand … at this time? What house do you work at?'

'Apologies, but time is of the essence, and I must hurry.'

'As you wish, but it's a pea-souper of a night and getting foggier by the minute.' He scowls at the weather. 'Be mindful – there are plenty of unsavoury characters about. And these London streets ain't no place for a young lady. Down the road is a pub called The Rose and Crown. It should still be open.' He points into the murkiness. 'It's only fifteen lamp posts away. If you come across any trouble, head inside. The drinkers will more likely cause you other problems, but at least you'll be in the warm.'

'Thank you for your help,' I reply, grateful for his kindness. I edge past him and onwards. As I turn to cross the street, it is true. Now I can only make out a few steps in front of me; the smog is getting worse. The watchman stays where I left him, the fog consuming his figure, and then his footsteps start again, this time more purposefully, directed towards me. He muffles a cough as he gets closer. There was a time when I might have trusted a stranger, but not anymore. My stomach churns with unease as I quicken my speed along Grosvenor Place, my heavy skirts and cloak whipping about my legs, slowing me down.

Around the corner, under Wellington Arch, a single hansom carriage awaits business. The driver's face is hidden, his collar turned up against his pale cheeks. Only the curling smoke of a pipe from his grey fingerless gloves gives the notion he is alive, a living statue.

'Will you take me to Camden?'

He sighs and sizes me up, checking that I am alone, no doubt, so he can ask for a good amount, for these streets are too dangerous for anyone; the number of grisly murders has increased. They are happening all over London, and not just the East End. Hannah relishes describing the grim details of the dismembered victims, passed on from her policeman companion.

'Two and six.' His breath steams in the air.

I almost catch my finger on the sharp thorns, barely constrained by the handkerchief as I remove my purse from my reticule. A mix of excitement and danger pulses through my veins.

The coins chink together. I have enough for a return fare. 'Number forty-eight Doughty Street, please.'

I climb into the cab, closing the door with a firm slam, finally blocking out the icy chill and the nightwatchman. The horses start to move, and the carriage jumps forward as their hooves hit the cobblestones. We pass a couple of women huddled in doorways, waving at the carriage to stop for their services. In only a few hours, the dawn street sellers with their donkey carts will tread the same streets with their signs for oysters and pea soup. But now it's too cold and foggy for customers, unless they are too drunk to feel the biting weather. Perhaps ghosts walk the empty paths at night. Who's to say they are all kept within walls?

We arrive at Mr Witherfield's house in no time, for there is hardly any other traffic on the deserted roads. It is unlikely they will admit me into the house at this late hour, but the boundaries of social etiquette are blurring in my quest for answers. Time is running out, and as selfish as it might seem, I won't hesitate to wake them if I need to.

'Can you wait for me?' The words are feeble and shrill as I call up to the driver. 'I should be less than an hour. There is an extra shilling for the wait?'

He leans back, pulling the reins into the seat, and takes out his tobacco box. 'I'll wait. But it'll cost you if you take longer.' His voice is gruff, unsympathetic.

He takes the money for the journey and more. I hope I can trust him; I do not fancy walking home in the early hours.

The house appears to be shut up for the night, except for a faint light glowing in the top-floor window through the lace netting. A surge of optimism rises in my chest as I walk around the side of the building to see if the servants are still awake. After knocking twice, someone scrapes the bolt back. The servant's door opens slightly, showing what looks like a housekeeper in her dressing gown, her thick charcoal hair swept back into a net, ready for sleep. She scowls at me, holding a small gas lamp up under my face. I can smell the paraffin burning.

'What do you want at this ungodly hour?'

'Apologies. My name is Miss Ivy Granger. I am so sorry to disturb you at this hour. It was my hope that Mr Witherfield might still be awake, and he would not mind my late-night intrusion. I sent a letter, I would not have turned up like this, only—'

She peers at me further. 'Yes, I remember you sent a letter. I am his housekeeper, Nancy. What on earth are you doing walking the streets at night? Are you in trouble?'

'I…' Her earnest, kind face breaks through my false confidence and I suddenly start to doubt myself for coming at all, the words lodging in my mouth, unwilling to continue.

'Oh dear, you best come in. I can see you're in a bit of a state.' She stands aside, opening the door wide enough for me to squeeze past. 'Settle yourself down by the fire and get warm.'

I walk into the narrow kitchen and take a seat, relieved to be inside, my hands numb with cold.

'I'm about to take Mr Witherfield his hot cocoa. A cup might calm you down too, or … perhaps a glass of sherry is better?'

I have never drunk alcohol before, but I nod yes, hoping it will quiet my emotions. And within a few minutes, I am sipping the small measure she has poured into a glass. The red liquid is pleasant and warms my throat.

'He doesn't get many guests. He will be pleased to receive one, even at this hour. The professor often sleeps during the day and is up during the night. But I have to warn you, he is getting more confused and has not been himself today. Would you believe it?' She says with a tired smile. 'He thought I was the flower girl in the street. Perhaps a new face might sort him out. If not, show him a smile, and I'll see if I can do my best to help you.'

She finishes making the cocoa, and I leave the comfort of the cosy kitchen to follow her up the main staircase, where she leads me to his room on the first floor.

Mr Witherfield doesn't hear us enter as he sits by the fireside with an open, unread book in his lap, his attention focused on the flickering flames in the grate. On his wall are many hand-drawn illustrations of various birds, such as blackbirds, robins, finches, and tits. But disturbingly, most of them are magpies, surrounding the other birds with their beady red-brown eyes. The scene reminds me strongly of Blackham House. The pictures are so lifelike, it's as if they could almost fly out of the frame and devour their prey in one swoop. I am taken aback at how similar they are to the drawings in Miss Earnshaw's house and in my mother's sketchbook.

'Professor,' Nancy says, speaking loudly. 'I've brought your hot cocoa and a visitor for you.'

He turns his head towards us. 'Oh goodness, my cocoa and a guest. What a double treat! Perhaps they could stay for lunch. Is it a Sunday roast we shall enjoy today? Tell the cook I'm in the mood for a trifle with lashings of cream.' He picks up his spectacles from the arm of his chair and puts them on the bridge of his nose, attempting to focus. As he looks at me, his jaw slackens and his bottom lip trembles. 'Why, do my eyes play tricks on me? My God, I always hoped one day I would see you again, but after all the...'

'I wrote to you last week on account of a relative.' I say, hoping he will remember.

'Why Lillian, you granted an old man his dying wish? Come closer, you haven't changed at all.' He takes out a crumpled tissue from his smoking jacket and dabs it against his eye. 'You must excuse me. I am quite taken aback.'

I edge forward. 'You knew my mother, Lillian?' The shock that he knows her name sends a tremor down my spine.

'Lillian was the sweetest bird of all.' His watery eyes glisten in the firelight. He motions for me to sit in a leather-backed chair opposite him. 'Such a mystery, our beautiful Lilly. You know, lilies are still my favourite flower, but they are so delicate.'

'They crushed you.' He stifles a sob into his handkerchief.

'I... I don't understand what you're talking about.' The wine must be strong because I cannot make sense of his words.

'I'm sorry, his mind is not what it was,' the housekeeper interrupts, moving to his side protectively. 'Come back downstairs, Miss Granger, and we can finish our drinks.'

'There, there.' She pats his arm. 'There's no point getting all upset now. This young lady is not Lillian. This is Ivy. She came to ask you for advice on a personal subject. It is late, and she travelled quite a way to talk with you.'

I am aware that the carriage is still waiting outside the front of the house. This could take more time than I thought, and I scold myself for not bringing out more money.

'It is Lillian! There is no mistake.' He strains forward in his chair, his mouth gaping in shock, revealing his teeth, stained brown from years of smoking tobacco. 'I turned my back on politics after I found out the truth. Tell me, after what that brute of a man did, do you forgive me for my part in such a terrible misfortune?' He starts to cough, spluttering in his handkerchief.

Before me is a confused old man. Should I have come? But Lillian is my mother's name; the coincidence is too great.

'I would do anything for you, Lillian, my dear, anything for your forgiveness. I cannot believe you are here. It is so long ago we said goodbye. Since we worked together, I feared I would never speak to you again.'

'But sir, I am Ivy, Lillian's daughter... We have never met before. What happened to my mother? You said you worked with her?'

'It is too painful to recall. Is Lillian here with you?' He looks past me to the door.

'I am sorry, but she passed away this last October.' I pause; the pressure to use the right words, to not waste this opportunity, washes over me. 'Is it true that you are connected to the spiritualist, Miss Earnshaw? I met her recently at my mother's funeral. I am trying to find her and learn why anyone might want to keep her quiet.'

He sighs. 'That is sad news. I don't like to attend funerals myself.' He coughs, a harsh sound resonating deep in his lungs. It is probable he will attend his own service soon. 'It has been many years now, but, yes, I am acquainted with Rosetta. She is a powerful woman, and I expect there are still people who would sleep easier if she retired.' His thick, grey eyebrows knit together in thought. 'Who did you say your mother was? I am so sorry for your loss.' He has become confused again. His pale blue, red-rimmed eyes watering as he looks at me in earnest.

'Lillian Granger,' I reply, trying to keep the frustration out of my voice.

'I told you he is a little out of sorts,' his housekeeper whispers in my ear.

'Lillian.' He pauses, rolling the name around on his tongue. 'Oh, that is sad. Terrible news, after all she went through.' He reaches for his handkerchief again and dabs at his face, which is moist with fresh tears. When he has composed himself, it appears I am no longer a stranger to him.

'Her daughter, eh? Now I see the likeness. Goodness, you are a mirror image of her when she was your age, with your thick hair and those sea-green eyes... So, she could keep you, after all! I am glad; at least I helped a little in the end.'

He reclines in his chair, taking a sip of the cocoa. The housekeeper bends down and shovels more coal onto the fire. What did he mean, keep me? My mind races with this new information.

'Such a long time ago now, but when I saw you standing at the door, you transported me right back. I kept all the drawings for the company.' He gestures to the artwork. 'How was I to know what the corvids signified until it was too late? Their special pact between life and death? I should never have doubted her. The guilt has never left. The whole ordeal haunts me to this day. I still talk about Lillian, don't I, Nancy?' He throws his question to the housekeeper, who is sweeping up the coal dust from the hearth.

'Yes, you do ... but let's not dwell on that now. Is it not wonderful news that Ivy is here?'

'Tell me.' I lower my voice to the housekeeper. 'What work did Mr Witherfield do? What connection could he possibly have had with my mother?'

She wipes her hands on her dressing gown. 'He was a famous professor in scientific research. I don't know about your mother, but I believe he took on the case of Miss Earnshaw when she was a girl. He tried to debunk her abilities to communicate with the other realms.' She rolls her eyes. 'Apparently, he failed in his intentions. Something unfortunate happened.'

'Who is Ivy?' He searches the room, his face bewildered when he finds me. 'No more students today, please. I am so dreadfully tired, and I have a lecture in the morning.'

'It's best we leave him now. He is getting worse,' says the housekeeper.

'Just one more question, if I may?' They both look at me in anticipation. 'Would you know of any reason why the Blackham family might wish Rosetta harm? She is missing, and I am convinced that they are responsible.'

'The Blackhams?' His face pales as he mumbles the name. 'You must stay away from them; they are very dangerous.' He becomes agitated, the book sliding from his lap to the floor.

I am stunned by the confirmation of his warning, my mind whirling, trying to add all the pieces of information together.

'Come now, that is enough,' the housekeeper says softly as she takes me by the arm and ushers me out of the room. I manage to say a quick good night before I find myself outside on the doorstep again. 'I am sorry, my dear, that he couldn't help more.' She gives me a thin smile. 'I'm afraid his moments of clarity are becoming less frequent. His memories are all mixed up with the present. 'Tis a shame. He was once so highly thought of.'

But before the door closes behind me, I hear him call out urgently down the staircase: 'Take care my dear – for they will hunt you down as they did your mother!'

Chapter 36 ~ Freedom Curtailed

The carriage I paid to wait has gone. I find another in Camden, but the driver charges an extortionate amount and drops me off at the top of a street near Blackham House, for I have run out of coin, and the driver his charity. Hurrying across Grosvenor Place, it is only a short walk, but I already know the nightwatchman will be in Chester Square, waiting.

As I reach the corner, I instinctively glance over to the square garden, and to my dismay, my worries are confirmed, for the form of a male figure appears amongst the trees. Trails of fog distort his features, but I know it is him. Picking up my skirts, I hurry, pushing forward against the frosty night. The nightwatchman stays motionless, but I sense him invading my space, even from a distance.

When I reach Blackham House, I turn and see the man walking back into the fog. Now frozen with cold, my fingers fumble with the lock. I let myself into the scullery and, after locking the door, I lean on it with relief, satisfied with the night. The kitchen is as I had left it, with the faint smell of suet and raisins. I return the key, but something makes me keep the knife as I hear hushed voices coming from the basement hallway – the blade is cold and metallic, a comforting weight in my hand, and I am glad of my decision. I pause in the kitchen, hidden in the shadows.

'I don't want anyone to know where you've been.' Mrs Higgins hisses the words through her teeth. 'The less you're involved, the easier it is for everyone.'

'You can't protect me forever.' Mr Bancroft replies sharply. 'I'm my own man now. I can make decisions myself.'

'You don't know everything, you must not—'

'We can better ourselves in this house, Mother.' He interrupts her. 'They will reward our loyalty; I am sure of it.'

'But James, you need to take care. Sometimes I can't comprehend the jobs we do. I warn you, there are things you don't…'

The smell of alcohol reaches me before I have a chance to react to a sudden presence behind me.

'I thought it was you!' Exclaims Master Blackham.

His hands grasp me firmly by both shoulders, and I jump out of my skin at his touch. He holds me close to him in an inappropriate embrace. I dare not push him away; something about him is wrong; instinct warns me against angering him.

'I finally found the culprit making off with the silver!'

His laughter breathes fumes into my face. He must have been in the pantry searching for alcohol, for he holds an unopened bottle of whisky. His body staggers, almost pulling me down with him. He appears jubilant but he also emanates another emotion which simmers beneath the surface – anger, torment?

'I need this more than ever tonight!' He waves the bottle. 'Thought I'd give Bancroft a night off. You haven't been waiting up for me instead, have you?'

There is a raw wildness in his manner as he bares his teeth into the grimace of a smile. Any sympathy I had mistakenly felt for him has been replaced by the sinking certainty that he is unstable and capable of anything. The disappearance of Miss Earnshaw and the scratches on his wife are at least two crimes I am sure he has committed. His hands grip me hard at the waist; the strength of them increases beneath my cloak. Professor Witherfield's last warning rings in my ears: *The Blackhams will hunt you down.*

'What goes on here?' Mrs Higgins calls out, and the tense moment between us breaks. She stands in the kitchen doorway in her high-necked, long frilly nightdress holding a candle, aghast at the sight of me and Master Blackham, wrapped together in the dark. There is no sign of Mr Bancroft with her.

'Apologies sir,' she coughs as she recovers her polite tone. 'I did not see it was you with Ivy. I will return to my room at once.'

'There is no need, Mrs Higgins. I merely discovered this woman wandering the basement.' He lets go of me and moves to lean on the kitchen table instead. There is a lingering pause. 'Whatever shall we do with her?' He laughs, but it sounds slightly manic and Mrs Higgins nods slowly in response, as if they are having a private conversation, I am not party to.

'Here now, Ivy, why don't you have a nice hot drink to calm yourself?' Mrs Higgins says, coming in and guiding me to sit at the long wooden table as if I needed help. 'Fancy you up and about this time of night! We can't have that, can we? And you have your cloak on! It will do you no good, gallivanting around the city. A sure path to come to an untimely end if you're not careful! And we need you safe and sound here.'

She sets her candle holder down and examines my face. I think she wants to know how much I have heard of her conversation with Mr Bancroft. 'Just as well you were found – I was on my way to check on the plum pudding. We don't want it spoiling before Christmas. Don't concern yourself, Master Blackham. I will sort her out.'

'Thank you, Mrs Higgins. I am in your debt; we must not wake up Mother with trouble from the staff.'

The master stumbles over to the doorway as Mrs Higgins lights a gas lamp and pours hot water from the copper kettle resting on the stove into a cup. She takes a jar from the top shelf and mixes a spoon of its contents into the cup, the rising steam carrying the pungent smell of herbs.

'I know how to make this right.' She casts a look in his direction. It is firm and no-nonsense, like a nanny to a child. 'You can leave us now.'

'Goodnight, ladies.' He nods in return and then glances at me with regret or concern. I am not sure which, for I lose his expression in the shadows, and then he is gone, his heavy footsteps travelling back into the main house.

'Come dear, drink this.' She sits beside me, watching as I slowly sip the bitter brew. Something about this attention seems false and she smiles slowly as I swallow it all down. 'I'll help you upstairs; you must be tired from such a long day.'

As we progress up the servants' stairs, my limbs become heavier, my feet harder to drag up each step. She takes my reticule and my arm, guiding me further up until we reach the attic. My legs can barely stand, leaning on her for support as we shuffle into my room. The walls blur. My eyes no longer see her face – I only feel her breathing hard on my neck and her hands heaving me onto the bed.

I wake up the next day, groggy and sick. The effort to pull myself off the mattress is harder than usual. The chimes from the church bell are unusually deafening. Retching into my water bowl, I notice my lips taste of blood – from biting them in my sleep? My clothes for the day are laid out on the only chair, the way my maid Nelly used to, yet I have no memory of preparing for bed.

Next to my reticule on the side table is a new addition to the room: a small statue whittled from wood. It is a figure of a woman with long hair and a simple, plain face. Hannah's taunts about William's affection also ring in my ears. Could it be a gift from the gardener? Has he been in my room, watching me sleep? I grimace, reading the letters that are deeply etched into the body: *Ivy*.

Instinctively, I throw it into the nearest drawer, out of sight. I don't want it near me. Instead, I focus on the contents of my reticule. At the sight of the Devil's Thorn cuttings, I release a breath I hadn't realised I'd been holding. The find is astonishing, and I am already forgetting the statue and the unexplained nausea, daydreaming of studying and presenting my notes to the Royal College of Science.

I transfer the prickly stems into my tin vasculum, the safest way to store them. I wish I had my screw-down press, but I will have to make do without. Unfortunately, some of the berries have become damaged, the juice staining the handkerchief green. A sickly-sweet smell rises, and I recall the cordial on the top shelf in the pantry. Time seems to slow down, and my hands start to shake.

The thought that someone could have made a concoction from this poisonous plant so deadly that it could kill half the occupants of the street is frightening. Praying the cordial had nothing to do with Miss Earnshaw's disappearance, I place the green tin back inside my carpet bag, along with my treasured books, back into the cupboard.

It is only then that I see the scratched words scrawled onto the inside of the small, wooden door: *Help me!* My blood runs cold. For whoever wrote this message is long gone now.

I sit on the bed thinking about the message. No one comes to my room to scold me for being tardy, which is unusual as the day is almost Christmas. I somehow get dressed for the day ahead, with the scratched words repeating in my mind. At half past seven, I stumble downstairs into the kitchen, aware that I must look more worse for wear than normal. The events of last night, like an odd dream, return in fractured pieces. I remember travelling to Camden to visit Mr Witherfield, but everything blurs after that. Every time I try to dig deeper into my mind, it aches with the effort.

'Here you are, lovey.' Mrs Higgins puts a plate of fresh scones on the table and beckons for me to sit. 'I baked them especially for you this morning.'

I am surprised, for I was expecting discipline, not a warm welcome. I scrutinise her features. Could she be capable of making a poison tincture from the nightshades in the garden? Surely Hannah would not know of such things and still work here?

Slumping down on the bench, all my muscles feel loose, especially in my face. A flicker of a memory of sitting in the same place disappears before I can remember it clearly. I touch my skin with the tips of my fingers. Everything is numb or too soft. I am out of sorts, a reaction to the sherry at Mr Witherfield's house, perhaps.

'You were a bit unwell last night.' She adds butter and a pot of strawberry jam to the table, which is normally reserved only for Lady Blackham. 'Too much to drink on your adventures?'

I watch Mrs Higgins speak, her lips moving, her voice too loud like the church bells. It takes all my willpower to control my mouth. The scones taste delicious, but even the chewing motion of eating seems to be difficult to master this morning.

'I remember when I was young, always sneaking out too... Well, you need not know about the follies of my youth. Do you have a fancy man, someone special?' She doesn't wait for an answer but turns back to the stove, moving saucepans about. I try not to wince at the sounds. 'I know Hannah does. She is constantly with that handsome Irish policeman of hers on a Thursday night.' She smiles at me over her shoulder and continues her morning ritual, still asking questions without answers.

The scones accomplish their job of easing my stomach. Combined with a strong cup of tea, I am finally coming out of the fog in which I woke.

'Now then, I've spoken to Mr Bancroft, and they have given you a nice, easy morning. See, the work isn't all bad? I've been here a long time and never found a better place of employment; none that compares to here.'

Did I wake up in a different house? The change in this woman is almost laughable.

'I could go to the market, the fresh air would be good?'

'No need, Hannah has already gone. Besides, open a couple of windows and you'll get the benefits without freezing to death.'

I am disappointed. The trip out would give me a chance to process what I learned from Mr Witherfield last night and the muddled events that followed. Are his memories reliable anyway? He is a confused old man. My mother never mentioned him or London. Why couldn't she keep me if she stayed in the city? These thoughts turn over in my mind. How is my mother connected to Miss Earnshaw, and why are the Blackhams so dangerous?

I am on my guard and force myself into the chore of simple dusting, although I am clumsy and uncoordinated with my hands. And I know with certainty that something has shifted in the house.

Later in the day, I ask Mr Bancroft if I can visit the seamstress for Mistress Blackham's newest dress, which is waiting to be collected. He also declines my trip outside, providing a reason that only sounds half logical. As the afternoon progresses, I wonder if an unspoken agreement exists to keep me within the house.

A leaden unease laced with paranoia takes root in my thoughts. I am beginning to distrust the illusion of freedom they give, and perhaps I am in more danger than I thought. When no one is about, I take the sewing box kept in a scullery drawer up to the attic, wrapping my mourning ring in the handkerchief gifted to me by the man at the apothecary. I sew the small bundle into the folds of my skirt. It is a rough job. The stitches are not neat, but it will suffice; I need to keep my most treasured possession close to me.

How long has it been since the mistress left the house? Each day I worry more about her health. Her night terrors are draining her. Every meal time she eats less, and her strength fades a little more. Maybe, because of my own nightmares, I have found empathy with her. The doctor says the mistress is losing her mind. I am more uncertain than ever about the boundary between what is real and my own warped imagination. My nurse had said that we all have demons. Perhaps I have more than most. The Devil and his unseen companions continue to haunt me with their anguished voices and rapping on the walls. I expect there was an element of truth in what my father revealed about my mother; she must have hidden her bouts of hysteria from me.

Do I carry the same disease in my blood, slowly losing my grip on reality?

My skin prickles with unease as I look around the attic. Nowhere feels safe. I had believed the master was the puppeteer of this house, but now I am not so sure he is the only one. He seems to struggle as well. The tension in this building is taking its toll on each of us. It seems like we are all moving to music I cannot hear, playing our parts like actors performing on a stage, but we continue as if we are all waiting ... waiting for something to happen.

Chapter 37 ~ The Devil's Face

Ivy ~ Blackham House, 22nd December.

A full dinner tray rests on the kitchen table, carefully prepared and ready to be taken upstairs for the evening meal: beef stew and dumplings with a small bread loaf. It's a heartening sight, but I am sickened with the knowledge of its destination.

'You drew the short straw tonight.' Hannah calls out from the pantry. 'I'm not seeing her again today. She was in a strange mood this morning. Had me going up and down those stairs like a madwoman.'

'What are you saying? She is always like that.' The humour in my voice is false, though. It is time to face the old woman, and I am determined to ask her about Miss Earnshaw.

Hannah continues to shout from the other room. 'No, today feels different. She was all flustered, like a fat, crippled bird in her nest, fluffing her feathers, squawking for attention. Nothing was good enough for her.'

I smile to myself; the idea is a clever one. Hannah has a knack for turning people into animals. She is uncanny about the butler being an ox and the mistress a canary, pretty but delicate, like the bird caged above her bed. What would I be to her – a field mouse?

The old woman never strays from her room. The only time I saw her smile was when I presented her with Mr Godwin's brooch. It should have been a happy moment, but instead, my conscience was heavy as I passed it to her. As if, somehow, I had unwittingly committed a crime in this action.

She has so many shiny objects, and with her gnarled hands like claws, Hannah might say she is a corvid, not a garden bird like a robin or a sweet wren. She would probably eat them if they appeared, boiled in this stew, soft and tender between her crooked teeth. The stew has started to congeal, its appeal already lost, and my appetite with it.

'You never know, you might bring her some happiness with that meal.' Hannah walks back into the kitchen, wiping her hands on her apron, the smell of beeswax and polish hovering about her. 'Asking for you, she was. Right peculiar if I say so myself. She kept wanting to know if you were still in the house, as if you would leave us. You aren't planning on going away, are you? A little holiday by the sea planned?' The question sounds light-hearted, but her eyes flash hard. 'Mr Bancroft wants us to go through the whole house again before Christmas Eve, cleaning everything we see. I don't fancy being left on my own to do your work.'

Mrs Higgins glares at me. 'It would upset Lady Blackham if you left us, Ivy, disrupt her routine.'

I fiddle with the tray, adjusting the cutlery and napkin, avoiding her gaze. A bell for the second floor starts to ring.

'Like when Mr Bancroft left? Maybe it unsettled her routine with him leaving and then returning out of the blue,' I reply, pensive of her reaction.

'But he went nowhere.' Mrs Higgins inhales deeply and reaches for a carving knife on the table. 'He has his bedroom down here, as do I. Age is playing with her memory.' She cuts up the vegetables with sharp, repetitive strokes. 'That's what happens when you're left to your own devices with nothing but your own company.'

'But he wasn't here when I arrived … and you told me his shoes belonged to William?' I glance up, waiting for her response.

'Why would William ever wear smart shoes? I would never say such a thing. Have you been on the mistress's tonic, Ivy? Blackham House has always had a butler.'

Mrs Higgins holds the blade in mid-air and gives me the same look as the innkeeper's wife gave me on my way to London, viewing me as a troublemaker. Her conviction is so strong that I am already doubting my memories, my recollection of events. Exhaustion muddles my mind; I cannot think straight.

The service bell goes on ringing and my heart sinks as I see it is for Lady Blackham, her mood will already be dark if she has been waiting.

Hannah continues obliviously, unaware of the tension in the room. 'Anyway, Lady Blackham wasn't confused. In fact, she was more alert than ever, fussing over all the ornaments in her room, ensuring I dusted them properly; watching me with her beady eyes, checking I didn't break anything. It was as if she was expecting someone. Who would visit her in that smelly old room? No one has come calling or left a card for ages – perhaps she has an imaginary friend?'

Mrs Higgins bangs the copper pot holding the cut vegetables hard on the stove. 'Enough! Ivy, go before that bell rings itself off the wall. Hannah, shut your mouth and get on with your work. I expect this soup to be finished by the end of the hour.'

I jolt with shock. Mrs Higgins swivels on her heels and dares me to stay a moment longer with a harsh glare. The thick brown sauce spills over the lid of the bowl as I lift the tray and find its balance. I can sense her eyes boring into my back as I leave the kitchen to make my way up the servant staircase, the bell still frantically ringing in my ears.

By the time I knock on Lady Blackham's door, the stew looks even worse. Lumps of fat have curdled, floating together with the faded, boiled vegetables. I will have to force the leftovers down later for supper and be grateful.

'Enter,' her voice dictates, direct and strong.

The old woman sits in her chair next to the fireplace wearing her finest evening wear, something she never does. The scene looks as though she is clearly ready for a guest to arrive.

'Ah, finally. Does the bell not work in the kitchen? You may put the dinner tray over here on the table beside the mantel. I am feeling the cold and wish to dine near the fire.' True, the room holds a much lower temperature to the rest of the house. I swallow my dislike of her, for although she is a difficult character, she is still frail and elderly. I would not wish her to freeze to death.

'Would you like me to check for a breeze? Perhaps the sash did not close properly.'

I set the food down and walk over to the bay window. I push hard on the frame, but the glass pane is secured with no draughts escaping. The room temperature is bitter, the tips of my fingers are already numb, and my breath puffs out visibly into the air. I am relieved that today she is not insisting on opening the windows.

Her dressing table is in disarray, with lids and boxes discarded carelessly. I look her over again in surprise. She is wearing all her jewellery at once, with at least two rings on every finger and a handful of pendants draped heavily around her neck. The recently purchased brooch is in pride of place in the centre of her chest. All of the gold is fighting for space, layered over the material so it will fit. They all have the silver hair, which must be from her late husband, weaved into their designs. I replay Mr Godwin's preposterous words in my mind; his claim that these gems have the power to break through cracks in the afterlife, to conjure spirits back and fulfil their wearer's desires of being reunited with the dead.

A single candle is lit on the mantel. The fire in the hearth burns vigorously below, but still no heat permeates the air. The rest of the room is dark, but the fierce flames are still able to cast light on Lady Blackham's true age. Deep lines, cragged with grey smudges around her eyes, highlight her frailty and that she hasn't slept for some time. She has attempted to tint her cheeks and lips with coloured balm, but the bright-pink stain gives her a startling appearance; almost vulnerable with the haphazard application, like a child found playing with makeup. But when she looks at me, her eyes are still sharp and penetrating – the lack of innocence behind them alarms me.

'Are you expecting someone? Shall I ask Mrs Higgins to prepare another meal, or perhaps you would prefer to move to the dining room?'

'No, I am quite content here.' She pats the velvet arm of her chair. 'Do not be concerned, for nobody will call at the front door this evening. I have everything I need and am prepared.'

'Prepared?' The question falters on my tongue and lingers in the air.

'All I need is you, and you are here now.' She looks at me up and down like a long-lost friend. 'Isn't she a darling, my dear, the best one yet?' She speaks past me towards the flower-papered wall.

I turn, expecting to find someone standing behind me. Perhaps the master is included in this private joke, but only a dead badger mounted on a shelf above the piano looks back at me. Its dispassionate eyes shine out amidst the greased black and white fur. My skin prickles from the intensity of the unlit corner nearest the doorway. The darkness is so deep that I have to strain to see the furniture.

'I told you not to worry if she would come.'

I wrap my arms around me for warmth. Something in the room is wrong and out of kilter. As Hannah had said, the old lady's behaviour is peculiar today.

'Patience brings all good things to us ... didn't I say?' She continues to speak as if to another person as the door clicks closed. The single gaslight flickers with the movement. I step back involuntarily from her, in the direction of the hallway, wanting to open the door again. 'You will be careful with her, won't you?' She pauses. 'Not like the other ones.'

Still, no answer is returned to her rambling, but I know without looking that if I turned towards the shadows in the corner, a figure would be there now. The image of the warm kitchen and the cook still reprimanding Hannah only a few floors beneath us is hard to imagine. The presence of malevolence is so strong the taste manifests in my mouth like a bitter herb.

'This one is special.' She smiles as she looks me up and down again.

Tendrils of panic twine themselves around my body. Who would rescue me up here if I shouted out? The room seems to twist and shrink; the walls are moving in. Claustrophobia tugs at my limbs with the need to move and shake off this dread. I flinch as the snaps from the fire become abnormally loud, as if they are miniature gunshots. The presence of danger crawls beneath my clothes like a slick snake escaping from one of the glass cabinets. The scaled creature edges up my sleeve and under the bodice, burrowing into my chest until it squeezes my heart, constricting me from the inside out.

Inhaling a shallow breath, I attempt to stand taller. 'I shall go now… Mrs Higgins instructed me to return once I am done here. I have more errands to do – she is expecting me.' The end of my sentence falters as Lady Blackham shakes her head.

If I moved fast enough, I could open the door and run down the staircase, out into the street before anyone could touch me. But who could be waiting in the courtyard? Would the man guarding the house apprehend me – the nightwatchman? I hear the wind picking up outside and the pattering gush of rain as it sweeps hard against the window. The water would soak me within seconds, and without taking my purse, I would be in trouble.

'No, my dear, we are ready for you now. You will stay here with us. I am sure the cook will understand.'

The sensation grows that I am akin to a fly who has been caught unaware, thinking I was free to choose my flight, when in fact the web has enclosed me the entire time. I find myself standing in front of the old lady, realising my mistake. Is this what Miss Earnshaw experienced before her fate?

But I refuse to succumb to their wishes easily; my nature is stubborn. The small vegetable knife is still in my apron pocket. I grip the cold steel, angling my fingers to grasp the wooden handle. I will use the blade if the situation comes to it, a question of self-defence when protesting my innocence to the police. But against whom? The old woman, or worse – I still do not know who or what watches me.

I tilt my head slowly to follow the gaze of Lady Blackham, and to my horror, from the corner of the room, the shadows merge to form the shape of a man. He is part of this house, coming from its underbelly; this ungodly thing that has been hovering at the edges of my vision, lurking, waiting, watching.

'Have you met my husband, Lord Blackham? Of course, you must have done. He is almost ready to join us, to touch and claim what is his. You have been in his study and taken books from the library?' She raises one eyebrow in disbelief. 'But don't concern yourself now. We will overlook that indiscretion. The fact pleases him you are well learned. It makes you all the more interesting to him. He has always been fascinated by the unusual.'

She strokes her rings, admiring them glinting in the light from the flames. 'Bringing his little treasures back here to keep them safely away from the rest of the world. Have you seen all the collection? We have many private pieces as well.' She waves her hands, opening them to the room. 'It is a great body of work throughout the house. I am immensely proud of him, of how his efforts pressed on even after—'

'What do you want?' I ask, my legs threatening to buckle. This is no parlour game, and if this is not my imagination, it is a dream beyond nightmares.

'Resurrection! It is within our grasp at last.' Her triumphant voice adds to the sensation that I have lost at a game I had no idea was being played around me.

Still, there is silence from the shadow, which stands unmoving. I will my limbs to react, but my body and mind have become disconnected. Like a caged animal, I want to run, but my legs won't move.

At first, no sound comes. I fill my lungs with the frigid, cold air in the room and then the emotion erupts, the power coursing through me, strong and wild. The release is immense, ringing in my ears as I scream.

The old lady is bewildered and taken by surprise by the sudden noise. She turns to the presence in the corner. Perhaps she had assumed I would be compliant in this prearranged agreement, surrendering without a word. But I want to live, not disappear and become a forgotten name, like the servants before me.

'Help me!' I cry. *The message in the attic cupboard is also mine now.* I scream again, this time louder; my body has been woken by the piercing sound. Let the nightwatchman in the street know I am afraid. Someone, a stranger, might help, although the hope is futile. I am frightened to my bones, but I will not give myself over to this godforsaken house.

The bedroom door opens abruptly, spilling light from the hallway. The master stands there, surprised.

'What is the commotion? Mother, are you well? What a devil of a noise! I expect half the neighbourhood will be wondering about us.' His eyes drift towards me, standing by the fireside. 'Ivy, you appear stricken! What on earth is happening?'

Lady Blackham composes herself. 'Nothing is going on, Alexander. Just a bit of fuss, that is all – the girl has become quite hysterical. She must be overworked, such an inconvenience.' She huffs, sending me a withering look. 'I recommend giving her one of the drinks prescribed for your wife. That should settle her nerves and give us a respite from this unnecessary display.'

She eyes me with disgust. I have disappointed her, and she is angry. For a brief moment, I can imagine what it must be like to be her son, living beneath her scornful gaze. 'Take her now and make sure she sleeps. I will not have this house brought down by poor social graces. You know what needs to be done for the reputation of this family. Do I need to remind you?'

'No Mother, I am well aware,' he mutters under his breath, but drink slows his movements as usual. 'Come here, Ivy.'

He strides awkwardly across the floor, breaking the spell I could not, and grabs my arm. His fingers hurt with the pressure, but I let myself be taken. All my energy is expelled with the gratitude that I am leaving.

On the way out, I expect the master to lead me back downstairs to the kitchen to be addressed by Mrs Higgins, but as we walk down the corridor, I see Mr Bancroft is already waiting.

'Can I assist you, sir?'

'Yes, will you kindly give Ivy a tonic from my wife's room? She has become quite hysterical, screaming down the house and upset my mother.'

Is he aware of the shadows that exist within these walls? Is he part of it all? He stumbles and hands me roughly over to the butler.

I wish to stay in the light of the hallway. I want to leave this house at once, run away back to the comfort of the countryside. Even a hideous marriage would be better than this. The two of them talk over me, as if I am not real or a child to be dealt with without discussion.

'I heard the outburst, sir. It is most irregular, but I do not believe the neighbours would have noticed. It's raining hard tonight and any noise will have disturbed no one.'

He also considers me with contempt. I want to explain about Lady Blackham's ramblings and the shadow in her room, but I cannot find the words. I am taken, half-dragged, down to the first floor, to the mistress's room. The master enters before us, as we linger in the doorway. Mr Bancroft's firm hand moves to cover my mouth to muffle my protests. Will the mistress wake up and finally understand the house she lives in? But my fear grows as the mistress lies motionless in her bed, dead to the world in sleep; she wouldn't move even if half of London surrounded her. Suddenly, I am sure I too will share the same drugged fate. They intend to take my consciousness away from me.

I struggle harder as the master returns with her blue tonic bottle. He staggers across the room, removing the lid with clumsy hands. 'Here, this is what she needs. See how Angelica is resting?'

He gives the glass bottle to Mr Bancroft, who prises my jaw open with his thick fingers, forcing the contents down my throat. I gag as the bitter liquid spills out of my mouth and runs down my chin, dampening my neck and collar. 'No, no, let me free!' I splutter. 'I will tell no one about this house.'

Kicking out at the butler's legs makes no difference. I pray for the spirit of Miss Earnshaw to intervene, for anything or anybody to help. But then I remember again that it is not her presence that roams within these walls, but an energy far more sinister and I am truly alone.

I cough, searching the master's eyes for pity. But they are clouded with something else other than alcohol, opium perhaps? I doubt he will remember this episode at all in the morning. Will I remember? The question forms in my mind as the fight evaporates. I try to yell again, one last attempt at controlling my future, but the cry is trapped in my chest, the snake of fear pulling tighter as the laudanum begins to engulf me.

The master walks down the hallway, leaving Mr Bancroft cradling me like an infant. Leaning down, he puts his mouth to my ear. I can't push him away; my strength has been stolen. His words are soft and gentle, but they shoot panic through my last thoughts as I drift into nothingness.

'Now, Ivy, hush-hush … you must not resist anymore. You belong in the attic, don't you?' He lifts me up and I cannot move, pressed against his chest.

I know we are travelling back up the stairs to the attic. 'No, please…' My protests are tangled and caught, muffled noises indistinguishable in the night, mixing with the creaking of the house.

I have so many regrets. I should have gone to the detective with my suspicions. No one knows where I am. This is the end and I am to disappear as if I never existed.

Through heavy-lidded eyes, wooden floors pass beneath me, confirming my room in the attic, the threadbare rug, and the familiar creak of the bed frame as he lays me down. He covers me gently with the blanket. The action should be one of kindness, but it feels as if he is preparing me for something else.

My memory trips back to the farmer on our country land, how he would stroke and murmur to the spring lambs just before he killed them for our meals. His tenderness was just enough so the animal wouldn't bolt, making sure the whole deed was easier to accomplish. I understand with horrid dread what Lady Blackham was implying – I am a sacrifice … a lamb to the slaughter.

Chapter 38 ~ Voices

Ivy ~ Blackham House, 23rd December.

It must be morning, but my eyes are hard to open. Pain shoots behind my temples as I try to move my aching body. Nauseous and groggy, sliding between sleep and reality, I can taste the bitterness of laudanum from last night.

Easing myself onto my side, I look around – it's still the early hours. The curtains are wide apart, revealing the jet-black sky, but the window is closed. No gaslight or candle is within reach, and only the moonlight casts a dim light across the room. I am still wearing my maid's uniform under a single blanket. Finding the metal edge of the bed, I slowly push myself up into sitting, suffering the lead-heavy effects of being drugged again. All this time, I had thought Miss Earnshaw was guiding me in some shape or form. How foolish I had been to pull on the silk threads myself, inviting the spider to come out of the shadows without realising my stupid naivety.

'Ivy, Ivy…'

My name fills the room.

On instinct, I clamber out of bed and stagger over to the earpiece, holding it close to my ear. Silence, and then a crackle. A rush of whispers and moans spill out of the metal like a swarm of bees gushing into the room. Men, women, children – they scream out to me in pain and torment.

Then I see it again, an ink-blot shape, the shadow of a man. The same unnatural presence that appeared in Lady Blackham's room. An icy shiver runs from the nape of my neck and sinks down into the marrow of my bones. Is this the same spirit the mistress saw when she fell and lost her baby?

An abnormal vibration travels around the walls and surrounds me. An ancient dread has awoken in the depths of my soul; a knowledge of evil passed down by generations of a long-forgotten memory.

'A beautiful treasure…' The rasping voice comes from the earpiece like a death rattle in a dying throat. The other voices intensify, as though the attic is crowded with souls from the neighbouring graveyard.

Dropping the metal tube, I flinch as if I've been burnt and scuttle back across the floor. I try to open the door but it is locked.

In a panic, I close my eyes and I cannot avoid returning to the fear of my childhood, believing that a spectre hoovers above me now as it did then. Freezing draughts cascade down the back of my neck, the coldness enveloping me; my body reacts violently, convulsing with erratic shivers. I keep pounding on the door with my fists, beating the wooden panels until my hands hurt. My longing for my mother pervades every fibre of my being, and I yearn for the innocence and comfort she provided before her death. I would rather be ignorant of the secrets and cracks in this world, of how hell seeps into this life on Earth.

Where is my faith? Perhaps if I surrender now, I could join my mother, find her somehow. At least in the afterlife, I would cast off the burden of living without her. How could she abandon me to face my horrors alone?

The persistent whispers begin again; even at this moment, they demand my attention. For as long as I can remember, I have struggled to keep these voices at bay. Mother said they were figments of my imagination and when I was older I would understand. Perhaps they are calling me to my death. I exhale slowly. Fine then, I am broken enough; let them have me. My legs go limp and give way as I slump to the floor.

For the first time in my life, I disobey my mother. I break down the walls in my mind and listen. I finally allow the voices in. What have I to lose now? My sanity has already cracked. Either death or an asylum is my destiny; I have no strength to pretend otherwise. All these years I've spent forcing them away have taken their toll.

Loud and rough, like rushing water, their familiar voices bombard me. Wave after wave, hundreds of thousands of voices, many crying, some whispering softly – others yelling to be heard. They swirl and knit together until finally, they form a sea; a mass of noise and energy washing over my thoughts, drawing me into the centre of their existence.

I let go, giving myself over to their commotion. They have me now. I am theirs for the taking; such a sweet release from the effort of denying them. They flood into my body, my soul. They consume all the empty spaces, swallowing the loneliness within me.

But oh, their tormented despair, agony, grief, and regret. I cannot control them. They tear through me. Desperate to return, they demand my help, wanting to speak to their loved ones, friends, enemies, about unspoken last words, warnings, and broken promises. They fizz around me like gunpowder, all the colours I could imagine, an unrelenting display of raw emotion.

'I will try to help you - give me time,' I plead. They abate a little, pleased by my acknowledgement. Cracking open my eyes, even the dim moonlight in the room is painful. The ominous shape has gone. Relief is bittersweet. I am alone, but not quite. The voices hum around me, waiting for their chance to come forward again, pacified only for the moment. Amid this darkness, there is still hope; my journey does not end here. I have a new direction; the spirits are calling and they need me. Perhaps, in time, I might even hear my mother's voice.

The door finally opens in the late afternoon, as twilight steals the last of the winter sun. I suddenly recall that it must be Christmas Eve. How life can change in a year. Hannah stands with a simple meal of bread and butter and a steaming cup of tea on a tray. I must have slept for most of the day, but still my stomach rolls at the notion of food.

'Mrs Higgins thought you might be hungry. Don't know why you're so special – none of the others got fed up here.'

I speak slowly, forming the words one by one with effort. 'Hannah, how many people have stayed in this room before me?'

She puts the tray down onto the bedside table, and then looks at her fingers as though counting each name in her head, and then seems to reprimand herself for indulging my question. 'That's none of your business.'

I push myself off the bed and weave past her, stumbling along the corridor and then down the narrow, winding servant stairs to the ground floor. With my heart in my throat, I try all the doors - the front door, the library, the dining room, but to no success. I am standing by the collection room when I hear her familiar footsteps behind me.

'What do you think you're doing?' Hannah asks curtly.

'It is locked,' I reply. 'I need to get on with my chores.'

My instinct warns me to act normally. Hannah must be unhinged to still be here; surely, she knows what is going on in this house. But then again, perhaps her obsession with the master has blinded her to the truth.

'Stand aside, I have to go in there first.' She pulls a large steel key from her pocket. 'They have given me an important job in the master's most treasured room.' She waits for me to move before turning the key. 'If you were less of a weak dormouse, perhaps they'd give you more responsibility, like me.'

Something inside me snaps, and I am no longer afraid of her disapproval. 'Are you frightened Hannah? Is that why you stay? Have they threatened you?'

She looks at me up and down. For a moment, I see the vulnerable girl she must have been before life hardened her. 'I'm not scared of anything, unlike you,' she scoffs.

'We could have been friends.' I say, trying to appeal to whatever kindness still remains between us.

'Friendship is a weakness… Trusting people only brings pain.'

'But you can trust me.'

She pauses, and I hope she might be considering my words, the offer of friendship. I have never been so bold with anyone.

'Everyone I've ever trusted has either deceived me or left me. Now, they've sent you to the attic, your days are numbered. You won't last long.' She pouts her lips. 'So, please, if you don't mind, my work doesn't involve the likes of you.' She slams the collection room door in my face. The lock scrapes shut.

I will try to get out through the kitchen. The stairs to the basement are in shadow. My head is beginning to clear from the laudanum, but despondent from Hannah's rejection, my concentration falters and I slip, falling down a couple of steps and catching my uniform on one of the rusty nails in the wall. I recover myself and yank it free quickly. If I break my leg now, that would be the end of me.

The kitchen is unlit, no one is about, and the aroma of cooking is unusually absent. My anxiety increases as the scullery door to the outside is also secured, and the key hooks are empty.

My attention is caught by the sound of faint footsteps, but they don't come from above – they're from the ground below, under the basement. They encroach closer. Puzzled, I dart into the pantry and hide behind the door.

From the pantry, I see a hatch in the kitchen floor open up in front of the fireplace. Mr Bancroft carefully closes the entrance with Mrs Higgins beside him. How had I missed this hatchway built into the floor? But this part of the kitchen has always been covered with an old rag rug.

'The preparations are nearly done. I know, I understand... I won't forget.' Her voice is high-pitched, almost whining.

'We cannot afford to have any...' he pauses. 'More mistakes. Everything must go smoothly this time.'

'Where is Ivy?' He demands and walks out of sight.

My blood runs cold at the sound of my name.

'She is still in the attic or somewhere else in the house. Don't worry, she can't escape anywhere. I sealed the whole place shut. I will fetch her when the time comes.'

'And Hannah?'

'A simple enough errand occupies her. She knows the routine.'

'Has Ivy come round to the ceremony? Everything would be easier if she did.' His tone is terse.

'She will. How can she not? It's only a matter of waiting.'

'Until then, we will continue with our work. There is still lots to do before we are done.'

Their voices make me nauseous, the way I'm being discussed like an object.

'I must go and get more herbs and ingredients for the special meal.'

There's a clash of pans, as if one of them has banged something in anger.

'I'm sorry, the fruit turned mouldy. I only got them yesterday, or I could ask Hannah if you prefer?'

'We cannot entrust the task to Hannah. She has not yet proven herself, and anyway, she might still be needed for tonight.'

'They wouldn't use her? She's all I have. I can't do all the cooking as well as the cleaning.'

'She's no longer the master's favourite and there will be a new servant soon enough to replace her. What about Lottie?'

'I told you she was off limits. I only employ her when I'm desperate. Besides, she's much too young. You go too far, James. This has all gone too—' There is another bang of a pan against something hard.

'Just get to the market before it closes and be quick about it.'

Gone is the private tenderness between mother and son. The kitchen door opens and a cold blast of air whips at my ankles from outside. The door slams shut and the lock turns. Mr Bancroft leaves the kitchen, but he is still in the house.

I know I must be mad, blinded by optimism to venture down into the depths below, but determination spurs me on, and if there's a last chance to escape or of finding answers, I need to take it.

Chapter 39 ~ The Crypt

Old wooden steps lead down further into the ground. There's only a faint light below. As I pull the hatch shut behind me over my head, I can still make out either side of the brick walls. The temperature drops. I smell the aroma of burnt herbs; rosemary and mugwort, and something else that's bitter; not quite the stale air I expected.

I arrive in a small corridor, no more than six feet wide, with three doors before me. The two next to me are closed; the one furthest away is ajar. I try the door to my left and it opens easily. The inside is simply furnished: a cot bed sits parallel to the wall, and there's a chest of drawers with a handful of small wooden-handled tools set out on top. A candle is lit with only a third burned, indicating someone has been here recently. Perhaps this is where William sleeps.

Door number two is stiff; the wood has warped with the underground damp. After a shove, it opens, and I almost fall into a large solid object on the floor. The scene makes my skin crawl: seven coffins line the walls; they are all shut except for the one open at my feet. The case is elaborately decorated, engraved with hieroglyphics, and lined with luxurious black silk.

I tremble at the unsettling sight. What is this place? Inside the coffin is a bundle of crimson cotton sheets embroidered in gold thread with the Egyptian hieroglyphs I recognise from the wall of Mr Godwin's jewellery shop. Birds, feathers, and planets adorn the fabric, but in this version, along the hem, there are also the shapes of people, waiting in line, looking up, as if in rapture, at the stars above. I touch the soft cloth, and out tumbles a handful of carved wooden figures, all female, with names inscribed on each base: Alice, Sarah, and Hattie. My breath becomes strangled; they are the same as the one I found with my name engraved on it. Each carving has a different face. They must be gifts given to the servants before me and I can almost imagine how the women looked; such is the careful detail of their features. A grim thought squirms in the pit of my belly like the maggots that appeared in the apple by my bed. I think of all the belongings which remain in Hannah's storage box unclaimed.

The other servants never left the house.

I lean forward and open another coffin, but it is empty, as are the others I can reach. There is nothing living or dead in this room, only the notion of something in between. The door creaks in protest as I close it.

Stepping through the last doorway, there is a change in the atmosphere, a foreboding sensation. The walls narrow into a smaller bricked passageway, forcing me to stoop as I move forward. I must be under the garden now. Beneath the diseased trees and the birds that feed on the dense soil. These grey bricks, damp to the touch, are a larger, heavier type of stone, like the slabs in the neighbouring graveyard.

Something down here is more frightening than that in the house above. Only the desire to find the secrets kept in the hidden depths of this building drives me on. As the confined tunnel twists ahead, the scent of burnt herbs becomes stronger and a panic induced by the small space starts to take hold; my mouth becomes so dry I can barely swallow. I cannot even make out the outline of my own fingers.

Tentatively, I feel along the stone wall edges with my other hand in front of me, reaching out into the unknown, hoping to protect myself, bracing myself for whatever might be waiting. *What lies beneath this building?* I recall the vicar's words again: the history here, the sightings of people when the house was empty, the ghostly visions at the windows.

The tunnel opens out into a large room with a solitary stone table. Four struggling gas lamps attached to each wall barely break the gloom. It appears to be a church crypt, but it is decorated strangely; old tapestries depicting what look like forest scenes hang from the far wall but bring no comfort to the space. There is no fire, no warmth. My arms are trembling with the icy temperature. The smell of burnt herbs is now almost overpowering, with no windows for fresh air. The need to run, the urge to escape this place is strong, primal. No God of mine directed me here.

The stone table is part of an embellished tomb, decorated with familiar glittering patterns. I take a step forward towards it. What is underneath? Not a normal grave. Lines of jewels encrust the stone: pearls, opals, rubies, topaz, amethyst, and lapis lazuli. Their order of placement is repeated again and again, the same arrangement of jewels worn by Lady Blackham in her mourning jewellery. The wealth spent on this grave is astonishing.

Someone sits in the far corner. They have been watching me the whole time but making no sound or movement. My eyes focus in the dim light and I find William looking back at me. He smiles slowly. For the first time, I notice one of his teeth is missing. He almost looks pleased to see me and his emotion catches me off-guard. I waver between being relieved at recognising him and startled by his presence. This is where he disappears to – this is his place.

He brings his finger up to his lips. 'Shhh... Don't disturb what is resting.'

And suddenly, I am unprepared for whatever exists here. 'Miss Earnshaw?'

'You won't find her here, not anymore, but she is closer than you imagine.' He glances around the room. 'Why don't you come and sit with me? It's nice to enjoy some company for a change.'

His features look different in the shadows, his sockets receding deeper into his skull, taking on the appearance of a gaunt face. He pats an empty chair beside him. 'You are early. I admire your enthusiasm. Not like the others.'

He muses to himself and then turns away to scrape at a piece of wood in his hand, the pale shavings falling into a scattered pile on the floor. 'Did you appreciate your gift?'

I refuse the seat but move closer to see what he is holding, watching as he carefully slices at a wooden figure, his fingers creating what is beginning to look like a female form. 'You want another?' He gestures towards the lump of wood.

I shake my head, unable to speak, to find the words that would make all this go away.

'Sorry Miss, I can't give it to you anyway. This is for the next. I do the faces later...' He grimaces. The rotten stub of his missing tooth moves as he talks.

Decay, death, it is everywhere.

'The one after you,' he continues. 'Although perhaps this time it might be different. I heard you are special. No matter, I am always prepared. That is why they chose me.'

He widens his bloodshot eyes. He must be half-blind, but his fingers continue to work on the wood with expert ease.

Then he stops.

'Told you not to mess with the birds; they've got their sights on you now,' he exclaims, and then throws back his face, opening his jaws wide. 'Cha – cha – cha – cha – cha!' The jagged sounds that erupt out of his mouth are loud and unnerving in their realism, capturing the raspy chatter of the magpies.

I expect the birds to appear, responding to his call, and swarm down on me; to peck and pull at my skin and my eyes, just as they did when they tore the poor cat apart in the garden. I turn away from him and scrabble back as fast as I can through the tunnel. My teeth clash together with the cold, but I am sweating in fright. I trip and fall, scraping my knees. Chancing a glance behind, I see he has not followed, but I am sure I am not alone.

I rush up the steps and push open the hatch. For one heart-wrenching moment, I panic that someone has locked me down here, trapping me to face the terror. But I am free and back in the kitchen, another world within a second. I slam the door back into the floor, shutting the gardener in the underground vault.

My legs give way, and I slump into a chair at the table, the skin on my neck slick with moisture. It is then that I see her.

Mrs Higgins stands slouched in the corner facing the wall. Her usually busy hands are idle, hanging limply by her side. I can hear water gushing from the tap in the scullery. As if my presence has woken her, she slowly turns around.

'You found the crypt then. I'm glad you came to your senses. You cannot fight it and there is no use in hiding. We all have a job to do. Make yourself useful and take this to the mistress.' She thrusts a tray of cold leftovers towards me across the table.

It is a pitiful sight, only fit for a dog. Her face shows no expression. She could be a stranger, for there is no trace of the woman I knew.

Chapter 40 ~ Quest for Help

I run to the mistress's room. No one is around, but the house creaks and moans as I hurry along past the papered walls. I pass the cabinet containing the grave doll – the ceramic face with real flaxen hair, the blue glass eyes almost forlorn, appealing to be released from the display coffin. The image makes me shudder; nothing in this house is at rest. I was expecting the door to be locked, but the handle opens. The mistress is lying on the bed, drifting in and out of consciousness, her eyes roaming the room deliriously. Dusk has drawn in early and the room is ice cold, my breath clearly visible in the crisp air. All of her usual lamps are unlit, as is the fire. Only a single candle flickers on her mantelpiece. The canary, suspended in its cage near the top of her curtained bedstead, has dropped from its perch, frozen stiff.

'Ivy.' The mention of my name is broken, strained.

Rushing over, I try to pull her up from her slumped position. Her head flops to one side, her eyes rolling back in their sockets. I shake her, no longer restricted by the constraints of being a servant. My grip tightens in desperation. I must get this woman out of this place.

I pity her. This will not be me in an opium stupor, waiting for whatever the house has planned for us. I cannot let go so willingly.

For a moment, the mistress awakens again and vomits over the edge of the bed, narrowly missing my feet but ruining the embroidered rug. It is not the first time she has been unwell, and the floor needs cleaning. She has been alone for a while; an unpleasant aroma of sweat and bile sits oppressively around her.

Mrs Higgins was acting strangely, but where is Hannah or even Mr Bancroft or the master? There is no one to help. A loud thud sounds from above us and scrapes across the ceiling, followed by a crash of furniture and the dragging of something heavy.

'We must leave the house together, mistress. You are not well.' I wipe her mouth with the towel from her bedside table. 'Your medicine is too strong.'

I don't say my greatest worry: that this house is evil, that she will end up dead like all the women before us. The stuffed animals imprisoned by the collection are not a curiosity, but a warning.

A slow, melodic thumping comes again from above. There is not much time. She looks down at her stained nightdress, shocked to find herself in such a state. 'Can you not understand I need help? Get some hot water at once.' Her words are barely audible. 'My husband can never see me like this.' She turns desperately looking around the room. 'I hear something. Is there someone coming?'

'It is not anyone you want to have in here, mistress. You must ignore the noise... It is no one you can trust. This house works against us. Don't you observe anything strange? Have you not felt yourself becoming weaker each day?'

'Where is Alex?' Tears threaten her sad eyes.

'Your husband is haunted. He is in his own world, and you are alone here. We must leave at once!'

There is a shift in her expression. Suddenly, her expression fires with a spark of rage. 'How can I leave? Is it not enough that I must compete with his first wife? The photos in his library, and the child doll, they do nothing but taunt me.' She spits the words with venom. 'But I am all he has now: real flesh and blood. He is my husband. He belongs to me, not to his ghost of a wife or a simpering maid. You have plotted against me with Hannah. No! I will not go; no one will have him, he is mine.'

'I don't even know where Hannah is!' I cry, exasperated. 'If you come with me, I can help you. Women die in this house, Angelica! Have you not noticed? You are in grave danger!'

'If I require protection, my husband will provide all I need. This is his home, not yours. Who are you to instruct me? You have overreached your station.' She pulls the bedspread high under her chin.

The banging noise is getting louder, and I have to raise my voice to be heard.

'You are a fool to give yourself completely to him. He has never been in control of this house! He has brought you into this place knowing what lives here. There is an ungodly grave buried beneath the foundations and its evil is spreading up into the garden, into this building. Miss Earnshaw knew about the Blackham's secrets and something ominous has happened to her – as it will to us if we stay.'

I pull at her hand, forcing her to give me a response. 'What about the figure of a man, you see? You told me he appears to you at night. He was the reason you fell down the stairs, wasn't it?'

'You are mad,' she barks at me, unable to look at my face. Her voice is rough, harsh. Her inky black hair falls loose about her shoulders, her eyes are wild and feverish. 'He doesn't exist … the doctor promised me!'

'I never believed I heard anything real either, but once inside this house, I realised that we are never truly alone.'

The banging suddenly stops and an eerie silence fills the room.

'There are no ghosts, only bad dreams. The mind plays tricks. The doctor knows better than you, Ivy.'

I look at her, a shell of her former self, an example of what will happen if I stay. She leans back against the headboard, her locks of hair damp against her face. 'Alexander takes care of me. I trust him. This is no business of yours.'

'You are mistaken, you are a prisoner. Can you not understand? When was the last time you went outside and stood in real daylight away from all these gas lamps and candles? Life carries on out there, the people who walk past. They are free of the evil that surrounds us.'

The mistress shakes her head towards the shaded window, blinking at the weak light that filters through.

'We must leave now. I beg you. This is our only chance!'

'How on earth can I go out into the street looking like this? I could never live down the scandal. Alex would never forgive me! You know the servants gossip about you and your unnatural ways:

making strange voices when you are alone, searching for secrets in private papers. They said you would be dismissed tonight. I believe them now. It is you who is not to be trusted.'

We both look back at the adjoining door, which links her to her husband's room. The silence is weighted between us. It is too late. The trapped panic is back and the instinct to run builds, to find somewhere safe to hide, to curl up in my mother's arms and turn away from all that is bad in the world. The mistress reaches over to pull the bell chord.

'No, no, you mustn't!' I shout. 'They will come! They will all come.'

The tone chimes faintly in the room, and I can imagine the bell ringing out in the kitchen, demanding attention.

'What have you done? You have summoned them here... I have tried to help you!' I shriek, raw distress in my voice. 'Come with me now – quickly, we don't have time for this.' I lean in and grab at her hand, pulling her out of the covers.

She pushes me away with surprising force. 'Don't touch me. Leave me be. A servant will be here soon, and normality will resume.' She looks unsure but folds her arms still resolute in her decision to stay.

'Hannah? You would trust her over me? Even though you know why she stays, how she tries to seduce your husband at every opportunity?'

'Get out!' Her face twists in anger. 'I regret ever taking you into my confidence. This is the repayment I receive. Help will come and then you will be sorry,' she mutters, her eyes narrowing as she glares at me.

There is a noise at the interconnecting door.

'You may enter!' She calls out clearly.

The door edges open, but no one is there. The temperature plummets further. I have lost. The voices of unseen bodies rise again in my ears.

'You have invited the spirits in.' The air rushes over me in a glacial blast.

'But what I see is not real. They told me...' She whimpers as she retreats further into the blankets. 'Ivy, before you go, please light the fire. I'm so terribly cold.' All her angst has passed, and she is like a vulnerable child again; the small body in the centre of the bed, hiding from the rest of the world.

I stagger about, holding my head. The sounds of anguish in the room are overwhelming. The candlelight flickers … I strain my eyes to see properly, for there is a mist forming in the corner like the freezing fog outside. Separate from the voices, the vapours twist and contort manifesting into a shape which my mind cannot make sense of. Suddenly, in one heart stopping moment the shade breaks free and lurches forward revealing the disturbing doglike face from my nightmares. The glowing orange eyes fixate on me as it forms its mouth – all pointed teeth and blackness into a hideous smile.

I scream, and my body jerks to the exit, making the decision for me. Running out into the hallway, I am forced to leave her behind if I am to save myself.

Chapter 41 ~ The Nest

The safest place to go is the vicarage. Blackham house hints at an understanding of my plan. Walls and doors rattle around me, and the gilded picture frames threaten to fall from their fixtures. I see the magpies have increased their unnerving presence at the windows, frantically flying against the panes as if trying to break the glass.

The doors remain locked, as Mr Bancroft had stated, but I remember the set of spare keys cast aside on the library table. The room is dark, the fire barely throwing out any heat or light. Master Blackham is leaning against the fireplace, watching the struggling flames. The floorboards creak under my weight as I tread lightly, but he does not acknowledge me – too drunk, perhaps.

Stealing the keys, I hide them within my skirt. He gulps back the remaining whisky and refills the glass. The bottle clinks against the lip of the crystal, and the liquid spills over the top, splashing onto the carpet.

Just as I move to leave the room, another bird crashes into the window. The violent sound startles us both. He turns and his clouded eyes try to focus. I start to warn him about the state of the mistress, but he waves me away. He stumbles and falls heavily into the leather armchair; drinking has been his only activity for some time.

I leave the master fixated on the dying flames of the fire. The outline of him looks to be blending into the walls. My heart hurts at the waste of life in this house. Holding the keys, I know which one I am looking for. The one engraved with a bay leaf for the morning room door opening onto the garden. But there is also a small, unusual-shaped key concealed by the others, just like the key my father had. Squeezing the steel in my fingers… I must try to unlock the secret panel within the collection room desk. It is the only place left to search that I can think of.

Staying away from the dimly lit corners, I take a gas lamp from the entrance table and unlock the collection room door. All the dead animals await me. The suffering eyes, replaced with glass beads, glimmer from the small flame of light in my hand.

I put the lamp on the desk. The room is claustrophobic. The familiar smell of decay is in the air, but no flowers or plants are wilting this time to explain the scent.

Searching along the ledge for the secret compartment, I manoeuvre the delicate wooden leaver and release the catch. The panel slides across and reveals a tiny lock embedded in the wood. The key fits perfectly, and the drawer opens.

Inside are many documents, some bound by string, others by leather folders. There is also money, and several small hard objects concealed in a bundle of black silk. As I push it aside, strange figurines made from marble – ugly looking creatures escape from the fabric. They roll around, seemingly so by themselves. Remarkable in their detail, they are examples of the finest craftsmanship, but their forked tongues and ghoulish expressions diminish whatever beauty they had. I discover six of them, all sculpted in a different position. But although they each have an unsettling human face; their bodies are carved into the shape of birds. There is the magpie with the fanned wings, the marbling black and white. I shrink back from the sight of them. It is a private corvid nest.

I listen out for footsteps, but instead I hear the notes of a piano start to play, drifting throughout the rooms, lingering and oppressive. I open the folder on the top, but nothing holds my attention – there are only house and stock deeds. The next document is a list of artefacts categorised by country of travel, stating their value and origin. I look up as the magpie above the door appears to return my glance. He is like the others outside. They are part of something bigger, linked to these grounds. Was he the first, I wonder? He is so much larger than an ordinary bird. They have conquered this place, this house of collections and death. Instinctively, I look for the mask weaved from magpie feathers, but the glass cabinet is empty.

I continue rifling through the pile of papers. At the bottom is a slim envelope with the name Blackham scrawled on it. Inside is a folded note. I open it with shaky hands. On first impression, the page looks like a standard letter, but the date is the same as the night of the parlour game: 11th November. As I read on, I realise that it is a receipt for an institution called Bethlem and the entry cost of a woman named Rosetta – the Christian name of Miss Earnshaw. It must be the place I heard the master and Mr Bancroft discussing, but part of the information and address has been ripped from the corner. I release a long-held breath. I finally have confirmation that she is alive, but she is still out of reach, hidden away somewhere, possibly in London. If I could learn where the building is, I could finally find her.

Vindication mixes with the adrenaline pumping through my blood. So, this was the truth I had been searching for: not a murder, but a kidnapping. They had taken her against her will, but why?

Now I have my proof. My body is already propelling me outside. I reach the morning room within moments. My hands are trembling too much to unlock the door, my fingers clumsy. Shaking the bunch of keys, I find the one with the leaf. On my third attempt, the lock clicks and the doors swing wide open.

I am free.

I run across the garden beneath the dominating chestnut tree towards the rose bushes. The magpie's constant chattering and squawking is deafening in my ears. They swoop to the ground from their branches. The batting of their wings is so close, I can almost feel their frenzied beaks and claws in my hair and face. Flinching and ducking low, I make it to the secret door.

I glance behind me at the building. It is no surprise that someone is watching me; they no longer hide. The shape of a man is standing at an upstairs window. It is not the master; the figure is taller, the true owner of the house, Lord Blackham reclaiming his control – summoned back into physical form from the dark realms.

Chapter 42 ~ Battle Plan

The vicarage is hidden behind the thick arms of the elm trees. For a brief moment, I think of the trees at home, but then trails of thin moonlight illuminate the headstones like bones in the ground. If I stumble, my instincts tell me I will lose myself in the shadows and drown, sucked down into the earth by the cold clasp of the dead. I race through them, trying not to picture the bodies rotting beneath my feet. The charm of the place has vanished, and at night has brought all the terrors of my nightmares to life.

I fall upon the cottage. 'Hello… Please, is anyone there?'

Mrs Guilden opens the door and the cosy scene of a well-run home lies before me. My resolve breaks and tears come before I can stop them. I wipe them on my sleeve, an act I would never have done before moving to London. I am beyond etiquette.

Her arms wrap around me, pulling me into the warmth of the kitchen where the fire is still burning. She smells of cinnamon and cloves: Christmas baking. A reminder of happier times as a child is a knife to my gut.

'Whatever is this? Come now, it can't be that bad?' She lifts my chin gently in her hand.

'Norman!' she calls over her shoulder. 'It's the young woman from Blackham House. Something must have happened. She is in an awful way.'

It is hard to tear myself away from her embrace. 'I would have come earlier. Only William warned me not to – he threatened me.' I splutter between stifled sobs.

'Who's William? He doesn't sound like a nice man, scaring you like that.'

'The gardener... I'm sorry, I had nowhere else to go.'

The murmur of a gentle male voice comes from the bedroom.

'Now, I'm sure everything will be well in the morning. Follow me. Norman has already retired for the evening. This cold weather is bad for his health, and he complains when he moves, which is not like him at all.'

She guides me to a small, simply furnished room leading off the narrow hallway. Vicar Evans is sitting up in bed, reading a leather-bound book by the light of a lamp. He rests his glasses on the open book in his lap. 'Good evening, my dear. I'm sorry you find me in a much-reduced state of affairs.'

'I'll fetch some hot tea,' says the housekeeper. 'You tell the vicar here what disturbs you. He prides himself on solving problems. Nothing a good chat and a brew can't fix.' She smooths down the bedspread and pats his shoulder as though to bolster him up for a trial ahead and then hovers in the doorway.

'Is the door locked?' I ask.

She turns in the direction of the front of the house. I cannot hide the alarm from my voice. 'I am not sure if someone followed me.'

'You're safe here, Ivy,' the vicar insists. 'This is a house of God. We are under his protection.' Still, he motions to the housekeeper to check, concerned about what might be outside. 'Best bolt the back door, too, Mrs Guilden. We want none of those winter winds invading us on a cold night like this.'

The housekeeper nods in agreement, and satisfied, the vicar beckons me closer. 'Ivy, sit down and tell me what troubles you.'

I take a chair beside his bed and the words spill from my lips in a mix of relief and exhaustion. 'They sent Miss Earnshaw to an asylum. It is the house, the birds... There is something sinister buried in a vault under the garden, something evil, a spirit.'

'A woman in an asylum ... spirits? The truth is often stranger than fiction.' The vicar leans forward and takes my hand in concern. His skin is cool and papery. He barely has the strength to grip my fingers. 'What is this spirit you see?'

'I am not the only one. I have heard the mistress speak of it as well. It is a shadow, but the form can change from a man to a beast.' My breath shudders at the memory. 'Her health is getting worse, and she cannot comprehend the danger that surrounds her.'

'You talk of a reflection, a trick of the light. You must be mistaken, Ivy. Perhaps you are running a fever?' He looks over my shoulder for the reassurance of another opinion, but we are still alone.

'Old Lady Blackham believes it is her husband. She spoke as though he was alive, and suddenly, a fearful shape appeared before us. At first, I believed my senses were deceiving me.' I pause to catch my breath. 'But it is as if she never let him go and called him back ... or something else back from the dead.' I search his watery eyes for validation.

The recent terror pricks at my skin, and I jump as the housekeeper bangs a pot in the kitchen.

The old man sighs. 'This person cannot be Lord Blackham, for I conducted his funeral myself.' He reclines on to his pillow. 'If anything, the apparition you saw would be a servant of the devil. It is not unheard of, but ghosts do not exist. Only spirits from Hell doing the devil's work.'

'But what about Miss Earnshaw? I thought she was dead, that she was trying to communicate with me. To think the rapping was not her, that she has been suffering, locked away against her will all this time...' Mrs Guilden passes me a hot cup of tea. The liquid scolds my lips as I try to drink it too fast.

'Who is this Miss Earnshaw to you?' He asks.

'She is the reason I came to London – why I was in the house, searching for any trace of her. It is important I must find her. She told me we were related, and that she could help me.' I falter. 'I was struggling after my mother's death; I cannot return to my father; my life would not be worth living.'

The vicar considers my words. I expect him to be surprised, to contest the negativity against my own family, but he nods at me to continue.

'However, by the time I had travelled here from Godalming, she had disappeared. She was never seen again after their séance. I am sure the Blackhams locked her away to conceal a secret.'

I watch as his expression sours at the mention of a séance. 'You have found proof?'

'I have a letter admitting her to an institution at the request of Blackham House.' I pat the pocket of my apron.

'The news of the missing spiritualist was in the papers!' The housekeeper moves to pick up the teapot. 'Nothing good ever came of that place. It gives me an uneasy feeling whenever I look over to those dying trees.'

The vicar picks up his cup from his bedside table and sips some of his tea. 'They are a most disturbing family, dabbling in evil for their own gains.'

The housekeeper almost overfills the cups as she tops up the drinks, the steaming liquid sloshing precariously close to the edges. 'I wouldn't be surprised if that house is haunted; two women and a child died in that room. It cannot be a coincidence?'

'Nonsense, Mrs Guilden. Let's not get carried away with ourselves.'

'But what happened to the master's first wife?' I ask.

'Miranda was not well, Ivy. He lowers his voice to a gentle murmur. She took her own life and that of her child's – an atrocious affair. We shall never know what drove her to such drastic action.'

'She jumped like the first woman you told me about?' I stammer, folding my hands around my cup for comfort.

'No, it was poison, not an easy death to choose.'

'It must have been her I saw at the window one night – her spirit is trapped in the house!'

'Hush, come on now … these are nonsensical ideas. Once we die, our souls go to either Heaven or Hell.' He says softly, trying to soothe me.

'But the voices I hear, they are not from people who have died?'

'It is all an illusion to distract and confuse. You have been tricked by the Devil, my dear.'

His words catch me off guard, the open omission again that the Devil is amongst us. My thoughts race like bolting horses, and the cup begins to feel too heavy in my hand. An element of truth is fracturing and reinventing itself as something different; the threads of my life are weaving together to create a bigger tapestry, a picture too hard to bear. Blackham House has only increased the number of voices I hear. The full realisation that it is not my nerves nor my imagination curls and twists my insides into a deep knot. I am not mad but cursed. Evil has always surrounded me.

'The Bible is what we need.' He slaps the leather-bound book in his hand, the sound bringing me back to his voice. 'I have seen none of the Blackham family in attendance at my services. Do the women wear a cross and chain? Are there any symbols of religious artefacts in the house?'

'No, only Lady Blackham's mourning jewellery ... nothing else.'

I picture the ring with my mother's hair woven into a forget-me-knot flower, secretly stowed away in the seam of my dress. Although I wish for the comfort of wearing the band now, I am comforted to still have it close to me. In my bleakest moments, I can understand the old woman's need for the link to the afterlife. The last physical connection to a loved one who has gone where we cannot follow.

'Mourning jewellery?'

'Yes, she is covered in necklaces, bracelets and rings. She worships the gems and dotes on them like children.'

'Surely it is normal to own a piece or two as a keepsake?' He questions.

'She owns an unusually high number of pieces, and they all contain the same silver strands of hair woven into the decoration. She keeps them in a jewellery box next to her bed. When the shadow appeared, she spoke as if it were her husband, implying he was almost ready to take physical form.' I glance at Mrs Guilden who looks horrified. 'Lady Blackham was wearing all her jewels, like she was dressing up for him. The presence came from nowhere, as though she had conjured him. They speak of a ceremony and so many servants have left before me.' I hesitate, not wanting to admit my fear. 'But now I think they never went anywhere.'

'What are you saying, Ivy?' He asks.

'Unholy ceremonies involving the deadly nightshade plants in the garden. It is my judgement that they use the poison as a cordial ... in murderous doses.'

His eyebrows rise in puzzlement. 'I find the possibility hard to believe. Naturally, it would have been reported to the police and we would have heard of servants disappearing in the news.'

I interject. 'But Miss Earnshaw was famous enough for her absence to be noticed.'

'Could it not be just an unsettling coincidence? I am familiar with the supernatural, but not murder. I think you have been through a great deal and are consequently suffering from an extreme case of nerves.'

'But you believe me, their actions are strange, terribly wrong?' I exclaim, frustrated by his sense of logic.

'Yes, I agree, something spiritually is amiss with that house.' He puts on his glasses again. 'Perhaps there is a connection between this jewellery you talk of and the strength of this shadowy figure who has manifested in the face of grief.'

The housekeeper gasps and makes an exaggerated sign of the cross over her body. 'Mrs Drysdale, down by the market, said a curse, or a hex, has always been on that house – sounds like what it is.'

'Come on, Mrs Guilden. We don't believe in curses, do we? That's just plain old superstition.' The vicar nods, confident in his belief. 'Remember, the Devil tries to mislead us. Ivy is frightened enough already. It is not unusual to have coffins in a family vault. We have a number of mausoleums in the church yard, but the existence of such a place under Blackham House is alarming. I don't believe a man of God has been in there, certainly not linked to this parish. There are no records, which is unusual indeed.'

The housekeeper clears her throat. 'I'm only saying what others are thinking.' She stands up straighter, almost in defiance at the vicar's rebuff.

He puts his drink on the side table and leans forward, interlocking his fingers together.

'This unconsecrated vault, it is possible that there is evil buried within it. Many lost souls would be buried next to the cemetery, unable to rest on Holy land for their sins. And now the Blackhams have discovered it. Meddling with the afterlife is a perilous affair, with unknown consequences.'

'Lady Blackham said they wanted…' My voice cracks.

He keeps his eyes locked on mine. 'What did they want?'

I can barely utter the word. 'Resurrection.'

'They want to bring back the dead?' His jaw becomes slack. 'It is not possible without resorting to the darkest of arts. This is blasphemy of the worst kind. We need to destroy the hold evil has on this family.' He rubs his face, holding his chin in his hand, frowning, thinking hard. 'If what you say is true, it seems this jewellery is at the root of it all. Can you bring me this collection you speak of? I have heard tales before of gems being used to conjure the dead; stories that were written in a scroll, hundreds of years old, discovered in Egypt. But we, the Church, questioned the translation as the language was so ancient and went against our teachings.'

'Are you talking about stealing?' The housekeeper is almost breathless with shock.

'We have to act fast. Perhaps, if we separate them from Lady Blackham, she cannot summon whatever creature the Devil is using as a vessel. We could cut off the serpent's head, so to speak. I can bless the jewellery and keep them in the safety of the chapel.'

'But the police?' Mrs Guilden moves next to me and squeezes my shoulder firmly.

'This is God's work. The police will understand. I know people in uniform I can trust. Besides, once I cleanse the pieces, it might be possible to return them, breaking any influence the collection once had.'

'You cannot expect the girl to go back into the house?'

'I don't want to,' I say in agreement, folding my arms like a petulant child, although my insides reel at the thought of leaving my precious vasculum and my beloved books behind.

'God will give you the courage you need, Ivy. I will come with you. History must not repeat itself. If the mistress is in danger, I have a duty to act. I have never forgiven myself for failing Mrs Geffrey.' The old man tries to sit up straighter, but he lacks the strength to move his body and slumps back down.

'You will do no such thing, Norman.' Mrs Guilden moves to tuck the blankets in around his frail body. 'He took a turn, Ivy, yesterday. Collapsed in my kitchen, of all places. He is too weak to even walk.'

His fingers try to grip my wrist; the skin on his hand is almost transparent. His expression acknowledges the truth of his housekeeper's meaning. He is not able to come with me. 'We must help the mistress.' His voice wavers as his breath wheezes in his chest, and despite my protests of not returning, I know with certainty he is right. I am not the coward I once was, and I must go back for her and for Hannah – the only two women I have ever come close to calling friends.

'I hate to ask something of you that I can't do myself, but trust in yourself. We will pray for you. You have come here for a reason – this is a chance to do God's will.'

You have a purpose. Miss Earnshaw's words from the funeral come to me again.

'I shall return,' I reply, my pulse already quickening before my courage wavers. I grasp the hem of my dress for the reassuring weight of my mourning ring, but there is nothing but torn material. Every fibre in my body heaves with dread. 'My ring! It's gone, I must have dropped it somewhere in the house.' I cry, searching my dress again. 'I have to find it! Otherwise, I truly have nothing. It means everything to me.'

'Then God has given you an answer, my dear girl. He is testing you and will protect you one last time in the mouth of Hell. You must try to get the mistress and any servants you can find to leave. I fear there is no hope for them if they stay.'

'But what if the same thing happens to Ivy?' The housekeeper interjects worriedly. 'What if they put her away like they did with Miss Earnshaw? I will not be responsible for an ungodly end.'

At the back of my mind, I cannot help but think of the many hidden passages in these big houses where the servants walk alone; secret places where anything can happen. I am putting faith in myself and a God, neither of which I have ever felt inside those walls.

'Ivy, take this with you.' The vicar opens the drawer next to his bedside and takes out a small box. He hands me a gold crucifix on a chain. 'This belonged to my wife. Wherever you travel, so shall God. Put this around your neck and you will be protected. Mrs Guilden, please, could you go quickly and call on some able men in the parish to send to Blackham House at once? You must convince them! They might be reluctant to at first, but I am sure they will not be far behind you, Ivy.'

'I shall leave now,' she says, reaching for her coat in the hallway.

'But what about William the gardener? He warned me about bringing insiders onto the grounds.'

'He was just trying to frighten you,' the vicar replies. 'Why, a handful of strong, good Christian men could easily rectify the situation. And you are a child of God – do not doubt your ability.'

I am not convinced I am a child of God, but this could be a test. Once I have proven myself a true believer, I pray God will release me from the voices I hear. So I can finally escape from the demons that haunt me.

Chapter 43 ~ The Mistress

Blackham House looks desolate when I approach it through the garden. Every instinct steers me away, to take my chances on the streets at night, to go anywhere but there, but I cannot bear to leave my only keepsake of Mother and guilt courses through me at leaving the mistress and Hannah. But when I think of Mrs Higgins, I no longer see her as innocent of the happenings in the building – she must be working with her son.

There is no evening birdsong and yet, when I steal a glance into the thick branches of the gnarled chestnut tree, the magpies sit together side by side, watching. There are at least fifty gathered tonight. I knew they would be there waiting; it is like a homecoming. But they do not fidget or fight for space amongst themselves. They should fly, catching their last meal of the day, but they are eerily stationary. I resist the urge to run and draw attention to myself, so I walk almost painfully slowly and try the morning room door I escaped from earlier. Thankfully, it is still unlocked. I open it quietly and step inside.

The silence takes me by surprise. Curiously, nobody moves through the rooms on the ground floor; everywhere is empty. I must find the mistress and Hannah, and then the jewellery box, but first my mother's ring – if I have that, I will have the courage for anything.

But my plan is tinged with madness, for what can I wield against these strange people and in the face of their ungodly power? I wipe my clammy hands down my uniform, my legs turning weak at the possibility of confrontation.

Maybe the prayers from Vicar Evans have worked. I touch the crucifix around my neck for reassurance. Retracing my steps, I go back to the top of the basement staircase, where I remember catching my dress on a nail in the wall. It is gloomy, but I see the ring glinting from within the apothecarist's handkerchief, lying crumpled halfway down the stairs. Dashing forward, I snatch it up, concealing the small bundle securely inside my bodice, close to my heart.

Now, I must try again with the mistress one last time. I hasten up the main staircase, but as I reach the first floor, a blood-curdling scream echoes throughout, bouncing off the walls. I falter on the last step. The cry stops as abruptly as it began, as though cut short by an unseen hand. The sound seemed to come from the back room. I find the door is no longer closed, and I nudge it further ajar, expecting to find someone inside, but it is empty. Instead, the bay window is wide open, the white net blowing in the night with a glacial breeze. Shards of moonlight reflect off the panes of glass as they swing on their hinges.

I cannot fight curiosity. Edging across towards the gaping window, I see the vicarage in the graveyard's midst, but it is unreachable now. Would anyone react if I called out? It is unlikely, for nothing is happening from the nearby houses in response to the scream I just heard. No distressed whistles are blown by nightwatchmen or police running down the street. This house is cordoned off from the rest of the world, the neighbours blind to the evil residing here.

I stand at the sill and look out. Despite already being full of berries, the Devil's Thorn plants have all suddenly bloomed, smothered with clusters of bright violet flowers. They reach up to the moon in celebration, defying the natural order of seasons.

To my horror the mistress is lying beneath me in the garden, her body at an odd angle glowing white against the murky ground, her nightdress spilling across the soil. Her delicate neck lies twisted like a broken marionette puppet cast aside.

My legs almost give way at the terrible sight, as a strange sensation begins to overwhelm my senses. The desire to climb up onto the narrow ledge and join her body on the ground surges through me. The magpies break their silence and begin incessantly screeching as every nerve in my body is being pulled, driven forward. What unseen force is pushing and summoning me to this doomed fate? William steps out from the shadow of the chestnut tree. His eyes glare at me in the dim light. He is the caretaker of the grounds and whatever comes into it.

My mother's ring inside my bodice becomes hot, burning my skin, bringing me back into the moment with a sharp slap of clarity that is too painful to comprehend. The body on the ground suddenly looks like me. The same brown hair unravelled from its pins, a slender frame sprawled over the damp earth, scarlet blood pooling around the head. But I check myself. I am still alive. It is the mistress who is dead. Did I fail her? I tried, but I could not save her. Guilt is already seeding itself into my heart.

I sense the bird's expectancy: they are waiting for me to fall too. They want to steal the life from me, to add my soul to the others who have died in this house. The magpies are the true masters of the Blackham collection. They have their own unnatural agenda.

The unwavering gaze of the gardener does not leave my face. He makes no sound, nor shows any concern for the corpse before him. A ripple of movement runs through the branches of the tree. The birds are in motion. One by one, the magpies swoop down, landing haphazardly over the garden. So many feathered bodies; there must now be a hundred or more. They land on the grass and the body as though they are feasting on it. Until just the figure of the old man remains standing in the centre of a mass of heaving black and white feathers – blanketing the ground, covering all that existed before. The sight sickens me as I force myself away from the abhorrent scene before me. I race for the door; time is running out.

A tall lamp on the first-floor landing sheds enough light to guide my way. The piano music becomes increasingly louder from the floor above. The melody should be soothing but the haunting sounds make my skin crawl. The flame flickers and dips as the gas runs low, casting shadows on the wall. My mind races as I imagine hands reaching out – the shapes and faces of the voices I hear when I'm alone; the whispers and weeping of strangers from the dead. Blackham House has succeeded in releasing them permanently from my imagination, and now they are stronger.

The stench of rot and stagnant water overpowers the air all the way up from the entrance hall. The fresh flowers I arranged yesterday on the sideboard are already decaying. It is impossible not to gag as I continue up the servant stairs to my room in the attic, hoping to find Hannah. All the while, I try not to think of the mistress outside on the ground. Dead.

If I die or disappear, I would like the vicar to tell my father I was brave; that I did not cower away from my fears and simper. I am more than that – I am equal to my brother, David, and any man he would have married me off to. But now I am here alone, am I truly prepared for what could be waiting in the darkness?

The attic room is empty, but I am met by the sound of buzzing. A mass of fat bluebottles hovers at the window. Fruit flies swarm over the newly mouldy bread Hannah left on the table, like a dead carcass. I have never seen so many, especially in winter.

To my dismay, the door of the small cupboard does not budge like it did before. With every second, the attic becomes increasingly suffocating. The flies are multiplying; they buzz near my face, getting into my eyes, my ears. They are erratic, frenzied, trying to escape the room just like me. I try again pulling at the small brass handle, desperation giving me more strength. It is a few heart-stopping moments before the wood eventually surrenders. Grabbing the carpet bag with my vasculum and most treasured belongings inside, I forsake my clothes and everything else. No doubt an item of mine will be added to the trunk in the servant's quarters. I stumble out of the doorway, the humming insects still vibrating behind me.

The disquieting piano music continues to play on the second floor, but before I think about the jewellery, I must search for Hannah and something better for protection. I need a kitchen knife.

Chapter 44 ~ Jewels

Desperation claws at me, for I cannot find Hannah anywhere. Mrs Higgins must have been in the kitchen recently, for there is a single tray set out with the finest crystal glasses and an open bottle of champagne on the table. I have just picked up the sharpest knife when the service bell on the wall rings for Lady Blackham's room. It keeps up with an incessant clamour and doesn't stop. Then I hear a shrill whistle as someone blows down the speaking tube. Against my better judgement, I bring the mouthpiece to my ear.

'Ivy?' Lady Blackham's voice drifts down the pipe from upstairs in the warm tone of a friend, not an employer or enemy.

'Come now, we are awaiting you. We understand you have questions. Bring the drinks and we can have a civilised conversation.'

An overwhelming sense of foreboding engulfs me, but resolve has settled in my gut. I need answers and the jewellery before I leave. An idea takes hold of poetic justice and retribution. I go to the pantry and lift down the glass bottle containing the green cordial. Ten to twenty berries would be enough to kill someone, but diluted in a bottle of champagne, ten drops might disorientate Lady Blackham sufficiently to tell me the truth. I disperse the thick droplets into the champagne, watching as the bubbles mix with the green poison, but my fingers tremble and the dosage increases beyond what I intended. I waver a moment in my decision. But it is too late now. Let God decide her fate.

I will not abandon this concoction here for the next victim. Hiding the bottle in my carpet bag I tuck my belongings into the kitchen corner, an easy place to retrieve them. Then I take the silver tray with the champagne upstairs to the second floor, the chilling piano notes leading the way.

The source of the melody stops abruptly as I open the door to Lady Blackham's room, and I see the music stool is empty. The fire is alight. Many candles are grouped in clusters; a hundred tiny flames flicker as one. The atmosphere is all wrong, the heat staggering. A sheen of sweat passes across my upper lip. I falter, for there are no signs of Hannah here either. I hope she has finally come to her senses and left already.

The old woman sits in front of her dressing table with the large walnut jewellery box in the middle, set up like an altar, the sparkling ornaments displayed in their open velvet trays as offerings. Her appearance is younger somehow, full of vital energy. I fight down my terror at entering again, and the shadowed man who may appear in the corner again.

'Ah, there you are. What a busy evening already, and we haven't even started. Why don't you prepare the drinks and make yourself comfortable?' She laughs and cracks the thick powder on her face. The sight is unsettling; the act breaks the illusion of youth.

I put the tray down on the side table and pour her a glass, my fingers trembling on the engraved crystal as I think of the droplets mixing with the champagne bubbles. Will they hide any bitterness?

'How did you like your gift?' She glances over her shoulder at me, beckoning for the glass to be placed on her dressing table. 'William is so thoughtful and talented. Apparently, the birds tell him who is lucky enough to be bestowed the gesture. All the little keepsakes are made from our own chestnut tree in the garden.'

Lady Blackham's hands flitter about the table, dabbing the scent onto her neck. She adds pins to her grey hair, which is swept back and decorated with jewelled clips more suited to the opera or ballroom. Her appearance is altogether different from her usual attire. She looks like a peacock in a blue and green evening dress. The gems glisten and shimmer inside the box before her. They look to be vibrating and moving, as if a snake is writhing underneath the bracelets and brooches.

'You appreciate my gown.' A statement rather than a question. She turns on her stool and properly acknowledges me standing in the centre of the room. 'Is it not exquisite? This was one of Henry's favourites. He chose the material for me on a trip to Italy. Venetian velvet.' She smooths down the fabric over her breasts, preening herself.

Tissue paper lies strewn across the bed, and I catch the musky scent of mothballs and lavender. The dress must have been in storage for years.

'No need for black mourning clothes anymore! What a fine occasion and a celebration at last.'

'But Mistress Blackham is dead!' The words tumble like stones from my mouth.

The old woman looks at me sternly. 'I am Lady Blackham, the true mistress of this house, and the Italian girl is not dead, dear. She is quite all right, I assure you.'

'I saw her… She fell from the back-room window into the garden. William must have seen and did nothing to stop her.'

'Oh dear, she was always impatient.' She presses her lips into a regretful smile. 'Too impulsive and selfish for her own needs and not Alexander's – not good enough for a Blackham. But what can you do when a son takes his own path against his parents' better judgement? I advised marriage, but she wasn't the right one.' Lady Blackham mutters as she leans over and pulls the bell chord on the wall for service again.

Who will answer her bell this time? I hope it will be Hannah.

'At least she was attractive. I can't blame my son for being seduced by her. Henry also admired his selection, being European.' She pauses, supposedly to recollect a memory. 'He said she added a certain beauty to the house. I suppose I must adhere to Henry's better judgement, for he showed a refined eye for the finer items to add to the Blackham collection. Still, a failure is a failure. That is two wasted opportunities at marriage and a legitimate heir. But why am I not surprised? I hope Alexander doesn't see this as another opportunity to sulk again. He has forever been the weak one, failing us time and again with his lack of backbone.'

'But she is dead. Don't you care?' I am taken aback by her lack of empathy towards her son and his wife.

'Now, do not go upsetting yourself. If she has indeed left us already, her death can only add to the power of tonight. We need to savour this evening, to relax and be merry.' Again, the white dusting powder on her face creases into the deep lines in her skin, marking her like an old painting badly restored. 'I think I shall enjoy this champagne.'

She puts the glass to her thin lips and takes a long draught of alcohol, closing her eyes and savouring each drop. My fingers twitch, and I almost move to stop her. If my hand had not slipped, the dosage would have been just enough to induce sleep, perhaps a temporary mild paralysis. But now it is much more potent, and my conscience pricks at the repercussions. *Could I be capable of murder?*

But I remind myself it is their own fate. They have brought this on themselves. I have used what knowledge I had to put an end to their scheming, to buy enough time to steal the jewellery box.

'How about a glass, Ivy? Do join me in a drink ... a toast to a new beginning?'

I shake my head. 'I found this.' I remove the folded envelope from my apron pocket and hold the paper up for her to see the precious evidence to expose the truth. 'Tell me about Miss Earnshaw and why you imprisoned her somewhere against her will?'

She puts down her glass, already half-drunk, and raises an ossified hand. 'Of course, all in good time. Now help me with my jewellery. I must wear all the pieces tonight. It is of the utmost importance that I get everything right. See the way they glimmer in the light? I could never imagine the force they hold. That jeweller is a genius.'

'I demand to know where Miss Earnshaw is—'

'Tell me, what is your life worth, Ivy? Do you believe you have a greater purpose? Were you following a particular mundane path before you came here?' She scrutinises me, her eyes narrowing as if trying to read my thoughts. 'You only pretended to enjoy working in this house. Your focus was never on your duties. I hear you weren't particularly good at your job, anyway. You will not be missed in the running of the place.'

I am about to protest, but then for what use? The more she speaks, the more I might learn.

'Whatever your reason for coming here, we can help you achieve your real and truest potential. It would not even be a big sacrifice on your part.' She takes out a pair of sparkling diamond earrings and adds one to each ear. 'All you have known will become insignificant in the light of what is about to happen. Becoming part of something bigger, of magnificent importance for all history. And to think my husband is such an integral element of it all. We should all be grateful to him. He deserves our faith and admiration. A brilliant man – in life and now, also in death.'

'I came here to find out the truth about Miss Earnshaw. There is a malevolence within these walls. I feel the evil and have seen the vault, the coffin filled with your so-called gifts. I believe she knew something too, and that is why you had locked her away.'

'What is this woman to you? How much do you imagine you truly know?'

'She uncovered the secrets of this house on the night of your parlour games. It was enough to merit her disappearance. Everyone thinks she is dead. Even the papers proclaimed to have given up hope. You deceived them all, and for what reason?'

'I will enlighten you, Ivy.' She gives me an indulgent nod. 'Sometimes, only a little knowledge can be the most dangerous. I am sure the story will be most interesting to you. Come here and drink with me.' She looks at the carriage clock on the mantel; the timepiece is working again – tick tock, tick tock. In fact, all the clocks within the room are now ticking, no longer stopped at five minutes to midnight but telling the correct time of half-past eleven.

'And it is not yet the hour; we still have some minutes to play with.' She pats the chair next to the dressing table and motions for me to pour her a second glass of champagne. I watch the small bubbles as they surface, fighting for their release. *How much of the dose is too much?*

I sit uncomfortably near her but am desperate to know the answer. The jewellery box is so close now; perhaps I can take it and run but I fight the urge and bide my time, humouring the old woman to tell me more.

Lady Blackham takes a long breath before speaking. 'Apparently, the Earnshaw woman was not the type of fraudulent spiritualist who usually conducts these tedious nights of entertainment. Quite by accident, my poor daughter-in-law booked a woman of real talent. A true, loyal spiritualist could have been useful to us under different circumstances. But unfortunately, she was intent on bringing up the past and revealing some sensitive information which we would rather keep inside the family.'

'What information?'

'All families hide secrets, Ivy. You, of all people, should understand that! And these are personal affairs, not to be the subjects of gossip. It is of absolute importance that our Blackham name remains unblemished; that the work within this house continues.' She sips from her glass again. 'Had she just provided a suitable evening of party tricks and games, no doubt she would be at another house this very night, continuing on with her dramatic behaviour and selfish quest for attention.'

I am so hot I can barely breathe, but the old woman is still seemingly unaffected by the drugged champagne and is strangely calm. The room swims before my eyes. Pinching the skin on my wrist returns me from the point of fainting. I must not be a coward. Any weakness could be the death of me. I have to stay vigilant. Nothing is to be trusted within these walls.

'But...' she continues, her face hardens, displeased at the memory. 'She exceeded reason that night, prying and exploring the rooms, asking questions, opening locked doors. We lock things away for a reason. It is unforgivable to trespass into another's world, another's belongings. Especially Henry's great collection. The artefacts are what we stand for. Rosetta Earnshaw will not stop or undermine us!'

Her hand shakes, her crystal glass spilling droplets onto the lace cover of the dressing table. Anger radiates from her as she spits the name in disgust. 'The collection must remain together; to keep on growing. Part of my son has come back to me after all.'

'What?' I ask, suddenly confused.

'Look at the portrait of my beloved Victor above the fireplace. Don't you see a similarity in your profiles?'

The question hangs between us. The room tilts in the heat of the fire, her words not making sense.

'I am not sure what you are implying?' I turn towards the painting of the young man.

'Why, you even look and act alike – both stubborn and defiant. It is uncanny. Fancy, after all this time and effort to remove ourselves from the past, you come knocking at our door.'

She pauses, her eyes trailing every inch of my face. 'At first, you were a nobody. You turned up out of the blue with your country accent, only days after that spiritualist, and then I saw you standing next to his painting in my room. I made some enquiries about your history and confirmed my suspicions. The Blackhams are still powerful with connections. There is no such thing as coincidence.' She looks again at the portrait. 'And I grant that you are not blessed with his good looks, but you do share the same sharp eyes, and the way he always motioned his head to one side when judging a situation. So, yes, you are my granddaughter, no matter the questionable affairs of my son. You are still part of the bloodline of this family.'

She reaches out to touch my hair, and I flinch in trepidation, nearly knocking the chair over as I stand up and take a shaky step away from her outstretched hand.

'You are indeed a real treasure and must take your rightful place in the collection. Just when we needed you most, you found your way back. You know your purpose now, the house called to you, didn't it? Summoned you from whatever grubby village you grew up in. Naturally, a scrawny baby girl like you did not concern us then, but times have changed, and you are of great value to us now.'

I am still mute, absorbing her words, watching the smudged rouge on her lips contort into a thin smile. This is beyond any nightmare that I am part of this monstrous family.

'My son Victor, that was a true tragedy. A real loss to the world. Such a fine, capable man. Unfortunately, his brilliance was not repeated in my second child.'

I look again at the picture of her dead son; his sorrel-brown hair, his angular face, his prominent green eyes … my eyes?

'I don't understand. We are not related. I was born in the countryside. My father is Mr Edward Granger. My mother was never married before him.'

'Minor details, my dear, but not the reality. Victor's blood runs in your veins. You are a fortunate child and should be grateful for your birthright. And now, you can only strengthen our work, and the timing is perfect. I believe the gods conspired and returned you.'

'The idea is absurd!' My voice rises in hysteria. 'Is this what Miss Earnshaw knew?'

'You understand, we only wanted what belonged to us.' She takes another sip of champagne, ignoring my question. 'Before, this would have been a private business, a situation to be kept secret at all costs. We did not count on her arriving after all these years and challenging us on the matter. Why now I ask?' She leans forward. 'We had been quite clear with Lillian. Neither she, nor her family, were ever to be seen or heard from again, lest we take action to silence her once and for all.'

'My mother is dead, this autumn past.'

'Well,' she hesitates. She does not show any empathy for my loss. 'Even if Lillian has passed over, her sister should still know better. An arrangement is binding, especially in death.'

'Rosetta is my aunt?' I slump down on a nearby chair, my legs buckling from the shock. She said we were related, but this was so close, true family.

'Unfortunately, yes, it's an inconvenience for us all. I was confident we had solved the problem some twenty-five years ago... How time passes. My son became infatuated when he met your mother at the theatre.' She scowls. 'I expect she enticed him, sordid creature of the night that she was. Little did she know, he was already engaged to a fine woman of our choosing, and we would never allow him to play around with a mere actress on the stage.'

'I don't believe it. You are telling me nothing but lies.'

'I imagine my butler at the time was very creative in his method of intervening. Pay a little extra, and servants strive to prove their loyalty.'

'What did you do to them?'

'Only what a sensible mother would do to protect her son's reputation – to clean up the mess he left behind. We needed you both to disappear permanently.' She glares at me. 'We assumed you had died, gone to the foundling house, or been abandoned at some other back-street orphanage. It was of no interest to us. But it appears that you landed on your feet and your whore of a mother found another fool to bring you up. But after consideration, we

349

have graciously had a change of heart and decided to welcome you into the Blackham family.'

Anger surges through my veins. I want to lash out and slap the face of the old woman before me. 'You have no heart, and I have no wish to be part of this. Where have you taken my aunt?'

'She was swiftly dealt with. Don't worry about her. You are with us now. If we had kept the body of my son, we could have been a family again, but that ignorant fool of a captain gave him a burial at sea. I grieved his blunder more deeply than the death of Victor. I will never forgive him for not bringing my first born home to me.'

'What are you raving about now?' I exclaim.

'My dear, we need his hair to complete the ritual. It is almost the new moon and time for the ceremony.' She glances over to the window; the curtains are open to the night sky. 'My husband was fortunate to find the perfect jeweller for the work.' She smiles smugly. 'Mr Godwin was passionate about the art of resurrection, and his talents have been put to good use. Wouldn't you agree with me, darling?'

Despite the ticking clocks, time seems to stand still as a tall man appears in the doorway. I grab my knife from my apron pocket and hold it in front of my body.

He towers above me, wearing the magpie mask from the collection room. It covers the top half of his face, the protruding beak forming a sharp profile against the wall. The holes cut for his eyes reveal nothing but pools of a starless night. Over an expensive dinner suit, a heavy cloak hangs, clasped together by a bejewelled gold pin, cascading from his shoulders to the floor. The material of the cloak shines like silk and is adorned with more feathers, changing shades in the candlelight, fading from blue to green to black. All the elements of his outfit blend to create another creature. A dark type of beauty, the true essence of a magpie. I hold my breath, waiting for him to speak.

'Pearl, opal, ruby, topaz, amethyst, and lapis lazuli: such a clever, powerful arrangement of mourning jewels.' He rasps the words slowly, and the decay of death fills the room, reminding me of the stagnant flowers in the entrance. It is an old, dry, cracked, ugly voice, at odds with the strong body it seems to emanate from.

'Each first letter,' he continues, 'spells out the only artefact missing in this earthly realm. The reason for the whole Blackham collection: to summon the departed back into the physical plane of the living.' He brings his arms wide, the feathered cloak acting like wings, casting a sinister silhouette against the wall. 'Binding the jewels with the strands of hair from the deceased allows us to create the ultimate spiritual bridge.' He bellows as if for the whole world to hear. 'A portal!'

Chapter 45 ~ The Corvidae Coven

'Rejoice, for my husband has returned,' Lady Blackham's excited voice breaks through the unsettling silence that now lingers in the room. This cannot be the late Lord Blackham standing before me, the true master of the house, for it appears the Devil has conjured a breathing demon before me.

The costumed figure lowers his arms. 'We need you, Ivy. This is the perfect night. We are nearly complete.' His speech is strange, hoarse, but there is something familiar about the inflection of words. 'With each ceremony, the collection grows stronger, and us with it.' The iridescent green and navy feathers of his magpie mask almost seem to be alive.

'Whom do you speak of? There are more of you?' I ask, still shaken at the vision before me, searching for others in the shadows.

'We are the Corvidae Coven; I am but one of a unique handful, working together. You are fortunate to be taken into our confidence and bask in our achievements.'

'But Lord Blackham is dead; you cannot be him.'

'This body may have changed, but my soul remains the same. I have existed in this world and the next. There are many more secrets, Ivy, but you must join us. We can strengthen the bridge and increase our power. Death will no longer be the end. The time to break free of our cursed mortality is now.'

He takes a step closer to me. 'Come now, put the knife down. We are your family. You need not be afraid. The ceremony shall proceed ahead as planned. We have the jewellery and now all we require is you.' He reaches out his hand and I shrink back in abhorrence.

As though I had opened a window, the voices which visit me become clearer and louder until their sounds fill the room. Male and female, young and old, the voices are shouting - competing and frantic to be acknowledged. Dropping the blade, even with my hands over my ears, they are overwhelming just like in the attic.

'What do the lost souls ask you to do?' He asks. 'What do they say to you in the depths of the night? You have a unique ability - for I hear them too. I share their world, the place where the dead are trapped between Heaven and Hell. They are reaching out! They will not cease demanding your attention until they find peace.'

A revelation resonates throughout my bones. I should have understood years ago, before I came to this house, that the only way to make them stop is to do their bidding. Acknowledging them is not enough - I must help complete their dying wishes.

The man claps his hands, and the voices abruptly cease.

'I possess the ability to stop them, Ivy. I can give you silence. Surrender to me now and your connection to the lost souls of the afterlife will be broken. I am Lord Blackham; I have returned, and you will experience a destiny you can be proud of.'

He moves away from me and pours himself a glass of champagne, deciding instead to stand next to Lady Blackham. He places one hand on her shoulder and with his other, he caresses her brooch; the same ornate piece I collected from the jeweller. Everything about the scene unfolding before me is wrong, but there is something about his tall stature, the way his shoulders are set back, commanding the room that nudges at my senses.

I stare at the rugged floor, shocked into submission. It is then that I see the soft-leather black shoes. 'Mr Bancroft?'

It comes to me then; this ageing voice is encased in a familiar body of youth. The sight of him pawing at the old woman sickens me.

'What are you doing?' I demand. 'Why are you acting in this poor taste of a charade?'

Lady Blackham leans back into her chair, touching the man's hand on her shoulder. 'It is true – Mr Bancroft is here and yet he is not; he has given us a chance to wake the dead.'

There is no response from the butler or the strange voice emanating from him. Instead, he drains his champagne glass in one swift movement.

'What about the mistress? She lies dead in the garden. Is that what you want for me too?' I am depending on the cordial working soon. My words are almost a whine, pleading for sanity in this room.

'Not at all. You have only a small journey to make, and it need not be painful. Angelica was weak and would not wait until the midnight hour. It is regrettable, but hers was an unfortunate circumstance, another example of feminine weakness. No doubt she would have also failed in the ceremony like the other feeble women before her, but you have the Blackham blood coursing through you. You are different.'

My false bravado ebbs to nothing, as I realise this woman is indifferent to my life existing beyond this night.

'Yours will be a noble sacrifice and a great success.' Lady Blackham adds with a confidence that shakes me. This ceremony has happened many times before. I back away from them both, looking for the knife on the floor, but it has disappeared.

'Don't you want to see your mother again?' The unnatural voice speaks again. 'She is smiling, waiting for you. You only have to come with us. We will reunite you... and fulfil your heart's desire.' The form of Mr Bancroft tilts his head smugly, knowing he goads me with a bait I cannot resist.

I have a rush of conflicting emotions. Hope mixed with loathing at my weakness of wanting to know more. 'You can see her?'

'As clear as night and day. She is sketching under a tree full of birds. Isn't that what you like to do together? Come now, don't be afraid.' He reaches out his arms towards me as if we are to embrace. 'This will all be over soon, and you will thank me.'

I hesitate with my response. I can almost feel my mother in the room. Has she been calling to me amongst the mass of voices? A part of me knows she is within reach, and she said she would return. But at what cost? This is playing God… I think of the crypt under the house and the spirit which possessed the mistress. I would always be bound by whatever evil they unleash. If my mother is in Heaven, I would never see her again.

'Tell me where to find Miss Earnshaw!' I cry, pushing the thoughts of his proposition away.

'With your help, we can bring all our loved ones back. Death will not hold power over our mortal bodies anymore.'

'Where is she?'

'That is no concern of yours. Once you are with your mother again, you will forget these insignificant worries.'

His condescending words remind me of my father's. There is nothing else I can learn here; all they want is for me to submit. I dash over to the dressing table, grab the jewellery box and run from the room.

In the corridor, Mrs Higgins is waiting. She points down the marble staircase, and I flee, grateful for her help, but then I see William on the first floor below. He blocks my exit and steers me towards the direction of the back room, into a dead end. It is the only door unlocked; even the servant stairwell is bolted. I am like the grey cat bolting for safety with the magpie in his mouth. There is a punishment for theft.

Once inside the back room, my mistake is confirmed. A single gas lamp sits in the corner, casting a yellow glow over a new addition to the room. In the centre of the floor now lies a damsel-red silk sheet. It is a more expensive version than the one I found in the coffin below the basement. Ornately adorned with gold and silver embroidery, the patterns are similar to the designs from the strange backstreet jeweller's shop. Constellations of stars surrounded with angular lines mix with Egyptian hieroglyphic patterns to form a story of what looks like a journey of rebirth.

I try to open the window, looking for the mistress outside, but the sash is locked, and the body is gone. A sudden flap of wings at the windowpane startles me to the reality of my senses.

'What is this?' I turn to run away, but William blocks the doorway, he seems to rise up, filling the space with his frame, his milky eyes wide and ugly grin taunting me to challenge him. He rolls up his sleeves, flexing his hands to reveal the sinewy muscles in his arms. He may be old, but he still has the strength of a young man.

'Step aside, no need to scare the girl. She will cooperate, I am sure.' Lady Blackham passes by him, striding in with her stick.

I have never seen this woman out of her room, and I am taken aback at how youthful and energetic she has become compared to the bitter, lethargic person I have been serving these last few weeks. Surely the cordial must take effect soon. I berate myself for not reading more about the effects of dosages.

'Ivy, this is our gift to you.' She waves her stick towards the covering. 'It will be part of your resting place, of sorts. The birds favour this room overlooking the garden, and so they see their offering before the vessel is taken down to the crypt.'

My throat tightens. 'Is this what Miss Earnshaw saw before you took her away? She wanted to stop your ceremonies?'

'Oh no, that was quite different – coincidence or fate, no matter how you judge it. If she hadn't seen him at the séance, none of this would have been possible.'

'Who was it? Who appeared?'

'Why, Ivy, do you really have no idea?' She shakes her head in puzzlement.

I am exhausted with it all. 'No, tell me!'

'The spiritualist thought she had all the answers, thought she could control us! But she saw the person she least expected. Her arrogance was her own undoing!'

'Miss Earnshaw knew the spirit?' My maid's apron twists in my hand, the old woman's words drawing the air out of my lungs. More secrets, why am I always the last to know?

'Of course, you cannot truly ever forget your own family, your own blood.'

'Who did she see? Another tortured soul trapped in this house?' I scream at her.

Lady Blackham relishes the power of her information before she speaks. 'She saw your brother!'

The revelation strikes me like a slap to the face, my mouth falling open. I also had a brother, now in the spirit world. The extent of my mother's deceit and her concealed life keeps widening. My heart aches with the loss of more family; grief mixed with regret and anger for all the lost years.

But I barely have a chance to understand before I see Mrs Higgins hand a handkerchief to William, and he charges in my direction.

The sickly aroma of lemons drifts in the air and I understand a second too late this is the chloroform Mrs Higgins spoke of to the mistress. My attempt to find Miss Earnshaw and gain the upper hand has failed. The champagne concoction proved to be useless. Just as my father predicted, all my studies have come to nothing. The jewellery box becomes weightless as it slips from my hands, the rings, necklaces, and brooches spilling onto the floor.

This must be the end - I am not ready. My mind protests, as my senses become disorientated and the unfeeling faces of those around me blur together. But as my body succumbs deeper to the drug, the scent of my mother's violets wraps around me and overpowers the citrus. Their perfume so strong that I imagine the whole room is filled with the purple flowers and their soft, silky petals cushion my fall into obscurity.

Chapter 46 ~ Feathers

I find myself lying on a cold, hard surface, unable to wake properly. There is no difference between my eyes being open or closed – blackness exists in both worlds. My mouth is stale, with a bitter taste layered on my tongue. I need fresh air to fill my lungs and dispel this confusion. My body is wrapped tightly in what feels like the silk covering from the backroom; a silk cocoon, a butterfly waiting for transformation. The vapours of newly varnished panels are noxious, making my head spin. *I must be confined inside the coffin.*

The thought terrifies me as the confinement becomes increasingly overwhelming. I can barely move, but my fingertips work relentlessly until they find the edge of the smooth fabric and push at the layers until at last it loosens. I shove at the wooden ceiling bearing above me, but it is fixed tight.

As despair begins to slice at my nerves, I find two small objects beside my legs. The first is made of stone, the second from wood, and without setting eyes on them, I know one is from the collection of disfigured birds in Lord Blackham's desk, and the other is my parting tribute from the attic: the female wooden carving created by William. I smash the shapes onto the panel above me, not caring if they break. Again and again, I hit the wood with the inanimate objects.

'Help! I'm trapped. Please, someone let me out!' I scream, but I hear nothing in response. If someone is on the other side of the box, they are listening to my cries silently. I imagine William sitting overseeing this coffin, guardian of what is needed for the Blackham's unholy ceremony.

'William, please let me out. My father has money. I am not poor. They will pay you for my return.'

But still there is nothing.

I must not panic; I try not to think about the air disappearing as my breathing quickens. Mrs Guilden will be here soon with a group of men to help, but they are taking their time and my hope of them arriving is fading fast. Could she not find men willing to leave their warm beds at this hour? Or is it the Blackham name that is preventing them from coming?

A flash of memory interrupts my thoughts, triggered by the small space. I am nine years old again. I smell the damp shed walls and see my brother's face twisted with shame as he shuts the door on me – not by his callous act, but through his relation to me. His friends, standing a few feet away, are laughing at him, spurring him on to punish his half-sister, who has only invisible friends for company.

'If you hear ghosts, you should become one of them, for no one living likes you.' He had laughed heartlessly before leaving me all alone in the dark.

I had gone wild, abandoned with nothing but the voices for company, trapped for hours until Mother had finally found me, grubby and mute from the hideous ordeal. I couldn't speak for a week. In those few hours alone, I had somehow separated my mind from my body and was unable to find my way back without her help.

But I am a grown woman now, and my mother is gone. I cannot let go of what sanity I have left. I consider the decisions that brought me here – the illusion that my safest path was searching for Miss Earnshaw. How wrong I was. My tongue licks at the blood on my lips. I have chewed the soft skin raw already.

Could this be what Hell feels like? I rarely paid attention in church or to the scriptures. I had always known I was different, with voices tormenting me whenever my mind wandered on its own. The other children in the village never heard them as I did, and my half-brother was not the only one who was cruel to me as a child. I eventually learned it was best not to engage with anybody, to keep my peculiarities as hidden as possible, but Mother said not to worry. They were just bad dreams that had escaped into the daylight; another version of the truth she had kept from me.

Angst is building inside me. I want to kick and punch the wooden walls into splinters, but if I lose control, what comes next?

The usual voices in my head push at my conscience to be heard again. This time, I don't have the strength to ignore them. They have been waiting for so long, it is my turn to listen now. I drop the statues to my side. Linking my fingers together across my chest, I try to pull apart the sounds. I am surprised that the act of concentration slows my breathing, and with every small intake of air, the panic abates a little.

Slowly, I begin to discern between the voices. One, that of a young man, becomes clearer the more I focus on him. I expect anger, but instead I hear remorse for a wasted life, leaving those he had a duty to behind to fend for themselves when he was needed. He cries for Hannah; wanting her to know his regret. I feel his pain as if it were my own and want to console him.

'I will tell her,' I whisper into the darkness.

As if he hears my validation, the angst in his voice softens until the words fade with him, lost in his memories of a sister and family he once had.

Sharp scraping noises surrounding my head bring me back to the reality of my confinement. Recoiling at the thought of rats, I listen in horror as the faint sound of scratching builds, becoming louder until it transforms into a ripping crack, like thunder. A flash of lightning floods my senses, and for a moment, I am blinded, and then I see Hannah. The candle in her hand illuminates her face, and I try to focus on the surroundings: a murky stone room, cold and earthy. I recognise the smell of burning herbs at once.

'There you are. Blimey, you don't half look a state!' She exclaims.

Hannah puts down the light and grabs hold of my arms, dragging me out of the coffin. My legs, already stiff, struggle to find their balance. She grimaces at me.

'You came.' I mumble. My head is pounding, and I am disoriented but so grateful to be released that I could weep for days.

Her eyes become wide with panic. She looks behind her as I lean against her arm. 'We don't have much time. I … thought I heard my brother's voice again, and—'

She shakes her head. 'It makes no sense, but tonight I couldn't look the other way,' she huffs. 'I know I'm going to regret this.'

'Thank you,' I whisper, the sound barely audible. 'I think I heard him too... He was sorry he had to leave you and regrets not being there when you needed him most.'

Hannah gives me a puzzled look and then dismisses my words with a shake of her head. 'I am always a fool for a scrap of attention. My brother used to say, you're just like a stray dog, who will follow a kind hand blindly.' She is muttering more to herself than to me as she helps me to stand. 'I wish he was here now. He always tried to do the right thing, and a whole lot of good that did him. But you were kind to me. No one offered to teach me to read before, and I – I...' She hesitates. 'I didn't want any of your things to end up in the trunk.' She blurts out the sentence. The unspoken truth is that no servant would ever leave behind their valuables by accident, that they never had the choice. 'I want no part in it, I am not following anymore.'

Holding onto her arm, searching her eyes, I see her true character beneath the veil of anger she used against me. Before hardship had moulded her into the sharp-edged girl she had come to be. 'Let's be getting away. They will return at any minute. We have little time.' Her furtive glance returns to the doorway, our only exit.

'So, you do know about this place? What they use it for?'

She nods reluctantly. 'Best you don't find out.' She takes me by the elbow and tries to push me towards the crypt door, sharing my weight. But I am still weak from the drug-induced sleep and my movements are slow.

'Perhaps, if I can rescue one person, I might be forgiven for the others.' She gives a sad smile. 'A selfish act again, but it could be enough to right the wrongs of this house.'

'Why didn't you leave?'

'I was mistaken that in time the master would favour me again.' She pauses, her cheeks flushed. 'Anyway, their rituals are the only thing they care about. We are nothing but fodder for their experiments and games. I only wish—'

The sound of footsteps cuts her words short. We both watch in dismay as Lady Blackham and the figure of Mr Bancroft walk in, the old woman striking her cane hard against the stone floor as she takes the seat William usually occupies.

'It's the ceremony. We are too late,' Hannah spits out. 'They have cursed you and I have cursed myself by staying.'

Lady Blackham eyes Hannah with disgust. 'So, this is where we discover you. What a shambles. You have let yourself down and not fulfilled your duties. Now you are no longer required perhaps William can find a use for you. The birds are always more grateful at this time of year.'

The cloaked Mr Bancroft steps closer to Hannah, reaching out towards her. She screams in terror. His lips, not covered by the feathered mask, curl into a perverse sneer; his face, once a model of composure, twists and distorts into a grotesque visage. As he opens his mouth, a deafening sound vibrates into the room. A chorus of more dead voices screaming for peace. The unbearable cries feel like a thousand knives are falling from above as I drop to my knees.

Hannah whimpers as the noise rips through her, crumpling to the floor in agony, her eyes wide with panic.

Mr Bancroft turns his attention to me, stepping past Hannah on the stone slabs.

She looks back over her shoulder, and I know she is measuring her odds of escape without the drugged weight of my body to drag along with her.

'Don't leave me!' I try to grab at Hannah's ankle. My words become lost in the roar. I can barely see her as the pain also bursts into my ears.

'God forgive me, that I could help none of you.' She tears herself away from my grasp, managing to stand, and stumbles out of the crypt, leaving me to face my fate alone.

Fear crashes over me like waves. The stone ground tilts beneath my knees, as if I am balancing on the stern of a sinking ship, searching for a safe horizon in the midst of a violent storm.

Chapter 47 ~ A Reckoning

Master Blackham ~ Blackham House, 24th December.

A single piercing scream jolts the master awake from his drunken slumber, causing his pipe to fall from his grip with the remnants of opium spilling onto the carpet, still warm. With heavy eyes, he hears the unearthly noise again, summoning him from his sweet oblivion. Heaving himself out of the study chair, he reaches for his wine on the side table, finishing the burgundy liquid in one fluid motion. It dribbles down his chin, and he wipes it with the back of his shirt sleeve.

Leaving the glass and taking only the bottle for company, he follows the source of the noise down to the basement. The blurred figure of a woman appears from the kitchen.

'Angelica, is that you?' He blinks his eyes. 'Thank God.' He moves slowly, struggling to put one foot in front of the other. 'I dreamt I saw you in the garden, surrounded by the birds. It was awful.' He chokes. 'They were pecking at your beautiful body, consuming you. Stealing you from me forever.' He staggers forward, taking another gulp from the bottle. 'But here you are now. Come to me, darling. We will go back to Italy, just like you wanted.'

Holding his arms open wide, the woman runs into his embrace. He smells her hair, running the strands through his fingers until he gasps in confusion. 'Hannah?' He says, pushing her away. 'Where is my wife?'

Hannah grips his arm. 'It is just as you saw. But at least we can be together again now.' She rushes her words, her eyes pleading. 'Don't you understand? I knew your marriage was a mistake. You had to get married, didn't you? To please your mother.' She grabs his shirt, pressing her body against his chest.

He tears her away with his free hand. 'What are you doing?'

'This was why I stayed - why I waited for you. She was weak, but I can care for you the way you deserve, the way I did before, now that she's gone.'

'Angelica is gone?'

'Did you not hear what I said? Your wife is dead. You are free of her.'

'Dead?' A sob escapes his throat. 'No, no, no, you lie!' He throws his head back in anguish, closing his eyes, a silent wail passing between his distorted lips. 'Hannah,' he moans, 'this is too much. It is unbearable, I cannot catch my breath.' He pulls at the neck of his shirt.

Hannah leans forward and strokes his arm, but he shakes her off with a violent snap.

'Who is responsible?'

'Lady Blackham.' Her voice is barely audible.

'My mother?' He barks. 'Where is she?' The words are spat out between gritted teeth, rage coursing through his veins.

'Under the basement.' She steps aside, revealing the open trap door. 'But don't go down there,' she cries. 'Please, you must leave with me!'

'Leave? Why would I go anywhere? This is my house, and my mother should be in her room where she belongs.'

'She has changed, and so has Mr Bancroft. It is not safe here; you must believe me! I have some money saved. I sold that brooch ... got rid of the evidence.' Her eyes become alight with feverish excitement. 'I don't care if you were part of her murder. The police would never find you. It is them that are dangerous,' she points to the trapdoor, 'not you. I know you wouldn't hurt me.'

'What brooch? This is all ludicrous!' He leans into her face, spittle flying from his mouth. 'What in God's name are you talking about, girl?'

'The bird with the black gems – the one the spiritualist wore. I found it on the floor the night she disappeared.'

'Listen to me.' He slurs his words. 'I don't know what you imagined happened, but I never murdered anyone.'

She shakes her head, raising her eyes to meet his, but he can barely focus on her. 'I beg you, don't go down there. There's something bad. I tried to help Ivy, but it's too late.'

'Get out of my way, I need to see my mother. She might make more sense.' He pushes her aside. 'And what has Ivy got to do with anything?'

'They have chosen her. William made her a gift; her fate is sealed. I thought you were protecting me from them, but it wasn't you, was it?'

'What are you gibbering about now?' He sputters, squeezing his temples with one hand, the other still firmly grasping the bottle of wine.

'I was never moved to the attic; the other servants always disappeared soon afterwards.

'No Hannah, it was never me. You were only something to warm my bed on a cold night. Now, go! Nothing matters anymore, nothing good ever came out of this place!'

He stumbles on the steps, making his way down the narrow corridor, past the closed doors, and into the crypt, where there is a dim lamp shining. His jaw slackens at the sight before him: his mother and another figure standing by a stone tomb; Ivy lying slumped next to an open coffin. He rubs his forehead on his forearm. 'Bancroft?' He staggers into the light, examining the man looming over him.

'My son,' croaks the figure, the words guttural and low. He opens his arms wide, the cloak displaying the many feathers sewn together in beautiful detail; the jewelled magpie mask still concealing most of his face.

The master sways, glancing at the bottle in his hand. 'If I hadn't smoked and drunk so much wine, perhaps I would have been shocked to find you dressed in my father's ridiculous clothes, apparently raised from the dead. But this nightmare will end soon enough. They always do.'

'This is no dream, Alexander. Your father has returned.' His mother's voice is joyous, at odds with the oppressive atmosphere surrounding them.

'Bancroft, stop this folly at once. I demand it!' The master shouts at the masked man.

'My son,' the rasped words repeat. 'A borrowed body, but it is my spirit.'

'Ha!' The master's laugh echoes off the stone walls of the crypt. 'What a ridiculous scene for a Blackham reunion. All we need now is precious Victor to complete our loving family; a proper welcome back to the land of the living.'

He raises the bottle as he sways about, wine splashing on the floor as he turns to face his mother. 'I did your bidding with the spiritualist, arranging the asylum. Her treatment did not sit well with my conscience, but all the same, I followed your instructions, always trying not to upset you, Mother. To avoid your avid disappointment at all costs.' He sighs wearily. 'And did you thank me? No, not a single murmur of gratitude. And now, all this … madness.' He points at the tomb and the engravings. 'How can I have not known you were continuing with Father's insane plans, his desperate search to conquer death? This insanity must stop at once. I demand it! This is my house.'

His mother leans on her stick, her eyes steely. 'Thankfully, your claim on this house has been relinquished now that your father is here. You have always been a selfish, needy child, draining me since your disastrous birth. Constantly ill, making everyone come to your room – your nurse and I were run ragged. And now in adulthood, living in your own vacuum of drugs and alcohol. I am surprised you can barely dress yourself each day.'

'How dare you! How did you expect me to act? The tonics you gave me as a sick boy created the most terrifying hallucinations. I never knew what was real or fantasy. I believed this house was cursed and was too frightened to leave my room, even when I was well! And then, just when I believed life could be tolerable, my beloved wife and child were taken away from me.' His eyes fill with unshed tears. 'And now my second attempt at happiness with Angelica has also failed. I did her the worst wrong by bringing her here. It seems I am fated to be alone. God forbid I should come to you for empathy.'

She stands from the chair and stabs her cane in the air. 'Pull yourself together. You are a Blackham, part of one of the most important families in this country. You should take control of your emotions and stop feeling sorry for yourself. Act like a proper man, like your brother was.'

He laughs. 'Of course, I'm not as brilliant as Victor ever was.' The name is bitter on his lips. 'I expect he would have been the mastermind behind all of this.' Slurring his words, he staggers on the spot. 'Sorry to disappoint you again, but Victor is long dead, and so is my father. I am all you have left. This man before me is not connected to our family. God knows what you have managed to conjure up!'

'It is him, Alexander. All the sacrifices ... they strengthened him. This is the longest he's broken through from the other side and spoken with us.' His mother proclaims her words proudly, high-pitched and excited.

'Yes, it is true.' Lord Blackham raises his arms, the magpie cloak of feathers shimmering blue and green in the candlelight. 'And soon, with the power of the Corvidae, I will become stronger, to permanently stay and walk amongst you all, as I once did.'

'Sacrifices?' Ivy's voice pierces the conversation shrill with panic towards Lady Blackham. 'Was my brother one of them, too? You said Miss Earnshaw saw him in the séance!'

'Hush! Your brother is forever dead to you.' Lady Blackham snaps at her.

'I found the dolls wrapped inside the coffins... They were gifts, weren't they, for the servants before me? Where are their bodies now?' Ivy's words waver. 'What does William really do in the garden?'

Lady Blackham glowers at Ivy. 'Enough! Our most loyal servants, they have all provided their service to us – in life and also in death.'

'William looks after the magpies,' drawls Lord Blackham. 'He feeds them whatever they request. Nothing more, nothing less. Nothing is wasted in their plan.'

'You murdered them all ... the turned ground in the garden. The rats and birds are feeding from their graves! It is the most unholy and evil act against humanity!' Ivy screeches, clapping her hands to her face. 'How can you sanction such deeds?'

Lord Blackham turns towards the stone vault in the centre of the room. 'The birds are the messengers of the true master we serve. When enough of us return from purgatory, he will rise again. He has already managed to speak through one of you in this house, and soon his shackles to the other side will be broken once and for all. And all the boundaries between this world and the next will be ours to govern. True power at last.'

He gently touches the stone coffin in the centre of the vault, where a large ruby-jewelled dagger rests on a midnight-blue velvet pillow. 'Bancroft is refreshingly strong. This vessel suits me well, for we are similar in many ways. Of course, sometimes the birds get impatient and restless, calling for their own rewards from the house, for blood to spill on the earth. But they are a necessary part of the true master's grand design. We will all be free of this inflicted mortality soon enough.'

'Is that what happened to the women I loved?' slurs Master Blackham. 'They died in that back room, driven to death by witnessing your mad experiments, taking their own lives for the sake of your bloody birds?'

'Perhaps,' says Lord Blackham, his words slow and carefully measured. 'I am sorry for your loss, but death is part of this futile short life we are given. That is why the work of the Corvidae is so important: we unite for a greater purpose, where death no longer becomes the end, at least not for the chosen few.'

'You are an abomination! Not content with me living in the umbrage of your constant disappointment, you punish me by destroying the lives of anybody I ever loved!' He shouts out, his eyes wild with disbelief.

'It was you who took Victor away from me!' His mother cries.

The master swivels, spilling his wine again to face his mother. 'And so, you admit it at last, fifteen years later, you still blame me for the fact you had to stay behind because I was sick. You believe the absurd notion that he died because of me?'

'I could have saved him, I know it.' His mother's voice is distraught. 'If I had been on that ship, I could have done something. Instead, I was here with you … always ill, always whining. Victor was so strong, so magnificent. He should have lived, not you. It is your fault he never returned!'

Her face turns puce and then a deathly shade of white. She puts a gloved hand to her cheek. 'Even now you drain me. I must sit down. This is how you treat your mother after all I have done for you?' She stumbles back into the chair, dropping her cane.

'This is just another of your theatrics,' the master replies, watching as his mother appears to struggle for breath, her hand at her throat, her expression strained in the dimly lit room.

Lord Blackham holds out his hands as if in prayer. 'Hush! I never held you responsible for your brother's death. It is only your mother who harbours that notion. You have always been weak, but that is your burden. You must put all that aside now and resume the role of my son. I will forge a true man out of you yet. Your turn will come to make us proud.'

Lord Blackham raises his hands; the cloak slips around his arms, the heavy velvet draping his young body. His fingers glint with flashes of gems: more mourning jewellery. 'My strength is weakening. The ceremony calls to me. It demands to be completed! The power does not come from this human vessel, but from beyond.' He looks at the dagger glinting with rubies. 'It is my master's way.'

He waves his arms around the room at the hanging tapestries depicting all types of birds woven together. But flying above all the smaller birds is the family of corvidae: crows, rooks, jackdaws, ravens, jays, and magpies; larger and more terrifying with their sharp claws and beaks, ready for hunting.

'The corvids are such magnificent creatures. We are honoured, for Blackham House is under the rule of the majestic magpies. They collect what is necessary to make the ceremony complete. Your wives played their parts; we did not waste their deaths.'

Master Blackham sneers at him. 'Who are you to play God in a twisted game with nature?'

'You cannot doubt their power, boy. Am I not proof? They chose us, Alexander. They meant for us to live here on these grounds, to discover this tomb and the power inside. The inscriptions detail what we must do. Even the Egyptian Book of Death, my most valuable discovery and my biggest sacrifice, was crucial for the ceremony's success. For in losing Victor, we gained the knowledge to crack open the doors of purgatory, to communicate with the birds surrounding this house, and so we do their bidding. Have you been blind to the birds too?'

'Oh no, I'm well aware of the feathered demons. They arrived soon after we moved here; as a child I had no protection from them, not even from my own mother. Every day they appeared at my window with their horrific red eyes, their wings beating against the glass.' He sways, struggling to stay upright. 'But now only this keeps the madness at bay.'

He brings the bottle to his mouth, droplets of claret wine sloshing across his chest, staining his white shirt like a fresh wound. 'What have you done, Father, to come back from the dead? What evil lies buried in that godforsaken tomb?'

'We did what we had to; we must always be ready to serve and obey. Now bring the girl to the tomb. It is time.'

'Are you not listening to me? There will be no more spilt blood! You must stop this insanity.' He grabs Ivy's arm. 'You are still here? Run! Get as far away from this cursed house and my family as you can.' He pushes her towards the doorway.

'No, you cannot let her go!' Screams his mother. She is visibly sweating now, clawing at the neck of her dress. 'This one is different. The Egyptian book explains it. She is of Victor's blood and therefore your father's; the link will be stronger. Mr Godwin says she could complete the gateway. This could be everything we have been working towards.'

'It's lies, all lies. Ivy is not Victor's – this is nothing but a madhouse!' shouts the master.

'But she is. That's why we had to deal with that spiritualist – she knew too much.' His mother replies adamantly.

'So that was why she was familiar. She had been here before?'

'Unfortunately, yes, many years ago.' Her voice bristles. 'We thought we had dealt with the repercussions of Victor's actions then, but it seems everything is coming together perfectly now.' His mother's now bloodshot eyes challenge him. 'Do you not agree?'

'No, I most definitely don't.' He grimaces in response.

His mother inhales sharply, as if to gather her strength. 'Come now, Ivy, do not waste any more time. You are a gift from

Victor to his father. You must fulfil your fate; this will all be over soon.'

'You will not have me, nor anyone else again for your sordid games!' Ivy speaks out, her voice icy with contempt. 'I will find Miss Earnshaw and the whole of London will know of your crimes. Your punishment will come.'

She staggers towards the exit, faster than Lady Blackham can rise from her chair, but the masked figure is unnaturally quick, grabbing at her dress, her hair, until she is captive in his embrace.

Tearing at his mask, she screams as the person behind is revealed. Mr Bancroft's eyes are void of any colour; only an opaque whiteness reflects back into the room.

Ivy scrabbles on the floor, trying to find her footing. She tears at her necklace, the vicar's cross, breaking the gold chain. She throws it towards his blank face and bolts for the door. The fine links catch in the feathers of the cloak and a deep red stain appears on his neck from where the crucifix has touched his skin. He cries out in pain as though the necklace has cut him like a knife.

'No, stop her!' He groans. 'I cannot stay much longer. We must make the link stronger.'

Master Blackham lunges forward, blocking the path to the distress of his mother and the manifestation of his father, allowing Ivy to slip away. 'So, we must have a toast to cursed family reunions!' He laughs. 'And let's not forget those who cannot be here.' He holds the drink out before him. 'To Victor and my dead wives.' He consumes the remaining contents rapidly with familiar ease, eyeballing the empty bottle with regret. 'I welcome the next life. For Hell must be better than this.'

Chapter 48 ~ Mr Bancroft

Ivy ~ Blackham House, 24th December.

The mourning jewellery is the key to stopping the ceremony from ever happening again. A blessing is not enough. The vicar must destroy the complete collection for its power to be truly broken. I make a dash upstairs, fear dissipating the drugged after-effects from my body. My heart hammers in my chest, with their arguments still ringing in my ears. Judging by the behaviour of Lady Blackham, the champagne finally seems to be taking effect, but I do not know how much time the distraction will give me.

In the back room the gas lamp still flickers on the ground next to the empty fireplace. I am not surprised to find the silk covering has gone from the floor and all the spilt rings and necklaces have been tidied into the box and placed safely on the mantelpiece. I breathe a sigh of relief.

'What do you have there?'

I spin on my heels and sweep up the box into my arms. Mr Bancroft stands in the doorway, still dressed in the cloak, but he is missing the mask of feathers. He motions for me to stop moving with a flick of his finger. 'I believe you hold an important part of the collection, do you not?' His jade-green eyes have returned, but his face glistens with a fever of sweat, his ghoulish lips red against his deathly pale skin.

'You no longer speak with the Devil inside you?' I ask tentatively.

His smile is lopsided; the evening has taken its toll. I catch a glimpse of the raw man beneath his perfectly composed features.

Again, a familiar feeling washes over me that goes beyond this house. The sense of déjà vu keeps telling me I have seen him before, a pull in my gut that we should be working together not against each other. But I shake the strange notion away. I am in danger, for he is part of the dark forces working against me. This is what my aunt predicted – here, tonight; my death completing the ceremony is what she was frightened of. I was always destined to fight this battle, with or without her.

'They see fit how to use me for their purposes.' His own voice has returned but his neck is slashed, bleeding from where the cross and chain touched his skin. 'And also, you.' There is an unsettling silence between us as he catches his breath from the stairs.

'Get out of my way, whatever – whomever you are. I am leaving,' I say, raising my chin to him in defiance.

'I'm afraid that's not possible. No necklace or God can help you now.' There is a new anger in his eyes.

'I have the blessing of the vicar,' I stammer as he laughs in my face, dismissing me like a child. 'What is their hold over you? Can you not fight their magic?'

His lips curl into a sneer. 'Are you implying we're under an invisible control? You are more deluded than I first thought.' He stands taller and straightens his jacket and cuffs under his cloak. It is an expensive dinner suit that must have belonged to the late Lord Blackham, pressed and freshly starched.

'What is it then? Are you afraid? Have they threatened you to do their bidding?'

Again, he laughs to himself at a private joke beyond my comprehension. 'Let's just say the family has persuasive means. I am my own man and with my own ambitions. I am going to run this household, and in time they will value my loyalty above the mere status of a butler.'

He moves closer, invading my space. I can smell his sweat, stale and bitter – gone is the pretence of his impeccable mask. I glare at him, straightening my back, showing him I won't be intimidated. 'Where do you go, Mr Bancroft, when you disappear from the house?'

'Where I go and what I do is none of your business.'

'Ah, so, they are just insignificant household errands, then?'

He towers above me, being at least six feet four. 'On the contrary, Ivy. I work for the Blackhams, the most prestigious family in all the country – and one day this world will realise their greatness. They trust me with their most important jobs, ensuring their name is protected and still powerful in the city.

'But if you are indeed so important, why would Mrs Higgins pretend that you didn't exist when I first arrived?'

A nerve twitches under his left eye. A sheen of sweat appears on his forehead. 'We don't trust easily. Some mothers have a natural inclination to protect their children. There are many that would like to limit our ambitions.'

'Like Miss Earnshaw?'

'Yes, and she was dealt with.'

'And me?'

'You are special to them, apparently the final piece of the puzzle. But even with all your snooping, you cannot comprehend what will bear fruit when the time is right, when we are finally ready to unleash the old powers of this world. Why don't you let me return you to the attic where you can rest? Surely, that's the best place for you. A long peaceful sleep, doesn't that sound nice?'

I grip the wooden box tighter. 'The vicar told me to bring the pieces to him. He can stop whatever ungodly act this family is trying to do.'

'So, you have spoken to a man of God?' He laughs in mockery. 'He is nothing but an amateur, compared to the knowledge we have. Faith cannot protect you here. We will be the gods of this world soon enough.' He opens the drawers of the box held against my apron, running his fingers through the chains and brooches, the jewels of the collection.

'Mr Godwin, in the jewellery shop… It is the Devil's work.' I shut the drawers firmly and step back.

'You are not so naïve, after all. All this time, I assumed you were ignorant and perhaps a little dim-witted. This collection of gems is the most favoured treasure above them all. I can't imagine Lady Blackham would let you take her belongings so easily, or the spirit of Lord Blackham, for that matter.' He licks his lips, frowning at the apparent difficulty of the action. I hope the champagne is finally taking effect on him.

Instead of trying to pry the box from me as I expect, he moves closer and strokes my hair. His tenderness takes me by surprise. 'This could have been so different if only you'd let go of your foolish notions. Join us – this family has been good to me, and they will look after you. There are ways to survive the ceremony if you do not fight. You can rise above the role of a simple servant, as I have done. Do something purposeful with your life. Whatever you dream of, they can provide.'

His change in tone stuns me. 'Is that what you told the others before they must have died, frightened and alone? What have they promised you to turn you into such a monster?'

'That's a private contract, Ivy, between me and them, but their promise of reward makes all of this worth my while.'

'Well, they cannot buy me,' I snap. 'Your morals may be for sale, but mine are not. Now, let me pass.'

Rage flashes in his eyes; I see the muscles in his jaw clench. 'Then I will have to do this the hard way.'

He leans down, and in one fluid act, his arm slips behind my head as he grabs the back of my hair painfully in his fist, forcing me into the crook of his elbow. With his other hand, he grips my throat, his fingers tightening around my neck as he edges closer to my face, his features distorted with fury. 'You will not ruin this for me. What is one more sacrifice? No one will miss you. I have worked too hard for what I deserve.'

I can smell the sweetness of the poisonous berries on his breath. I know the cordial is working now, I see the beads of sweat on his forehead and his pupils dilating.

'I know your strength is fading. You should just let me go,' I say hastily. 'Just like Lady Blackham, you will soon be overcome with its poison. Just like the servants before you.'

He looks at me, confused.

'The champagne you drank was laced with the Devil's Thorn. I know you made a cordial from the poisonous plants in the garden. It is only fitting to be given the same fate as the servants before me and is the perfect justice for this occasion, is it not?'

'So, you found the ceremonial drink, not so dim-witted after all.' I wince at the pain as he digs his thumb into my skin.

The sickening panic returns of being trapped, of small spaces, sweaty hands, and hot breath.

I try to twist with a sudden jerk, and a flash of pain strikes in my hip from the awkward lunge. He doubles over as his stomach seems to be overcome with spasms. In his moment of weakness, I push him away as anger erupts, the rage rushing through me. *I will have no more bruises.*

'Leave me be!' I shout.

I step backwards, kicking over the lamp near my feet. The glass breaks, spilling the lighting fluid violently across the floor towards the window. Within a single heartbeat, the curtains become alight. He rushes forward to restrain the blaze, showing his loyalty to the house once more.

I watch the scene in slow motion as he tries to stamp out the burning fabric. In the light of the flames, the feathers on his cloak glimmer all the beautiful, iridescent colours of a magpie – stunning magentas and emeralds mixed with lapis blue. But the fire is hungry and his efforts are in vain. It burns with even more determination than him, devouring everything it touches. The curtains break free of their frame and engulf him with their weight. He wrestles with the heavy velvet, shouting in anguish at the scorching heat.

In the distraction, I bolt down the stairs with the jewellery box and into the kitchen to grab my carpet bag. Hannah must have unlocked the door, for I am able to run straight out into the street.

Chapter 49 ~ Rescue

The glacial air bites at my face but is a welcome sensation. A fine dusting of white powder covers the iron railings and the ground. It is almost Christmas Day. Shrill whistles pierce my ears as an urgent call for the fire service suddenly passes along the street. The speed of the flames is quick and relentless. Smoke is already escaping from the building, trailing upwards into the night sky as snowflakes tumble down.

I dart away into the square garden which is already filling up with people. Standing alone, I search the groups of people for anyone I recognise, the blood still pumping hard through my veins at the thought of what the Blackhams had planned for me. Thankfully, I see no one from the house, so I place the jewellery box carefully on the ground and remove the ripped piece of paper from my carpet bag with the details of where they took Miss Earnshaw. The bottom of the address remains intact: an institution in East London, an area I am unfamiliar with. But there can't be many asylums in that location. I have just enough coins to cover a cab; they can take me to each establishment until I find her.

Away from the light of the burning house, the city looks bleak and ominous. I have tested my luck enough today. I will return to the vicarage and deliver the hoard of jewellery. Picking up the box, even in this weather, the smooth walnut panels are almost warm to the touch. There is certainly a strange energy about its contents. After this godforsaken night, I never want to see it again. The vicar will be waiting for me. I hope he is still praying.

Curtains twitch with the people inside, the spectacle drawing the attention of the entire street. More crowds are gathering in the courtyard to watch the fire consuming the house. Some of them are probably the men Mrs Guilden roused to help, arriving too late, but now witnesses to the aftermath. The flames licking at the building deterring the bravest man. I am not surprised they didn't come faster or if at all. The house has a reputation, and I am a nobody.

The profile of the nightwatchman appears amongst the figures, and my chest tightens. But then the man turns, and it is not him. The flecks of snow must be distorting my vision. It is too dangerous to look in the crowd for the housekeeper. She will return to the cottage soon, but I dare not risk going through the back garden to get to the vicarage. I need to be as far away as possible from the front entrance, the doors of which are gaping open. The flames have become unconstrained, spreading to the other floors, the heat leaching out. All the collection is burning. There's a loud crash as something snaps within the building and gives way.

In the moonlight above the roof, a mass of moving shadows circle in a tight formation. The magpies – I count at least ten, but there must be more flying in motion, seemingly as one body. Hovering over the building for a moment, they look to be communicating. Then, in a single act, they suddenly disperse in all directions, morphing into an image of shooting stars as their black and white feathers disappear into the night sky.

Their innocence, like my own, has gone. For now, I know the sinister intentions they hold beyond their determined red eyes. The way they think and behave, they are not of this world. The magpies have driven the Blackham collection, propelled it into existence. They are part of the evil buried in the crypt, but it is too late to contain them; the birds are already set loose into the city.

I rush down the street and up the next parallel road to the direction of the church, making small footprints as I go. The safety of the vicarage pulls me onwards. Only then will I allow myself to rest. I can almost savour the delicious aroma of a hot pie and warm bread that might be waiting.

As I leave the nightmare evening behind, I am grateful that I ventured back into the sinister house and survived. I could not save the mistress, but I hope Hannah saved herself.

Fatigue weighs heavily on me, but the cottage is not far. I nearly slip on the icy pavement and wish I had my cloak and gloves. If I keep up at a fast speed, I can reach the building in only a matter of minutes. Figures occupy the spaces between streetlamps; I try to avoid them. I do not want to be a target, as certainly this chest must hold an extraordinary amount of wealth.

A lonely figure keeps pace behind me. *Had I truly seen the nightwatchman in the courtyard?* Already the fiery smoke is mixing with the increasing blizzard, creating obscure human shapes out of nothing. I hear a familiar melody, ethereal notes carried on the winter breeze. My tired imagination is playing tricks on me at this late hour.

I cut across the street and walk up the second road. The gate to the churchyard is in sight, but the sound of heavy footsteps quickening behind me causes me to doubt my decision. I must walk in the graveyard, through where no light shines before I can get to safety. How could I be so foolish to hope I could leave undetected? I am sick with dread, so close to the haven of the vicarage I could weep.

The boots come closer, crunching on the fresh snow. I turn, searching the fog for a figure, and my heart sinks as a large man rushes out of the vapours. The nightwatchman is finally coming for me.

In a last effort of defiance, I try to run, but the injury in my hip from evading Mr Bancroft is sharp. I drag my leg behind me, wincing as I imagine his breath hot and foul against my ear and a rough hand across my mouth.

Another look over my shoulder and I glimpse his scarred cheeks. He is even nearer. I am trapped with only the ominous graveyard before me. Either my father sent him, or he acts on his own, but he has followed me all this time, and now I must face him. The ethereal notes of a whistled tune begin again. Stumbling in panic, I slip on the cobbles and brace myself for the hard impact of the ground, but instead I am caught in the firm arms of a blue uniform and a strong policeman helps me to my feet.

'Now then, Miss Granger, where are you rushing to on an evening like this? We will need to take your statement regarding the fire and make sure we account for everyone.' His Irish accent, warm and friendly, is a comforting contrast to the chaos of the night. His face is hidden, half-shielded by his helmet. I cannot discern his features, but now I remember his whistle – it is

Hannah's companion, Frank, the man who meets her every Thursday.

'I am most glad to run into you.' My words rush together. 'I am being followed - there is a man.'

I look behind me as the nightwatchman stands across the road. His face is grief-stricken at the knowledge I have been rescued at the last moment, snatched away from danger. He hesitates, shuffling from side to side, his hands balling into fists as if he is considering confronting the policeman, but then he shakes his head and walks back into the smoke.

Frank seems not to notice. 'Nothing but your imagination, miss, but lots of people loiter when a house catches fire. No doubt a passer-by on their way to take a closer look – makes a good story at the local pub.'

His attempt to calm me is working. Looking closer I can see what Hannah likes about him; his face is attractive, and his wide smile is friendly. He takes in my appearance, my carpet bag, and the box I'm holding.

'What is this, belongings you've saved?'

'Yes, only at the last minute.'

'Must have been a frightful evening for you.'

He grimaces in the house's direction. The smoke from the fire is billowing into the night sky. The smell of burnt wood lingers. 'Let's get you to the station. This way is quicker.' He motions to the path in the graveyard, pushing open the iron gate. 'With no coat, you might catch your death in this weather. I would give you mine, but I'm not allowed when in uniform.'

We start to walk, but I waver at the entrance. 'What about Hannah and Mrs Higgins? Do you know if they are safe?'

'Did you see them still in the house?' He asks, his voice full of concern.

'No, but…'

'Well, then, I am sure they are. My men will take care of them.'

The entire experience feels like an impossible dream. Should I tell him about Mr Bancroft and what is in the basement?

'There are—' I begin, but he cuts my words short by holding up his palm in front of his face.

'Do not concern yourself with the house. You're bound to be in shock. Let the fire brigade do their job. Come now, let's get a hot cup of tea inside you.'

We walk up the path, passing each lonely gravestone covered in snow. My nerves are still agitated from the ordeal, but I'm thankful to have found company.

'I was on my way to the vicarage. I have friends there who will let me stay with them.'

'Don't worry, you're safe with me. Once we have your statement, you're free to go. I'll walk you back personally; I know how to take care of a lady.'

'Yes, Hannah talked a lot about you.' I look up, expecting to see him smile, but his expression is blank.

'Did she? That was careless of her.'

His smile returns, but without the warmth of before. He nods onwards towards the cottage, on the other side of the graveyard. 'Anyhow, I'll get you to the station and then bring you back here. As a friend of Hannah's, I'd better stay with you until you're settled.'

'Thank you. I would appreciate that.' I answer, falling into step beside him. The affliction in my hip is still angry, and I stumble again.

'Here, let me help you.' He takes my carpet bag and offers his elbow. Leaning on it eases the discomfort. His uniform and firm grip are reassuring, but something about him is wrong. The front door of the vicarage opens, and warm light cascades from the home as I see the vicar's stooped silhouette in the entrance.

'I will just give this box to the vicar, and we can be on our way to the station.'

I remove my arm from the crook of his elbow to wave. 'Vicar Evans!' I call out, but the words are distorted. Pain consumes me, spreading from above my right temple and splintering my vision as my eyes flash white. The shock is absolute, and I crumple like a discarded puppet. The ground is ice hard and unforgiving as I land awkwardly, my knees scraping on the earth.

Frank grabs my waist roughly, dragging me away from the path and behind the nearest headstone, hiding us amidst the graves. I struggle, dropping the jewellery box, gasping in dismay as he thoughtlessly discards my belongings, the magenta and gold tapestry bag thrown into the trees. I watch, horrified, as the sketchbooks tumble out and loose pages of drawings scatter amongst the frozen headstones. A blast of bright light flashes before my eyes as I glimpse the green tin of my vasculum strewn in the fresh snow, before he smashes another stone hard against my face.

'Hush now, you stupid woman!' The words hiss between his teeth, his spittle landing on my cheek. He curses, but the threats fade out as blackness mixes with the blind agony in my head. I am floating for an instant and then I remember nothing more.

The movement of the vehicle stops. I am in the back of a wagon; from the looks of it, a police cab. Inside are two wooden benches with steel rings, presumably for handcuffs. How long have I been here? A night at least, for the day already sounds underway. The shouts of female voices pass by the shell of the carriage. Some commotion is happening outside.

'We will have to stop here!' Frank's voice shouts from the front, heavy with his Irish accent. 'I can't get any further through this blasted march. Christmas Day, of all days. There are women all over the street; it's a bloody nightmare! Where are the bobbies? There's no one in uniform when you need them.'

I am relieved to find my hands unbound, although my whole body aches, and my head throbs with a dull, sickening pain, which radiates down my neck. This is not one of my usual headaches. My last memories run through my mind; the night of the fire flashes before my eyes, the search for safety … the graveyard, Frank.

'You will be no trouble, will you, Ivy?' He shouts again. 'Hannah was a disappointment to me, too selfish.'

The door opens and sunlight distorts my vision; the snow from last night has melted. My skin is tight from a throbbing cut, and my swollen cheek blocks the sight of my right eye. 'I know you're a good girl.'

I glimpse his face. He is smiling again, as charming as when we first met. Like a magician, his illusion is impressive but false. I don't struggle. It is safer to feign weakness, so I can bide my time to understand what is happening.

'I prefer women to be obedient ... as they should be.'

Frank pulls me out of the back of the cab without care, and the swift movement causes my stomach to roll with nausea and hunger.

It seems we are in the middle of a liberation march. I look for a friendly face from the Hanover Square meeting, hoping my luck might change, but all around me are unfamiliar faces in hats and rosettes. Some women sing together in groups, like the congregations of a church choir.

He pushes me through the crowd. I fall, losing my footing on the street cobbles. Women stop beside us, their expressions full of concern.

'What are you doing with her? She needs medical attention.' A woman with a large ribbon with "Right to Vote" takes my wrist.

'Help me, please!' I try to talk, but my voice croaks. But they must see the panic in my eyes. I don't need language to explain my bloody face and his tight grasp on my arm.

More figures crowd around. Flashes of purple, gold, and green sashes over white dresses swim before me.

'I am helping her, she got in a fight - out of my way!' Frank rebukes loudly.

'Give her to us. I am a nurse; she needs a bandage.'

'No, leave her be. She is in my custody.'

I let my body go limp and heavy as he struggles to hold me, the shift in my weight taking him off-balance. For a moment, he lets go to get a better grip. In the release of his fingers, I take the split-second opportunity to strain from his grasp.

He shouts – there is a space between us, only a hand's width, but it is all I need.

'That's it, run! You are free!' An older woman declares, ushering me away.

The women surround him, blocking his view of me, singing louder, allowing me to stumble onwards. Trying to regain my balance, adrenaline fuels me forward. Each step further from him is a relief.

I race to where the crowd is thickest, to lose him completely. Someone hands me a flag, and I am one with them, just a woman protesting as we march down the street in unison. But the sight of me must be grim as another lady passes me a handkerchief. Looking at me with pity, her eyes trailing the blood I can feel drying on my cheek. I hold the lavender square against my face; the scent uplifts my spirits.

At that moment, I understand I am part of something bigger than me alone. Together, women are stronger, as were my mother and aunt when they performed as one. Some men, like Victor Blackham and Frank, are afraid of the power women wield when they grow to their potential, when we are released from the confinement of social restrictions and political restraints. Is it fear that drives them to dominate the weaker sex?

I know his eyes are still on me; they burn on my skin. Frank won't let me go easily, won't let me slip away from the clutches of that family. What makes him do this – money, control? Did Hannah ever understand the truth of his character, the depths of his crooked nature? His handsome face disguises the ugly creature within.

The clear voice of Mrs Finch drifts across the crowd from a megaphone, urging the women forward. I see her standing proudly at the front. But then there is a glimpse of blue fabric and male voices. The shrill sound of whistles takes over, and the crowd is suddenly being parted by policemen. The singing and chanting dissemble, with only a few voices continuing solo.

'Break it up, ladies! This is over. Go home to your husbands and children.'

Black hats and polished silver belts are everywhere; policemen are leading women off in all directions, arresting, redirecting the traffic, and forcing normal life to resume in the street.

And then Frank is standing before me again. His face bears into mine with menace in his eyes. 'There you are Ivy. I nearly lost you, but there is no escape from where you're going.'

My body flinches as he grabs my waist. His fingers return painfully to my arm. 'Wait! Stop. What about Hannah … your mother?'

'What?' His tone rises in surprise. 'I have no mother,' he declares as he drags me along the pavement. 'She did me the courtesy of dying in a gutter, leaving me to grow up at the mercy of the backstreets.'

'Are you not going to the countryside with Hannah? If you are caught taking me against my will, how will that fare?'

He sneers. 'No one cares what I do with you. And Hannah?' He laughs. 'She must have bent your ear off with my stories. Women believe anything they want – doesn't make it real.'

'But you are a policeman. Doesn't that count for a shred of decency?' I squirm in his grasp, but he drags me in closer to his chest as though we were lovers.

'Thank God there are still wealthy families who rely on … well, helpful members of the police force to do their work and turn a blind eye to the law occasionally, for the right price.' He gives a heartless laugh. 'Bancroft almost works as hard as I do, running all their errands, delivering their letters of requests to me.' He throws me into a nearby cab. 'Come now, I have a debt and a card game waiting.'

We arrive at our destination sooner than I had hoped. This time he has bound my hands behind me, pushing my body forward in the seat. I ache all over from the strained posture. He's stuffed a dirty rag in my mouth; it almost reaches to the back of my throat. If I think too much about it, I gag. My eyes water as he sits beside me, his hand upon my knee. Every time I try to move, he squeezes it so hard I want to scream. He leans over, his face next to mine. 'Stop your antics. I caught you, little mouse.'

As we climb out of the cab and onto a narrow driveway, a large, old building looms over us, foreboding in the drab afternoon. He pulls the rag out of my mouth but holds a finger to my lips, warning me to be quiet.

'What do you want?' A gruff voice asks from behind a small, barred grate in the front door.

'Where is Mr Melville, the orderly? I have a special delivery, a Christmas gift.' Frank replies.

'Go to the back entrance,' the voice replies, sliding the grate shut with a snap.

Frank pulls me around the side of the building where an old man appears, shuffling from a small door in the wall; a hacking cough precedes his arrival. His face is pointed like a rat, his eyes shifty as he looks me over.

They appear to know each other, shaking hands. The policeman passes him a slip of paper. It is a business transaction; he has done this before.

'I've got the perfect cell for her.'

'Much obliged. Sorry for the late notice, but I've taken the initiative on this one. I think my boss will be very interested in learning that I caught her trying to escape the house, stealing from them.'

'Doesn't bother me,' the old man replies, 'long as my money is paid.'

Frank turns to me. 'And don't worry, I've stored the jewellery box somewhere safe … well, almost all of it, minus a small finder's fee,' he says with a gloating smile. 'And you will be here, ready and waiting, if they need you again.'

I panic as we walk down a drab corridor into the belly of the building. 'The sunlight is fading; I must have a lamp or a candle in my room.' The words are painful to utter. My cheek and lips are still swollen. I am sure the voices will visit me here. Even though I understand they mean me no harm, I can face them better with a little light for comfort.

'You will get nothing,' the old man snorts, 'just like the other one he brought in. Requesting things, as if we are here to service your needs. I'm not at anyone's beck and call.'

He stops walking, peering close into my eyes, searching for something in my features, his breath pungent in my face. 'But I swear she's not alone in her cell at night, mad like all the rest. This asylum was built especially for misfits like you.'

He continues again. His takes us deeper into what I now realise is an institution – *Bethlehem?* On and on we walk past locked doors and empty staircases. I hear the faint sound of sobbing and then it stops.

'Men's voices and screams, a hell of a racket. We draw straws to check on her, but she's always asleep. Calm as anything during the day, a funny creature that one. Still, I think this is the best place for her, and you too, by the looks of it. Frank, where do you find these women?'

Chapter 50 ~ Debt

The Nightwatchman ~ Bethlehem Asylum, 27th December.

The nightwatchman stands in front of the asylum. He knows Ivy is in there - both of them now. Finally, he had linked the disappearance of Rosetta to this location using his connections on the watch. It is a small comfort at least they are together, but he should have dealt with the Blackhams himself. His fingers flex, agitated at his failure to protect the girl. Although she had shown courage, she was no match against them.

He should have taken her back to his room when he had the chance. But he hadn't seen the policeman in the smoky night until it was too late. That copper was corrupt, and you can't confront someone shifty like that in public without a plan. The fire had disorientated him, his irrational fear of the burning house forcing him to hesitate, to sacrifice precious seconds. He berates himself for submitting to the power of a vague childhood memory. Nowadays, he usually surrenders to no one.

Rosetta's visit on the 11th of November had taken him by surprise. Somehow, she always knew where to find him. He was a creature of habit: the same whoring and drinking in pubs night after night. Although they moved in different circles, their friendship still existed, forged by the loneliness of their childhood at the foundling centre. A type of love he had never felt before or since he first met her. Now he had made her a promise, an offer of redemption, for letting her down when the Blackhams first crossed her sister's path. A time when he had youth but no courage.

'Watch her. You'll know her face – she will look just like Lillian.' She had paused briefly, giving a sad, beautiful smile in remembrance. 'Tonight, I disturbed a hornet's nest, and I fear the repercussions have been set in motion. Ivy could be in danger when she comes to visit me in London.'

'What danger? There are many people who owe me favours. You know, I'm not scared of trouble.' The role of nightwatchman suited him well.

Rosetta was one of the few that didn't flinch from his scarred body. Even as children, she saw his true self and not the skin ravaged by fire. No one had come to claim or adopt him, and no token of identity was left to give any hope for his parents to return. He had been truly abandoned, but not by Rosetta and her sister, Lillian. They were his only genuine family.

'If I must leave the city, watch her and keep her safe until I return. She is like you and me, alone now. She needs guidance, protection.'

'I'll take her to my lodgings and wait for you there. Do not fret, she'll be well taken care of.'

'Thank you, but perhaps it won't come to that.' Her hand rested gently on his arm, trying as always to reassure him that the world was not all bad.

'I am sure Ivy will have money to stay at a boarding house; otherwise, my housekeeper Mrs Forbes should look after her. We spoke of the girl, but she was against me finding Ivy and bringing her back to London.' She shook her head. 'Mrs Forbes even threatened to send her away if she did come.'

'But why not help, if only for your sake?'

'The cards also warned that death will follow.' Rosetta's voice wavered. 'Mrs Forbes is incredibly loyal; she wants to protect me, sometimes at the expense of others. I understand her fear; she is concerned history will repeat itself and knows the power of the Blackham family.'

He had whistled through his teeth. 'This is a story of nightmares. Lillian was the victim of the worst type of man.' His fingers clenched in reflex at the memory. 'How can his father, a dead politician, cause you more trouble now?'

'His legacy continues, and he is just one of their group. There are others in the shadows; the Crow, the Rook, and so many more; faceless men working together to unleash the dark arts into the city. A brotherhood of evil. My sister and I failed on our last attempt to stop the Corvidae from rising, but now the cards foretell Ivy must end it all. The delicate balance between this world and the next must not be damaged.'

'Then I should help her? You've told me often enough you cannot fight fate.'

'But she is not to know. It could make things more dangerous for her. Besides, the cards have been wrong on occasion. She could just be an ordinary girl.'

'You know those cards of yours never lie. She is your niece, so she would never be ordinary.'

Rosetta's face tightened. 'Whatever happens, we must not let the Blackhams find out who she really is. They took my sister from me. They will not win again.'

'You know, I'll do anything you ask.'

'Ivy is a protected girl. She has only ever trusted a handful of people, namely her mother. Ivy is bound to be nervous, maybe even frightened of you.' She touched his pitted cheek tenderly. 'So best keep a distance. But I trust you. I will be forever in your debt again.'

He remembers his face flushing with heat from the soft caress of her hand. He questions his decision again to let Ivy continue to work as a maid in the house, but he had hoped she might succeed where he had failed in finding Rosetta. If there is a Heaven or Hell, he'll be with Rosetta in this life and the next.

Chapter 51 ~ Fate

Ivy ~ Bethlehem Asylum, 31st December.

The room is small, six steps by six; if I stand, my fingertips can almost graze each wall from the centre of the floor. The bricked walls are damp and cold. A straw pallet with a blanket and bucket is my only company. The wool scratches against my neck as I pull the cover over my head, at once exposing my bare feet. The warden took my shoes, muttering about them being a danger. I would not have the strength to use them against someone, even if I wanted to. My shuddered breath mixes with the noise of my heart thudding painfully in my chest; my health is getting worse.

    Church bells ring in the distance, summoning the masses. It must be nearing New Year's Eve. I remember toasting the last new year in with my mother, just the two of us. The memory feels like a lifetime ago. This is the type of asylum I had always feared: soulless and bleak. It is a poor irony that, despite my efforts to avoid such a fate, this is exactly where I find myself now. A mouse scurries past my feet, and I think of the rats in William's garden that cannot help but eat the poison he gives them. Surely, they know to warn each other of the danger. But like those poisoned by the Blackhams, they all perished in the end.

    Lady Blackham's revelation of my brother and his untimely death plays on my mind. How life could have been so different if Mother had confided in me, told me her reasons for keeping him secret. Perhaps we might have been close – even kindred spirits before he died. The Christian side of me should pray the Blackham's made it out of the fire alive, but I can't stop myself from hoping everyone connected to the horrors of that basement perished, and the collection burned to ashes. I do wish Hannah managed to find a place of comfort away from the house and the grip of Frank, a true monster whose fate should have been joined with the others. I have not seen him since, so I am none the wiser about what will happen to me or if anyone survived.

My mind tries hard not to linger on Master Blackham, for I am filled with what feels like a mix of revulsion at his character and pity for his inner torment. I should banish him from my thoughts, but now, is he not also my uncle? Was the sympathy sparked by a bond with blood? Creatures of nature recognising one of their own, like my plants growing in clusters protected by the strength of numbers in their own species. But I will not grieve for the loss of my birth father. Victor Blackham is long dead and for all the pain he has caused, I will never resurrect his name into my life.

This place is run by money and threats. There are patients that go with the nurses for medicine and never return. They fill the empty seats with new bodies, only to have them become vacant again. Fear and unease have morphed into my constant companions. Mealtimes are the only occasions I am allowed out of my room. The blank eyes of the other women in the dining hall of this institution scare me, they remind me of Mr Bancroft when the spirit of Lord Blackham possessed him. But they are the true walking dead. No jewellery was needed to summon them, only the harsh treatment of the experiments on the lower floor.

The day I saw my aunt, Miss Earnshaw, sitting at one of the long tables in the dining hall, I wept with joy. Guards separated us, but she looked up as I was shuffled past, as if expecting me. A slow smile spread across her lips as we drank each other in. Gone are the fineries she wore at the graveside at our first meeting. She is thinner, drawn; her eyes are set deeper in their sockets. The last two months in this building have taken their toll on her, but they have not broken her yet. She is waiting, as am I, biding our time until I hope we will leave together. We do not speak. It is forbidden, but an understanding resonates between us, a hum of expectation of what is coming.

The joy of finding my aunt is mixed with the trepidation that I may indeed go mad before that time will come. I have been counting the days and only a week has passed, but it feels like a year. It is not medicine they practise here; only brutal, cruel treatments are prescribed to heal insanity. I am sure it must be my turn soon. I hear the screams, followed by weeping and then silence.

There is a guard on duty in the evenings. He is sly but slow-footed, limping heavily on one side. He walks across the stone floor, stopping outside of my cell each night for the briefest moment before continuing along. I sense him paying me extra attention; even my plain features do not protect me here. My skin prickles in disgust. He has told me what he wants, his lewd expression following me constantly. We came to an agreement that if he arranges for me to send a letter and I receive an answer, then I will agree to his demands. He wants nothing by force, which is a small mercy within these walls.

The arrangement is an insult of an exchange, but a currency that can buy freedom. My virtue is the only asset I have left to trade, as I will never give up my mourning ring, still concealed in my bodice.

Cousin Edith appeared in my dream last night. She was standing by the fireplace in my childhood home. She turned and fixed me with a concerned but judgmental look I recognised only too well. Perhaps, in my pride, I had overlooked a small degree of care that might have underlain her attention towards me. And so, my letter will be addressed to Edith. It is a humbling act to admit my circumstances. I am sure the letter will be read with a mix of interest and distaste. No doubt, my demise will be the talk of social events for some time, but I know I can trust her to influence my father and assist us, although the inclusion of my aunt in the request will displease him greatly. The shame of learning his daughter resides in an asylum, even if we are not blood related, should move him to act. Or would he leave me here as a penance for choosing my own fate? Daring to stray from his own rules, and Mr Whitlock, finding nothing but misfortune in London?

But he would be wrong in thinking that and predicting my studies would come to nothing. Even though I ended up in this lowly place for the lost and forgotten, this journey was entirely mine and mine alone. I found the missing parts of my family, and my knowledge of the botanical proved more useful than he could imagine.

Rough hands pull me up from the damp pallet, interrupting my wandering thoughts.

'No, leave me please ... I have not written my letter.'

My protest is feeble. In only a few days I have become weak and sick from the poor food and dirty surroundings. A candle glows painfully bright, forcing my eyes open.

'Ivy, we are leaving.' The shadowed face of my aunt, Miss Earnshaw, flickers before me. 'Can you stand? We must make haste.'

Steadying myself on the arm of my rescuer, I am shocked to find it is the face of the nightwatchman who greets me. He has finally found me, but I feel no joy at the prospect of returning to my father, only ensuring the safety of my aunt would make it worthwhile. I recoil at his closeness. His scarred face is only inches away from mine.

A female voice interjects. 'He is a friend, Ivy. You are safe with him.'

I double over as my stomach spasms from the effort of moving.

'She is too ill with fever. I'll carry her. We'll be faster.' His words are gruff but tender. He picks me up gently and holds me over his shoulder, smelling of tobacco and wood fire. I am taken aback but relieved to see him beckoning my aunt to follow with his other arm. She resembles a gaunt, haunting apparition, running behind us in the dingy corridor, carrying a single candle. The Blackhams turned her into a ghost, after all.

'This way, quickly,' he whispers.

We pass the slumped body of a night guard, the one with the limp. A smattering of blood covers his forehead. The nightwatchman has been busy.

A single cab is waiting outside on the wintry, bleak street. As we approach, the driver clicks his tongue to ready the horses.

I am lifted into the embrace of my aunt as the carriage jerks forward. This must be a dream, salvation from the confinement of the cell. The nightwatchman's gaze never leaves my aunt's; such is his devotion. He is a large man and fills the space of the two opposite seats. I have feared him for so long and yet it appears I was wrong, for he is a gentle giant.

His eyes crease with regret. 'I tried to get to you both sooner, but it took a few days to gather enough money to pay off the orderly and find out exactly where you were. That building is a maze.'

'We are so very grateful to you,' my aunt responds. 'Thank you.'

'The Blackhams?' I can't hide the anxiety in my words.

'Do not distress yourself. They have left the city. Now you must rest.' Her voice is tender, as she places her hand on my head. 'You are burning up.'

'They should have burned,' the nightwatchman mutters with a scowl. 'The fire escaped them, but if they return, I will not hesitate to punish them for what they have done.' He rubs his knuckles, the skin torn and bleeding.

'And what's buried in the crypt under their house – could that be stopped by a fire?' My body twitches with fever and the memory of the stone tomb. 'It has the power to control people, even the birds.' My aunt's hand stops abruptly mid-stroke of my hair.

'No, that dark spirit is very old and was born amongst flames, but there are other ways to overcome evil, and the Blackhams are weaker now, thanks to you. You succeeded where others failed, including your mother and I.'

'Others?'

'You and I are part of something much bigger. It seems your instincts and intuition are strong even without your mother's encouragement... I was sure the gifts of your birthright would have blessed you.'

'What do you mean?' I say, trying to sit up.

She pauses, trying to find the correct words. 'The women in our family have always had the gift of insight – generations, going back through the ages, linked by a purpose, an ancient language.'

'The symbols in your diary and mother's sketch book are connected?'

'Yes, there are many languages that belong to this world and the next. But only our sacred words can be used for protection, wisdom, and teaching. Your eyes have been opened. Now is the time to answer your own calling.'

My mind swirls with information. 'But how?'

She shakes her head. 'You will always be shown your path, but it is your decision whether to make the choice. I know it can be a difficult journey to meet your true fate. If you agree, I will teach you everything I have learnt. It will be worth the trials you have endured.'

'My mother, she was the same?'

A sadness passes over her features. 'Your mother decided to hide her abilities after you were born, but I continued to use mine.'

'As a spiritualist?'

'Yes.'

I want to tell her about the strange garden and the jewellery, which must still survive, but as she continues to smooth my hair, the right words fail me, and their importance diminishes. Closing my eyes, the comfort of her touch becomes overwhelming in the absence of tenderness these past months.

'Hush now, rest. You are with family. We are together, which is all I ever wished for. We will return to my apartment and start anew.'

'But I have no money and no means to support myself. I do not wish to be a burden.'

'That could never be, and it is no matter. In time, you can use your mother's money as you deem fit.'

'Father said there was no money,' I cannot hide the disappointment in my voice. 'Mother was lying about it.'

She laughs unexpectedly. 'In your mother's world, where do you think she would have hidden the money I sent her?'

I concentrate hard, but I am confused. And then I remember my mother's final words telling me to look to the ground, where we planted together. *The earth would provide for me.* 'She buried it!' I exclaim, stunned again by the secrets my mother kept.

'Of course she did, and you shall find it in good time, but for now you will stay in London with me as my special guest, my niece. I regret your journey was not easier and my prediction could not spare you pain, but it doesn't always work that way.'

I look up. 'So, you are not lying about the predictions and your abilities?'

She smiles ruefully. 'On the contrary, sometimes I wish I was.' She pauses. 'Have you ever felt that something set you apart; heard things, seen things that are concealed from others?'

I think of Hannah's brother when I listened to his murmurs with intent. His voice had become as clear as if his heart was beating next to mine. The whispers have always invaded my mind, but now I know they meant me no harm. 'Mother said it was all my imagination.'

'She was protecting you,' she says wryly. 'But you cannot hide from yourself. That is the path to self-destruction. It is necessary to embrace your differences. There is power in your gifts. To be both master and servant to the lost souls of this world is our greatest challenge.'

A silence hangs between us as I let her words sink in.

'But Father must have known about you and Mother?'

'Perhaps he had suspicions there was something more to my sister's story, but I think her beauty eclipsed her troubled past.'

'So, it's true he is not my real father?'

She looks at the nightwatchman before answering: 'A professor made the introduction to help Lillian get out of the city. It was all we could do at the time. Mr Granger took to Lillian immediately and managed to pass you off as his own. From what I know of him, he is a proud man and would not take well to scandal.'

'But how did you know where we lived?'

'Lillian wrote to me a single heart-breaking letter telling me where she was when you were still an infant.' She stops speaking and squeezes my shoulder. 'All I could do was send money each year, but the danger was too great to see each other again. She didn't want to lose you as well. I knew instinctively when she passed.' She sighs. 'My sister has not spoken to me yet from beyond the veil, but I couldn't stay away from you, knowing you were alone.'

The carriage continues through the quiet streets, the horse's hooves clattering loudly against the cobbles.

'Our family is what matters now, and we have hope,' she smiles, 'as your brother is no longer lost to us.'

'Brother?' I pull myself out of her embrace to see her face properly. 'But I have no brother. There has only ever been me. Lady Blackham told me he was dead and that you saw his spirit during the séance. But it sounded so absurd I couldn't possibly believe it was true!'

She smiles, cupping my cheek in her palm. 'You do have a sibling – born on the same day, at the same hour. I am so terribly sorry you were separated. We both were, your mother and I, but we were all pulled apart.' Her eyes glisten in the faint light from the passing streetlamps outside. 'The Blackhams both created and destroyed our family at their whim.'

'But he's dead. I couldn't see him in the afterlife even if I wanted to, as you can.'

She takes me gently by the shoulders, bringing her face closer to mine. I watch her lips move as the carriage continues to jolt us along, trying to understand every word she says. 'No, Lady Blackham misled you. It is true, I did see him that night. When the butler brought the lamp closer to me and the light shone on his features, it was your mother's eyes looking back at me. Hiding in plain sight, they had brought your brother up in service as their illegitimate heir. I don't think he even knows of his real identity.'

'Mr Bancroft is my brother? It can't be him; it doesn't make sense – we are nothing alike!' I am aghast. My thoughts, normally so logical, are now scattering, loose like the mice in the asylum. Then I think of his green eyes and the familiar feeling of déjà vu he gave me. Could it be true?

'Your lives have been very different, but there is no mistake.'

'But you didn't see him like I did. He became possessed, his loyalty is only to the Blackhams.' I am sick to my stomach, a heavy weight forcing the air out of my lungs. 'He could truly be dead now. The last time I saw him, he was in the centre of the fire I started.'

I strain to look out the window, trying to see which part of London we are in, almost expecting to witness the house still burning after all these days, but the effort is futile.

'Please don't fret, you were meant to find him, and brought an end to the Blackham's madness. He may come back to us; the rest is out of our hands. My predictions of your danger came true, despite my efforts. Fate is a fickle creature, but the cards have been pacified for now.'

I slump further into the seat. I think about Mr Bancroft, with his ambitious, cold eyes and impenetrable face: my own blood. About how the Blackhams manipulated him, and we were blind to the cruel truth. That the Blackhams robbed us both.

In my aunt's embrace, I find the validation I have been searching for. Frantic whistles blow in the distance. The fever tries to pull me back into blackness, but I am here in this moment – alive and no longer doubting my sanity. Grief and death have not conquered me yet, but I have lost my innocence of this world. My mother tried to protect me, but evil will not be content to be buried underground or hidden in the true nature of people. For where there is light, I know now, there must also be darkness.

Thinking of my belongings scattered in the graveyard I pray the vicar has discovered them. My pulse skips, remembering the Solanum pyracanthos plant cuttings. If they survived inside the tin of my vasculum, I could continue with my research, for I am certain the winter air would have preserved them for a time. Removed from the house, their abnormal connection to protecting the garden and what lies below should be broken. I refuse to feel guilty about using their cordial against the Blackhams. My fate would have only been the same if I hadn't acted.

I want to live. My aunt was right. I do have a purpose. I refuse to play the part of another. No longer can I hide or turn away from the lost souls I hear. I am listening now. They are just like me, searching, reaching out for someone to help them find peace. Let them come and surround me. I will conquer my fear in time. There is much work to be done, but my path will be my own.

I cannot hear the voice of my mother, but now as the weight of grief begins to lift, I feel her presence with me. Yesterday, in my windowless cell, I woke to find a glossy deep blue feather in the palm of my hand, pristine and soft, like the finest silk. We cannot fathom or control the bridges between life and death, but there are signs and miracles that slip through, guiding us and giving hope that our bonds to loved ones are not broken. Like a swallow returning to its nest after a season of winter, my mother never left me.

Coming soon…

Book Two: *The Crows - There is a thief in the night!*

Why are people disappearing from the asylums and who is stalking the London streets at night? Ivy's next mystery is even more dangerous than Blackham House...

I hope you enjoyed the first story in The Corvidae Series!

If you did, I would love to see your review on Amazon or Goodreads.

It is much appreciated!

Thank you,

Jen x

Sign up to receive news and updates about future releases, including a welcome gift of an original Victorian ghost story.

Sign up: www.JenniferRenshaw.com

Instagram: @jen_renshaw

Pinterest: jen_renshaw

I wish to thank the following people who have helped and inspired me along the way.

Claire Baldwin, Andrew Noakes, Sherron Mayes, and Lisa Edwards for their wonderful editing and advice! And anyone who has listened to me try to explain the Corvidae world over the last few years and added their thoughts.

Micaela Alcaino for her beautiful cover design and illustrations.

A special thank you to Angela for her support and for reading the earlier versions multiple times!

My friends, near and far, in the UK, Australia and Denmark.

To my much-loved parents, who believe in me and my ideas.

My fantastic sister, who always knows what to say. I wish we could spend every day talking about stories!

And finally, to my husband and boys: In all the chaos and love we share - thank you for cheering me on and helping me turn my secret writing into a book. I couldn't have finished this story without you.

Printed in Great Britain
by Amazon